04   05
H2

D1016906

THE HEARTBREAK *LOUNGE*

ALSO BY *WALLACE STROBY*

The Barbed-Wire Kiss

GLASGOW CITY - COUNTY LIBRARY

THE HEARTBREAK LOUNGE

WALLACE STROBY

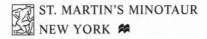

ST. MARTIN'S MINOTAUR
NEW YORK

THE HEARTBREAK LOUNGE. Copyright © 2005 by Wallace Stroby. All rights reserved. Printed in the United States of America. No part of this book may be used or reproduced in any manner whatsoever without written permission except in the case of brief quotations embodied in critical articles or reviews. For information, address St. Martin's Press, 175 Fifth Avenue, New York, N.Y. 10010.

www.minotaurbooks.com

Library of Congress Cataloging-in-Publication Data

Stroby, Wallace.
    The Heartbreak Lounge / Wallace Stroby.—1st St. Martin's Minotaur ed.
      p. cm.
    ISBN 0-312-30095-6
    EAN 978-0312-30095-1
    1. Private investigators—New Jersey—Fiction. 2. Ex-police officers—Fiction. 3. Organized crime—Fiction. 4. Ex-convicts—Fiction. 5. New Jersey—Fiction. 6. Revenge—Fiction. I. Title.

    PS3619.T755H43 2005
    813'.6—dc22

                                                  2004056472

First Edition: February 2005

10 9 8 7 6 5 4 3 2 1

For my mother, Inez Stroby, whose love and
support have made all this possible

ACKNOWLEDGMENTS

The author wishes to thank Kelley Ragland and Robin Rue for their unfailing patience, support, and enthusiasm.

THE HEARTBREAK *LOUNGE*

ONE

Two days out of prison and twenty miles south of Daytona, Johnny decided he'd walked far enough.

He slipped the duffel bag off his shoulder, dropped it in the parched grass. There wasn't much in it: two pairs of jeans, some spare shirts and socks and the books from his cell—paperbacks of Nietzsche and Sun-Tzu, the *Hagakure*. He'd given everything else away before being processed out.

He sat on the duffel, elbows on his knees. He knew there was little chance of getting a ride for the next few miles, especially the way he looked, and he was light-headed from the sun and lack of food. He hadn't eaten since the night before, eggs and coffee at an all-night diner in Melbourne. He'd slept in a park, taken his chances with the police, not wanting to spend any more of the little kick-out money he had left on a motel.

There was a single Camel in the bent pack in his shirt pocket. He shook it out, straightened it, lit it with the silver Marine Corps lighter he'd stolen off a bar in Boynton Beach. He sucked in the smoke, held it for a good long time before letting it out, then crumpled the empty pack, tossed it. He sat there smoking, his legs sore, his back stiff, feet blistered in the heavy work boots. He would hurt tonight. Hurt twice as much if he had to sleep outside again.

He heard an engine, turned to look back the way he'd come. A flatbed truck rumbled toward him in the heat haze. Without getting up, he held out his thumb. The truck blew by him, raising dust and grit from the road, leaving it suspended in the air.

Passenger cars were few on this stretch of Route 1, and he knew his best chance was a truck. Yesterday he'd gotten a ride all the way

1

from Fort Pierce to the outskirts of Melbourne in the bed of a pickup driven by two Mexican day laborers. He sat on stacked concrete blocks and when they let him off, the dust was all over his clothes, his skin. He'd walked into town from there.

He took off the Marlins cap he'd bought in a convenience store, rubbed at his stubble. In Glades he'd kept his head shaved, had only let his hair grow out in the month before his release. It was thickening now, itching as it came in, but it offered little protection. The cap helped keep the sun off his scalp and forehead, but he could feel the stiffness and burning on the back of his neck.

He finished the cigarette, watched a hawk glide in the thermal currents above the tree line. There was swamp on both sides of the highway, the air thick with the sulfur smell of it. Spanish moss hung from the cypress trees and it looked cool and dark among them, but the one time he had wandered in to get out of the sun, he had ended up knee-deep in water. So he kept to the road.

Out here, between towns, he knew he was running the biggest risk. He watched for the tan and black Florida State Police cruisers: if a trooper thought he was hitchhiking, he would be stopped, questioned, have to show ID. He was legal, free and clear, but that wouldn't matter. Cops were cops, and here it would be even worse. If he looked down-and-out—if he looked like what he was—they would fuck with him, make him spend a night in their drunk tank, cite, fine and release him. All by way of warning: *Don't come back.*

He wasn't coming back, he knew that. If he ever got out of this state, he was never coming back.

He brushed ash from his pants, stood up, his knees aching. He picked up the duffel, slung it over his right shoulder.

He heard the car before he saw it. Didn't bother to turn at first, until he heard the pitch of the engine change, slow. It was a dark green Buick Electra, sun flashing off chrome. He put his thumb out, saw a glimpse of blonde hair as the car went by. It was halfway up the rise when its brake lights glowed.

He watched the car slow, steer onto the shoulder, pause there as if the driver were having second thoughts. Then it began to slowly reverse, veering slightly from side to side. He could see the woman behind the wheel now, right arm thrown over the seat as she backed up, no one else in the car.

It stopped a few yards ahead of him, the woman looking back, sizing him up, her foot probably still on the gas pedal, ready to pull away in an instant. He knew how he must look, covered with dust and grime, his blue work shirt sweat dark. He walked slow, expecting the car to peal away, leave him breathing road dust. It stayed where it was.

As he got closer, there was a click from the trunk and the lid rose. He looked at her through the back window, saw her smile.

The trunk was big, empty except for a blanket and a white metal first-aid kit. He dropped the duffel in, shut the lid, heard the thunk as she unlocked the passenger-side door automatically.

He opened the door, said, "Thanks," and got in.

She was in her late forties, early fifties: frosted blonde hair, blue flowered blouse, designer jeans. She was toned and fit, her skin tan and slightly leathery. He saw all this in the moment it took him to slide onto the seat, pull the door closed.

The car was chill with air-conditioning and smelled of perfume, powder. The leather seats were cold through his jeans. She looked at him for a moment, put her blinker on and pulled back onto the road.

"Not many rides along here, I wouldn't think," she said. "And that sun . . ."

"You're right about that."

He shifted in the seat, shivered slightly as his sweat began to cool. "I appreciate your stopping."

"Is this too much AC for you? I can open the windows."

"No, it feels good."

He pulled at his shirt, tugged loose the wet patches where it clung to his skin.

"I don't usually do this," she said. "I haven't in years."

He took off his cap, ran a hand through his stubble.

"Well, I'm glad you did."

"Your neck is burned. It must be painful."

"I'll be fine. When I get where I'm going, I'll buy something, put on it."

"And where are you going?"

3

"St. Augustine. I'm meeting some friends there."

"That's not too far. An hour and a half at most."

"Then that's fine with me."

He looked out the window at the cypress trees rushing by. It was good to be in a car again, riding.

After a while, she said, "You're being rude."

He looked at her, saw she was smiling.

"Sorry," he said. "I think the heat's got me zoning a little."

"I can understand that."

"My name's John. John Harrow."

"Mine's Teresa. You from Florida, John? You don't sound like it."

"New Jersey."

"That's what I thought. New Jersey or New York. You get down into South Florida and everybody you meet is from one or the other. It's like the South just stops and the North starts up again. Where are you coming from?"

"West Palm," he said. "Had some work down there, but it ran out. And I wanted to get home for the holidays anyway."

"You planning on hitchhiking all the way to New Jersey?"

He shook his head. There was a silver cigarette case on the seat between them.

"Mind if I take one of those?" he said.

"Go ahead."

He opened the case. They were women's cigarettes, long, with a good inch of filter.

"One for you?" he said.

"No, I'm trying to cut back. Add a few years to my life."

He took a cigarette out and she punched in the dashboard lighter. He put the case back on the seat, broke the filter off.

"Sorry," he said. "Not used to them."

"That's all right."

He powered the window down, hot air rushing in, threw the filter out. When the lighter popped, she handed it to him. He got the cigarette going, dragged the smoke deep into his lungs, replaced the lighter himself. For the first time, he noticed the key chain hanging from the ignition. Along with the keypad for the alarm and locks, there was a rabbit's foot. It was the first one he'd seen in years.

He slid the window back up until it was open just a crack, blew smoke through.

"My friends in St. Augustine," he said, "they owe me some money. I'll take that, buy a ticket, get a plane out of Jacksonville, maybe a train."

"Plane's cheaper, and easier. You have family in New Jersey?"

"A little boy. I haven't seen him for a while."

"I'm sorry about that. Will you see him when you get there?"

"I hope so."

"How old is he?"

"About seven now. His mother and I . . . we're not together anymore."

"I guessed. Still, he'll be happy to see his father, I'm sure. With Christmas coming up."

"I hope. Ashtray?"

"Right there."

It was neatly hidden in the dash. He slid it out, tapped ash into it.

"I'm sorry," she said. "I shouldn't pry like that, asking about your family situation."

"It's all right."

"I can imagine how you feel. My children are all grown now."

"They down here?"

She shook her head.

"Connecticut. That's where we're from. But I live in Boca now."

He looked at her hands on the wheel.

"No ring."

"I'm divorced. Just last year."

"Sorry."

"My ex-husband built houses. We moved down here because he had so many projects going. Too many. He never had time for any-thing else."

They passed a state police cruiser parked on the shoulder. He watched it as they went past.

"It's better this way, though," she said. "It's like a new life, you know?"

"I know exactly."

They drove in silence for a few minutes.

"John, I changed my mind. Can you light me one of those?"

He did. When he handed it to her, her fingers touched his for an instant, then drew away. Smoke drifted across the inside of the windshield.

"When you get up there," she said, "will you stay?"

"I don't know. I don't think so. It depends what happens."

"You have work up there?"

"I will."

"And what is it exactly you do?"

He looked out the window, thought of the miles falling away behind him. The miles left to go.

"I can do all kinds of things," he said.

She smiled, kept her eyes on the road.

"I imagine you can," she said.

THE FUEL light went on just outside St. Augustine. He steered the Buick off the elevated highway and down a sloping exit ramp to a combination Waffle House and Chevron station, its two-story sign rising above the roadway. He touched the scratch on the left side of his neck, looked at his fingertips, saw the redness there.

At the pumps, he felt around beside the driver's seat for the fuel door lever. The first one he tugged unlocked the trunk, the lid rising. He was out of the car quickly, put a hand on the lid, thumped it shut.

He put five dollars' worth of super in the Buick, went inside and paid the attendant—a teenage girl—in cash, saw her looking at the scratch. He got change for the pay phone, felt her eyes on him as he went back out.

He made the call, traffic humming on the highway above. After he hung up, he went back to the Buick, got behind the wheel again, started the engine, pulled out.

Back on the highway, heading north, he smoked another of her cigarettes. He felt good. He'd seized the opportunity offered him, the car allowing him to cover more distance in an hour than he could in two days on foot. The moment the Buick had pulled onto the shoulder, he knew it was a sign. It was the universe aligning itself, paving his way. He could not be stopped.

WHEN HE hit St. Augustine, he found the courthouse, drove slow down side streets until he spotted the bail bonds office. He parked a block away, went in, the opening door setting off a buzzer somewhere inside.

There was a single desk out front, plastic chairs. Vertical blinds on the big window, late-afternoon sun flashing through; magazines and a fat dead fly on the sill. The door to the inner office was closed. The woman at the desk, red hair piled high, was talking on the phone in a Southern accent. She looked up at him and a moment later the inner door opened. A balding, middle-aged man in a short-sleeved shirt waved him in.

He went into the inner office and the man closed the door behind him, sat down at a paper-cluttered desk. A noisy air conditioner worked in one window, a strip of yellow ribbon fluttering from it.

"Good thing you called ahead," the man said. "Getting ready to shut down for the day, go hit some golf balls. You would've been out of luck."

Johnny waited, standing.

"You look like your picture," the man said. "I have to give you that. No sense asking for ID, I suppose."

He opened a desk drawer, came out with a legal-size manila envelope. He put it on the desktop, left the drawer open. Johnny knew there would be a gun inside, in easy reach. He came closer, picked up the envelope.

"Don't know who I'm doing this for," the man said. "Or why. But I know how to follow instructions. It's all there."

The flap was sealed. The man slid a silver letter opener across the desk. Johnny used it on the envelope, looked inside, counted. There were twenty fifty-dollar bills.

"Supposed to be more," he said.

"You'll have to take that up with someone else. A grand, that's what I was told."

Johnny looked at him, the letter opener still in his hand. The man scratched his elbow. His eyes flicked toward the open desk drawer.

"You'd never make it," Johnny said.

The man looked at him, said nothing.

Johnny set the opener down on the blotter, left the office. The woman was still on the phone, but she watched him as he went out the door.

He drove five blocks, found a coffee shop. He sat where he could watch the car and ate a steak with french fries and green beans. It was his first real meal since leaving Glades. He ate slow, washing it all down with swallows of sweet tea from a red plastic glass. When he was done he put one of the fifties beside the plate, went to a phone booth in the back.

From his shirt pocket, he took out the piece of paper with the ten-digit number on it. He fed in coins, dialed the number, waited while it rang. When the pager on the other end beeped, he punched in the number of the pay phone, hung up.

He waited there until it rang back.

"Yeah?" a voice said.

"It's me."

"Where are you?"

"St. Augustine."

"You get it?"

"I got it. It's shy."

"I had some second thoughts. We can discuss it when you get up here."

"This is a bad way to start."

"We'll talk about it later. I can't stay on. This isn't a secure line. Let me call you back from someplace else."

"No need. I just wanted to let you know."

"Let me know what?"

"That I'm on my way." He hung up.

Forty minutes later, he was at the airport in Jacksonville. He watched for signs, steered the Buick into the long-term parking lot. He got a ticket from the machine, waited for the automated gate to open. It took him five minutes to find an empty spot. He pulled the Buick into it, killed the engine, got the duffel from the backseat.

He took a white T-shirt out, used it to wipe down the inside of the car, the cigarette case. When he was done, he got out, hipped the door shut, wiped the outside latches, then the trunk lid. He put the T-shirt back in the bag, the envelope already in there.

He locked the doors with the remote, tore the ticket up, let the breeze take the pieces. Slinging the duffel over his shoulder, he started walking toward the terminal, heat shimmer rising off the blacktop around him.

There were buses waiting at the far end of the terminal. He would get one into town, catch a train north. Two, three days at the most and he'd be there.

Near the bus stand, he stopped, got the key chain out. He stripped half the keys off the ring, dropped them through the grate of a storm drain. He found another grate twenty feet away, dropped in the rest of the keys, stepped on the remote and kicked the broken pieces of it in after them. He kept the rabbit's foot.

TWO

THE WEEK AFTER THANKSGIVING AND IT SEEMED LIKE WINTER WAS already here to stay.

Even back here, in the cooler, they could hear the sleet rattling the plate-glass windows of the liquor store. The space heater at their feet glowed orange, but Harry could barely feel it. He knew they'd be there for hours, so he'd dressed accordingly—flannel shirt with T-shirt under it, boots, jeans with long johns beneath, black windbreaker with the RW Security logo front and back in white lettering.

Gray metal walls on three sides, cooler doors on the fourth. They'd assembled a makeshift table out of four cases of Miller Lite and a half sheet of plywood. On another case sat the closed-circuit monitor that was hooked up to the store camera.

Errol drew a card from the deck.

"Dealer takes one," he said. His breath misted in the air.

Harry looked at his own cards. They were playing five-card draw and he'd had a pair of queens to start with, had taken three cards, picked up a pair of threes and a five.

There was two dollars in change in the pot. Errol put in another quarter. Harry matched it.

"Call," he said.

Errol turned his cards over one by one. Queen of hearts, six of hearts, four of hearts, two of hearts. Harry didn't even wait to see the last card. He dropped his face-down on the table.

"Got lucky on that one," Errol said. He swept the change toward him, gathered up the cards and began to shuffle again.

10

"Going to stretch my legs," Harry said.

He got up from the wooden folding chair, checked his watch. Nine-thirty. They'd been here three hours. The store would close at eleven and they'd stick around another hour until the money was counted, then ride along for the night deposit. Already, his left elbow ached. It had been broken a little over a year ago, and cold and damp brought the pain back, along with the knowledge it would bother him the rest of his life.

"No one's going out there tonight," Errol said. "Not the way that shit's blowing. Black folks don't like this kind of weather."

Harry wandered over to the racks, looked past six-packs of Michelob, through the thick glass of one of the cooler doors. Chaney, the old black man who owned the place, was behind the counter ringing up a bottle of champagne for an enormous woman in Capri pants and a waist-length cape. This was Harry's third night here and he'd yet to see a single white customer. Chaney's nephew Lyle, a heavy, slow man with a lazy left eye, passed by, pushing a broom.

Harry dug into his jeans pocket, came out with the small twist of aluminum foil. Inside was a Percocet, broken into quarters. With his back to Errol, he slipped one into his mouth, dry-swallowed it, closed the foil again.

"What I still don't understand," Errol said, "is what the hell you're doing here."

Harry turned to him. Errol was one of a half dozen black cops Ray Washington employed in their off-duty hours. He was in his early thirties, fit and lean, with close-cropped hair and coffee-dark skin. He wore a thick commando sweater beneath his windbreaker, thicker still for the Kevlar vest under it. A Smith & Wesson .380 automatic in a clip holster rested alongside the monitor.

Ray had given Harry a weapon as well, a short-nosed blue-steel Colt .38. It was holstered on his right hip, a familiar weight beneath the windbreaker.

"Honest work," Harry said. "Just like you."

"You know Ray, what, ten years?"

"Closer to fifteen."

"You on the state police with him, right?"

"We were in the same class at the academy, worked the Turnpike together. He went on to MCU and I followed later."

"Major Crimes. Not many black men in that. I thought about taking the test once. For the state. But I hear they can still make it tough on a brother if they don't like him, even if he's lucky enough to get in the door."

"There's good people there. Bad ones too. Like everything else."

"But both of you quit."

"Different reasons."

"I know about Ray, all that bullshit he had to put up with. How about you?"

"I got shot."

Errol looked at him, said nothing.

"Can I use your cell for a minute?" Harry said.

"Sure." Errol took it off his belt, handed it over. Harry opened it, dialed his own number. When the machine picked up, he cut it off, punched in his security code. The tape rewound, hissing, stopped. Three hang-ups, one automated mortgage solicitation. Nothing from her.

He clicked off.

"Thanks." He closed the phone and handed it back. Errol set it on the table.

They heard the door chimes ring, looked at the monitor. Chaney had his coat on, was going out the door, Lyle behind the counter now.

"Coffee run," Errol said. "Right on time. Be a nice change, he ever asked us if we wanted anything."

He was feeling the Percocet now, the pain in his elbow fading. Errol picked up the cards, began to shuffle again.

"In or out?" he said.

"In."

Harry took the chair, turned it around, straddled it. He adjusted the holster so it didn't dig into his hip, picked up the cards he was dealt.

"Five-card draw again," Errol said. "Deuces wild."

Harry looked at his hand, eights and aces and a hanging six. He put a quarter in the pot to get started.

"So, a watch commander and two patrolmen are walking down

the beach," Errol said. "And one of the patrolmen finds this lamp in the sand, you know, like an old lamp. Arabian."

"Got it."

"So the one patrolman rubs it, and this big, black genie comes out, dressed in genie clothes, and he says, 'I've been trapped in that motherfucking lamp for two thousand years, and now you've freed me, so I'll give y'all one wish each, anything you want.' So the first patrolman thinks and he says, 'You know, I'm tired of sitting in a unit, freezing my ass off all winter. I want to go on a cruise in the tropics, all expenses paid, luxury accommodations, with a bunch of fine supermodels. And all we'd do is fuck all night and lie in the sun all day.' So the genie says, 'Okay, you got it,' and in a puff of smoke the first cop's gone.

"So the genie turns to the second patrolman and says, 'Your turn, bro. Anything you want. Say it and it will be yours.' So he thinks a little bit and he says, 'I want a big old house on top of a mountain in Jamaica, where it's warm all the time and I can just sit around, watch the sunset and smoke reefer.' And then *poof,* he's gone too, just like that.

"So, finally, the genie turns to the watch commander and says, 'You get one wish too. What do *you* want?' And the watch commander says, 'I want those two assholes back here *right now.*'"

Harry laughed, looked at his cards. Errol said, "Check out this shit."

Harry looked at the screen. Lyle had taken a pint bottle from beneath the counter. He unscrewed the cap, took a sip.

"Now, do you think that ignorant motherfucker does not realize we can see everything he does?" Errol said. "Or does he just not care?"

They watched him put the cap back on, replace the bottle under the counter. Errol shook his head, picked up the deck again.

"How many?" he said and Harry answered, "One," thinking for the first time he might have a shot at winning this hand, and then the chimes rang again and the door opened.

"Yo," Errol said. Harry dropped his discard, looked at the screen.

His first thought was that it was a kid, a boy. He wore a puffy jacket, hands deep in the pockets, baseball cap pulled low. Even with the distortion of the camera angle, he looked half the size of

Lyle. And then he took a hand out of his pocket and there was a gun in it.

"Goddammit," Errol said and dropped his cards on the table, reached for the holster.

Harry got up, looked out through the cooler glass. The kid had the gun, a short-barreled revolver, pointed sideways at Lyle's head, and was yelling at him. Harry couldn't hear the words.

He looked at the cell phone. He knew the drill, what they'd been told. Call 911 first, get the locals on the move before taking any action. But Errol was already at the door of the cooler, the Smith & Wesson out and up.

The kid was still yelling, the gun unsteady. Lyle punched at the register, screwing up the keys and having to do it again, the kid getting impatient, the wavering muzzle closer to Lyle's face. The register drawer popped open and the kid waved Lyle back with the gun, then leaned over the counter and started grabbing bills.

Errol looked back at Harry from the cooler door, hand on the latch, said, "Come *on,*" and then Harry was behind him, moving on instinct, his hand on the .38.

"It's a kid," he said, more to himself than Errol, and then the cooler door was open and they were hurtling through it. Errol was screaming commands, the Smith & Wesson in a two-handed grip, and the kid turned, surprise and fear on his face, and shot him twice in the chest.

The gun made a noise like firecrackers, two quick, unimpressive snaps. Errol sat down hard, crashed back against a promotional display of beer cases, said, "God *damn* it." Harry moved in front of him, shielding him, the .38 steady, pointing at the kid's chest, screamed, *"Put it down! Put it down!"* and the kid fired again, wild, and Harry heard the round punch through cooler glass. He yelled, *"Down! Down! Down!"* his finger tightening on the trigger, feeling the hammer pull. He had a clear shot, impossible to miss, less than ten feet between them. He looked into the kid's wide eyes—he was fourteen, fifteen at the oldest—and centered the front sight on his chest, began to squeeze.

The kid dropped the gun. It clattered and flew apart on the linoleum floor. His hands came slowly to shoulder height, the bills still clutched in his left hand.

Harry let his breath out slowly, eased off on the trigger. There was silence. Then, behind him, he heard Errol say, "Mother*fucker.*"

"On your knees," Harry said. "Slow. Hands behind your head."

The kid was shaking now, confused, not processing what had happened. Lyle backed away, lowered his hands.

"On your knees," Harry said again.

The kid's hands went higher, ear level, awkward.

"Relax, son. Do as I say and you won't get hurt."

The kid laced his fingers behind his neck. Harry let the muzzle of the .38 drop, spoke clearly, slowly.

"Now kneel down. On the floor. Do it now."

The kid started to obey and then, from the corner of his eye, Harry saw Lyle's hand go below the counter, reaching for the pint maybe, a drink to steady his nerves. Then the gun came up, a revolver, no bigger than a starter's pistol. The kid was still looking at Harry, not seeing the gun, and Harry only had time to yell *"No!"* once before Lyle leaned close and shot him in the head.

There wasn't much noise. A quick crack, the muzzle of the gun barely rising, and the kid fell instantly to the floor, everything loose. Lyle leaned his bulk over the counter, holding on with one hand so he didn't overbalance. The gun sparked and cracked again and the kid shook once and lay still.

Harry was moving now, closing the distance.

"Put it down," he said.

Lyle looked at him, his face blank.

"Put the gun down."

"Got that motherfucker," Lyle said and set the gun on the counter.

The kid moaned, one leg kicked. There was blood on the floor, blood on his jacket, blood in his hair. The baseball cap lay a few feet away. Bills were scattered on the floor.

The kid's gun was in two pieces, bits of black electrician's tape stuck to them. Harry scattered them with his foot.

"Call 911," he said.

Lyle didn't move.

From behind him, Harry heard Errol say softly, "Son of a bitch," as he got to his feet.

Harry holstered the .38, looked at Lyle.

15

"Good shot," he said. He slid Lyle's gun along the counter, out of reach.

"That nigga went *down*," Lyle said and Harry nodded, raised his right hand.

"Man, what are you . . ." Lyle started to say, and then Harry leaned over the counter and hit him as hard as he could in the face.

THREE

WHAT THE *FUCK*?" RAY WASHINGTON SAID.

They were out in the parking lot, getting wet, the building overhang blocking the wind only slightly. The sleet had turned to a steady rain. There were a half dozen cruisers in the lot, rollers flashing, red and blue lights reflecting off the wet pavement. Cops wandered idly through the store.

Harry shrugged. His right hand was swollen, stiff, but he wasn't feeling the pain yet. The adrenaline and the Percocet were keeping it at bay. But his stomach was sour, and every few minutes a wave of nausea would rise up in him that he had to choke down.

Through the window he could see two Neptune cops talking to Chaney. A few feet away, a plainclothes detective had Lyle off to the side. He had an ice-filled towel pressed against his face and occasionally cut an angry glance at Harry through the glass.

The ambulances had been and gone. He was starting to feel the fatigue now, the sleepy dislocation that always came after moments of high stress.

"How's Errol?" he said.

"Said he was fine, but I told him he had to go to the hospital anyway, get some X-rays. Insurance reasons. Now, listen, we need to get our stories straight here."

"It happened just the way I told it. Tell them to pull the tape. It's all on there."

"I'm sure they will. In the meantime, I have a very pissed-off business owner here. I don't think this is the way he saw things going."

"That Neptune cop, the first one I talked to, said he knows the kid. Said he's fourteen. His brother's in prison."

"Which is where he'll be himself someday if he lives long enough. Maybe Lyle did him a favor."

"You believe that?"

"Who am I talking to here, Jesse Jackson? Get your shit correct. He walked in there with a gun in his hand. He did it before, he'll do it again."

"If he lives."

He looked away at the cars on Route 33, most of them slowing down to see what was happening.

"Come on," Ray said. "Let's get out of this rain."

They went back inside. Chaney looked over at them from where he stood talking to the two cops. Ray took Harry's arm, guided him in the other direction. The blood on the floor was already drying, thick and tacky in the fluorescent light.

A uniformed cop escorted Lyle out the door, still holding the towel to his face. The plainclothes cop who'd been talking to him looked around, saw Ray. He was a heavyset white man in his fifties, wearing a satin New Jersey Devils jacket over a shirt and tie. Harry didn't know him.

He came over, shook hands with Ray, nodded at Harry.

"What a mess, huh?" he said, taking a pack of cigarettes from his jacket pocket.

"Ed Odell, this is Harry Rane. He works for me."

Odell looked at him but didn't offer his hand. He pried a cigarette out of the half-empty pack, lit it with a Cricket.

"Rane? I know you?"

"We worked together for the state," Ray said. "MCU. He's been with me about six months."

"And I trust those weapons are fully licensed, carry permits and all?"

"Of course," Ray said. "Happy to show you the papers."

Odell looked at Harry.

"Been a while since you've been in the middle of something like this, I'd guess," he said. "When did you leave the state?"

"Three years ago."

"Drummed out, huh?" He smiled.

"Something like that."

"Well, Ray." He turned away from Harry. "I know the mayor

okayed your being here and I know the Businessman's Association or Civil Rights Council—or whatever the fuck they're calling themselves these days—is paying for it, but aggravation like this I don't need."

He looked Ray in the eye. Smoke drifted between them.

"Don't mean to step on your toes here, Ed, but if these people feel they're not getting enough police protection, then they're entitled to bring in someone else. Every corporation and chain store in the area has private security. Why is this different?"

"Because I can't remember the last time I had to respond to a shooting at Sears, that's why. You state people, even after you leave the job, you've got the same attitude. Like the locals are some sort of Mickey Mouse outfit and you're going to come in and tell us how things should be run. I have to put up with that bullshit sometimes, no way around it, but I don't have to put up with it from you now."

"That's not the way it is, Ed, and you know it."

"Looks like we're stuck cleaning up your mess, though. And maybe I should be making a call to Errol Micheaux's boss over in Asbury too."

"He's been cleared to work for me. He's off-duty. No one's breaking any rules."

"Could be you need to hire some Neptune boys. Maybe they'd have had this situation under control a little quicker, with nobody getting hurt."

"How's the kid?" Harry said.

Odell looked at him.

"Kid? You referring to the shooter or the employee whose face you fucked up?"

"He shot that boy point-blank, unarmed. It wasn't right."

"Well, maybe that 'kid' will learn his lesson now."

"How is he?"

"Last I heard from the hospital, he was still unconscious. Twenty-twos, though, they can be bad with head wounds. Small slug, but it rattles around in there, bounces off the bone. Can do a lot of damage."

"Is he going to live?"

"Got a coin?"

Odell slapped Ray on the arm.

"Let's talk in the morning," he said. "Come by headquarters. And bring that paper."

He turned away, went over to talk to one of the uniforms.

"Prick," Harry said under his breath.

"You've been out of the Life too long," Ray said. "He's a prince compared to some I have to deal with. Come on, let's take a drive. We need to talk."

WHEN RAY went to use the phone at the back of the diner, Harry swallowed another Percocet quarter, washed it down with coffee. He looked out the window at the rain. They'd driven from the liquor store in Ray's Camry, left the Mustang there. He hoped there were enough cops still at the scene that it wouldn't be stolen.

Ray hung up, walked back to their table, sat down. A gust of wind blew rain against the windows, made the glass shudder.

"Well?" Harry said.

"The boy's name is Luther Wilkins. He's still in surgery. We'll know more later. The ER doctor says his signs were good, brain activity strong."

"And Errol?"

"Minor bruising to his chest. Nothing much, but he'll get a story to tell out of it. Never been shot at before."

"He did good in there. Moved fast. The kid panicked. There was nothing he could have done about that."

"He wouldn't be moving very fast now if he hadn't been wearing that vest. You should have had one too."

"Next time, I will."

Ray drank coffee.

"I don't think there'll be a next time," he said. He set the cup down. "At least not there."

"What do you mean?"

"I don't imagine that old man is going to invite us back. I don't think he was one hundred percent in favor of us to start with."

20

"So why were we there?"

"A dozen robberies at black businesses in Neptune and Asbury since August, no arrests in any of them. The Citizens Crime Watch Committee decided to pool their money, hire private security. I quoted them a good rate. It was important to them, I think, to go to a black firm."

"And then the white guy shows up and all hell breaks loose."

"There's some will look at it that way, sure. Doesn't make them right." He gestured to the waitress, who returned with the coffeepot, poured for both of them. "I've been rotating three two-man teams out of seven different businesses for a month, and that's the first time anything's happened."

"So you're going to retire me?"

"Hell, it's not like you did anything wrong. You probably saved a couple lives in there. But the neighborhood people . . . they can get unduly sensitive about white police in their midst. Even ex-police."

"I understand."

"After tonight, what actually happened in there won't matter. There'll be at least two other stories about it floating around on the street."

"In both of which, I'm at fault."

"This is a rumor community," Ray said. "Word-of-mouth. People don't always read the papers. And when they do, they don't necessarily believe what they read anyway. Black folks have a long history of mistrusting authority. Can you blame them?"

"So this isn't exactly a public relations coup for you. That what you're telling me?"

"Not what I said. I'm happy—grateful even—you took me up on the offer to come work with me. But maybe we should rethink this particular situation."

Harry sat back.

"Don't sweat it, Ray. I'm fine. You don't need to go out of your way for me."

"Did I say I was? We'll find something else for you to do. It isn't a problem."

"But is it worth it?"

Ray didn't answer, put his cup down.

21

Harry looked out at the rain.

"This weather's getting to me."

"Heard from Cristina?"

Harry shook his head.

"A letter about three weeks ago, that was it. Nothing since."

"You try to call her?"

"No."

"Why not?"

"When she's ready, she'll call me."

"With all that happened between you two, I can understand her wanting to get away, get some things clear in her head. But you act like she's never coming back. Like it's already a lost cause."

"Maybe it is."

"You should listen to yourself. You think you were going to come back here, do the happily-ever-after thing just like that? You got the crap beat out of you, got your arm broken, her husband got murdered. Not exactly your normal courtship."

"I don't know what I thought."

"You were doing well for a while, partner, and now you're sliding again. I can see it, hear it in your voice."

Harry shrugged.

"You ever consider seeing someone?" Ray said.

"What do you mean?"

"To talk with. You know."

"A therapist? I did for a while, a few years back. After Melissa died."

"And?"

"It was good for me at the time, I guess. But after a few weeks I felt like we were just going in circles. The pills didn't help either."

"What they give you?"

"Something called Paxil. I took it three times, flushed the rest down the toilet."

"Maybe you should go back. Find a different doctor."

Harry shook his head.

"Where did you say she was?" Ray said.

"Seattle. She has a cousin there."

"And how long's she been gone?"

"Two months this week."

Ray looked down at his cup.

"If I were you . . ."

"Yeah?"

"I'd go out there. Show up on her doorstep. Sometimes that's what women need, a gesture."

"Maybe I'm all gestured out."

Ray took out his wallet.

"Come on," he said. "Let's get out of here. I'll drive you back to the store, let you get your car. Then I'll call the hospital again. I have the feeling it's going to be a long night."

THERE WERE still a handful of patrolmen at the liquor store, but Odell and the other detectives had gone. One cop had a roll of yellow crime scene tape, was waiting for the others to finish up before sealing the place off.

The Mustang was intact. Standing in the rain, Harry got his keys out, unlocked the driver's-side door.

Ray slid the Camry's window halfway down.

"Give me a call tomorrow," he said. "We'll figure something out."

Harry nodded, got behind the wheel. As he started the engine, he looked up, saw the uniforms watching him from inside the store. The cop with the crime scene tape gave him the finger.

THE RAIN had slackened by the time he reached Colts Neck. He pulled up the long slope of driveway, left the Mustang in the side yard, not having the energy to push open the barn door, park inside. He was shivering now, with cold and post-adrenaline hangover.

In the kitchen, the answering machine was dark. He played the tape back anyway, listened to it beep, hiss, click, shut off again.

He hung the wet windbreaker on a peg by the back door. He'd left the .38 with Ray. He wouldn't need it anytime soon. And he didn't want it in the house.

There was half a bottle of red wine left on the counter. He filled a glass, took it with him upstairs. In the bathroom, he stripped off his clothes, tossed them into the corner, the hamper already full. He turned the shower on hot, set the glass on the sink and climbed into the needling spray, felt it loosen the muscles in his back and neck.

After a few minutes, he grew sleepy, twisted off the faucets. He got out, toweled off, took his first sip of wine. Almost instantly he felt his stomach clench, the nausea rise.

He barely made it to the sink. His vomit was thin and watery, dark from the coffee. He gagged as it came up, gripped the edges of the sink. When it was over, he ran water, drank from the faucet, spit and drank some more. He wiped at his face with a towel, then poured the rest of the wine into the sink. It splashed like blood on the porcelain. He left the glass there, walked naked and cold down the hall to his unmade bed.

There were traces of her everywhere: her jewelry box and makeup case on the dresser, a Chinese-print robe hanging from the back of the bedroom door. She had worn it the morning she'd left, hung it on the door before getting dressed. He'd left it there ever since, untouched. When he'd gotten back from taking her to the airport, the sight of it had made him cry.

He dressed for bed, sweatpants and T-shirt, listening to the wind. The farmhouse was more than a hundred years old, had belonged to his grandparents and their parents before them. No matter how much insulating or weather-stripping he did, the cold found a thousand places to enter. The hardwood floor was like ice beneath his bare feet.

In the hallway, he turned the thermostat up, heard the furnace thump and rumble in the basement. He got into bed, switched the nightstand lamp off, lay back on the sheets. When he closed his eyes he saw the muzzle flash of the .22, the kid's legs giving way, the blood on the floor.

After a while, he looked at the nightstand clock, saw it was almost three. He got out of bed, went down the hall to the bathroom. In the medicine cabinet was the Percocet bottle, two months past its expiration date. There were about a dozen left. He shook one out, snapped it in half, swallowed it with a palmful of water.

He'd needed her tonight, more than ever. Needed her to be here, needed her to care about what had happened. To tell him that every-thing would be all right, whether either of them believed it or not.

When he went back to bed, the sheets had already given up their warmth. He pulled the comforter across him, trembling with cold and more, closed his eyes and let the night take him.

FOUR

IT WAS IN JAMESBURG THAT HE FIRST SAW THE VALLEY. HE WAS FOUR-
teen and it was his second jolt there, nine months for aggravated
assault.

How it had happened, why the vision had come to him, Johnny
didn't know. He'd been in isolation, a one-bed cell, after his second
fight in as many weeks. Lying on the thin mattress, coils pushing
through it, he closed his eyes and tried to ignore the noises that fil-
tered in from the hallway: yelling, the blare of a TV from the common room and, from the cell next door, the steady crying of a
young boy.

The vision came suddenly. A mountain green with trees, so green
nothing could be seen through them. He saw it as a bird might,
swooping easily, silently. And there, at the base of the mountain,
was the Valley, white with mist.

It had calmed him, settled him. And after a while he had tuned
out the noise, tuned out that world. His cell had vanished. He was
borne on the wind, dropping slowly into the comfort of the Valley.

Where the vision came from, he never knew. But it had come to
stay. There in Jamesburg and later on, in other cells. In Glades,
there had been times when the idea of spending a single night more
behind those walls made him want to open his own throat with the
homemade knife he'd kept beneath his mattress. It was those nights
he would close his eyes, listen to his own breathing, find himself
floating above the mist, the trees.

Later he found he could do it almost anywhere, in seconds,
even with his eyes open. In the cafeteria, the weight room, the
showers. The vision steadied him, soothed him, told him he would

26

survive. That, no matter what, the Valley and its peace always waited for him.

When the train pulled into Newark, he opened his eyes, felt the Valley fade. The doors had slid open, people were moving down the aisle. A chill breeze blew through the car. He got up, stretched his legs, took the duffel down from the overhead rack.

Home again, he thought. The longest he'd ever been away. But everything was different now. *He* was different. And nothing would ever be the same.

HE KNOCKED twice on the trailer door with his fist, loud enough to wake anyone inside. He listened, did it again.

On the street behind him, the cab driver was watching, restless. He knocked a third time, waited, heard a muffled, "Who the fuck is that?" from inside.

It was ten-thirty in the morning. He knew Mitch would be asleep, unless he was still partying from the night before. Johnny knocked again, louder.

"It's me," he said. "Open the door."

Movement inside, then locks being undone. He stepped back, waited. The door opened out a few inches, the length of the chain. His brother looked out at him, unshaven and bleary-eyed, most of him still hidden behind the door.

"Hey," Johnny said.

"Son of a bitch. Hang on."

The door closed and the chain slid off. Johnny turned and waved at the driver. He pulled away, happy to be out of there.

Mitch opened the door wide.

"Come in, man, come in."

Johnny slung his duffel over his shoulder. Mitch wore jeans, a white T-shirt, was barefoot. He stepped aside as Johnny came in.

The front room was a mess. Clothes on the floor and furniture. An ashtray full of cigarette butts and burned-out roaches. The smell of stale incense and last night's pot hung in the air.

"You should've called me, man," Mitch said as he closed and locked the door behind him. "I could have picked you up. How'd you get here?"

"Train," Johnny said, looking around. There was a widescreen TV in one corner, a stack of unopened stereo component boxes beside it. A tumble of videotapes and DVDs on the floor, kids' movies, a handful of titles he recognized—*Pinocchio, The Little Mermaid*. Seven years inside had given him a sense of order and space, of organization. He had lived like this himself once, but now what he saw offended him.

"Let me take your bag, man."

Johnny let him take the duffel, unzipped his black field jacket. Somewhere in Delaware, he'd stolen it from the train's overhead rack, bundled it beneath his arm and carried it back to his own car. Three people had watched him, but no one said anything. It was a size too big, but he was grateful for its warmth.

"You got my letter, right?" Johnny said.

"Yeah, but I didn't think you'd be here so soon, bro. I mean, if I knew . . ."

"It's okay."

Mitch, still slow with sleep, set the duffel in a corner, began to gather discs and tapes off the floor, stuff them into an open compartment in the TV console.

Johnny heard movement behind him, turned to see a black woman standing in the doorway that led to the back of the trailer. She was in her early twenties, thin, her once-dreadlocked hair now matted and lank. She held a blue terry-cloth robe closed around her, but a small rip on one side showed a patch of mocha thigh. From a room beyond came the sound of another TV, cartoons.

She looked at him, said nothing.

"Sharonda," Mitch said. "Go get dressed."

She looked at him, then back at Johnny. She slowly pushed off from the door frame, turned and went back down the hall.

"Go on, man. Have a seat."

Johnny slipped the jacket off, dropped it on the arm of the sofa. He moved a stuffed dog aside, sat down.

"I was expecting you to call, man," Mitch said. He sat on a recliner opposite the couch. "I would have made you something to eat or . . ."

Johnny shook his head. He'd slept little on the train and the

28

fatigue was on him now. He rubbed the stubble on his chin, took off the Marlins cap, set it beside him.

"Oh, man," Mitch said. "What happened to you?"

"Shaved it all off." He ran a hand through his thin hair. "In Glades."

"What for?"

Before he could answer, there was a noise in the hall. Johnny turned to see a black girl of about six standing there, wearing pink zip-up pajamas, bows tied in the rattails of her hair. She looked at him, rubbed sleep from an eye.

"Hi, there," he said to her. "How you doing?"

She looked back at him without expression. Sharonda appeared in the hallway behind her, dressed now in jeans and a knee-length blue and gold basketball jersey. She took the girl by the hand, gave Johnny a look he couldn't read, then wheeled them both back down the hall and into a bedroom. He watched her go, heard a door close.

"Yours?" Johnny said.

"What? Treya? Oh, no, man. Sharonda had to leave her place. I'm just letting her stay here a few days. It's not what it looks like."

"I couldn't care less, Mitchy."

"I know, I'm just saying—"

"You should crack a window, let some air in."

Mitch got up quickly, went to the window beside the front door, undid the latch and fought with the pane until it opened. Cold air wafted in.

"I can't tell you how good it is to see you, bro," Mitch said. "Let me get you a beer." He started toward the kitchen.

"Little early for that. Maybe later."

Mitch sank back down in the chair. He leaned forward, forearms on his knees, scratched the wiry red hairs on one arm. Johnny looked at him, sensing his discomfort. Seven years since they'd seen each other, and Mitch not knowing how to feel, how to react.

"How you been getting along?" Johnny said.

Mitch shrugged.

"You know. Same old, same old. Couple bucks here, couple bucks there. Enough not to have to go to bed sober at night if I don't want to."

"That thing work out for you? What I told you about?"

"With Joey? No, man, he just . . . I don't know. I guess I just wasn't cut out for it. He said the words but he acted like he didn't want anything to do with me. Had me selling phone cards on the street, believe that? Bogus phone cards like I was some sort of punk-ass scammer. I hung with him a couple months and then I said adiós. He wasn't sorry to see me go."

"I'll talk to him about it."

"No, man, don't bother. It just wasn't working out."

"I wrote him from Glades when I went in, asked him to look after you, throw you something now and then."

"And he did, man, and now it's over. I already forgot about it. Ain't no thing."

"You should have told me about it. Wrote me."

"Like I said, it didn't matter much. All that matters now, man, is having you in the flesh right here. And you look good."

"I was in the same place a long time, Mitchy. You could have come to see me."

Mitch shook his head, looked at the floor.

"I thought about it. A lot. But it's just . . ."

"What?"

"The idea of seeing you like that. In that place . . ."

"In a cage."

"I just couldn't handle it. I don't know if that makes any sense. But it's true."

Johnny got Camels from his jacket pocket, lit one with the Zippo, sat back.

"You look like you could use that beer yourself," he said. "Go ahead."

Mitch got up, went into the small kitchen, got a can of Budweiser from the refrigerator. Johnny could see a sink full of dishes. Mitch popped the can, came back into the living room, sipping foam.

"I don't know how long I'm going to be around," Johnny said.

Mitch sat back down.

"Where you going?"

"I've got some business to take care of. And when it's done I'm probably going to take off for a while. In the meantime, I'm putting something together, little by little. You could have a piece of it."

"I appreciate that, man, but really . . . you don't need to. I mean, me and Sharonda . . ."

"Yeah?"

"Well, I'm doing all right. Not getting rich but I'm doing okay, you know? Like maybe for the first time in a while."

"Feels good, doesn't it?"

"Yeah. It's just that . . . I guess I was getting a little old for all that bullshit." He grinned. "Now all I want to do is sit around and watch the flat-screen, you know? Scratch my nuts, drink some beer. Go out and get paid every once in a while. Ain't bad."

"I guess not."

"So you thought about it?" Mitch said. "What you want to do now?"

"Thought about it quite a bit."

Johnny pinched the cigarette out. When it was cold he put it back in the pack.

"If there's anything I can do for you, just say it," Mitch said. "Anything. You need a little cash, a place to stay, I'll find you one. I'd let you stay here, man. But the way it is . . . you know, with Sharonda . . ."

"That motel still open? In Asbury? Near the beach?"

"Which one?"

"The big one. Across from the boardwalk."

"As far as I know, yeah."

"Got wheels?"

"Outside."

"Drop me there. Let me get settled. I may need to borrow your car now and then for a little bit, till I get set up. That all right with you?"

"Anything, man. Whatever you need."

Johnny stood up, put his hands in the small of his back, stretched, felt joints creak and pop.

"Let's get going, then. I'm ready to crash."

Mitch disappeared into the back of the trailer. Johnny could hear voices, muffled, then slightly louder. He shrugged into the field jacket, pulled the cap on. As he hoisted the duffel, Mitch came back out. He wore the same jeans, boots, a hooded sweatshirt under a denim jacket.

They went out the door and when Johnny saw the old Firebird

31

parked two spaces down, he knew it had to be Mitch's. It was a faded bronze, the right front fender primer gray. Mitch locked the trailer door behind them.

They got in, the cracked seats stiff and cold, and Johnny slung the duffel into the backseat. When Mitch turned the key the engine roared, rattled, and Johnny could hear a loose manifold under the hood. Mitch gave it gas, racing the engine, warming it up. The smell of exhaust filled the car. Johnny rolled his window halfway down.

They drove slow out of the trailer park, easing over the speed bumps, the Firebird's engine low and throaty. Some of the trailers were decorated for the holidays, lights in the windows, paper Santas. Just as many weren't.

They turned south on Route 9 and Johnny looked out at strip malls, office buildings. He knew they were passing through Englishtown, where they'd both grown up, but nothing was familiar to him.

"Changed a lot, hasn't it?" Mitch said.

"It has."

"No more trees. Just in the last few years, fucking developers. Half those places are empty, man, but they just keep building more."

Mitch turned the radio on and heavy hip-hop beats filled the car. He turned it down quickly, reached behind the passenger seat without looking, fumbled through some cassette tapes.

"Forget it," Johnny said. "Let's just talk." He switched the radio off. "You ever see Frazer?"

Mitch didn't answer. Johnny watched the side of his face.

"Yeah," Mitch said finally. "Every once in a while."

"Where?"

"Around. I'll walk in some joint and see him there. We don't talk. Shit, sometimes I don't even think he remembers me anymore. He had some heart trouble a while back—or maybe it was his lungs, I don't know. I think it did some damage to his brain too. That and the liquor."

"He still live at the house?"

"Far as I know. I mean, where's he gonna go?"

They were on Route 33 now, heading east toward the ocean.

"I thought he'd be dead by now," Johnny said.

"Not far from it. He was never the same after the old lady died."

"You feel sorry for him? After what he did? Three little kids, weren't even his own?"

"I didn't say that. I hate that bastard. But you know, at least he was around most of the time."

"Been better off for us if he hadn't been."

When they hit Asbury Park, Mitch turned east on Lake, took them down to the boardwalk and onto Ocean Avenue. It was wide and empty, windblown trash in the streets. They drove past the crumbling Casino, its roof partially collapsed, walls covered with graffiti. The shops on the boardwalk were shuttered and dark, some burned out.

"It's a shame, isn't it?" Mitch said. "Remember what it was like here when we were kids?"

The stoplights above Ocean Avenue blinked yellow, swung in the wind. There were no other cars in sight.

"Things change," Johnny said.

He looked out at the desolation. Even in the seven years he'd been away, things had gotten worse. The Ferris wheel and rides that once lined the boardwalk were gone. Up ahead, near the squat bulk of Convention Hall, were two cranes, and the boardwalk around the building had been torn up. Sawhorses and yellow tape blocked the way. Across the street were empty lots where buildings had once stood.

"What are they doing up there?" he said.

"Redevelopment. They finally got the go-ahead. They're going to tear all this shit down, build condos. No surprise, I guess. Took them long enough, though. Here it is."

The Sea Vista was a six-story motel across from the boardwalk. Each room had its own terrace, a sliding glass door. But now some of the glass had been replaced by plywood, and there were letters missing from the sign on the roof.

They pulled into the gravel lot. Only three cars in it, one with flats all around.

"You sure about this, man? You can do better than here. There's a MacIntosh in Eatontown, like forty bucks a night. I'll take you there."

Johnny shook his head, looked up at the building.

"I want to stay here," he said. "Sentimental reasons."

Windblown grit rattled against the car windows.

"Can I ask you something, John?"

Johnny looked at him.

"I know it's none of my business and all, but . . . what are you going to do?"

"Right now? Sleep for a couple hours. Get some food. Maybe walk down to the Heartbreak later."

"She ain't there, Johnny. She's long gone."

"Might be some people there who know her, know where she is."

"Why bother, man? People don't stay around here like they used to. And that was a long time ago."

"I guess it was," he said and opened the door. "She always did want other things." He got out, pulled the duffel after him.

"You gonna call me?" Mitch said.

"Tomorrow. I need to get my shit together. Get some things straightened out."

"I hear you. And Johnny . . ."

Johnny stopped, his hand on the door.

"It's good to see you, man. Good to have you back home."

Johnny shut the door, stepped back. The Firebird wheeled in the lot, exhaust billowing white in the cold, pulled back onto the empty length of Ocean Avenue.

Johnny lifted the duffel, watched him drive away. Salt wind blew hard from the ocean, flapped his jacket, swirled trash in the lot. He could hear the waves, the crash of spray on the jetty. Gray clouds scudded by overhead. He felt like he was alone on the Earth.

FIVE

ERE'S THE TRUTH ABOUT THAT," RAY SAID. "FORGET ALL THAT BULL-
shit you see in the movies, read in books. Falling in love isn't
always a good thing."

He was leaning against the right front fender of the Mustang,
hands buried in his overcoat pockets. Harry had the hood open,
was using a wrench to tighten the spark plugs he'd just installed.
Wind swept through the bare willows in the backyard.

"You speaking from experience?" Harry said. He secured the last
plug, put the wrench down on the towel that protected the fender.

"I'm just saying it can be some complicated shit. And everybody's got an agenda. Everybody. Whether they admit it or not."

Harry fit the rubber boots over the spark plugs, wiped his hands
on the towel he'd slung over his shoulder. His right hand was stiff,
the first two knuckles still slightly swollen.

"Why don't you pay someone to do this shit for you?" Ray said.
"You've got the money."

"It relaxes me." He sat in the driver's seat, cranked the ignition.
The engine caught, fired. He listened to the sound of it, the cylin-
ders firing smoothly, gave it gas. The pitch of the engine rose and
fell evenly. He switched it off.

He got out, shut the hood. High above, a massive V of Canada
geese squawked, headed south, outlined against the gray clouds.

"Come on in," he said. "I'll buy you a beer."

They went in the back door and Harry washed his hands in the
kitchen sink.

"I'm guessing you haven't heard from her since we talked," Ray
said.

Harry shook his head, dried his hands on a paper towel.

"She's all right, as far as you know, though, right? I mean, you have no reason to think anything's wrong out there, do you?"

Harry got two Coronas out of the refrigerator, opened them on the counter.

"I don't know."

Ray sat at the kitchen table and Harry put a beer in front of him, took another chair.

"What's that mean?" Ray said.

Harry drank beer, shrugged.

"What? You think there's some guy involved?"

"I don't know."

Ray watched him.

"You have any evidence?" he said.

Harry looked away. "Let's just drop it for now, okay?"

"Up to you, partner. All the more reason you should take a run out there, though, show the flag, claim what's yours."

"Maybe it's not mine anymore. Maybe that's the problem."

They drank beer, neither of them speaking. The thermostat on the wall clicked and they heard the furnace kick in downstairs. Outside the wind picked up, shook the windows.

"Heard from Errol?" Harry said after a while.

"Talked to him today. He's fine. Back at work."

"And the kid, Wilkins?"

"I spoke with the hospital yesterday. He'll live. They're not guaranteeing he'll ever see again, though."

"He was fourteen."

"I know."

Harry shook his head, looked away.

"Thing about Errol is, he's still a little embarrassed about the way it went down. How he ended up flat on his ass while you dealt with the situation."

"Those were lucky shots. That kid was shaking so bad he couldn't have hit him again if he tried."

"Maybe, maybe not. But the fact remains he didn't get hit again. You saw to that."

"That whole situation was a fuckup from beginning to end. You said the same."

"Not quite. I said it was the aftermath that was problematic."

"So I'm still fired?"

"You were never fired. You're still on the payroll. I'll find something for you to do. In the meantime, you're consulting."

"Consulting on what?"

"Consulting on how long it's going to take me to get another beer. And why does this house stay so cold with the heat on."

"I can answer the first one right away," Harry said, getting up. "But for the second one, who knows?"

LATER THAT night, wind rattling the house, he felt the pull. He had stopped the driving for a while, when Cristina was here, but in the last few weeks he'd drifted back to it. He'd take late-night drives in the Mustang with no destination, just an aimless run up the Turnpike or Parkway, an hour in one direction, an hour back, stopping only for gas.

He had done it constantly in the months after Melissa died, and then again after he'd recovered from the gunshot wound that retired him. He knew why he did it. It gave him a false feeling of transition, of moving forward, leaving the sad places behind, bound for something better, even if it was only a moonlit stretch of road in the middle of the night. It was motion, it was movement. It helped.

A little after eleven, he put on his leather jacket and gloves, went out to the Mustang. The night was cold and clear. A moon bow glowed above, a single star shining within it.

He started the engine, let it warm up, the heater on full blast. He tuned the radio to an all-news station, swung around in the side yard. At the end of the driveway, he turned right on 537, headed west.

He listened to the radio without hearing it, the night bright around him. He wondered if Cristina was looking up at the same moon. If she knew he was out on the road again. Alone.

THE NEXT morning he slept until noon, woke with a headache. He'd taken the other half of the Percocet after he'd gotten home, washed it down with another Corona. For the first time in weeks, he'd slept straight through the night.

He showered, pulled on jeans and a sweatshirt. He knew he should go for a run, get his blood pumping, chase the fog from his brain. But his limbs felt like lead, his muscles ached. He made instant coffee, slumped on the couch, watched television, found himself drifting into sleep again.

The cordless phone woke him. Moving slow, he reached over, got it from the end table.

"Hey," Ray said. "What are you up to?"

"Right now? Not a whole hell of a lot."

"You got a couple hours for me this afternoon?"

He looked at his watch. It was a little after one.

"Sure. Why?"

"Something came up. Somebody I want you to meet. Can you be at the office by three?"

"I guess. Who am I meeting?"

"Does it matter? Trust me. And it might be the answer to our problem."

"How's that?"

"We'll talk about it later, partner. Get your ass in gear. I'll see you at three."

RAY WASHINGTON'S office was off Route 18 in East Brunswick, in a building he shared with a dentist and a computer repair shop. Harry popped two Aleve before he left the house, but the headache was still with him. The flesh around his eyes felt tight, and a vein throbbed in his right temple.

The receptionist buzzed him through into the inner office. There was a coffeemaker in the hall and Ray was filling two blue ceramic mugs that bore the yellow triangular State Police logo.

"Only fifteen minutes late," Ray said. "That's not too bad. Couldn't find a razor today, huh?"

Harry shrugged. Ray handed him the mug.

"You look like you could use this more than me."

"Thanks," Harry said. Ray waved at the open door to his office.

"Have a seat," he said. "I'll introduce you."

Harry sipped the steaming coffee, went in.

The woman turned as they came in. She was in her early thirties, light brown hair cut short, almost raggedly. She wore a tight black turtleneck sweater, jeans. A brown leather car coat hung from the back of the chair.

"Who's this?" she said to Ray.

He handed her the second coffee.

"An associate of mine," he said. "Harry Rane. Harry, this is Ms. Ellis."

"I thought it would just be you," she said.

"Harry's worked with me a long time. I want him to hear all this."

He went to his desk, sat down.

"Money is an issue," she said. "If there are more people involved . . ."

"Relax," Ray said. "Like I said, this is just a consult. It won't cost you anything. If it turns into something else, we can work those terms out."

Harry drew a chair away from the wall, sat down, sipped coffee.

"First things first," Ray said. "I want to bring Harry up to speed on what you told me. He might have some ideas."

Harry looked around the office. The walls were decorated with framed photos: Ray with governors, senators, civil rights leaders. On the wall behind his desk was a photo from the State Police Academy in Sea Girt, Harry and Ray standing with a group of cadets on a cold morning, halfway through their training. Harry had owned a copy of the photo once, lost it long ago.

"This is kind of unique," Ray said to him. "I'm interested in your input."

"Happy to give it." He set his coffee mug on the floor.

"Stop me if I get anything wrong," Ray said to her. "Jump in when you want." Then to Harry: "Ms. Ellis has an estranged husband."

"Not husband," she said. "We were never married. I said that."

"Sorry. Boyfriend, not husband."

"Not even that anymore."

"Whatever," Ray said. He looked at Harry again. "This individual is also father of a child they had together. Up until recently, the father was incarcerated. He's just been released and Ms. Ellis fears he's going to make an attempt to locate the child, whom Ms. Ellis gave up for adoption as an infant. And she doesn't want that to happen."

Harry looked at her.

"Was the adoption open or closed?"

"Closed," she said.

"He knows where the child is?"

"No."

"*You* know where the child is?"

"No."

"Then I'm confused. What's the problem?"

She looked at Ray.

"Maybe I made a mistake in coming here," she said.

"Easy," Ray said. "You're here now. Let's take it one step at a time." He looked at Harry.

"The father is apparently a multiple felon. His most recent conviction was for attempted murder. He was already in custody at the time the child was born."

"But he knows there was an adoption?" Harry said.

She nodded.

"I told him," she said. "In a letter. Afterward."

"How did he take it?" Ray said.

"Not well." She set the mug on the carpet, the coffee untouched. "He wrote me back. He said I had no right to do it, that it was his child too. That I should do whatever I could to get him back. And that if I didn't he would never forgive me. That he would hold me responsible."

"What else?" Ray said.

"He called too. Left messages. I didn't answer him. But I guess I shouldn't have been surprised by the way he felt."

"Why?" Harry said.

"He always wanted a child, a son. Always. His family had been . . . troubled."

"I can imagine," Harry said.

"Go on," Ray said.

"We talked about it, but I wasn't ready. It didn't feel right. When it happened it was almost an accident. We hadn't planned it. When I told him I was pregnant . . ."

She picked the coffee cup up again, didn't drink.

"Take your time," Ray said.

"He was happy. Happier maybe than I'd ever seen him before. He started making plans. Talked about buying a house, everything. I couldn't tell him how I was feeling. Then . . . everything fell apart. When I wrote him, told him what I'd done, I don't think he could handle it."

"What exactly did the letter say?" Ray said. "When he wrote back."

"Like I said. That I was making a mistake, that I had no right. That I would pay for what I did. That he'd make sure of it."

"I guess you could safely call that a threat," Ray said.

"How long ago was this?" Harry said.

"Almost seven years," she said.

"People say things, write things, in the heat of the moment," he said. "Doesn't mean they have any intention of following through. Especially after all this time."

"You're not listening to me, are you?" she said.

"Just making an observation."

"Ms. Ellis was telling me earlier," Ray said. "She feels he might have the resources to track the boy down."

"After seven years?" Harry said. "I'm no expert on adoption law, but that sounds like it might be difficult."

"You say that," she said, "because you don't know him."

"Let's back up a little," Ray said. "You gave the child up immediately after delivery, right?"

"Yes."

"So the father's never seen him? Has no legal claim on him?"

"No."

"Where was he incarcerated?" Harry said.

"Florida," Ray said. "A place called Belle Glade."

"And he just got out?"

"Last week," she said.

"How do you know that?" Harry said.

"Thank the Florida Department of Corrections," Ray said. "They have a system you can access online. I had a look. It's unbelievable. Everything's right there. Arrest records, sentencing, date of incarceration, date of release. All public record. You can type in a name, get it all in a few seconds."

41

"I was registered with them," she said. "As someone to be notified when he was released. I got a letter two weeks ago."

"So you knew this was coming?" Harry said.

"No. Not this soon."

"It looks like he swung some sort of early release," Ray said. "Not sure why. He was sentenced to nine years, did a little short of seven when they released him."

"Parole?" Harry said.

Ray shook his head. "Not in Florida. They eliminated parole per se, War on Crime and all that. They've got a similar system—a tougher one—called Gaintime, but that's not the case here either. Whatever the reason was, it's not part of the public record."

"And how do we know he's back up here?"

"If he's not yet," she said, "he will be."

"You had any communication with him in the interim? Threatening letters, phone calls?"

She shook her head.

"No. Not since that last letter. I never wrote back."

Harry picked up his mug, sipped cooling coffee, looked at Ray.

"What I need to know," she said to Ray, "is whether you're going to help or not. And if not, tell me that right now."

"Let's slow down a minute. . . ."

"From what I know of the adoption process," Harry said, "there are already a lot of safeguards in place, for mothers who change their minds, that sort of thing."

She looked at him.

"What makes you think they won't work?" he said.

"Do you have a problem with me?" she said. "Because if so, why don't you just say it?"

"No problem," he said, shaking his head.

"Whoa," Ray said. They both looked at him.

"Chances are," he said, "Harry's probably right. I mean, the system's in place for just this kind of thing. There's likely no chance at all of him being able to track the boy down to his adopted family."

"I need to be sure," she said.

"I understand that. And it's not like you're exactly helpless here. We can look into it, at least make some sort of notification to the agency about a possible threat. Give them a heads-up. That's a start."

"And you could do that in a letter," Harry said to her, feeling Ray's eyes on him. "You don't need us for that."

"But the bigger question," Ray said quickly, "is, do you feel like you may be in danger yourself?"

"Maybe. I don't know."

"Because that's an issue we *can* do something about. And that's pretty straightforward. We can look into it, find out where he is, if he's in the area or not. Do what we call a threat assessment. And we can keep you safe."

"How much would that cost me?"

"It would depend," Ray said. "We'll draw up a regular contract, but it's negotiable. It all depends on what's involved."

She gave that a moment, looked out the window, then back at Ray.

"You could find him?"

"We could try. Then the issue would be keeping him away from you. And there are ways to do that."

"The reason I came to you," she said, "was that I heard you did work that some agencies wouldn't, for people who didn't have much money."

"That's true," Ray said. "Sometimes."

"I have some money saved, but not a lot."

"Or," Harry said, "you could just do what most people in your situation would do. Go to your local judge, get a restraining order. And that wouldn't cost a cent."

She rounded on him.

"What is your fucking problem?"

He raised his hands, palms out.

"Who are you to judge me? What do you know about me, my situation?"

Harry felt his face growing red.

"Listen—" he said.

"No, you listen." She stood up. "Don't you patronize me, you ass-hole." She looked at Ray. "I guess I did make a mistake."

"Hold on," Ray said, getting up. "Just hold on."

"How much do I owe you?"

"Just wait a second," he said, coming around the desk. "Let's just everyone calm down and we can finish talking here. Because—"

"I don't think so," she said. She snatched the coat off the chair, walked quickly out of the office.

Harry sipped cold coffee.

"She'll be back," he said.

Ray stood there, hands on his hips, looking out the door. Then he crossed to the window.

"Explain that," he said, without looking at Harry. "And do it slow, so I understand."

"I appreciate the gesture, Ray. But it's not necessary."

Ray turned to look at him.

"What?"

"Hard to consider that a coincidence. I get bounced from your street team and then a day later you're trying to find busy work for me, with a client you wouldn't take on in a hundred years. You give me something to do, charge her practically nothing. It's a good arrangement, I guess, but—"

"What did you just say?"

Harry saw the anger in his eyes.

"Ray, if you're pissed, I'll run after her right now, apologize, bring her back, if that's what you want. But if this whole thing was for my benefit, you needn't have bothered."

"I don't believe you," Ray said. "I really don't. You think *every-thing* that *anybody* does is some sort of a reflection on you?"

"I know the way you are. The way you handle things. You wouldn't even have had her in here if it weren't for me. How long ago did she first call you? Two weeks? Three?"

Ray turned away, looked out the window again.

"Well?" Harry said.

"Last week. I told her we couldn't help her, told her to write a letter to the agency, talk to the local cops about a restraining order. I called her back this morning, asked her to come in."

"That's what I thought."

"There's a blue Blazer pulling up outside. She's getting in it."

"You do too much," Harry said to his back. "You're looking out for me, I know. But I'll get by."

"There she goes."

"Sorry."

Ray turned to him.

"It's not like you to be that rude," he said. "Under any circumstances. I couldn't believe what I was hearing."

"Something about her. It just rubbed me the wrong way. I couldn't explain it."

"Let *me* explain something about clients: You don't have to like them. In most cases you don't. And you know something? It shouldn't make any difference."

Harry raised his hands, let them fall.

"I've put up with a lot of moods from you, partner," Ray said. "You know that? And most of them I've let slide by, haven't even acknowledged—"

"I know."

"—because you've been through a lot. So I guess you have the right to be a disagreeable son of a bitch every now and then. But lately, I think you're taking on the role for life."

Harry put his elbows on his thighs, rubbed his temples, still feeling the pressure there.

"I'm sorry," he said again.

"All the years I've known you . . . You're like family to me, you know that? So, yeah, every once in a while I try to help you a little, drag you out of that hole you dig for yourself when you want to feel bad. And you fight me on it every step. And that, I don't understand."

"Where's her number?" Harry said, getting up. "I'll call."

"And say what?"

"I don't know. I'll tell her I'm sorry. I'll tell her we can work something out."

"And you think that'll fly, after what happened in here?"

"No, I don't think it will. But I'll do it for you."

Ray sat back down at the desk, sighed.

"Fifteen years," he said. "And sometimes I feel like I don't know you at all."

He tore off a sheet of notepad paper, dropped it near the phone. Harry went to the desk, sat on the edge, picked up the paper. Written on it was the name Nicole Ellis and a ten-digit phone number.

"I think that's a cell," Ray said.

Harry pushed the speakerphone button. The dial tone was loud.

"Nine first," Ray said.

Harry looked at the paper, punched in the numbers. It buzzed twice, three times. There was a click as the line was opened.

"Yes?" A man's voice.

They looked at each other. Ray shrugged.

Harry said, "I'm looking for Ms. Ellis."

"She's right here. Hold on a minute."

A pause as the phone was handed over.

"Yes?" Her voice.

"Ms. Ellis, this is Harry Rane. I just want to say—"

"I'm glad you called."

He looked at Ray, raised an eyebrow.

"Good," he said. "Why's that?"

"Because I didn't get a chance to tell you to go fuck yourself."

The line went dead.

The speaker hissed, clicked. The dial tone returned. They listened to it without speaking.

"Well," Harry said finally. "There you go."

SIX

THE HEARTBREAK LOUNGE WAS DECORATED FOR CHRISTMAS. THERE were cardboard cutouts of smiling reindeer on the walls, fake snow sprayed on the mirrors that lined the room. On the stage behind the circular bar, two women in thong bikinis moved slowly to an old Motown song. Inlaid on the stage floor was the green neon outline of a heart, an illuminated crack running through it. A rear-projection TV on the far wall was showing a hockey game.

Johnny sipped his Heineken, looked around, the place less than a quarter full, the game getting more attention than the girls. A pack of college kids to his right, baseball caps reversed, doing shots and high-fiving one another afterward. To his left, a handful of young Mexicans, restaurant workers maybe, keeping to themselves. On the other side of the bar, two men in suits and loosened ties, money in front of them, eyes on the dancers.

He'd been here almost two hours, but it was only his second beer. The barmaid had come by several times and he'd shaken his head. She was ignoring him now.

One of the girls made eye contact with him, smiled, almost sadly. She was barely into her twenties, with short dark hair, breasts so small she hardly needed the bikini top to cover them. She did a slow turn around the silver pole, eyes half closed. Stoned, he guessed. Couldn't climb up onto the stage without something to give her distance, soften the edges of the world.

He lit his fourth cigarette, separated a twenty from the wet bills in front of him. The barmaid, a bleached blonde in her late thirties, saw it and moved toward him.

"Heineken?" she said.

He shook his head.

"Got a question."

"A what?"

"A question. If you can help me out, this is yours."

"Give me a break."

He folded the twenty.

"If you don't want it, give it to one of the girls."

"What's the question?"

"Used to be a girl danced here. She called herself Jasmine sometimes. You remember her? Her real name was Nikki."

"Jasmine? Do you know how many Jasmines have been through here? Or Nikkis, for that matter? And Britneys and Brandys and Willows?"

"You remember that Jasmine? Long brown hair? A tattoo of a butterfly"—he reached around, touched his lower back—"right here?"

"You're kidding, right?"

He looked at her for a moment, sat back.

"Never mind," he said. "Keep the twenty. And bring me another beer when you get a chance."

"Anything you say, sport," she said and took the bill.

The music had changed—fast and loud now, thumping bass and distorted guitars. Two new dancers took the stage. One was tall and black, with a full natural, tight leather pants, a white halter top and hoop earrings. The other was older, red hair in a ponytail, wearing a T-shirt cut raggedly just below her breasts, a dark bikini bottom lined with sequins.

The barmaid brought the Heineken, opened it and set it in front of him, moved away. The first two dancers were working the bar now, talking with the drinkers, pushing their breasts together for money, then moving on.

The sad-eyed girl came over to him, walking gingerly on high heels, and he took another twenty from his pile. She leaned over the bar and hunched her shoulders to create cleavage. He shook his head, took her hand, put the bill inside and closed her fingers over it. She gave him a stoned smile, slid her other hand into her bikini top and pulled the material away slightly to give him a flash of nipple. She blew him a kiss and moved away. With her back to him, she looked at the bill, saw it was a twenty. She looked over her shoulder, gave him another smile.

Of the two women onstage, the black one was clearly the favorite. The hockey game was forgotten now, hands holding out singles and fives. She ground her hips slowly as if in defiance of the faster pace of the music, intently watching her own reflection in the mirrored wall. She was someplace else, away from the catcalls and offered bills.

The red-haired woman worked the pole at her end of the stage, worked it hard, knowing she was being ignored, putting effort into it anyway. At first he didn't recognize her. She was thinner than he'd known her, almost gaunt, her muscles toned from exercise, the baby fat gone. Struggling to hold on to her looks, he thought, her ability to make money, while an endless supply of girls barely out of high school came through the door every day.

He fixed his gaze on her and after a while she became aware of it. She looked over at him, no recognition in her eyes, then swung into another routine, using the pole as an axis point. When she slowed, she looked over again and he gave her a lift of his chin. It threw her. She missed a step, almost lost her balance, then recovered, fell back into the practiced movement.

The song ended and she slowed and stopped, looked at him. She stepped down from the stage carefully, ignored the men gesturing to her, made her way behind the bar to where he sat.

"Hey, Sherry," he said. "Looking good."

"Johnny Boy."

"Long time."

"You almost gave me a heart attack, seeing you there."

The black dancer had left the stage as well, was talking to the suits, leaning close.

"All the years since I've been in here," he said, "not much has changed."

"I don't know where she is, John. I haven't seen her in years."

He raised an eyebrow.

"Who?"

"There's only one reason you'd come back here. I know that."

"Maybe I'm just here to see you."

"Not much chance of that, is there?"

The barmaid came by, took a bottle from the speed rack. Sherry stepped aside to give her room.

"Come on, Sherry," the barmaid said without looking at her. "Spread the wealth around. You know Sahid gets pissed about this. He'll be on my ass again." She moved away.

"I'm not supposed to talk to the same customer for too long. Bad manners."

"Who's Sahid?"

"Manager. He and his brother bought the place when Joey sold it. About three years ago now. A couple of pigs. Lebanese."

"Maybe it's time to look for another career."

"Doing what?"

He shrugged.

"What time you wrap up here? Maybe we can take a few minutes, catch up on old times."

She looked toward a bouncer standing near the door, shaved head, massive arms folded, wearing a yellow polo shirt that said STAFF on the back. But he was watching the game, oblivious to her.

"Just a few minutes, Sherry. To talk."

She looked back at him.

"I'm not going to be any help to you, Johnny. Really."

"What time do you get off?"

"Two."

"I'll meet you here. You have a car?"

"Yes."

"Then I'll wait for you outside. We can sit, talk."

He gathered his cigarettes and lighter from the bar, picked up the rest of his money. She watched him.

"Just talk, Sherry, that's all," he said. "See you at two."

HE HELD her head down, his hand on the back of her neck, feeling the heat rising inside him. Sensing he was close, she tried to raise up, get her hand on him to finish him off, but he tightened his grip, his fingertips buried in the muscles of her neck.

He tried to hold off as long as he could, but then his breath was hitching, his hips arching off the seat, and it was all over. He held her there until he was done, then sat back, breathing slowly, took his hand away.

She sat up in the passenger seat, pulled away from him. There was a small pack of tissues on the console near the gearshift. She pulled one out, wiped at her mouth.

He tucked his limpness in, zipped up and resnapped his jeans. They were in the front seat of her Honda in the parking lot of the Heartbreak, the engine running, heater on. The club was dark, the parking lot empty except for them. The wind off the ocean rocked the car slightly.

She'd changed back into her street clothes: a T-shirt, jeans and high-heeled boots. Her work outfits and the money she'd made that night were in a gym bag in the back, next to a child's car seat.

"Been a while since I felt that," he said. "You're as good as you always were."

She was looking out the window, not letting him see her face.

"I'm going to get married," she said after a moment. "He's a good man. He runs his own business."

"Congratulations."

"He's buying a house. For Janey and me."

He took a pack of her cigarettes from the dashboard, shook one out.

"Why did you come back?" she said.

He left the filter on, got the cigarette going with his lighter, drew in smoke. He felt relaxed, loose, for the first time since he'd walked out of Glades.

"What else was I going to do?" he said. "Seven years is a long time. I had business to settle up here."

"What kind of business?"

He didn't answer, blew smoke out.

"She hasn't worked here in a long time," she said. "Maybe six years. She just sort of dropped out of the scene. I don't know where she went."

"She didn't tell you?"

She shook her head.

"I don't believe that," he said.

"It's true."

"I want to talk to her."

51

"About what?"

He turned to her.

"What do you think?"

"She had nothing to do with what happened to you down in Florida, John, nothing at all. She loved you."

"Every day of the trial, I sat at that table, looked out at the people there. Every day I looked for her."

"She didn't have the money to go down there, John. She wanted to, but she couldn't. Not then."

He shook his head slowly, rolled the window down. Cold air filled the car, fought with the heat from the vents.

"When was the last time you saw her?" he said.

"Like I said, five years at least, maybe six."

"Which is it?"

"At least six since she worked here, Johnny. Maybe I saw her once or twice after that."

"And all this time, she hasn't called you? Written?"

"She wanted to get away from all this. Hard to blame her. All I would have done is remind her."

"It's not good to forget about your friends like that."

"I wanted her to go, Johnny. She had a chance. She had to take it."

"Was she with somebody? A guy?"

"I don't know, Johnny. Why are you asking me these things?"

He felt the anger then, reached over, caught her ponytail, pulled. She made a small noise, stiffened, raised her chin as he wound the hair tighter.

"Why am I asking you? Why the fuck do you think I'm asking you? Was there a guy?"

He twisted, felt the hair grow taut, saw the tears bloom in the corners of her eyes.

"Johnny, please . . ."

He pushed her away lightly, let go, turned to look out the window again.

"Seven years," he said. He flicked the cigarette out the window, watched it spark and glow on the blacktop.

They sat in silence for a moment.

"There's no stopping you, is there?" she said. "No matter how things really are, no matter what the truth is, you only believe what you want to believe. You get something in your head and that's it."

"I want to see my son. I have that right. And I'll do whatever it takes to make that happen."

She turned away from him.

"Maybe you haven't heard from her in six years," he said. "And maybe you have, but you're trying to protect her. I understand that, respect it even. So I want you to understand this: I don't want to hurt her. She wants me out of her life now, that's fine. But she can't keep my son away from me."

"Johnny, I haven't—"

"Let me finish. There's something in it for you too, if you help me out. More than you'd make in a month here shaking your tits at strangers. You tell me where she is, or how I can find her, and I drop the money on you and walk away. You never have to deal with me again."

There was a pack of matches on the console, black with a green broken heart on the front flap, no words. He reached across her, opened the glove box, rooted through the clutter there—another package of Kleenex, makeup, a small stuffed animal—until he found a ballpoint pen. He shut the glove box, opened the matchbook, wrote Mitch's phone number inside it.

"Here," he said. He took cash from his jacket pocket, pulled off a hundred-dollar bill. He folded the bill tight, slipped it inside the matchbook, held it out.

"There's a number you can reach me," he said. "I won't be there but they'll know where to find me. I'll get your message."

She looked at the money, not touching it.

"Take it," he said.

When she didn't respond, he slipped the matchbook and bill into the visor above her.

"There it is," he said. "You can use it or not, I don't care. But keep that number."

He opened his door. In the glow from the dome light he could see the streaked mascara on her face. She was looking straight ahead.

"Johnny."

"What?"

"Please don't come back here."

He looked at her.

"If you want me to come to wherever you're staying, do things for you, I'll do it. But please don't come back here."

"You afraid I'll run into your boyfriend?"

"Please, Johnny."

He got out of the car, shut the door, leaned slightly through the window, his hands on the lip.

"Fair enough," he said. "But you should know this too. If she is around here, if you know where she is and you're not telling me, the last thing you want to do is tell her about this conversation, give her the chance to go somewhere else. If you do that and I find out about it—and I will—I'll hold you responsible. If she calls you, if you hear from her at all, the first thing you do is call that number, right?"

She didn't answer, didn't look at him.

"I keep my promises, Sherry. I pay my debts. Help me out with this and you'll be glad you did. But at some point you're going to have to choose a side, one way or another. It can't be helped. So choose carefully."

He looked at her, half-lit in shadow, saw she was sobbing softly, trying to hide it from him.

"You're thinking it's not fair," he said. "And you're right. But it's just the way it is. One side or the other."

He took his hands away.

"Safe home, Sherry," he said. "I'll see you soon."

SEVEN

WHEN RAY ANSWERED THE PHONE, HARRY SAID, "I FEEL BAD."

"You should."

Harry looked out the kitchen window to the backyard. The willows moved in the wind, sunlight glinting off the creek beyond.

"I want to try to reach her."

"Why?"

"I was out of line. I guess I need to tell her that."

"Call. You still have that cell number, right?"

"I tried. Three times today. The first time she answered, hung up on me. The second and third times that guy's voice mail picked up. I left a message with my phone number. No response."

"So what do you want me to do?"

"She leave you any other numbers? An address? Anything?"

"No. She called that first time, I talked to her and she gave me that cell number. That's how I called her back. Never got any further than that, thanks to you."

"So you don't know where she's living? Or who picked her up? Or whose cell that is?"

"All I know is what I told you."

"Your building still have that security camera outside? At the entrance?"

"What about it?"

"Could be it got the license number of the car she drove away in. You said it was a Blazer?"

"Yeah, a Blazer. I'm not sure about the camera. I'd have to check."

"And you still have that Red Line to DMV, right? If you can read

55

the plates on the tape, we can find out who it's registered to, where. It's a lead."

"Maybe you should consider a career in law enforcement."

"No, thanks. Too much politics."

"I'll see what I can find out. What prompted this change of heart?"

"Like I said, I was out of line. You were right. I was wrong. I shouldn't have sent her off like that. And maybe there's something we can do to help after all."

"So, how long have you been dealing with this multiple personality disorder?"

"What?"

"Sometimes I feel like I need a psychic to predict your moods. They don't have any logical progression."

"I know."

"You home?"

"Yeah."

"I'll let you know if I come up with anything," Ray said and hung up.

There was a fifty-pound bag of birdseed in a black plastic container near the refrigerator. He got the sawed-off plastic jug, scooped some up. He opened the back door, went into the yard and tossed the seed in a series of splashes on top of the hard ground. Birds swooped down—starlings, blackbirds, the occasional crow. He went back inside, closed the seed up, watched through the kitchen window as more birds arrived, the yard full of them now.

An hour later he was out by the barn, quartering split logs into firewood, when he heard the phone ring inside. He set the ax against the barn wall, went back in.

"Yeah?" he said, still breathing heavy.

"After I hung up I went down to the security desk," Ray said. "They pulled that tape, fast-forwarded it. It's all time-coded, so it was easier than it sounds."

"The Blazer?"

"Got it. It was on-camera long enough to get a pretty good shot of it."

"Hang on," Harry said. He opened a drawer by the sink, found a pen. There was a newspaper on the table and he tore off a corner of it.

"Go," he said.

"Jersey plates. KMC-13K."

He wrote it down.

"Good," he said. "Now all we have to do is run it with DMV."

"Did that. What, do you think I sit around here all day, waiting for your guidance?"

"Sorry. What did you get?"

"This address, it's in Ocean Grove." He read it off and Harry scribbled it onto the paper.

"And the name?" he said.

"William Clancy Matthews. DOB eleven-fourteen-seventy. It's a new registration, less than a year."

"Phone number?"

"None listed. I called Directory Assistance too. No one with that name and that address. What are you going to do?"

"Try the cell again. If no luck, stop by, try and talk to her. Apologize."

"And if all she has to say is 'Go fuck yourself' again?"

"I'll take the chance. I figure I owe it to you, to take it that far at least."

"You're right, you do. If you talk to her, see if you can get her back here for another sit-down. Maybe we can start all over again."

"It's probably too late for that."

"Yeah, I know," Ray said. "It almost always is."

OCEAN GROVE was only one square mile, the streets lined with Victorian houses on narrow lots. It had been founded as a Methodist camp meeting center in the 1860s, and the Methodists still controlled it, owned the land. When a house was bought here, the homeowner had to take out a renewable ninety-nine-year lease on the lot itself. Houses could be sold, or new ones built, but the land belonged to God.

He drove down Ocean Avenue, the beach to his right. The waves rolled in thick and heavy, spray leaping up through the boards of the fishing pier. At the far end of the pier, an American flag snapped atop a pole.

He remembered the last time he'd been here. He and Cristina had come to this beach often during that first summer, because there was less chance of running into anyone they knew. They'd been as careful as possible and it had still gone bad.

One-way streets here. He turned left, went up three blocks and came back down Bath Avenue, which ran west to east, ended at the ocean. He slowed, watching house numbers. Some of the houses had been converted into bed-and-breakfasts, most of them closed for the season.

He almost missed it. It was a classic Victorian, crisp green and white, freshly painted. A blue Blazer was parked directly in front. He braked when he saw it, rolled by slowly. The plate number matched. A rainbow-flag bumper sticker on the back read, *Hate is not a family value.*

He went down to the ocean, swung around onto a parallel street, came back to make another pass. He pulled to the curb a half block from the house, left the engine running. Lights were going on behind windows up and down the street. The day was growing grayer, the night coming fast.

He took the container of take-out coffee from the console, folded the plastic lid back. He'd come all this way but he still wasn't sure what his approach would be, why he was even here.

He sipped sweet coffee, watched the house. A few minutes later, the front door opened and a slim man with feathered blond hair came out, wearing a waist-length jacket, green scarf, matching gloves. Harry watched him unlock the Blazer, climb behind the wheel. He started the engine, idled there at the curb. Harry could see him talking on a cell phone. After a moment, he pulled away.

Harry drank coffee, looked at the house. After about five minutes, the door opened again and a man in a yellow warm-up suit and wide headband came out. He was big, over six feet, with the V torso of a weight lifter. He hit the sidewalk, turned in Harry's direction and started jogging. Harry looked straight ahead as he ran past the Mustang.

He watched the windows of the house, saw no movement inside.

In his rearview, he saw the jogger thump down to the end of the street, turn left.

He'd call first, he decided, find a pay phone, dial the cell again. Tell whoever answered who he was, where he was, why he was calling. Try to get her on the phone. If there was no answer, he'd come back, knock.

He pulled away from the curb, drove past the house and back down to Ocean Avenue. He parked near the fishing pier. Out on the water, the wind was shearing the tops off the waves.

He looked out at the beach, pictured it in the middle of summer, a long stretch of umbrellas and blankets, radios playing, children laughing. He remembered swimming with her out past the breakers, kissing her as the swells gently lifted them together. He thought about the touch of her skin, the lilac smell of her perfume.

Full dark now, his the only car on the entire length of Ocean Avenue. He saw movement from the corner of his eye, turned, and then the jogger was standing by his window, lit by a single streetlight.

Harry looked up at him. He had light crew-cut hair and a wide jaw, arms that hung away from his body. He made a circular motion with his right hand.

Harry rolled down his window.

"Yeah?" he said and the jogger leaned in, reached for the ignition, switched it off. When he pulled his hand back the keys were in it.

Harry yanked up on the door latch. The jogger dropped the keys into a warm-up pocket, put both hands on the lip of the door, leaning into it, pushing it shut again, holding it there. His hands and wrists were thick with veins.

Harry let go of the latch.

"What are you doing around here?" the jogger said.

Harry met his eyes. He reached behind the passenger seat with his right hand, found the long aluminum flashlight there.

"And what would it be to you?" he said.

"You'll tell me unless you want me to drag you out of that car, break both your arms."

Harry looked through the windshield, let his breath out.

"My name is Harry Rane," he said. "I work for RW Security. I drove out here to talk to Nicole Ellis."

"About what?"

"That would be between us, wouldn't it?"

"Answer the question."

"I just did."

"You got any ID?"

"I do," Harry said. "And a couple minutes ago, I would have shown it to you. But now you're just pissing me off. You want to give me my keys back?"

"I'm pissing *you* off? Tough shit."

"I guess that's a no."

He brought the flashlight up, pressed the button, shone the bright halon beam full into the jogger's eyes, blinding him. The jogger's left hand came up to block the beam and Harry reversed the flashlight, cracked the base of it across the hand still on the door.

The jogger pulled his hand away and Harry shoved the door open, drove him back. He got out, the flashlight at his side.

"And don't touch the fucking car," he said.

He saw what was going to happen, knew there was no way around it. The jogger recovered his balance, swung at him, a big, strong right, and Harry dropped, let it pass over him, snapped the heavy flashlight hard against the point of the jogger's right knee.

Harry had learned the move years ago from a veteran trooper, practiced it with a baton until he could do it without thinking. He had taken down angry drunks with it, men twice his size, because the pain it produced was sudden and intense, in a place they hadn't expected. You could disable a man immediately or, if you weren't careful, break his kneecap into so many pieces he'd walk with a limp for the rest of his life.

The jogger cried out, grabbed at his knee, fell heavily onto his side, hugging his leg. Harry leaned over him quickly, batted one of his hands away, reached into the warm-up pocket and came out with the keys. He stepped away, trained the flashlight beam on the jogger's face. The jogger squinted up at him.

"I don't know who you are," Harry said. "And at this point, I don't really give a fuck. But I guarantee you I'm not who you think I am."

He turned the flashlight off.

"You broke my knee."

"Probably not. I will next time, though. I promise you that. Is she home?"

"Who?"

"Give it up. You did your duty. You can lay there all night or we can drive back, talk to her."

The jogger looked away, his shoulders rising and falling as his breathing settled.

"I need you to help me up," he said after a moment.

"No chance. Now, you can ride with me or walk. I don't care. Up to you."

"Don't hit me again," the jogger said.

Harry had to smile.

"Come on," he said. "Get in the car."

EIGHT

WHEN THEY PULLED UP OUTSIDE THE HOUSE, THE BLAZER WAS BACK.
"You first," Harry said and shut the car off.

The jogger got out, limping. He went slowly up the walk to the porch, opened the front door. Harry followed him.

The woman and the blond man were waiting. It was a simple living room, hardwood floor, a bookshelf against one wall, a black leather couch. Glossy decorating magazines fanned out on the coffee table.

The woman wore jeans, a man's blue work shirt with the tail out. When she saw him, she said, "It's you."

The blond man looked at her. She shook her head.

"No, Jack," she said. "Not him."

"I've been calling," Harry said. "But I've been having some trouble getting through, it seems."

"Who is he?" the blond man said and as Harry started to answer, the jogger looped a thick arm around his neck, jerked him back.

It took him off his feet, left him without leverage. He pumped an elbow back into a solid stomach with no effect.

"Reggie!" the blond man said.

Harry kicked back, felt his boot heels meet shins. Reggie bent him forward, swung him around like a wrestler so that Harry was facing the floor in a reverse headlock, held him there.

"Jack, get his wallet," Reggie said. "Check his ID."

Harry felt blood rush to his head, pain in his lower back. Jack came tentatively forward and Harry back-kicked at him, his boot hitting nothing but air. Jack retreated and Reggie hauled up, big arms tightening around Harry's neck, cutting the air off. He saw

62

flashes of light around the edges of his vision. He stopped struggling, felt the wallet pulled from his back pocket.

Jack took the wallet to the other side of the room. Reggie eased the pressure.

"Check his license," he said. "Who he is."

Harry looked at Reggie's legs, ankles.

"Well?" Reggie said.

Jack said, "I'm looking, I'm looking."

"His license. What's it say?"

Harry spread his feet for balance, looped his right fist up hard into Reggie's groin. He heard Reggie's breath go out of him, felt the grip on his neck loosen. He reached down, caught both ankles, pulled up.

Reggie went over backward, crashed down onto the coffee table, smashed it. Harry straightened, saw him roll quickly back onto his feet, faster than he'd expected, too fast. He backpedaled, trying to put distance between them, catch his breath. The backs of his legs met the couch. On the end table to his left was a fluted glass vase filled with baby carnations. From the corner of his eye, he saw the woman run from the room.

There was no boxing, no feinting. Reggie moved forward, planted his feet and drove a thick fist at Harry's face, his whole body behind it.

Harry ducked, felt the fist pass above him, reached across with his right hand, gripped the vase, brought it around backhanded. Reggie's arm came up, blocked him forearm to forearm, and the vase flew from his hand, shattered against the wall, spraying glass and water.

Reggie's fist cocked back again and Harry kicked out, caught him in his injured knee. When he bent, Harry grabbed at his warm-up jacket, yanked it down over his head, tangling his arms, blinding him. He brought his right knee up once, twice, a solid impact each time. The jacket tore as Reggie pulled away and Harry got in a final knee, let go. Reggie flew back, fell onto his side, and Harry heard the unmistakable sound of an automatic pistol chambering a round.

Everything stopped. Harry looked at the woman, tried to catch his breath. She held a small .25 automatic pointed at his chest. It was a Phoenix Raven, nickel, with imitation-pearl grips, a junk gun. The muzzle was small, but her grip was steady.

"Put that away," he said. The gun didn't move. Behind her, the blond man stood white-faced.

"Sit down," she said.

Reggie moaned, rolled onto his knees. His jacket was in rags, blood dripped from his nose. He looked at Harry, then at the gun.

"Sit down," she said.

Harry locked his eyes on hers, measured the distance.

"Don't try it," she said. "Please don't try it."

"Point that somewhere else." He took a step forward.

"I said sit the *fuck* down."

"That's a tiny gun," he said. Another step. "I don't think you could even—"

She lowered the muzzle and fired once into the couch near his right leg. The noise was no louder than a stick breaking, but he felt the movement of the bullet past his leg, saw the impact as it slapped a hole in the leather. He froze. A thin mist of smoke and gun oil drifted from the muzzle. A shell casing rolled across the floor. She raised the gun again.

"Sit *down*," she said.

He lowered himself slowly onto the couch, his eyes on her. Broken glass crunched beneath his boots. Flowers lay on the hardwood like fish out of water.

There was silence in the room. Reggie started to get to his feet. He pulled the remnants of the warm-up jacket off, exposing a bloodstained white T-shirt beneath. He touched his nose, looked at Harry. But the violence was gone from the air, the gunshot ending it as quickly and finally as a door closing.

"Nikki," the blond man said finally, "you know that's Italian, don't you?"

"Jack," she said, not taking her eyes off Harry, "take Reggie into the kitchen. Make sure he's all right."

She lowered the gun until it was pointed at the floor. For the first time, Harry could see she was trembling slightly.

"Nikki, are you sure?"

"Go on."

Reggie had taken his headband off, was holding it up to his nose to staunch the blood. He looked at Harry until Jack took his elbow, started to lead him away. He limped as they went down the hall into the kitchen.

"Maybe I should call the police," she said.

"Call whoever the fuck you like." He saw his wallet open on the floor where Jack had dropped it, contents spilling out.

"Jack saw you parked outside. He panicked, called here on his cell. Reggie went out to take a look. They thought . . . well, you know what they thought."

He nodded at the floor.

"Can I get my wallet back?"

"How'd you find me?"

"License plate. Like I said, I've been trying to reach you. I called that number you gave Ray. Left messages."

"That's Jack's cell. I use it sometimes. Why were you trying to call me?"

"To apologize for the way I acted that day."

"You can't be serious."

"Believe what you want. I'm going to get my things."

He got up and she took another step back. He leaned over, pain in his back, picked up his wallet, the things that had fallen out of it—a credit card, a small color snapshot of Cristina on the beach, taken when they were in Captiva last year. He slid them back in the wallet, replaced it in his jeans pocket, stood up. His neck ached.

"I'm sorry if you got hurt," she said. "He was just protecting me."

"Whatever. I'm leaving."

"Wait."

He shook his head.

"I've had enough. Fuck this. And fuck you. I won't call again."

Jack appeared in the doorway, looked from her to Harry then back.

"Nikki," he said, "we need to get Reggie to a hospital. I think his nose is broken."

"Go ahead," she said. "Take the Blazer."

He looked at Harry.

"It's okay," she said. "It was a misunderstanding. Go on."

A minute later, Jack led Reggie through the room, a bloodstained dish towel held to his face. He glared at Harry as Jack got coats from a closet, helped him into one. Harry watched him. Jack caught Reggie by the arm, led him through the front door. After a moment, they heard the Blazer engine start, watched through the window as it pulled away.

"Who's William Matthews?" he said.

"What?"

"The Blazer is registered to a William Matthews. That's how I found this address."

"That's Jack. His real name is William, but nobody calls him that anymore."

"That makes as much sense as anything else around here, I guess."

"I'm sorry about all this. Reggie can be a hothead. He comes on too strong sometimes. And I guess we're all a little on edge."

"Because of Harrow?"

"Yes."

"Well, good luck with that."

He went to the front door, had it open when she said, "Hold on." He looked back at her.

"You're serious?" she said. "About why you came here?"

"Forget it," he said and went out the door. He stopped, looked back at her.

"This your package out here?"

"What?"

"On the porch. You didn't see it?"

"What package?"

"Right here."

He held the door open. When she started to move past him, he threw his weight into her, pinned her hard against the left door-jamb. He caught the wrist of her gun hand, twisted. She flailed and he leaned into her.

"Let *go* of me."

He got both hands on the wrist, bent it until she gasped and her fingers opened. He took the gun away from her, spun her around and put the fingers of his left hand between her breasts, shoved. She took three off-balance steps into the living room, sat down hard on the floor.

"Son of a *bitch*," she said, and then he stepped back into the room, pushed the door shut behind him.

She froze, looked at him, the gun.

He ejected the magazine, worked the slide. The chambered shell flew out, hit the floor and rolled beneath the couch. He put the gun in his jacket pocket, then thumbed the shells out of the magazine one by one into his left hand. When he had all four out, he opened the door again, went onto the porch. He shook them like dice, the brass clinking in his grip, then tossed them out into the yard. He looked back at her, still sitting, then flung the magazine away in another direction, heard it land in winter-bare bushes.

He went back into the living room. She'd made no move to get up. He felt his anger start to fade. He held up the Raven.

"Never point a gun at someone who you're not ready to shoot," he said.

He lobbed the gun at her. It thumped against her chest, fell into her lap. She didn't try to pick it up.

He went back out, left the door open behind him, went down the walk to the Mustang. He didn't look back.

NINE

AT LEAST TEN YEARS SINCE HE'D DRIVEN THROUGH NEWARK, BUT LITTLE had changed. Johnny steered the Firebird through block after block of brownstone tenements with boarded windows, trash-strewn empty lots. When he hit red lights, he slowed only a moment before driving through.

When he saw the sign for Frelinghuysen Avenue, he turned left, went up a block and turned left again onto a street of warehouses and garages. The address he'd been given was on the right, halfway up the street, next to an auto body shop with a sign that read COLLISION SPECIALISTS.

He steered into the narrow lane between the two buildings, the Firebird's engine chugging as it crawled along. At the end of the alley, he turned right into the warehouse parking area.

The lot was fenced with chain link and razor wire, windblown plastic bags trapped in the coils. There were a dozen vehicles here, mainly SUVs, lit by a floodlight mounted over the loading dock. Most of the SUVs had cages in the cargo area, the rear seats taken out to make room for them.

There was a single door next to the loading dock and two black men stood there, watching him. Johnny pulled the Firebird up beside a Lexus jeep, cut the engine, wished he had a weapon.

He got out of the car, locked the door. The two men watched him come toward them. The one on the left was tall, wearing a leather jacket and pants, his hands gleaming with gold jewelry. His partner was shorter and heavy, dressed in a suit with a topcoat over it. Both their jackets were open despite the cold.

Johnny stopped about six feet from them.

"Here to see Lindell," he said. "He's expecting me."

The men appraised him. Topcoat reached inside his jacket, scratched. Johnny watched his hand.

"Lindell, huh?"

There was nothing to say to that. He waited.

"Chill here," the tall one said to his partner.

Topcoat nodded and the other man opened the door, went through.

They waited like that, the wind picking up, whistling through the razor wire. Topcoat was looking at the Firebird.

"Looks like you need you some new wheels," he said.

Johnny looked at him but didn't answer. He got his cigarettes out, lit one. He was halfway through it when the door opened again.

The tall one held it open, cocked his head inside. Johnny gave Topcoat a last look, stepped in. It was a narrow cement corridor lit by fluorescent tubes. At the far end was a dark green metal door.

"Go on. He waitin' for you."

The tall man went back outside, shut the door behind him.

Johnny started down the hall. There was a surveillance camera bolted high on the wall halfway down. He could already hear the noise, muffled through concrete—talking, yelling, barking.

When he got to the door, it swung open, a heavy black man holding it wide. He went through, saw the door had four different deadbolts and a police lock that fit into a plate in the floor. Mounted on the wall behind it was a closed-circuit TV screen showing the corridor he'd just come down.

Now the noise hit him fully, along with the smell of smoke and sweat and urine. He turned right into a small anteroom lined with lockers. A dead pit bull lay on a tarp thrown in one corner, its gray coat matted with blood, eyes half open.

He went through into the main room. The warehouse was a single open space, maybe two hundred feet in each direction. Metal-shaded bulbs hung on cables from the ceiling and smoke moved in their light.

There was a ring marked off in the center of the floor, bordered by wooden shipping crates. About twenty men in the room, all black, some sitting on metal folding chairs, some standing, all watching the ring where two men held back snarling dogs. The dogs—one a rottweiler, the other a pit—were raised up on their chains, snapping at the air, barely a foot of space between them. The pit's handler wore a black vest with no shirt, a black cowboy hat. The kid holding the rott was barely out of his teens. He wore a white knee-length T-shirt, a gold medallion and a black nylon stocking cap that lay like a mane on his shoulders.

Johnny stayed where he was, the others oblivious to his presence. A white-haired man in a suit spoke quietly to the handlers in turn, got nods from both of them. They pulled their dogs back, crouched beside them, began to unsnap their collars.

"Let 'em go," the white-haired man said, and in a flash the dogs were at each other, colliding in midair. As the handlers stepped back, the rott snarled, snapped, caught the loose flesh around the pit's throat, bore it down. But the pit twisted free, bit the rott deeply behind its left ear. First blood. Some of the men began to shout.

The rott pulled free, leaped again, caught the pit's ear and shredded it, but lost its hold almost immediately. The dogs fell and rolled. The rott snapped, drew blood from the pit's muzzle, then released its grip to find a new target. In a flash, the pit was in, locking its jaws on the rott's muzzle, its flat dinosaur face impassive.

The rott kicked, squealed, but the pit held on, its front legs braced against the floor. It dropped, bringing the rott down with it, and Johnny heard the sharp crunch of bone. The pit released, lunged again, buried its muzzle deep in the rott's throat, bore it down once more. The kid shook his head, looked away. The rott's bowels emptied, the smell sharp in the air. It kicked almost reflexively until its struggles slowed, stopped.

"God*damn*," one of the watchers said loudly. Johnny looked up. Lindell had been standing with his back to him the whole time, but now he stepped into the light wash from the overhead bulb, peeling money from a roll. He wore a black pinstriped suit, his hair straightened and pomaded back, goatee neatly trimmed. He counted off bills, handed them to a fat young man in a black sweatshirt and camouflage pants who took the money with no expression. He counted it as he moved away, then handed it to Cowboy

Hat, who folded the bills, nodded at Lindell, tucked them into a vest pocket.

The pit was still holding on, though the rott wasn't moving. Cowboy Hat took a wooden breaker stick, forced it into the pit's mouth like a shoehorn, levered up until it let go. Then he caught the pit and pulled it back to the edge of the ring.

Lindell turned, saw Johnny for the first time. He replaced his roll, started toward him. Johnny finished his cigarette, stepped on it.

In the ring, the rott's handler picked it up almost gently, the dog dead weight in his arms, carried it away.

"Johnny Too Bad," Lindell said. He showed flawless white teeth in his smile. He put his hand out and Johnny caught it in the soul shake. They embraced quickly, slapped each other on the back.

"Lindell. Looking slick as always."

"Did you see that? That was some sorry shit. Cost me five bills."

The rott's handler had carried the dog into the anteroom. Now he came back out to stand in the doorway, his T-shirt stained with blood.

"Lindell," he said.

"Excuse me," Lindell said. Johnny followed him.

The rott had been laid out on an army blanket, the material already darkening with blood. It lay on its right side with its eyes open, breath whistling through its cracked muzzle, wheezing as its chest rose and fell. The pit had crushed its throat.

"He's alive, Lindell," the kid said. "I told you he was tough, that he was dead game." There was water in the kid's eyes.

Lindell crouched beside the dog, far enough away to keep blood off his suit.

"Yeah, he was game, all right. Not game enough, though. And he may still be alive, that little motherfucker, but he never gonna fight again."

"We gotta get him to the vet right away, Lindell. Get him fixed up and shit. We gotta get him there now."

Lindell shook his head.

"Not this time. Not worth it. Give him the shot."

"But he's trying to get up, can't you see?"

"He's done, boy. Give him the shot. Get it over with."

Lindell stood, looked at the kid. He was still kneeling on the concrete, a leather case open beside him. Inside were a syringe, three dark brown ampules. One of them would be penicillin, Johnny knew. The other B_{12} or another vitamin booster to prime the dog on fight day. And the third an anesthetic to put it down.

"What are you waiting for?" Lindell said.

"There ain't none left."

"What do you mean?"

"The bottle's empty. I was going to get more from Rakim this week. But I didn't think there was any way T-Boy could lose tonight. Not like that."

The dog gave a hitch, its legs working for a moment in slow motion. Johnny watched it, could see its system shutting down piece by piece.

"Yeah, well, he lost, all right. And cost me five hundred dollars. Step out the way."

Lindell reached under his jacket, came out with a silver automatic. He pointed it at the floor, worked the slide. The kid stepped back. When Lindell crouched again, the dog rolled one rheumy eye up to watch him. The nub of its tail moved slowly from side to side.

"Don't look at me like that, you stupid-ass lame motherfucker." He caught the edge of the blanket, pulled it over the top half of the dog's body.

"Which side is the heart?"

"I don't know," the kid said.

Lindell put his left hand on the blanket. It rose and fell under his palm.

"I feel it," he said. He took his hand away, held the muzzle of the gun four inches away from the spot he'd touched.

"Lindell . . ." the kid said.

He fired twice, the shots loud in the concrete room. Casings hit the floor. The dog spasmed beneath the tarp, one leg kicking slowly, then was still. Urine pooled between its legs, the ammonia smell of it filling the room. The holes in the blanket smoked, the tang of cordite drifting in the air.

The men in the other room had turned at the shots. Handlers had brought in two new dogs, were holding them at the outside of the ring, waiting. Lindell stood, put the safety on the automatic, made it disappear under his jacket again.

"Go on," he said to the kid. "Get him out of here before he stinks up the place any more."

The kid looked down at the dog, didn't move.

Lindell turned to Johnny.

"Come on," he said. "Let's go where we can talk."

The kid knelt, began to fold the edges of the blanket over the dog, bundling it to be carried. Johnny followed Lindell back into the big room.

"My nephew," Lindell said. "Trying to school him, but he ain't getting it yet. It ain't no motherfucking game."

Johnny felt the eyes of the men on him as they walked past, wondering what this white boy was doing in their midst. Lindell gestured to a stairwell in the far wall. Johnny followed him. Behind him, he heard the referee call and then the snarling and snapping as dogs met in the ring.

They went up a short flight of stairs into an office with a window that looked out on the floor. There was an old refrigerator along one wall, a filing cabinet next to it, drawers bent and half open. On top of the cabinet was a color TV, DVD player beside it. On the screen, a blonde woman was performing oral sex on a muscular, tattooed black man. The sound was turned off.

Lindell opened the refrigerator, took out two Michelobs, nodded at a wooden chair near the window. There was a single desk in the room. Atop it were a half dozen DVD cases, the women on them in various states of undress.

He opened the beers, handed one to Johnny, then sat behind the desk. Johnny pulled the other chair closer, sat down. He nodded at the cases.

"What are those?"

"DVDs, man. Get that shit free. One of the perks of the job."

He moved a newspaper aside, found the remote.

"Video was better, though. This digital technology is no good for porn, man. Lets you see all the lines in these bitches' faces, pimples on their ass. It's depressing." The screen went gray, then black.

73

"I wouldn't know."

"Yeah, I guess you wouldn't, being away all this time. I should have thought of that."

Lindell put the remote down, sat back.

"You talk to the man yet?" he said.

Johnny shook his head.

"Figured I'd talk to you first, see what the situation was."

Lindell nodded. "Smart."

"Funny, though. Last time I was around here, 'the man' meant someone else."

"The times has changed. *That* man is *re*tired. And those times ain't never coming back, I'm happy to say." He took a sip from the beer. "No shit, Johnny. Things are good and gonna get better. Joey been waiting for you to get out, help him get busy."

"I called the store. They danced me around. Then they gave me a number for you. No one answered. I was starting to feel like people were avoiding me."

"Everything's mobile these days, dawg. I ain't never in one place for too long. Got your message and got back to you soon as I could, though, didn't I? I knew you'd be ready, hungry to get down to it. And as far as the store, man . . . Joey don't hardly go there no more. He still got the office upstairs and all, but mostly does his business elsewhere. Couple different places. Keep a jump on the suckers, you know? But here, I got something else you gonna like."

He reached into a pocket, came out with a small vial of cocaine, waved it once in the air, put it on the desk. The vial was sealed with a metal screw cap, a tiny spoon inside.

"Take a blast of that," Lindell said. "Shit will open your eyes but good."

Johnny shook his head.

"No."

"What? You used to love that shit, dawg. Suck it up like an Oreck."

"No more."

"I hear you." He slipped the vial back in his pocket.

Johnny took a sip from his beer.

"You looking lean and mean, man," Lindell said. "They make you cut your hair inside?"

"Did it myself."

"Got yourself an early release too. How that happen?"

"My lawyer pulled some strings. Made it work. Walked out of there with nothing but my kick-out money, though. Spent most of it getting up here."

"I hear that." He stroked his goatee.

"I could use a little of what's owed me."

Lindell shrugged.

"Hey, that's up to Joey, man. I mean, the man's business is his business. I don't question how he runs it. But if you asking me, 'Lindell, do you think he owes me money?' then I gotta say yes. But it ain't up to me to give it to you."

Johnny said nothing.

"Now, some things have changed since you been away, that's true. Most of those old fucks, they long gone. Ain't no OGs left among the spaghetti benders, man. They in the pen or they headed for the pen or they in the ground. What we got now is a wide-open market. No more bullshit, no more hogging the tit. These days everybody get paid."

"That's good to hear."

"No doubt. And you gonna get your share too. Ain't nobody gonna keep it away from Johnny Too Bad. If they do, he just gonna go take it anyway, right?"

"I only want what's mine."

"Like everybody. And Joey gonna get it to you too, man. He don't forget nothing."

"Good."

"So what you need? Some snaps to walk around with? Get your swerve on? 'Cause I *can* help you out with that."

He got up, went over to the filing cabinet, pulled out a drawer. There was a metal strongbox inside.

"We keep some petty cash in here, cover the betting money," he said. "Not too much, though."

He opened the box, took out two bound bundles of cash, held them up, looked at Johnny.

" 'Bout six hundred here I can spare," he said. "That do it?"

Johnny looked at him.

"Six hundred?"

75

Lindell didn't answer.

"You know where I been the last seven years? And why?"

Lindell lowered the money, shook his head, put it back in the box.

"Like I said, man. It's all I got right now. If you don't want it—"

"Give it here."

Lindell smiled, took out the bundles again. Johnny caught the first in midair, let the second fall into his lap.

"Joey want to see you," Lindell said. "He gave me the word. We gonna set it up for tomorrow. Tuesday at the latest. He happy you out. And I think he gonna have some good news for you." He closed the box, pushed the drawer shut.

Johnny thumbed through the money.

"Let's hope." He put a bundle in each jacket pocket.

"Get yourself some pussy yet?"

"Why?"

"You want some, I hook you up. Fine sistas. Work your jimmy like to make your head spin."

"I'll keep that in mind."

He got up.

"Listen, Johnny."

He stopped halfway to the door, looked back at Lindell.

"I know you're mad. About what happened and all down there. But Joey gonna make it up to you, man. I guarantee."

"Give me a number where I can reach you without getting jerked around."

Lindell took a business card from his jacket pocket.

"My cell, man," he said. "Now you got the access."

Johnny took the card. It was blank except for a handwritten number.

"I'll call you tomorrow afternoon," he said.

"You got it, bro. I have some word for you then."

Johnny turned and went back down the stairs. There was a lull in the fighting and the bettors watched him as he walked past. At the doorway to the anteroom, he turned and saw Lindell standing at the office window, looking down at him.

Topcoat and the tall man were still outside. They watched as he walked to the Firebird.

He was at the driver's-side door, key in hand, when he saw movement in the jeep next to him. He turned, saw the rottweiler's body laid out in the back, the blanket open, the kid sitting Indian fashion with the dog's bloody head in his lap. The kid looked at him and Johnny saw tear lines running down his smooth face. Johnny held his glance for a moment, then turned away and got in the car.

BACK AT the motel, he sat on the edge of the narrow bed, pulled the phone into his lap. A sticker on the front of it said it belonged to a Best Western in Myrtle Beach, South Carolina.

He dialed the beeper. At the tone, he punched in the motel number, the pound sign and then the room number. He hung up, set the phone beside him on the bed, lay back. The ceiling was spotted with water stains, but there was no sound from the floors above or below. Besides the Korean man at the front desk, he had seen only two other people since he'd been here, both welfare residents. As far as he knew, he was the only person on the floor. At night, he heard only the wind.

The phone rang less than five minutes later. He put the receiver to his ear.

"Yeah?"

"About time," Connor said. "I was worried you hadn't made it. This where you're going to be staying?"

"For now."

"You had contact?"

"With Johnson. In Newark. I just came from there."

"What about Joey?"

"Tomorrow. Lindell's setting it up."

"He's screening you."

"Maybe."

"Where's the meeting?"

"I don't know. Maybe the place on Twenty-Two."

"The porn shop? He hasn't been there in weeks."

"That's what Johnson told me. Said Joey's been keeping a low profile."

"That's a laugh. Low profile? It isn't in his personality."

"I'll call you afterward."

"Be careful," Connor said. "You can't trust either of them. Keep your eyes open. Look and listen. How you doing on cash?"

"I could use some more. A grand doesn't go very far."

"I'll see what I can do. Might take a few days."

"What about that other thing?"

"I'm working on it. I told you."

"I'm worried you're not properly motivated."

"You start showing me results, John, and I'll get motivated."

"That wasn't the deal. I told you I wanted one thing out of this. That hasn't changed."

A pause on the line.

"I'm expecting some news soon. It's tough. Records are sealed, there's privacy issues involved."

"But you can do it?"

"I can do it."

"Good, because if you can't, if you're jerking me around, then the whole thing's off. I vanish and you're on your own."

"Don't talk foolish, John. You already owe me. You want to go back to Glades?"

"You know the deal. You know what we agreed."

"I told you. I'm on it."

"Then make it happen. When I call you tomorrow, I'll more than likely have something for you. You should have something for me."

He hung up.

TEN

"NFW," HARRY SAID. "NO FUCKING WAY."

They were in Ray's office, bright sun pouring through the window.

"You're the one went chasing after her," Ray said.

"I learn from my mistakes."

"She called me again. She has a valid situation there. You said so yourself. And we might be able to help her."

"Send Errol."

"She wants you."

"Why?"

"She says she liked the way you handled yourself."

"Bullshit."

"No." Ray raised a hand. "God's honest. That's what she said."

"Then that makes no goddamn sense at all. Did she tell you she pulled a gun on me? That I had to take it away from her?"

"She alluded to that, yes."

Harry got up from the chair, went to the window, looked out.

"Explain this," he said.

"What's there to explain? She wants to contract with us. She wants you to be the point man. Client's request. You won't be solo on this, but she insists you stay in the picture."

Harry looked at him.

"What's going on behind the scenes here? What hasn't she told us? And what am I supposed to do for her anyway?"

Ray shrugged.

"As far as what she isn't telling us, I don't know. Maybe nothing. But I've been giving quite a bit of thought to what we can do for her. And the first thing is to go down to that agency, talk to some people there. Let them know the situation."

"She couldn't do that herself?"

"She could, but it'll bring more weight to bear if we're there with her. They'll be more inclined to listen, get a sense of the gravity of the situation."

"Which I'm still not convinced of myself."

"The woman's worried. That part's real, regardless of whatever else may be going on. Even if we just look into it a little, convince her there's no reason to be worried, then that's a service too. She buys herself a little peace of mind. And there's nothing wrong with that."

"She's already on board, isn't she? You already signed her. Regardless of what I might say."

"If she's not happy with our efforts, she can terminate the contract. But I wasn't going to jerk her around another week before giving her an answer."

"You were that convinced I'd say yes?"

"Let's just say I was hopeful."

"When does she want to go to the agency?"

Ray sat back.

"We were just talking about that on the phone before you got here," he said. "And it occurred to me there's no time like the present. How's this afternoon sound?"

THEY RODE in the Mustang.

When he'd gotten to Ocean Grove, the Blazer was gone. He'd waited in the car, engine running, sounded the horn. After a few minutes she came out the front door and down the walk, wearing a green sweater, jeans, leather car coat. He leaned over, unlocked the passenger's-side door. She got in, shut the door, and he pulled away from the curb without speaking a word.

They drove the first few minutes without speaking. When they hit Route 33, heading west, she said, "You know where it is?"

"Yeah. Ray gave me the address. They know we're coming?"

"He made an appointment for me."

"Ray did?"

"Yes, why?"

"Never mind. I should have guessed."

They drifted into silence.

"I'm sorry," she said finally. "About what happened the other day."

He gave that a nod.

"Reggie shouldn't have done that," she said.

He didn't answer.

"But you overreacted."

He looked at her.

"Excuse me?"

"You could have seriously hurt him."

"He could have broken my neck. Without even meaning to or knowing he did it. I could have ended up in a nursing home with a feeding tube and an adult diaper. He didn't seem too concerned about that. You either."

"He was protecting me."

"So I was supposed to stand there, let him use me for a heavy bag?"

She looked out the window, didn't answer.

"And that stupid stunt you pulled—"

"I wasn't aiming at you."

"And if you'd clipped my femoral artery because your hand shook, and I'd bled to death right there on your nice hardwood floor, how would you have felt about that?"

"You were scaring me. I thought you were going to kill him. I wanted to stop it."

"Never point a gun—"

"Yes, yes. Never point a gun at someone you're not ready to shoot. You told me."

"That's not what I was going to say."

She looked at him.

"Then what?"

"I was going to say, Never point a gun at *me*."

She looked out the window again.

"I'll try to remember that."

The agency was in a building off Main Street in Freehold, across

81

from the Hall of Records. He parked in a municipal lot a block away and they walked against the wind.

They rode the elevator up to the fourth floor and the doors opened onto a small foyer with a reception window. Behind the glass, a young black woman was talking on a headset. She didn't look up as they came in. On the shelf outside the window was a clipboard with a sign-in sheet, a Bic pen attached to it with string.

After a few minutes with no eye contact, he tapped a knuckle on the glass. The woman looked up at him, frowned. He raised his hand again and she reached up, slid the window open.

"Please don't do that."

"We have an appointment," he said.

"Who with?"

He looked at Nikki.

"My name's Nicole Ellis," she said. "We had an appointment for four?"

"Did you sign in? You can't see anybody unless you sign in."

A well-dressed black woman in her fifties came up behind the receptionist.

"Ms. Ellis?" She looked at him. "Mr. Rane?"

"Yes," he said.

"Right on time. I'm Rosetta Harper. I'm the managing director here at Second Chance. Let's go back to my office."

The receptionist buzzed them through into a long room divided into cubicles, each with a desk and filing cabinet. He could hear phones ringing, printers clacking.

They followed Harper down a narrow aisle into a cubicle that was slightly larger than the ones around it. Inside was a desk, two plastic chairs in front of it, a filing cabinet and coat rack behind them. There was a computer on the desk, the screen showing animated fish chasing one another silently back and forth in bright blue water.

"Have a seat," she said. "I pulled your file earlier."

They settled down into chairs. Harry unzipped his jacket, but didn't take it off. Nikki hung her coat on the back of her chair.

"Now, if I remember correctly," Harper said, "this concerns a child you've given up for adoption?"

"Yes," Nikki said.

"And Mr. Rane"—looking at Harry—"is your husband?"

"No," she said. "I thought you read the file."

"My mistake. So what can I do for you?" Sitting back in her chair, putting distance between them, Harry already feeling the whole thing going south.

"I've hired Mr. Rane and his company to help me out, because—"

"What company?"

Harry took an RW card from his shirt pocket. He'd grabbed a handful before leaving Ray's office. He leaned forward, handed it to her. She took it, looked at it skeptically.

"I don't understand. . . ."

"Ms. Ellis is a client," he said. "I don't know how much you were told over the phone—"

"Not very much." She put the card down, picked up the phone, dialed a three-digit extension.

"Who are you calling?" Nikki said.

Harper didn't answer. After a moment she said into the phone, "Mr. Simmons? Rosetta. Sorry to bother you. But we're going to need you in here when you get a chance."

"So YOU understand our dilemma," Simmons said. "As executive director of Second Chance, I have to tell you that confidentiality comes first, always. It's the bedrock on which we work. Without it, the whole system would crumble, there'd be chaos."

"I understand," Harry said. Simmons was a tall, skinny black man in a dark suit and yellow bow tie. Harry had taken an almost instant dislike to him.

"We're not asking you to tell us where he is," Nikki said.

"And we wouldn't," Simmons said. He'd pulled in a chair from another cubicle, positioned it alongside Harper, facing them, his elbows on the arms, his hands clasped in front of him.

Nikki looked out of the cubicle, then back to him.

"You don't seem to understand what's going on here," she said.

"I'm trying to, but you have to see it from my perspective. And the fact remains, I really don't know who either of you people are, do I? On what grounds should I just accept what you're telling me?"

"She pulled my file," Nikki said. "Read it."

"I will," he said. "Later."

Harry leaned forward.

"Go ahead and call the number on that card," he said. "I work for a licensed security agency. Personal and professional protective services. Call the number, they can give you references: lawyers, people they worked with."

"Be that as it may," Simmons said, "you're asking me for something I can't do."

"No, we're not," Nikki said.

"Now if you were with an actual law enforcement agency," Simmons said, ignoring her, "that might be different."

"I was with the New Jersey State Police for twelve years."

Simmons shrugged.

"But no longer, right? And that's why I'm afraid I don't know what to say to you."

"Our feeling is there's a risk situation here," Harry said. "You must have some procedure when there's a threat, when a family or child is in danger. When a birth mother or father decides to come looking for their child."

"There is, of course, but I'm not at liberty to say what that is."

"You don't need to. But whatever that procedure is, it might be a good time to get it up and running. Whether it's up to you or someone above you, look in your files, your database, find out where the boy is, the family, find the caseworker if there still is one. Warn them. You owe them that."

Simmons sat back, looked at Harper, and Harry realized he had misplayed it.

Simmons turned back to him.

"I'm happy to hear you have such a clear picture of how I should do my job," he said. "But even looking objectively at what you said, I have to ask—and you should ask yourself—'Owe them what?' To frighten them, turn their lives upside down because of some rumor?"

"It's no rumor," Nikki said. "If he's not back here already, he will be soon."

Simmons looked at her.

"You've seen him? Talked to him?"

She shook her head.

"Not yet."

"All we're asking," Harry cut in, "is that someone get the word out through the system, let the family know."

"I told you confidentiality was the bedrock of our work," Simmons said. "And it always has been. There's no way the father—unless he had access to our records, which I can assure you he does not—would be able to find out where the boy is."

"I'm sure you're right," Harry said. "But if he got pointed to the right person, a person who knew or could find out, someone who had access to those files, I doubt he'd be as polite about it as we have been."

"Is that a threat?"

"Please," Harry said. "Listen to what I'm saying."

"I've been listening."

"What possible reason would we have for coming here, feeding you this story, if it wasn't true? What purpose could possibly be served?"

"I don't know."

"Then why don't you believe us?" Nikki said.

He looked at her.

"Did I say that I didn't?"

"You're acting like it."

Harry held up a hand.

"Let's everyone relax here," he said.

Simmons slid a sleeve back, looked at his watch.

"We've told you the situation as we know it to be," Harry said. "Do whatever you think is best. That's all we can ask."

Simmons looked at him, waiting for him to finish.

"But there are some key things to keep in mind," Harry said. "John Harrow is a multiple felon."

"I understand that."

"Knowing him, Ms. Ellis is convinced he's going to try to find the boy. I think we have to trust her on that. Because she doesn't want that to happen, the boy's adoptive parents wouldn't want that to happen, and I'm sure *you* don't want that to happen."

"Of course not."

"So I think we owe it at least to those parents—and to the boy—to let them know what's going on, so that they can be aware of what the situation is, what the potential dangers are."

Simmons reached over, took a pencil from Harper's desk, looked at it, tapped it lightly against the edge of the chair, looked finally at Harry.

"Let me think about this," he said.

"That's fine," Nikki said. "Only thing is, I get the impression you're the kind of man that thinks a lot and ends up doing nothing."

Harper turned to her.

"Now, you just wait a minute, honey. Who do you think—"

Simmons reached over to touch her arm, calm her, looked at Nikki.

"I'm sorry for your situation, Ms. Ellis," he said. "But maybe there are a few things I need to remind you of. When you gave your son up for adoption—which I'm sure was the correct decision—you renounced all rights to him, maternal or otherwise, as I'm sure you fully understood when you signed those—"

She stood up quickly and for an instant Harry thought she was going for him. Simmons reared back slightly.

"I'm sorry we wasted your time," she said. She pulled her jacket off the chair, slung it over an arm. "I guess I should have known better."

She started to leave the cubicle and Harry reached up to touch her, stop her, but she brushed by him and out.

Simmons looked at him.

"She's upset," Harry said.

"Obviously. But when people behave like that, it's difficult to have much sympathy for them."

"It's not about her," he said. "It's about the boy."

He stood, zipped his jacket up.

"Call the number on the card," he said. "Ask about me. Ask around about the agency. Then, when you're comfortable with that, all I ask is that you get on the phone to whatever regional office is closest to where the boy is now. Tell them what's going on."

"Mr. Payne—"

"Rane."

"I do my job as I see fit. I don't answer to you."

"I know you don't," he said. "But if anything happens to that boy, you will."

86

ELEVEN

WHEN THEY WERE BACK ON THE ROAD, HE SAID, "WELL, I THINK WE can safely say that was a disaster."

She didn't answer.

"I'm afraid you didn't help your case much."

"I was trying to stay calm. It didn't work. Those people are idiots."

"Just bureaucrats. Following rules."

"Assholes."

He faced her.

"I think the lesson you need to learn here is . . ." he said, and saw the tears.

"I'm sorry," he said.

She took a tissue from her pocket, wiped her eyes quickly, put it away.

He turned the radio on low to an all-news station, the weatherman predicting below-normal temperatures, snow flurries into the night.

They were stopped at a light on Route 33 when she said, "Do you have children?"

"No."

"Married?"

"Widowed."

He looked up at the light, expecting the standard response, some variation of "I'm sorry." Nothing.

He shifted into first, waited for the light.

"Then you don't know what it's like," she said.

The light changed. He went through, shifted gears.

"Maybe not," he said. "But there are certain cases—and back

there was one of them—where a little diplomacy wouldn't hurt. Might actually get you closer to what you wanted."

"What am I supposed to do? Blow him to get him to do his job?"

"I'd like to think that, even though we left on bad terms, it doesn't mean they're not going to do anything. At the very least maybe they can put some sort of red flag on your file in the system, in case someone starts digging around."

"Do you really think they'd do that? After that conversation, do you really think they'd care?"

"Maybe. There's one thing I don't think anyone asked—did Harrow know what agency you used?"

"I don't know. If so, it didn't come from me. It wouldn't be too difficult to find out, though. There aren't that many around."

"Chances are slim, though."

"I guess. He had other things on his mind at the time. He was in the middle of his trial when I went into the hospital."

"And you've had no contact with him since?"

"Like I said, he wrote me for a while, from Belle Glade. I didn't write back. When I went to California, I didn't leave a forwarding address. I wanted to put everything behind me. So I guess if he wrote me after that, the letters would have been returned."

"And that's what I don't get."

"What?"

"Why you were together in the first place."

"I was twenty when we met. I didn't know any better. At that age sometimes, you're looking for someone to come along, take you out of the situation you're in. Show you a different world."

"That what he did?"

"That's what he promised."

"What happened?"

"What always happens? He loved me, maybe. But he loved what he was doing even more. It was him against the world, you know? That was the way he saw things. You were either with him or against him. 'Part of the solution,' he used to say, 'or part of the problem. Pick your side.'"

"And you did."

"No. I just opted out. His going to prison, it was an opportunity for me to get away, get clear of all that. Some people offered to help me out, get me settled somewhere else."

"So you went to California?"

She nodded.

"And what did you do there?"

"Lots of things."

They were in Ocean Grove now, almost night, purple streaks in the west marking the end of day. He found the street, pulled up to the curb, engine running. The Blazer was still gone.

"Thank you," she said. "For coming with me. I should have said that before."

He looked at her, not sure how to respond.

"Can you come in for a minute?" she said. "I want to show you something."

"Are your friends here?"

"No, no one. I won't keep you. It'll just take a minute."

He shut the engine off. She got out of the car and he followed her up the walk to the house. They went into the warmth of the living room and he closed the door behind him.

"Wait here," she said. "I'll be right down."

She went into the hallway and he heard her footsteps on the stairs.

He looked around. The glass vase had been replaced by a ceramic one, filled now with yellow roses instead of carnations. The tiny hole in the couch had been temporarily patched with clear tape.

After a couple minutes, she came back down. She had a leather wallet, a small manila envelope with a clasp. She unsnapped the wallet, looked through it and slipped a Polaroid out of a plastic sleeve. She looked at it for a moment, then handed it to him.

"I wanted you to know," she said.

It was a photo of a newborn baby, wrapped in a blanket. Pink skin, the tuft of hair on its skull matted and damp.

"They don't like you to do that," she said. "Take a picture. They think it makes it harder to let go. But I did it anyway. A friend of mine snuck a camera in, took it right there in the hospital room."

He looked at the picture, unsure what to say, handed it back.

"And does it?" he said.

"Does it what?"

"Make it harder."

She looked at the photo again, carefully slipped it back into its sleeve.

"Nothing makes it easier. But I did what I had to do. I wanted the photo, though. I didn't want to be left with nothing at all. I didn't want to ever forget. . . ."

"What's in the envelope?"

She handed it to him. He undid the clasp, opened it. Inside was a color snapshot of a dark-haired man in his late twenties, leaning back against a bar, the flash of the camera reflected in the mirror behind it. He had his arms crossed, the hint of a smile on his face. His hair was long, tied in the back, and even with the poor color reproduction, Harry could tell his eyes were a dark blue.

"You take this?" he said.

"Yes. I don't know why I kept it. Maybe I knew it would come in handy someday."

He turned the photo over. *New Year's '93* was written on the back in red ink.

He slid it back in the envelope.

"I'll need to keep this," he said.

"Go ahead. I don't have any use for it anymore."

He put the envelope in an inside jacket pocket.

"We'll shake some trees," he said. "See what we can come up with, what we can find out. I'm meeting with Ray tomorrow."

"And then?"

"And then we'll figure out what comes next."

He was at the door when she said, "I'm sorry."

He looked at her.

"About what?"

"Your wife."

He nodded, watched her.

"Thanks," he said and went out.

THE FLURRIES began on his way home, flecks of white swirling in his headlights. He stopped at a liquor store on Route 537, bought a bottle of red wine. By the time he got back to Colts Neck, the snow was sticking, the temperature dropping.

He stacked quartered logs in the fireplace, got a fire going, then went into the kitchen. He took a skillet out, found a plastic-wrapped package of ground beef in the refrigerator, sniffed it to see if it had gone bad. He set the skillet on the stove, turned the heat up. When the surface started to smoke faintly, he dropped the beef in, hissing, pushed it around with a plastic spatula until it was done.

He scraped the beef onto a plate, opened the wine, poured a glass. He ate standing at the counter, watching the snow swirl around the security light over the barn.

When he was done, he filled the glass again, took it into the living room, added more wood to the fire. He sat on the couch, put his boots up on the coffee table. Despite the fire, he could feel the cold settling on him, the ache in his left elbow growing. He got the remote, turned the TV on, channel-surfed randomly for five minutes, watching four seconds of a program here, ten seconds there. Finally he switched the TV off, watched the picture fade to a dot and then blackness. He listened to the wind.

THE BOTTLE was almost empty when he made the call. Glowing embers in the fireplace, the room cold again.

"Hello?"

"Ellen? It's Harry Rane."

"Harry?" A pause. "Hang on. Cristina's upstairs. We were just getting ready to go out to dinner."

He waited, heard footsteps, muffled voices, then the phone being picked up.

"Harry?"

Something pulled inside him at the sound of her voice.

"Yes."

"What time is it out there? What are you doing?"

"Just sitting. And thinking it's like the song."

"What song?"

"It's the coldest night of the year . . . and you're not even here."

"What are you talking about? Are you drunk?"

"Maybe."

"You don't know?"

"I've been working on it, but it's not coming very easily."

Silence. Then: "Harry, I can't talk right now. We're on our way out."

"Who?"

"What do you mean?"

"On your way out with who?"

"Ellen and I. Who did you think?"

"Never mind."

"Don't start on this, Harry. Not now."

"When are you coming back?"

"I don't know. Soon."

"When is soon?"

"Harry, this isn't the time or place to have this conversation. Let me call you back."

"When?"

"When I can talk. And you're sober."

"I need you."

A pause.

"This isn't fair, Harry."

"No, it isn't."

More silence. Regretting now that he'd called, feeling the whole thing falling apart.

"I have to go," she said. "Ellen's waiting for me."

"Call me."

"I will."

"I love you."

Static on the line, the hiss of the wires.

"I love you, Harry. But you've got to give me time."

"You said that to me once before. And I told you that you had all the time you needed, all the time in the world."

"I remember that."

"But I'm not sure if I can say that anymore."

There was no answer except the hiss of the line, the distance.

"I have to go."

"Then go," he said and ended the call. The dial tone buzzed in his ear.

He put the phone facedown on the coffee table, looked at it, willing it to ring back. He poured the last of the wine, thought of the Percocet upstairs. After fifteen minutes, he picked up the phone, returned it to its base on the end table. It took him two tries to get it to stay.

He sank back on the couch, looked up at the ceiling. When he closed his eyes, he saw her face.

TWELVE

WHEN THEY PULLED UP TO THE TRAILER, THERE WAS AN OLD RED Chevy pickup parked out front.

"Who's that belong to?" Johnny said.

"It's Frazer's."

Mitch pulled the Firebird in behind it, shut the engine off. The car chugged with preignition, shook and was silent.

"What's he doing here?" Johnny said.

"I don't know."

Johnny got out of the car, looked the truck over. It was pitted with rust, the tires almost bald. There were empty beer cans in the bed.

They went up the stairs and into the trailer. The old man was sitting on the couch, Treya on his knee. He was bouncing her, holding her hips, but she wasn't smiling. Sharonda stood in the hallway, looked at them as they came in.

Frazer saw them, his knee slowed and stopped. He lifted the girl, set her on her feet. She ran to her mother.

The old man wore stained pants, a dark blue work shirt with his name over the pocket. What was left of his hair was white, and there were patches of eczema on his cheeks and neck, the skin pink with it. A grease-stained John Deere cap was on the couch beside him.

Mitch closed the door. Sharonda took Treya, disappeared into the back bedroom.

"There they are," Frazer said. "My boys."

He started to get up, wincing with pain. He limped toward Johnny, put out his hand. Johnny looked at it.

"I heard you were out, back up here," Frazer said. "I can't tell you how good it made me feel to hear that."

94

Mitch went past them into the kitchen. The old man smiled at Johnny, dentures yellow with nicotine.

"You look good," Frazer said. "Healthy. Like you're ready to kick ass and take names."

Johnny looked at him, remembered the man he had feared, wondered where he had gone.

"Something wrong?" Frazer said.

"No." He nodded to the kitchen. "Come on. Let's go sit down."

The old man followed him in, hips canting from side to side as he walked. Mitch was leaning against the counter, looking at the floor.

Johnny pointed at the table, opened the refrigerator door. There was a cardboard pizza box inside, an untouched six-pack of Budweiser. He pulled three loose from the plastic collars.

"It's been a long time, Johnny," Frazer said. "When I heard you were here, I couldn't wait to see you."

Frazer sat down at the head of the table, wheezing with the effort. Johnny looked at Mitch, tossed him a can. He caught it. Johnny put another in front of the old man, pulled out the chair opposite him, sat down. The chair was thin aluminum with cheap padding. It sagged under him.

"How'd you know I was here?" Johnny said. A faint odor of sweat came from across the table.

The old man shrugged, picked up the beer.

"Word gets around, that's all."

He popped the beer, brought it to his lips, siphoned the foam. Johnny opened his, set it down without drinking. Mitch watched them.

"What do you mean?" Johnny said.

Frazer put the beer down.

"You've got a lot of friends around here, Johnny. That's all. And you've been gone a long time. Only natural that people would be happy to see you, tell others about it. Like I said, word gets around."

"I guess." Johnny took a pull from the beer. "You get to the cemetery much?"

"What?"

"The cemetery. Visit Mom and Belinda. You ever go there, clean the place up, leave some flowers?"

Frazer looked at the floor.

95

"Well, I do what I can," he said. "But these knees . . . it's not so easy anymore. Makes it tough to get around too much."

Johnny nodded, drank beer.

"You'll want to take care of that," he said. "Not let it get worse."

The old man looked at him.

"Too much fucking standing up, I guess," he said, smiled. "I guess I fucked my knees out of commission somewhere along the line. Gettin' old's a bitch."

Johnny looked at Mitch. He was still at the sink, looking at his unopened beer.

"Mitch," he said, "why don't you go check on Sharonda and Treya?"

He nodded, put the can on the counter, left the kitchen.

Frazer drank beer, watched him go.

"Hard to believe," he said. "That boy taking up with a nigger like that."

Johnny shrugged, rocked back on his chair slightly, boots braced against the floor, one hand on the table to steady himself.

"You'd think he'd know better," Frazer said. "Way he was raised and all."

Johnny lifted his beer, swished it.

"What did you come here for, old man?"

"Want to see my boys. Isn't that enough?"

Johnny drank, put the can back down, waited.

"Mitchy tell you I got the emphysema?"

Johnny shook his head.

"Been in and out of the hospital. I got the oxygen at home when I need it. Quit the cigarettes. Christ, it seems like I quit everything that ever give me the slightest amount of pleasure. Can't work anymore either. And you know me, John. I was always a worker."

"How much do you need?"

The old man rubbed his chin, his whiskers making a faint bristling noise.

"Come on, Johnny. You don't think I came here just to—"

"How much?"

"I know you're just out and all . . . probably need time to get back on your feet. But if a man can't ask the son he's raised, who can he ask? So I was thinking, maybe when things get going for you again, when you get a little something for yourself—"

"I don't need to wait. I can help you now. How much do you want?"

"They turned the phone off, and I'm two months behind on the electric. They'll be shutting that off too before I know. And that Jew doctor . . . they're going to turn it over to a collection agency if I don't pay the rest of what I owe them. They don't care if I can't work, if I'm sick."

Johnny let the front legs of the chair touch down. He took money out of his left jacket pocket, looked for hundreds, found five of them. Frazer watched him.

"There you go," Johnny said. He folded the hundreds, slid them across the table. "Go pay your phone bill, your electricity, whatever else you need to. That should set you for a while. You need more, you let me know."

The old man looked at the money, didn't touch it.

"Go ahead," Johnny said. "It's a gift. For taking care of us all those years. Raising us right."

Frazer touched the money tentatively at first, then drew it toward him. He unfolded the bills, smoothed them out on the table one by one.

"That enough?" Johnny said.

"You're a good boy, John. You always were."

He watched the old man look at each bill, then fold them again, put them in his shirt pocket.

"But don't come here anymore," Johnny said.

"John, I only—"

"You want to talk to me, you call Mitch. I'll meet you some-where. But I don't want to see you here again."

"Can't a father see his sons?"

"You want to see us, talk to us, you call. You don't come by. That clear to you?"

Frazer met his eyes, then looked at the floor, nodded.

"Now finish your beer. Have another if you want. But it's the last time you set foot in here."

"There's no cause to act this way, John."

"Drink your beer. Then go pay your bills. And buy yourself some new clothes. You look like shit, old man. And you smell."

Frazer scraped his chair back from the table. Johnny watched him, seeing something familiar in those eyes, the way they narrowed before the first blow hit. He remembered the fear, the taste of it like pennies in his mouth. Those same eyes, but a different man now.

"It shouldn't be like this, John." He got to his feet, winced, one hand on the back of the chair for balance. "After all these years not seeing you. It ain't right."

Johnny looked at him, sipped beer.

"You should come by the house," Frazer said. "It's been a long time since you been there. Lot of memories there for you. For both of us."

"Maybe I will."

Johnny watched from the kitchen window as he drove away, the truck belching gray smoke, engine backfiring in the cold. He heard Mitch come into the kitchen behind him.

"What was that about?" Mitch said. "What did he want?"

"What do you think?"

"I don't like him here."

There was a pack of menthol cigarettes on the counter. Johnny shook one loose, sparked his lighter.

"Don't worry," he said, exhaling smoke. "He won't be back."

IT WAS a two-story concrete-block building off Route 22, red neon signage, blackout curtains. A little after midnight and the parking lot was half full. Johnny pulled the Firebird in behind the building, swung around and parked so that the nose was facing the street again. Reserved spots in the back here. Lindell's Lexus jeep. A Cadillac Escalade. A Ford Cherokee.

He cut the engine, listened to the car tick and cool around him. There was a single lighted window on the second floor, blinds drawn, figures moving in silhouette behind them. The office.

He watched it for a few minutes, then got out of the car. There was a fire door in the back wall, a delivery bell alongside it. He pressed it with a thumb, stepped back. The light from the window fell on him.

Footsteps on stairs inside, then the door cracked open, a line of yellow light falling on the blacktop. The man in the doorway was heavy, a hard Indian face pockmarked with acne scars, black hair slicked back off his forehead. He wore a dark silk shirt open at the neck, a gold crucifix on a chain.

"Tuco," Johnny said.

The Mexican looked at him. Johnny raised his hands at his sides to show they were empty, let them fall.

The Mexican nodded.

"How you doing, homes?"

"He here?"

"Yeah, man. Waiting for you."

He pushed the door wider. There was a narrow stairwell inside, concrete steps leading up. Johnny started up without waiting, heard Tuco pull the door shut.

The layout was as he remembered. Two doors off the landing, both open. One led to a stockroom with one-way mirrors that looked out on the store, the other to a brightly lit office. Johnny heard Tuco's heavy breathing as he came up the stairs behind him.

"What you waiting for, homes? Go on in."

When he walked in the office, Joey Alea stood up behind his desk, opened his arms.

"Look at him," he said. "Just look at him."

He started around the desk and Johnny looked him over. He wore a gray blazer and black turtleneck, his jet black hair moussed perfectly in place, but his hairline higher than the last time Johnny had seen him.

"Come here, you," he said, and pulled Johnny to him, clasped him in both arms, then pulled back to look at him. Johnny could smell his cologne.

"Look at this guy," Joey said. "Johnny Blue Eyes in the flesh." Then to Johnny: "Do you know how long I've waited, watch you walk through that door?"

"It's good to be back," Johnny said.

Joey stepped away. Lindell stood behind the desk, suit and open shirt, medallion. He raised his chin in greeting.

Johnny looked at the third man in the room. He sat on a chair in the far corner, crew cut hair, impassive Slavic face. He wore a leather jacket, sweater, jeans, elbows resting on his knees. He looked at Johnny, nodded. The room smelled of cigar smoke.

"Come over here," Joey said. "Take a seat." There was a cushioned chair facing the desk. Johnny went over to it, started taking his field jacket off. On the desk was a computer terminal, wire trays with papers, invoices, a glass ashtray with a thin cigar smoking in it.

Johnny felt Tuco come into the office behind him, close the door.

He folded the field jacket, laid it across the back of the chair. Joey watched him. He caught the bottom edge of his sweatshirt, pulled it up and over his head.

"This isn't necessary," Joey said.

He laid the sweatshirt atop his jacket, knew they were all looking at his tattoo. He put one foot up on the chair, pulled the cuff of his camouflage pants up to knee height, pushed his sock down to the boot, showing the bare skin. He did the same with the other foot, then smacked his crotch to flatten out the material, show there was nothing hidden there. Joey looked amused.

"You're a good man, Johnny," he said. "Always were."

Johnny picked up the sweatshirt, pulled it back on.

"Lindell," Joey said. "Viktor, Tuco. Give us a moment. Please."

Lindell came over to him, put his hand out. Johnny caught it in the soul shake, and Lindell pulled him close, patted him on the back. It felt stiff, formal, as if done for Joey's benefit alone.

"Catch up with you later," he said. Then to Joey: "I'll be downstairs."

When they were alone, Joey gestured at the door. Johnny closed it. Joey sat back down behind the desk.

"United Fucking Nations," Johnny said.

Joey laughed.

"Yeah, land of opportunity, right? Have a seat, man. It's been a long time."

Johnny pulled the chair closer to the desk, sat down. Joey picked up the cigar, then seemed to think better of it, put it back in the ashtray.

"First things first," he said. "I'm sorry."

"For what?"

"What happened down there."

Johnny shrugged, took his cigarettes out of the field jacket.

"They offered me a deal," he said. "I told them to go fuck themselves."

"I know."

Johnny got a cigarette lit. Joey pushed the ashtray toward him.

"I had no idea what was going on down there," he said. "With Cardosa. I should have figured he'd be a fucking rat too, on top of everything else."

Johnny looked around the office.

"Don't worry. I get it swept once a week. Phones too. We're clean."

"New faces around."

"Not that many. You know Tuco, right?"

"Looks like he's come up in the world since I've been away."

"You left a vacuum, Johnny. Big shoes to fill. Not that anybody could fill them. But you were missed, you know? So I brought him up a little. Balls like a bull, that guy. Not the smartest, but he'll do any goddamn thing I tell him and not ask twice."

"That what you used to say about me?"

"That's not even funny, John. There's no comparison."

"What about the other one?"

"Viktor? Just over here a year or so. Only twenty-eight but he was in the Russian Army. Tough kid. Came over here not speaking a word of English. Now he runs this place for me. Fast learner."

"Russian."

"Yeah, but none of that *Organizatsiya* bullshit. Just a guy looking to make a living. His girlfriend was over here, working at one of my places up in North Jersey, dancing. He used to come around. That's how I got to know him. Half of the girls in those places now are Russian, Polish."

"I wouldn't know."

"But Viktor, that guy never took a fall in his life—at least not in the States. He's got a green card and everything. That's why he's useful to me. Things are a little different around here now."

"That's what Lindell was telling me."

"That bullshit in Florida, with Cardosa, it was like a wake-up call. A fucking twenty-grand deal and the whole thing blew up in our faces. I mean, look at what you went through. And for what?"

"I wondered that same thing myself."

"The way it fell out . . . it made me reevaluate some things. I mean, guys like Cardosa, you deal with them, you don't really know what you're getting into, do you? Who could have known the guy was working for the Feds down there? Lowlifes like that, there's no sense of honor. Who could believe the guy would get up in open court, testify against you?"

"Maybe he felt he didn't have anything to lose. Being as how I tried to kill him."

"Regardless. You trade with people like that, you run a risk. You're better off without them."

"Too bad you didn't figure that out before I went down there."

Joey raised his hands.

"Who knew? Like I said, if I'd had any idea, I would have done things differently. But if it's any consolation, that fucking guy got what was coming to him anyway."

"I heard."

"And nobody shed a tear, including the Feds. They probably felt he'd served his purpose anyway, you know? So they saved the time and expense of putting him in the WitSec program, starting a new life for him out in Bumfuck, Iowa. They'd probably thank me if they could."

Johnny nodded at the door.

"Tuco?"

Joey smiled.

"Balls like a bull, like I said. But the point is, that lying mother-fucker Cardosa is never coming back. And I did that for you. Out of respect."

"Thanks."

"At that point, the other things, the money, I could have written it off to experience, you know, moved on. It wasn't worth the trouble. But what happened with you . . . there was no way that was going to stand. Even with the risk. There was a principal involved. Loyalty."

Johnny leaned forward, tapped his cigarette in the ashtray. The cigar had gone out.

"It hurt me when you took that fall, John. Nine fucking years. I couldn't believe it."

Johnny shrugged, sat back.

"Lindell talk to you?" Joey said.

"A little."

"Then you know things have changed. I used to have to ask permission, get blessings, to make a move. I don't anymore."

"What about your uncle?"

"What about him? He's still around, but for how long, who knows? He's practically retired already."

"That's hard to believe."

"Believe it. I mean, don't get me wrong, he's still my uncle. He hooked me up in the past, protected me when I needed it. And hey, I'm not foolish enough to think his name didn't grease some wheels for me. But that was then. The landscape's different now."

"Hard to imagine Tony Acuna like that, retired."

"There's nothing wrong with it. Someday, maybe, I'll want to do the same. He stays at home, grows his grapes, takes his cut, what gets kicked up to him. He doesn't deserve it, doesn't work for it. But what are you gonna do? He gets to relax now, go back to Italy once a year. He's happy. He leaves me alone to do my business."

"What about his crew?"

"You can hardly call it that anymore. The ones around him—that fucking Frankie Santelli and the others—they're all old men, like him. So my uncle keeps a small slice of the pie, some stuff out at the Port, but it's nothing. A gesture. It just rolls in; he doesn't have to do shit."

"So who's calling the shots these days?"

"Nobody. That's the beauty of it. Those old parasites are off our backs. The Scarpettis, they used to have their hands in everyone's pockets. You couldn't do shit without them taxing your ass. They're out of the picture almost totally now. That crazy old fuck, Paulie One-Eye, he's under indictment. If he goes in, he ain't never getting out. His crew's a shambles. So there were all kinds of things on the ground, waiting to be picked up. And other things they'd never even thought of."

"Congratulations."

"Hey, when I started putting things together, I did it my own way, handpicked my own people—by reputation, by brains. Not because of their uncle's mother's maiden name or what part of the Boot they came from. What I've got going is business—a real business. And I run it that way. I'm into a lot of things now, Johnny. Things that were just a dream a few years back."

Johnny lit a new cigarette off the old one, pinched out the butt and put it in the ashtray.

"But being able to get to that position . . . I owe a lot of that to you. You gave seven years of your life to solve a problem for me, let me get another couple of rungs up the ladder. I took advantage of that opportunity. I won't forget your sacrifice."

He opened a drawer in the desk, took out a bulky manila envelope and a cardboard box the size of a hardcover book, set both beside the ashtray. The box had weight to it.

"Go ahead," Joey said, pushing the envelope forward. "Have a look."

He sat back again, smiling.

Johnny left the cigarette in his mouth, took the envelope. He looked at Joey and then undid the clasp. Bank-wrapped currency slid into his lap.

"I still owe you fifteen for what you did down there," Joey said. "I put it aside, computed the interest, seven years at the current prime rate as of Monday, plus a bonus. So that's twenty of what I owe you."

"Thanks."

"And there's another fifteen there as well."

"What for?"

"A gesture. And a retainer."

Johnny looked at the stacks of money, riffed the edges of one of them. Hundreds.

"If you want me to put some of that to work," Joey said, "I could double it for you in six months' time."

"On the street?"

Joey shook his head.

"I have so little money on the street now, I couldn't care less. It's a fraction of what I've got working for me."

"Then what?"

"Real estate. In terms of the investment-to-profit ratio, you can't touch it. Things are going through the roof in this state now, and land is the one asset that never depreciates. I own about a dozen properties in Monmouth County alone. Christ, I own half of Asbury Park. With the redevelopment that's going on there, it's a gold mine. Already I've got a couple deals that are turning over money like somebody was printing it."

"Scams?"

"Little of this, little of that. Most of it's straightforward. Quick things, though. In and out and cover your tracks afterward. I have a sweet deal I've been working with properties in niggertowns all over the state. It's absolutely untouchable. And no one has any idea it's happening. I even have an office in Middletown. Mortgages and shit."

He waved a hand to encompass the room.

"I almost never come to this place anymore. No reason to. Only reason I did tonight is because I thought you might be more comfortable here, since it was a place you knew."

Johnny put the money back in the envelope, worked the clasp.

"What's in the box?"

"A present. Go on, open it."

Johnny bent forward and picked up the box, knew what it was. He set it in his lap, opened the flaps, lifted the lid. Inside was a thin sheet of gray packing foam. Beneath it, nestled in more foam, was a Sig Sauer 228, nine-millimeter, flat black with plastic grips. Alongside it, resting in silhouette grooves, were two clips.

"Sweet, isn't it?" Joey said. "Your favorite, right?"

He had used a Sig in Florida, had been forced to drop it into a canal near his motel a half hour before the Feds arrested him. They'd dragged the canal but hadn't found it. The gun in front of him was a mirror image of the one he'd lost. He took it out, hefted it.

"Brand-new, at least as far as it goes," Joey said. "I've had it for three years, waiting to give it to you. Never been fired."

The Sig was unloaded, the clips empty. Johnny pointed the muzzle at the floor, worked the slide. The action was smooth, easy, oiled.

"Well?" Joey said.

"It's good." He put the gun back into the foam. "Thanks."

"Least I could do. So what are you thinking?"

"I'm thinking there's a reason you gave this to me. And it's got nothing to do with real estate."

Joey laughed, sat back.

"It's a gift. Really. To replace something you lost. That's all."

He opened another drawer, took out two cardboard boxes of shells, set them on the desk.

"Almost forgot these," he said. "Save you some trouble trying to buy them."

Johnny took one of the boxes, slid it open, looked at the brass cartridges standing nose up inside. He closed the box.

"I need another favor too," he said.

"Name it."

"I'm looking for Nikki."

"Who?" A pause. "You mean that chick you used to be with? Back in the day?"

"Yeah. Her."

"If you want a woman, John, I can make a phone call, take two seconds."

Johnny shook his head.

"It's not that way. I want to talk to her. She used to dance the circuit—Partylights, the Heartbreak. You owned a bunch of those places."

"Not anymore. I sold off the last one a couple years ago. And I haven't had a piece of the Heartbreak in five or six. I don't do business in a strip club anymore, you know? I do it in an office."

"You still know people. You can ask."

"John, I hardly remember her. I met her once or twice, but that's it. Tell the truth, I probably wouldn't know her now if I saw her. You might not either. Chicks get old fast in that business."

"Do me that favor, though? Put the word out low-key. I don't want her to know I'm looking."

"She worth the hassle? After all these years?"

Johnny didn't answer.

"Okay," Joey said after a moment. "I think it's a waste of time, but if you want that, you got it. I'll have Lindell look into it. If she's around, he'll find her."

Johnny stood up. He pulled his field jacket on, slipped the boxes of shells into his pockets.

"Lindell has my number," he said. "Where I'm staying."

He tucked the box with the Sig under his left arm, picked up the envelope.

"Thanks for this."

"I wish I could do more for you, Johnny."

"You said the money's a retainer."

"Something like that."

"You need some work, you need me to prove myself to you—"

"John, I don't need—"

"What I'm saying, you have some work for me, then you just tell me what it is. I'll take care of it."

Joey nodded.

"We'll talk soon," he said.

Johnny started for the door.

"And John . . ."

He stopped, turned.

"It's good to see you. Take care of yourself."

"I will," he said.

THIRTEEN

THE FACE ON THE COMPUTER SCREEN WAS OLDER THAN THE ONE IN THE photo, harder.

"That's him," Harry said.

Ray scrolled.

"Harrow, John D.," he read off. "DOC number 672775. Birth date 11/23/69. Release date, November 23, this year."

"Can you print all that out?"

"I will. Let's see what else we've got here."

They were at Ray's desk, chairs pulled close. Once they'd gotten onto the Florida Department of Corrections site, Ray had punched in the name and the page had come up immediately. At the top of it were three pictures of Harrow—left profile, right profile and front—taken the day he was booked into the Glades Correctional Institution.

"Tattoos," Ray said. " 'Sacred Heart. Left chest.' What's a Sacred Heart?"

"It's Catholic. The heart of Jesus." He traced a figure on his chest with a finger. "You've seen it. A heart with a crown of thorns around it."

"Religious man then. Here's his sentence and offense history, but it's only Florida. Attempted murder, assault with a deadly weapon. Convicted, sentenced to nine years. Out in seven."

"Why?"

"Don't know. It's not in here. Seven years for attempted murder isn't bad, though. I know people have done less for first-degree in Jersey."

Ray touched a button, pointed to a printer on the credenza next to the window. It began to chatter, spit paper.

Harry walked over, picked up the first sheet, the photos in color, looked at that face again.

"What about his New Jersey record?" he said.

"Had it faxed to me," Ray said. "It's right here."

He sat back, took a pair of faxes from a plastic "In" basket, put them on the edge of the desk. Harry went over, picked them up.

"Not a whole lot on there," Ray said. "Did a juvenile stretch in Jamesburg. Not sure what for. Record's sealed. He was only nineteen when he went down for grand theft auto, did nine months at Southern State in Cumberland. Twenty-two when he shot a guy in a bar in Keansburg. Gun charge and attempted murder, but the guy ended up refusing to testify. He got three years on the gun charge."

Harry looked through the sheets.

"Three years in Rahway," he said. "That's hard time. That's like ten somewhere else."

"Yeah, you get old there quick."

"So, guy's in his mid-thirties, most of his life has been spent behind walls in one way or another."

"Old story," Ray said. "You go into Jamesburg at fifteen, sixteen, you don't come out a Boy Scout. Your options are limited."

Harry put the papers back on the desk.

"So here's how I read him," he said. "Guy's in and out of stir his whole life. One of his brief periods out, he meets a girl, they get something going, she gets pregnant. Then he throws it all away by shooting some guy down in Florida, goes back to prison. Why?"

"You're trying to put normal logic to work here, Harry. This guy's a career felon. Do you think he even knows why he does what he does?"

"So he gets out finally, the girl's gone, the baby's gone. His youth is gone. And he's pissed off about it all. Hard to blame him."

"No, it's not. You can play psychologist all you want, but he made his choices. You start feeling sorry for these guys, you can feel sorry for everyone—Hitler, Bin Laden. Everybody has their reasons."

"I'm just thinking. Putting myself in his place. Threat assessment."

"Whether he's an actual threat to this woman or not, I think we have to deal with it as if he were. My gut feeling? We wait long enough, the situation will take care of itself. These kind of people chase their own destruction like they're on a game show. We protect the woman, wait for him to fuck up on his own, end up back in stir. Give him enough time, it'll happen."

"If it was parole it would be different," Harry said. "He could get violated just for leaving the state or on some bullshit 'associating with known felons' charge. But if he maxed out in Florida—which is what it looks like—then he's free and clear. He'll have to do something, get caught at it."

"He will. This guy is no citizen. You think he's going to take some factory job when he gets back here? No. He's going to go back to making a living the only way he knows how."

"And someone else gets hurt in the meantime."

"We can't protect everybody in the state of New Jersey—or Florida. We're protecting our client. She's writing the checks. Our job is to keep him away from her. Anything else is a little out of our realm of responsibility, don't you think?"

"So how do we deal with this guy?"

Ray leaned back in his chair.

"You know, you constantly amaze me," he said.

"What do you mean?"

"A couple days ago, you didn't want anything to do with this situation, or this client. What happened?"

"I guess I'm looking at things a little differently. Anyway, we're in it now, right? You took her money."

"I did."

"So we look forward, not back. Think it through, check out the angles, the best way to handle the situation. Assess and eliminate the threat."

"That's what I like about you, Har. Just when I think I know where you're coming from, you switch directions. And somehow, in your mind, it all fits together. You don't see the conflict at all."

Harry shrugged.

"We work with what's in front of us. When the situation changes, it changes."

"Lieutenant Rane, the philosopher king of the MCU. Reborn. Good to have you back."

"You know what I used to say back then."

"You used to say a lot."

"The only way to do it . . ."

". . . is through it. Yes, I remember."

"And some things," Harry said, "don't change."

HARRY LAID the sheets of paper on the table in front of her. He'd made copies of the printouts, the fax.

"I want you," he said, "to fill in the blanks."

They were in a coffee shop in Ocean Grove, fashioned from the shell of an old drugstore. The decor was small-town 1930s, a half dozen tables, a lunch counter with stools along one wall, an ice cream and soda fountain with a walk-up window that opened onto the street. Christmas music played softly from ceiling speakers.

She moved her cup of coffee to the side, looked at the pages one by one, read through them, expressionless. She wore a sleeveless black sweater despite the cold, jeans. He could see the vaccination mark high on her left shoulder, the fine blonde hairs on her arms.

"There's more than what's here," she said.

"I figured."

"I'm not sure what you want."

"All we really know about him is what's on those. I want you to tell me the rest. When did you meet him?"

She put the papers down, stirred more sugar into her coffee.

"I used to dance at the Heartbreak Lounge. Do you know where that is?"

"In Asbury? Yeah."

"That's where I met him."

She lifted the cup, sipped. He waited.

"I'd just turned twenty. A kid still. A friend of mine was dancing already, told me how much she was making—four, five hundred a night. So I gave it a shot. Went in for an audition and they hired me."

"Tough way to make a living."

"Not if you know how to draw boundaries. I would get on that stage and my brain would leave the building. It was like I was watching somebody else in the mirror, dancing. I'd count my money at the end of the night, but the rest of it would be a blur. It beat waiting tables, though, I can tell you that."

"You ever wait tables?"

"Like I said, I've done a lot of things."

She put the cup down.

"I worked the whole circuit, up and down Jersey, like everyone does. But the Heartbreak was where I danced most of the time. One night he came in, alone. He just sat at the bar, watched me. Never gave me a dime. He told me later it was because I was different, that giving me money would have been an insult. I was young and stupid. I believed him."

"So he swept you off your feet?"

"You're making fun of me."

"No," he said. "Just curious."

She sat back, ran a fingertip around the rim of her coffee cup, not looking at him. He could smell the faintest trace of her perfume.

"I got into some trouble there," she said. "He helped me out."

He drank coffee, let her take her time.

"One of the girls there," she said finally, "convinced me to do a bachelor party. Said it was easy money, a guaranteed twelve-hundred-dollar take, just to do the same things I was doing at the Heartbreak. Like I said, I was young then, stupid."

"What happened?"

She looked at him.

"You really want to hear it?"

"If it'll help."

"I don't know that it will."

"We'll find out."

She tilted the cup, looked into it, swirled its contents.

"It went bad quick," she said. "It started out in the basement of this firehouse. I was scared. I found out later that none of the girls ever do those gigs—for anybody—without bringing somebody along. So I guess I learned the hard way. I woke up the next morning in a motel room, naked, alone and sick, the cleaning lady banging on the door."

"You don't remember what happened?"

"Not past a certain point. It occurred to me later that somebody must have put something in my drink. I remember wanting to get out of there. Then I just blacked out. I had only myself to blame, though, for getting into that situation."

"Like you said, you were young, you didn't know any better."

"I should have."

"Did you tell anyone? Afterward?"

"Like the police? No. The definition of rape gets a little cloudy, don't you think, when it's a woman dancing half-naked in front of a bunch of drunk men?"

"No, it doesn't," he said. "Not really."

"That's easy for you to say. Luckily I was on the Pill. I don't know what I would have done if I'd gotten pregnant. I never knew how many of them took their turn."

"I'm sorry."

The waitress came over, filled their cups without being asked. He waited until she moved away.

"So you were on your own with it," he said.

She nodded.

"I was young, but I was smart enough to know that making an issue out of it would only make things worse. My word against theirs, and I took their money. The last thing they needed at the Heartbreak was a prostitution beef. They would have fired me in a second."

"So what's all this got to do with Harrow?"

"Two of the men from the party—the ones who hired me—started coming around the Heartbreak. I guess they were looking for a repeat performance. I was terrified of them. I'd get onstage, see them at the bar watching me and I'd just freeze up. And the way they looked at me . . . I'd see them talking to other men at the bar, laughing, and I knew they were talking about me."

"What happened?"

"They kept showing up. It got to the point where I didn't even want to go into work, because I was terrified they'd be there. They'd say things to me, offer me money to go out to the parking lot with them."

"You told Harrow all this?"

"Eventually. He cared, you know? And who else was I gonna tell?"

"What happened?"

"One night, closing time, I went out and they were waiting for me, drunk, waving cash. They wanted me to go to a motel with them. I got away, but I was shaking so bad I could hardly drive. I almost wrecked on the way home. The next time Johnny came by, I told him everything."

"And?"

"At first, I was worried, you know, that he would get angry, angry at me. Some men are like that. But he just listened. And he told me the next time they came into the bar, I should call him."

"And did you?"

"Yes." She met his eyes. "I couldn't live like that anymore."

He sat back, waiting for her to tell the rest.

"He came in, sat across the bar from them, didn't say a word. They were drinking a lot. After a while they got bored, left. He followed them to another bar, caught them in the parking lot. He knew if anything happened at the Heartbreak it would cause trouble for me."

"Considerate of him. What happened?"

"He only told me part of it afterward. But I read it in the *Asbury Park Press* the next day. He left one of them in a coma."

"How did that make you feel?"

"You sound like my shrink. Is this going to cost me one-fifty an hour?"

"Like I said, just curious."

"It made me feel a lot of things. It scared me, and maybe made me feel a little sorry for those two men. But I didn't have to be frightened of them anymore either. I was terrified of them and then one day they were gone and they never came back. How do you think it made me feel?"

"Nothing came of it?"

She shook her head.

"He said they wouldn't go to the police. That they knew better. And he was right."

"Because if they did . . ."

"He'd kill them."

He let that hang in the air.

"And had he?" he said.

"What?"

"Killed anyone? That you know of?"

"I never asked him. But there were times . . ." She looked away, then back at him.

"So he did?"

"Do I think he did? Yes. Did I want to know about it? No."

"Did you know he'd been in prison?"

"I suspected. Later, he told me. I can't say I was surprised."

"Is that where he got the tattoo?" He touched his chest.

She shook her head.

"Johnny would never let one of those prison artists touch him. He got that done in Asbury. I got one myself that same night. It felt like a bond, you know? A promise. Like I said, I was just a kid."

"Why did he go to Florida?"

"I don't know all of it. I only know what he was convicted of."

"He was working for someone, wasn't he? He wasn't down there on his own."

The waitress came back with the coffeepot, saw they hadn't touched their cups, went away again.

"Have you ever heard of Joey Alea?" she said.

He shook his head.

"He's from North Jersey. His uncle was some big mob boss up there back in the day. Joey owned a bunch of places. Had a piece of the Heartbreak. That's how Johnny got to know him. Then he started doing some work for him, here and there."

"What kind of work?"

"What do you think?"

He sipped coffee, waited.

"All I knew, there was some guy down there owed Joey money. He'd been up here a couple times, at the Heartbreak. A loudmouth, couldn't keep his hands off the girls. I think he owned a club down in West Palm. One night, he and Joey had a screaming fight in the back room at the Heartbreak. Then he left."

"And Harrow went after him."

"Not until a month or so afterward. I'd just found out I was pregnant. I was still dancing, counting the days until I stopped. We were living together by that point. Then one morning Johnny told me he had to go down to Florida for a couple days, nothing big. But I had a bad feeling about it. I asked him not to go, for me, for the baby. He went anyway. I never saw him again."

"So you don't know what happened down there?"

"Only what I read. The club owner was involved with the FBI, some sting or something down there. A drug thing. They had agents working undercover at his club. Nothing to do with Johnny or Joey or anyone up here. It was just bad luck. Three days after he left, I got a call that he'd been arrested, charged with attempted murder, assault. On the day he was sentenced, I went into labor."

"How well did you know this Joey Alea?"

"Well enough, I guess. I worked for him. He's the one that hooked me up with some people in L.A., to get me started out there. He said he was doing me a favor. That's not the way it turned out."

He let that sit.

"He know you're back?"

"Not as far as I know. But I've had no contact with him—or that world—since I've been here, thank God. I'd like to think that part of my life is over."

He sat back, pulled an earlobe, trying to put it all together in his mind.

"You have friends?" he said. "Back then?"

"One or two. Why?"

"Any of them still around?"

"Maybe."

"I was thinking what we need is an early warning system. If Harrow was back in this area, asking around, he'd start with people you knew. We can talk to them, see if they've heard from him. Chances are he would have gone back to the Heartbreak at some point too."

"There's only one person from those days I kept in touch with after I left," she said. "And I haven't even done that in a couple years. She was in Jersey at least until then. I know that. She danced at the Heartbreak too. She might still be around."

"Can you give me her name, the last address you had for her?"

"I can do that."

He gathered up the papers. The waitress saw them, came back and left the check at his elbow. He got his wallet out.

"You're different," she said.

He took a five out, looked at her.

"Than what?"

"Than the way I thought you were when we met."

"We didn't quite get off on the right foot."

"No, we didn't. And it was my fault as much as yours. I'm sorry."

"Forget about it. There's one thing I agree with Simmons on, though."

"What's that?"

"Even if Harrow's looking for the boy, the chances he could find him—that he could navigate that system and come up with a name and address—are pretty slim. He doesn't have those types of resources."

"But Simmons does. And if Johnny got ahold of Simmons, it wouldn't take him long to find out everything he wanted to know, to get him to look up whatever he wants him to look up."

"Maybe you're giving him too much credit."

"Maybe I am. But you don't know him."

"I'll take your word for it. He have any family up here?"

"A brother, half brother, really. Mitchell. He might still be around, I don't know. He had a younger sister too, Belinda. But she died in a car accident while he was in Rahway. They wouldn't let him go to the funeral."

"Parents?"

"His mother's been dead a long time. He had a stepfather, but I don't know if he's still alive."

"That would be Mitchell's real father?"

"No. Mitchell and Johnny grew up together, but their mother remarried when they were kids. Johnny never spoke much about it, so I don't think I ever got the whole story. But I don't think Johnny or Mitchell ever knew their real fathers."

"Mitchell older or younger?"

"Younger. I didn't know him well."

"They get along?"

"As far as I could tell. I think Mitchell always looked up to him."

"I guess what I'm wondering is, even if he did find out where the boy was, what would be the purpose? What's he going to do, kidnap him? Go on the lam with a seven-year-old in tow? It doesn't make any sense."

"I don't know. But I don't want to just wait around to find out either. Giving my baby away was the most painful thing I've ever done in my life. But it was the best thing too, and the only thing I've done in the last twenty years that I'm even slightly proud of. I gave him a chance to grow up and live a life without people like his father around him. And I won't have that threatened. I won't let anyone take that chance away from him."

He looked into her eyes. She didn't look away.

"Come on," he said. "I'll give you a lift home."

"No, I can walk from here. It's only a couple blocks."

"It's cold."

"I'll be fine."

He paid at the register and they pulled on their coats and went out into the darkening afternoon. The trees on Main Avenue were strung with Christmas lights, already glowing. The Mustang was parked up the street, outside another restaurant, in front of which a white-haired man, bundled against the cold, was playing "Have Yourself a Merry Little Christmas" on a saxophone. A handful of people stood around listening to him. The open instrument case at his feet was half-full of bills.

Harry stood on the sidewalk, people moving around him, and watched her walk away. Then she turned at the corner and was gone.

He got the Mustang keys out, dropped a five into the saxophone case. The man nodded at him, never stopped playing. As he pulled away, the street lamps started to go on, one by one, as if lighting his way.

FOURTEEN

WHEN THE PHONE RANG IN THE MOTEL ROOM, JOHNNY WAS CLEANING the Sig on the bureau top. He had a sheet of newspaper spread out, the gun's disassembled parts gleaming with oil. He'd bought a cleaning kit and a can of gun oil at a sporting goods shop that afternoon, along with a Buck knife with a five-inch blade.

He wiped his hands on a rag, picked up the phone. It was Lindell.

"Yo, Johnny Boy. We need to talk, man."

He pinned the phone between shoulder and chin, wiped oil from his fingers.

"Who's we?" he said.

"You, me and the J Man."

"When?"

"Tonight. Soon as possible. Some shit went down today needs to be discussed."

Johnny looked at his watch. It was four-thirty.

"Where?"

"Find a pay phone, ring my cell. I'll let you know."

"What's going on?"

"Phone's not cool, bro. We'll talk later, fill you in." He hung up.

Johnny replaced the receiver, went back to the Sig. He finished cleaning the barrel with the push brush, then began to fit the pieces back together, snick them into place. When he was done, he shook the box of cartridges onto the newspaper, felt each individual shell for imperfections. He loaded one of the clips, thirteen rounds, slid it into the grip of the weapon until it locked in place. He racked the slide, felt the shell chamber, the mechanism working smoothly. He lowered the hammer.

119

Out on the balcony, he lit a cigarette, watched the gray waves. The wind pulled at him. He looked across at the darkened board-walk, the gutted carousel house of the Casino. Somewhere, a loose drainpipe rattled and banged. He thought about Frazer.

After a while, he flicked the cigarette away, went back through the sliding glass door, shut it behind him. He got the Sig from the bureau top, sat on the edge of the bed, pulled the phone into his lap. He felt in his pocket for the slip of paper, touched the rabbit's foot. He'd forgotten it was there. He pulled it out, turned it over in his hand. Wind shook the sliding glass door.

He put the rabbit's foot down, picked up the Sig. He ejected the clip, worked the slide again. The chambered shell popped out of the breech, fell on the sheets. He let the slide clack home, the ham-mer up.

He looked at the rabbit's foot, then snugged the Sig's muzzle into the soft skin beneath his chin. His index finger slid over the trigger, felt the pull. He could smell the fresh oil.

He closed his eyes, imagined the path of the bullet. Up through his jaw, his tongue, the roof of his mouth. Then exploding through his sinuses, up into his brain and out. He squeezed the trigger. The hammer fell dryly on the firing pin.

He sat that way for a while, his eyes closed, then took the gun away, set it on the sheet beside the rabbit's foot. His hand was slick with sweat.

He picked up the phone again, dialed the number, punched in his own and hung up. Five minutes later, while he was rinsing his face at the rust-stained bathroom sink, the phone rang.

He dropped the wet towel on the bed, picked up the receiver.

"What've you got?" the voice said.

"Meeting tonight."

"Again? So soon?"

"Something's up. I don't know what."

"Who? Where?"

"Lindell, Joey, maybe the others. Don't know where yet. I'm sup-posed to call later, find out."

"No clue what it's about?"

"Probably just some bullshit."

"Maybe not. You've got time. Come by here, we'll gear you up."

"Not yet."

"Why not? We could be wasting an opportunity here. Take five minutes to get you set up."

"Too soon. He's still wary. We could blow the whole thing."

"When then?"

"Next time maybe."

"Don't dick me around, John."

"No one's dicking you around."

"We had all this straight down in Florida. That's why I got you out of that shithole. You want to be back there tomorrow? I can arrange it."

"Don't threaten me."

"Then don't fuck around."

"I know what our arrangement is. But I have to run it the way I see it, or neither of us is going to get what they want. I'll let you know when the time is right."

"The time better be right soon."

"What have you got on that other thing?"

"Working on it. Like I told you, it takes time. There's lots of issues involved."

"Now who's dicking around who?"

"Don't like the way it feels, huh? Then I guess my answer to you is the same as yours to me: patience."

"Just find him," Johnny said and hung up.

HE WATCHED snowflakes blow against the windshield, only half listening to what Joey Alea was saying. They were in Joey's Cadillac Escalade, parked behind the office of a limo company he owned in Plainfield. Tuco was at the wheel, Johnny beside him. Lindell and Joey sat on opposite sides of the wide leather backseat, Lindell reeking of cologne and the faint sweet scent of marijuana.

"You dreaming up there, John?" Joey said.

Johnny turned toward him.

"I heard every word you said."

"And what do you think?"

"I think you already know what you want to do."

Joey smiled, looked at Lindell.

"Cuts right through the shit every time, doesn't he?" he said. "That's what I missed about you, John. It's good to have you back."

Johnny got his cigarettes out. Lindell was looking out the window, as if wishing he were somewhere else.

"No smoking in the car, homes," Tuco said.

Johnny stopped, Camel halfway to his mouth. Tuco was facing forward, not looking at him.

"I let Denise drive this sometimes," Joey said. "Take the kids to soccer practice. I let someone smoke in here I'd never fucking hear the end of it."

Johnny put the cigarette back in the pack.

"Shit'll kill you," Tuco said.

Johnny looked at him, put the pack away.

"I need your counsel here, John," Joey said. "These are rough people. Hard-core scooter trash. I've butted heads with a couple of them in the past, but this shit today was bold."

"How badly is your guy hurt?"

"Bad enough. Two broken arms, some cracked ribs. And his eye's all fucked up. He may lose it."

"He use your name?"

"If he did, I guess it didn't do him much good. But I'm not worried about him. He knew the risks. There's a principle at stake here."

"If he did say your name," Tuco said, "shit should have been over with right there."

"What's your history with them?" Johnny said.

"Couple years back maybe, they moved some product for me," Joey said. "But they're unreliable, these people. And once they started producing themselves, they didn't need me anymore. Fine. Live and let live, you know? What the fuck. It's a big market."

"They say anything to your guy?"

"He'd just made a drop-off in Keyport," Lindell said. "They followed him home from the bar, pushed their way in. They busted him up, took the rest of the crank and his money. Told him he best not be moving any more shit unless he was getting it from them."

"Guy's only worked for us, what"—Joey looked at Lindell—"two, three months? I could give a fuck. But there's a larger issue here. If

I do nothing, then the next thing I know it's not just the crank they're cutting in on. It's the pot, the coke, the E maybe. These fucking guys are ruthless."

"I thought you wanted to get away from that shit," Johnny said.

"I do—and I will. But on my own terms, in my own time. And yeah, six months from now, I might not give a shit who moves meth and where. It'll be a fucking memory to me, and good riddance. The money's not worth the trouble. But in the meantime, I'm not going to have it taken away from me by a bunch of white-trash Neanderthals who don't even bathe."

Johnny thought about the thirty-five thousand, how Joey had called fifteen thousand of it a retainer. It hadn't taken long.

"When and how?" he said.

"What?"

"You want to send a message, right? So it comes down to when and how."

The snow was starting to stick. Johnny looked out the window, watched it settle on the parked limos.

"What are you thinking?" Joey said.

"How many of them? Altogether."

"I don't know. Ten, maybe fifteen at most. They're independent."

"You know where they operate? Their clubhouse?"

"Down South Jersey somewhere, I don't know for sure. But there's one thing I do know."

Johnny turned to face him.

"What's that?"

"I know where they cook."

Joey was smiling now.

"Guy who works for us now," he said, "used to work for them. Knows the whole operation. Back of his fucking hand."

"There you go," Johnny said.

"What? You thinking we should go down there some night?"

Johnny shrugged.

"Why wait?" he said.

FIFTEEN

IT SEEMED LIKE THE DAY HAD GIVEN UP. BY NOON, IT WAS DUSK DARK and overcast, with the occasional spit of snow. Harry felt sleepy as he drove north, wished he'd had another cup of coffee before leaving the house.

In Newark, he parked in a Kinney lot off Broad Street, walked the block to the federal building. He went through the checkpoint downstairs, showed his driver's license and was given a visitor's card. Saturday afternoon and most of the offices he passed were dark. He rode the elevator up to the ninth floor.

The Strike Force office was at the end of the hall, door ajar. He knocked twice on the glass. A voice inside called, "Come on in."

He went past empty desks, down a short hall to another office. It was small, two desks pushed together head to head, a table, a filing cabinet and a water cooler. A man in jeans and black sweatshirt was going through desk drawers, putting their contents in a brown banker's box atop the desk. Another box, already full, sat on the table. Harry tapped a knuckle on the door frame.

"Yeah," the man said, turning to face him. He was a head shorter than Harry, compactly muscular, short black hair. He wore a laminated Department of Justice ID on a cord around his neck.

"You Rane?"

"Yes, thanks for seeing me."

The man put out his hand.

"Vic Salerno. Ray called yesterday, but I told him today would be better if this was going to be informal. Fewer people around. Just give me a second here."

124

He put a bronze fishing trophy in the box, a framed photo of a man and woman on a small boat, smiling at the camera.

"I was sorry to hear about your partner," Harry said.

Salerno shrugged.

"I knew Sully twenty years, partnered with him for six. Right here in this office. And this is what it all comes down to. Somebody throwing all your shit in a cardboard box. Someone will do it for me someday."

"Was he ill?"

"I played one-on-one with him just last week, over at Rutgers. He ran my ass all over the court. He'd just turned forty-two. Three years younger than me, but in better shape than I've ever been in my whole life. You know what they say—in thirty-five percent, or something like that, of heart disease cases, the first symptom is sudden death."

"I'm sorry. He have kids?"

"Two girls, nine and ten. Divorced, but he and the ex were talking about getting together again." He gestured at a chair by the filing cabinet. Harry rolled it over, sat down.

"You always think you'll have time," Salerno said. "To put your affairs in order, get your shit together. Fix things in your life that aren't going well. But you don't always get it. It's like, every day, life goes on. And then one day it just goes on without you."

He sat down.

"So how is Ray?" he said. "I talk to him occasionally, usually when he needs something. But I haven't seen him in months."

"He's fine. Doing well. Asked me to say hello."

"And Edda?"

"She's fine too. Their daughter's at Cornell now."

"I heard. Smart kid. My son's seventeen. He'll be lucky if he gets into Fairleigh Dickinson. You got kids?"

Harry shook his head.

"Can't blame you. The way the world is now, it's like, why the fuck would you want to? It has its rewards, though."

"I guess."

Salerno looked at him for a moment.

"Stop me if I'm out of line," he said. "But I'm curious."

"About?"

"You ever catch any fallout over what happened to those two whyos? The ones from Paulie Andelli's crew?"

Harry shook his head.

"You closed a lot of case files when those two went down, you know that? Saved a lot of people a lot of work."

Harry said nothing.

"Sorry," Salerno said. "I shouldn't have brought it up."

"It's okay. I just don't know how to respond."

"You don't need to. Like I said, I shouldn't have brought it up. So, Ray was pretty cryptic on the phone. Said there were some people you wanted to ask me about, off the record."

"Joey Alea."

"That little shitbag? You involved with him?"

"Not really. This has to do with a client of Ray's."

"And this person is mixed up with Joey Alea?"

"Secondhand. What can you tell me about him?"

"Well, you know who he is, right? I mean, who his uncle is?"

"No."

"Tony Acuna. Tony and Joey's mother were brother and sister. Joey's father—Sam Alea—ran a shy operation Down Neck for many years. That was the bone Tony threw him, I guess—I hear Sam was no genius. You know what happened to him, right? Joey's father?"

Harry shook his head.

"He got nabbed by the Feds on extortion charges, must have been in seventy-two, seventy-three. He cut a deal, agreed to testify against Tony and his people. Supposedly they'd already made a place for him in the WitSec program—state, not federal. This is all before my time, of course."

"What happened?"

"Pretty much what you'd imagine. Every skipper Tony had on his crew was going batshit, waiting for the ax to fall. There was a lot of pressure on him to do something. He didn't want to, brother-in-law and all, but he had no choice. Supposedly the word came from the Commission itself, via Carlo Gambino. So Sam disappears, and a couple years later they're digging up a chicken farm down in Jackson Township that a friend of Tony's used to own and what do they

126

find? Joey had to be a kid when all this was going on, though. I mean, we're going back more than thirty years here."

"I understand. So what happened to Joey after that?"

"Well, here's the funny thing. And again this is just what I've been told. Tony took him under his wing, but he was dead set against Joey getting involved in the Life. I mean, he went out of his way for the kid. Even sent him to college—Montclair State. The family never wanted for anything."

"Guilt?"

"Maybe. But maybe something more than that. Tony's an interesting guy. How much do you know about him?"

"Not much. I know he's semiretired."

"Yeah, pretty much. Tony's a legend, you know? But he always kept a low profile. And when the young Turks started coming to power—Gotti over in New York, Scarfo down in Philly—and people started to get whacked all over the place, Tony took a dim view of it. He thought it would be the ruin of Their Thing. And he was right. It was the beginning of the end for most of them. Look at where they all are now. The Scarpettis are away on long federal jolts, Paulie Andelli's got so many indictments on him he can barely afford to pay his lawyers. Gotti died in prison and Little Nicky probably isn't far behind him. But Tony's still out there. I've met him a few times. And you know the weird thing? I like him."

"How's that?"

"Well, he's a product of his environment, you know? He, the Scarpettis, Andelli, they all grew up in the North Ward, in Newark. Not too far from here, actually. And most of them were Calabrese, just like my family. From the *Mezzogiorno*. Their families were poor there, they came across the ocean looking for opportunity and they ended up poor here too. My grandfather was a tailor, had a shop down on Sheffield Street. He knew of all those people. And back in the thirties, it wasn't so much an Italian thing. It was mostly Jews running the show—Longy Zwillman, people like that. Dutch Schultz came to Newark after Dewey chased him out of New York. Schultz got clipped about a half mile from here, on Park Street. Used to be the Palace Chop House back then. Now it's a bagel shop, fittingly enough. Sorry. You're not really interested in all this, are you?"

"That's okay."

"Personally, I'm fascinated by this shit. I consider myself a student of it. Sully used to say there was a great book to be written about the New Jersey mob someday."

"Maybe you should write it."

"You kidding? I type up a 10–14 report, I have a headache before I'm done."

"So you like Acuna?"

"Well, as far as it goes, you know? Met him four, maybe five times. Always a gentlemen. You know, for fifty years people like me have been trying to put him away and not one of us ever succeeded. He beat every case ever built against him. And he had no taste for violence. I mean, when someone had to go, they had to go, and I don't think Tony ever had a problem pushing the button on them, but in general he'd go to it only as a last resort. And that's one of the reasons he flourished the way he did, quite frankly. Guy ran the port here—controlled almost everything that went in and out of it—from the sixties on and no one ever touched him. It's when bodies start turning up that the heat comes down, state and federal. So Tony avoided all that.

"And you know, he was what he was. But he's got three kids— two daughters and a son—and who knows how many grandchildren. His kids never even had a whiff of the Life. The son's a doctor in Millburn. Tony's thing was he always wanted something better for his kids. He felt the same way about Joey too, you know? Why it didn't take, who knows?"

"Joey worked for him?"

Salerno shook his head.

"No, never. Tony wouldn't have it. So instead, Joey started hanging out with other wiseguys, running errands. College boy, you know, totally out of his league. But trading on his uncle's name. I think they humored him, threw him some bones here and there. No one took him seriously. Plus, nobody ever forgot his father was a rat."

"Was he ever made?"

"In his dreams. He ran a few places, probably still does. Turned out to be a pretty good businessman, from what I remember.

Owned some strip clubs, a porn shop, that type of thing. Rumor was he was in the video business, financed some skin flicks. And he dabbled in other things too—meth, I'm sure. Coke when it was big. He came across our radar a few times, but that's it. Last time we were looking at him it was in connection with a shitload of Ecstasy tabs that ended up at Rutgers. Nailed the kids that were distributing it, but couldn't work our way up the ladder, so the case stalled out."

"His uncle doesn't mind he's involved in all this?"

"At this point, who knows? Maybe he's given up. The old guard tolerate the kid because of his connections, I think, which they might not do for someone else. They let him run his business. Joey's strictly small-time anyway, so why bother? And frankly, we've hit the OC guys so hard the last few years that their whole infrastructure's falling apart. It'll never be the way it used to be. Those days are over."

"You sound confident."

"LCN these days—traditional LCN—is like the Soviet Union. Geographically, it's still there, but the structure's collapsed. Despite the name, it was never very organized, you know? And it's even less organized now. Yeah, the Commission still sits and passes judgment when it needs to, but there's no one watching the shop all the time. So there's a lot of loose cannons out there as well."

"So Alea's an up-and-comer?"

"Barely. I mean, this guy isn't exactly going to the top of the class anytime soon. Those old-timers—Acuna and those boys, that whole generation—they had balls, you know? Say what you want about them as human beings—and some barely fit the term—they didn't get where they were by running scared of anybody. Tony and his right-hand man, Frankie Santelli, they been together since the forties. They fought their way up and took their beatings along the way. That's what makes them leaders. That's what draws people to them. Alea? Dope and pussy, that's all he's got going for him. Yeah, you can always attract people with that, keep them hanging around, telling you how great you are. But respect? Loyalty? That's something else entirely."

"You know of a guy named Johnny Harrow?"

"Heard of him. Why?"

"He work for Alea?"

"He did, at least. But last I heard, he took a fall for Joey, ended up with a jolt in Florida."

"He's out."

"That what this is about?"

"More or less."

Salerno sat back, interested.

"Go on."

"Someone's worried about his being back up here. They're concerned about his being a possible threat."

"Business or personal?"

"Personal."

"Well, this Harrow guy, if I remember right, was Joey's heavy hitter, or as close to one as he came. Popped some people for him, maybe. From what I heard, Joey had a difficult time keeping him on a leash, was maybe even a little scared of him himself. But muscle's muscle. You need it if you want respect, so it will always have value. You think Harrow's back in the mix?"

"Maybe."

"Up here?"

"Looks like it."

"And he's hooked up with Joey again?"

"I don't know that."

Salerno nodded.

"Thanks for passing this on. I'll look into it. So where's your client fit into all this?"

Harry raised his hands, dropped them.

"Can't tell me, huh? I figured that. Had to ask, though."

"I know."

"I'll say this, though, as far as Tony Acuna is concerned . . ."

"Yes?"

"He may be an old man, but he's still got a few teeth left in his head. He wouldn't be happy about Joey Alea stirring up the pot, making muscle moves, if that's what's going on. And yeah, he's kept the peace for many years, run his operation with a minimum of drama, but he's not a guy to fuck with. Even now. You ever hear the story about the guys who robbed his house?"

"No."

"Well, this goes back about ten years now. Not that long, really. Tony had some contractors working on his house in Holmdel, doing some plumbing, putting in a new bathroom downstairs, whatever. So apparently, the contractors are in the basement and they come across a safe, set right into the concrete floor, covered up by a humidifier or something. All this is just kind of pieced together after the fact, by the way. We never got the whole story."

"I understand. Go on."

"So one of the contractors tells some friends he found Tony Acuna's safe, loaded, no doubt, with diamonds and cash and heroin or whatever the fuck they thought they were going to find in there. And he tells them he can get them in the house, because he's there all the time doing work and has to shut the security system off, so he knows how to deactivate it . . . Like I said, this is all conjecture."

"Got it."

"These guys—a real group of white-trash losers, petty housebreakers—decide this is going to be the score of their lives. So, two weeks after the contractors are done, Tony's got his new bathroom, he and his wife are away for the week. They come home and the house has been broken into, alarm turned off, and the safe is popped, contents missing.

"What I heard later was there were three of them did the actual job, plus the contractor who set it up. The contractor—a guy named Hurst—disappears like two days later. No one can find him, he just stops showing up for work. His girlfriend reports him missing, nobody knows a thing. Some people thought he just got smart, hit the road. But less than a week later, two of the other guys end up in the back of a shipping container in Kearney, burns on their hands and faces—an acetylene torch, likely—and two each in the back of the head.

"So the last guy tries to make a deal—he'll give everything back, pay up an extra fifty K and leave the state if they just let him go."

"What was in the safe?"

"What I heard was some jewelry, not much. Family things, heirlooms. Apparently Tony'd been keeping them there because he was worried about the G coming in with a search warrant someday, taking that stuff with everything else, make him fight to get it back.

Probably not worth a whole lot moneywise. Sentimental value, though, who knows?

"So this last guy gets in contact with one of Tony's people, says he has everything in hand, nothing's been sold, and let's work out a deal. Tony gives the go-ahead—he wants the stuff back. So the guy turns over the fifty K—who knows how many other people he had to rob to raise that—and he ends up getting a personal audience with Tony at some warehouse somewhere. He hands back the stuff and Tony tells him, sure, a deal's a deal. He can go wherever, they won't bother him. He can go to California tomorrow if he wants—but his dick has to stay in New Jersey."

"What?"

"That's the deal they gave him. Lose your dick or your life. If he lets them take it, they won't touch him again. He's free to go. If he doesn't, he's dead. Because one way or another, he becomes a message. So the question is, does he want to be alive or dead at the end of that message?"

"What happened?"

"What would you choose? You got a guy with a Skilsaw on one side of you, guy with a thirty-eight on the other?"

"Is there much difference?"

"Depends how certain you are you're going to die, I guess. He must have been pretty certain. He let them take it off with a power saw, halfway down the shaft. Then they put a tourniquet on him, dropped him off at the hospital. He lived, poor bastard. And Tony kept his word. He never went after him. The guy—his name was Warren, Jimmy Warren—spent a month in the hospital and then fled for points unknown, as they say."

"And the first guy, Hurst?"

"He ends up on a roadside in Sussex County, out in the sticks, two in the head. They held him that whole time, to find out about the others, then popped him when they were done with him. Nice story, huh?"

"And you said you liked this man."

"That's the odd thing. I do. Aside from those four fuckups, I could count on two hands the guys Tony's had whacked in his entire career as boss. He was always the Great Negotiator, always trying to bring warring parties to the table. He was a little like Angelo

Bruno down in Philly, but unlike Bruno, he managed to stay alive. And he kept a lot of people from being taken out, spoke up for them. Because his word was respected and he knew blood on the streets was no good for business. But with the robbery, that was a very public thing. So the response had to be equally public. It was a matter of honor. And he can be a cold son of a bitch when he needs to, even now."

"Sounds like. So what you're telling me is, aside from that, his tenure has been a model of efficiency?"

"To a certain extent. Which has made it twice as hard to get him. And at this point, you know something? We're never going to get him. And he knows that. But his days are over, and he knows that too. He just wants to drink wine, sit in the sun, play with his grand-children. He's been going back to Italy a lot in the last few years, back to Calabria. My feeling? He's getting ready to die."

"And the nephew?"

"Who knows? Maybe Tony still feels guilty enough about what happened to Sam that he lets the kid have his leash. I don't know. Maybe he just doesn't care anymore. But Tony's worked his whole life to get to the point where he is right now—alive and free and enjoying the fruits of his labor, as it were. And if the kid even comes close to fucking that up, there's going to be trouble."

Harry nodded, looked out the window onto the empty expanse of Broad Street. A police car flew by, lights flashing, siren fading as it headed across town.

"Thanks," he said finally. "I appreciate your taking the time to talk with me."

"No problem. Let me know how things work out with your client. And if it gets serious, you need to come back and see me. But you know that already, right?"

"Yes, I know. And I will. Thanks."

He nodded at the box.

"You need a hand with those things?"

Salerno looked at it.

"Nah. I'm going to sit here a little while with them, I think. I'm supposed to take them up to his ex-wife in Little Falls. But it's strange. I'm in here sometimes and I think I hear his voice in the hall. I expect him to come walking in. It's like this stuff is the last of him, you know? Two weeks, maybe less, there'll be someone else at this desk, somebody else's pictures on the wall."

"I'm sorry."

"Thanks. And tell Ray he should give me a call. He still play ball?"

"Not too much these day, I don't think. Knees."

"Well, tell him to lose some goddamn weight. I can't have friends checking out on me right and left. There aren't enough to go around."

SIXTEEN

TUCO DROVE. THEY RODE IN A BLACK FORD EXPLORER WITH TINTED windows, made good time down the Parkway and into the Pine Barrens. The sky had cleared and the moon was a cold blue circle. They pulled into a rest stop outside Atlantic City and Johnny used a pay phone to call Lindell's cell.

"What's the word?" Johnny said. His breath frosted in the air.

"Where are you?"

"Near AC. We're turning west, should be there in about an hour, less if we can find the place easily enough. The moon will help."

There was a pause as Lindell covered the mouthpiece, spoke to someone else. They would be together, Joey and Lindell, waiting to get the call that said everything had gone all right. Or that it hadn't. Or waiting to get no call at all, and knowing what that meant as well.

"He says go ahead. Call when you get clear. And be careful."

"We will," Johnny said and hung up.

He climbed back into the Explorer, pulled the door shut.

"Let's go," he said.

Forty minutes later, they pulled down a dirt road wide enough for only a single vehicle, the woods dark around them. Ahead, a wooden fence blocked the road, red emergency reflectors set into the wood. Their headlights lit up the snow and bare trees beyond. Tuco slowed to a stop.

"Kill the lights," Johnny said.

The darkness fell around them. Tuco left the engine running. Johnny turned on the dome light, spread the hand-drawn map on the dashboard.

"There's a trail out there," he said. "Straight ahead. We'll follow it, bear to the west. Supposed to be reflectors in the trees, every couple hundred yards or so. That's how we'll know we're on the path. A mile and a half in and we should be able to see the first signs of the lab, if it's still there. Smell it too."

"How do we know that map's right? We could be out there for hours, walking around in the snow. Freeze our ass off."

"Only one way to find out."

He watched a bead of sweat creep out of Tuco's hairline, roll down the side of his face. Tuco wore a flannel shirt buttoned up to the neck *chulo* style, jeans and snowboots, black gloves. Johnny wore his own boots and jacket, cheap cotton work gloves he'd bought at a convenience store.

"You okay?" Johnny said.

"I'm okay. Worry about yourself, homes."

"Then shut it down. Let's get moving."

Tuco turned the ignition off. They got out, boots crunching in the snow. Tuco used the keypad to unlock the back hatch. It rose slightly.

Johnny pushed it all the way up, pulled away a blanket to expose the wheel well. Inside was a black nylon gym bag. Johnny unzipped it, took out the two Mini Mag flashlights, high-intensity bulbs in black aluminum tubes. He twisted one on, played the light over the contents of the bag. He handed the other to Tuco, who put it in a pocket without checking it.

Johnny put the cold metal of the flashlight between his teeth to free his hands. He took out the Mossberg shotgun with the pistol grip and folding stock, handed it over. Tuco grunted, took it. Johnny gave him the box of shells that went with it. Tuco pointed the muzzle at the ground, opened the box and began to thumb shells into the receiver. When the magazine was full, he pushed the rest of the shells into the right-hand pocket of his parka, dropped the box in the snow.

There were four sticks of dynamite in the bag. He wondered where Joey had gotten them. With them was a metal box containing blasting caps and fuses, a small chamois pouch. He opened the pouch. Inside was the flat black Aurora silencer he'd asked for, barely three inches long. He rolled it into his hand, reached under his jacket and took the Sig out of his belt. Tuco watched while he

136

threaded the silencer into the barrel. When it was tight, he put the gun in the right pocket of his field jacket.

He rooted in the bag, came up with two small illuminated compasses, a pair of green ski masks. He handed over a compass and a mask, took the flashlight from his mouth. Tuco looked at the compass.

"In case we get separated," Johnny said. He zipped the bag back up, pulled it out. Tuco leaned the shotgun against the bumper, began to pull the mask on.

"Wait on that," Johnny said.

"Why? It's cold."

"You're going to have a hard enough time seeing as it is. Put it on when we get there."

Tuco looked at him, then wadded the mask up, pushed it into the pocket with the compass. Johnny swung the hatch shut. The doors clicked as Tuco locked them.

Johnny took the Sig out again, pointed it at the ground, worked the slide. Then he lowered the hammer, ejected the clip. He took a loose shell from his left jacket pocket, rubbed it free of lint, pushed it into the clip to replace the one he'd chambered. Then he slid the clip home again.

"You ready?" he said.

"Just waiting on you, homes," Tuco said and picked up the shotgun.

Johnny slid the Sig back into his pocket, hefted the bag.

"Let's go," he said.

They walked for fifteen minutes, the pinpoint beams of the Mags lighting up the ground in front of them, before they found the first reflector. It was a simple lens from a car's brake light, nailed into the trunk of a scrubby pine tree. Johnny took the compass out, checked to make sure they were still facing west.

"This is the way," he said.

"You sure of that?"

Johnny didn't answer, kept going, his boots breaking through the crust of snow. Every few minutes he would stop, play the light across the snow around him, looking for other footprints. Nothing.

Cold and silence fell around them as they walked. Tuco's breathing got heavier, his feet scuffing in the snow. Johnny had slung the nylon bag over his shoulder to keep his hands free, could feel the dynamite sticks bouncing off his back with each step.

Five minutes later, they found the next reflector. Johnny stopped. He could feel the adrenaline working inside him now, the slow and steady beating of his own heart. His mind was clear. He didn't feel the cold.

"What's up?" Tuco said and Johnny raised a hand to silence him. He twisted his own light off, waited for Tuco to do the same.

"Follow me," Johnny said in a low voice. "Don't use your light."

They moved forward again, the trees thinner here, moonlight shining off the snow. He could see the path clearly now, even without the reflectors to follow. He stopped again, listened. Faint at first, then clearer. The distant thump of a generator.

He put the flashlight in his pocket, took out the Sig, held it loosely in his right hand, muzzle pointing at the ground. He moved forward slowly, knowing noise would be a factor now, flicked the safety off.

Another five minutes of walking and the sound was louder, unmistakable. He could smell gasoline. A cloud passed over the moon and dropped them into darkness. He stopped, felt Tuco bump into him from behind. He waited, and after a moment the cloud was gone and the moon lit their path again. They went on.

Ahead, the glow of a light. He stopped, listened, heard faint voices.

There was a gentle downhill slope ahead. Johnny motioned Tuco to stay where he was. He moved closer, watching his step.

At the rim of the slope, he stepped behind a tree, looked down. There were two shacks laid out in an L in a clearing below, plywood and tar paper with corrugated metal roofs. There was light coming from the nearest one, illuminating the snow around it. Beside the shack, a gasoline generator chugged irregularly. Alongside it were two fifty-five-gallon drums. He could smell the generator exhaust and a harsher chemical odor that made his eyes water. He blinked it away, eased around the tree to see what was beyond the shacks.

There was an outhouse there, slapped together with boards and canted drunkenly to the left. Near it, a motorcycle and pickup were parked side by side. There would have to be a road from the west, he knew, so that equipment and vehicles could be moved in and out. The footpath they had come in on would be an escape route only.

He waited, watched. Figures moved in the lighted shack, threw shadows on the snow. He heard voices again, then a back door opened. A big, bearded man in a leather vest with a blue bandanna on his head came out, stood next to the pickup and urinated loudly into the snow. He zipped up and went back inside.

Johnny eased the bag off his shoulder, set it at the base of the tree. He retraced his steps, found Tuco standing on the path with the shotgun at port arms. He came up close to him before speaking, his voice low.

"Two huts. At least two people inside, maybe more."

Tuco nodded.

"I'm going to find another way down the slope," Johnny said. "You move up to that tree there, wait for anybody trying to run out the back."

Tuco shook his head.

"What?" Johnny said.

"Joey says I shouldn't go in. Said I should watch your back, but not get into it."

"Are you shitting me?"

"No, homes. Way it is. You're the fucking ninja anyway, right? He told me not to go, so I'm not going."

Johnny looked at him.

"That prick . . ." he said.

"Shouldn't call him that, homes. He'd be angry if he knew."

Johnny shook his head slowly, looked back toward the clearing.

"I'll be right here," Tuco said. "Watching your back. Like the man said."

"Good," Johnny said. "You stay right there. And don't you fucking move."

Tuco said nothing. Johnny gave him a last look, then moved back to the slope.

More shadows on the snow below, voices. He began to make his way to the right through the trees, stepping carefully over frozen roots that had pulled from the ground. The longer shack was dark, with a row of windows. He could hear voices clearly now from the front one, could see the flickering blue glow of a television through a curtained window.

He started quietly down the slope, boots sliding in the snow, his eyes on the lit windows. At the bottom, he stopped, pulled the ski mask on, adjusted it so he could see clearly.

He went to the dark shack first, shone the Mag-light through the window. There were cheap canvas curtains inside, but enough of a gap that he could see most of the room. He walked the beam of light across the floor, saw the tables laid end to end, the beakers and paint masks and cans of denatured alcohol atop them.

Beyond were the plastic vats, six of them. Even through the glass he could smell the sting of the chemicals. He raised the beam, bounced it off the back wall. There were exhaust fans built into the windows there, a fire extinguisher propped in a corner.

He shut the light off, slipped it back in his pocket, moved along the wall of the shack until he reached the corner. He switched the Sig to his left hand, flexed the fingers of his right to loosen them.

There were voices from the other shack, close. The rear door opened again, spilled light onto the vehicles and the outhouse. A second man, bald, wearing an identical leather vest over a rebel flag T-shirt, stood in the doorway. He tossed a beer can into the darkness, unzipped his pants.

"Do that shit out in the yard," a voice said from inside. "I don't want to be slipping on your frozen piss in the morning."

The biker laughed.

"Fuck you," he said.

"And close the fucking door."

The biker spit on the ground, pulled the door shut, walked out into the yard, pants still unzipped. He went up to the outhouse and began to urinate against it, the stream smoking in the cold.

With the moon, Johnny could see as if by daylight. He switched the Sig back to his right hand, felt the adrenaline, the tightening in his groin, the thrill almost sexual. He stepped away from the corner, silently crossed the distance between them, the Sig coming up as if on its own. At the last moment, his right boot snapped something beneath the snow and the biker turned quickly to face him, looked into the muzzle of the silencer.

The Sig made a whooshing *chug* and blood spattered the outhouse wall, steamed there. The biker fell hard onto his side on the frozen ground. Johnny pinned him with a boot, leaned over, picked a spot behind his right ear and fired again. The biker shivered and lay still.

He pointed the Sig at the closed back door, waiting for someone to come out. When no one did, he flicked the safety on, put the gun back in his jacket. He stepped over the widening patch of red snow, caught the biker by both wrists and dragged him around and behind the outhouse, left him slumped there.

He counted to ten, catching his breath, then stepped out from the cover of the outhouse. He could still hear the TV. His breath misted in front of him as he took the Sig out, crossed the yard.

The door opened easily. Inside was a single large room. The first biker sat in a rocking chair, back to the door, watching a color TV atop a wooden crate. The TV had a set of rabbit ears, foil wrapped around them. There was an electric space heater beside the chair, coils glowing. Propped against the wall, within easy reach, was a pump shotgun.

"Jesus Christ," the biker said without turning. "Shut the fucking door already."

Johnny eased it closed, pointed the Sig at the back of the rocker. To his left was a dark hallway. To the right a kitchen area with a rough table and chairs, hot plates, cases of beer stacked against the wall.

His finger was tightening on the trigger when the woman came out of the hallway. She was dope skinny, long black hair streaked with silver, eyes deep-set. She wore leather pants, a denim shirt. She looked at him and, without a word, turned and ran back the way she'd come. He heard a door open and slam shut.

"What the fuck?" the biker said and got up, turning. He saw Johnny, then calmly took the shotgun from against the wall. He racked a shell, aimed.

Johnny's first shot caught him in the right hip, spun him slightly. He grunted, brought the shotgun back to bear, and Johnny fired twice more, the Sig jumping in his hand. The biker took both hits without falling, stumbled back slightly into the crate. The TV fell backward onto the floor, the picture tube exploding with a pop and a burst of white smoke. Johnny fired again, saw the bullet strike the stock of the shotgun, splinter it. The gun flew from the biker's hands, hit the wall and fell to the floor without going off.

The biker looked at the shotgun, then at Johnny. Then he noticed one of the entry wounds in his shirt, touched it, brought his fingers away red and sticky.

Johnny aimed again, left hand wrapped around right wrist, and fired four times in quick succession. Smoking shell casings flew out of the breach, clattered on the plank floor. The biker grunted again, went back over the crate. He grabbed for the chair, took it down with him as he fell. The room shook.

Johnny faced the hallway. He ejected the clip, replaced it with a full one from his back pocket. He could feel it now, moving through him, the surge of adrenaline giving way to the coldness of control. Everything fell away from him except the corridor ahead, the weapon in his hand.

It was a narrow hallway, a closed door at the end of it. To the right, another door halfway down, ajar. He pushed it open with his boot, pointed the Sig inside. It was empty except for an unmade bed, a mattress on a simple metal frame.

Back into the hall, the silencer pointing at the far door. The only sound was the muffled thumping of the generator outside. He took aim, fired once at chest height. The round punched a neat hole through the wood, showed light on the other side. The casing jingled off the wall next to him.

Three quick steps to the door and he flattened himself against the wall beside it. He touched the knob with his left hand. Listened, heard nothing, began to twist.

The top panel of the door exploded into the hallway. The boom of a shotgun, two barrels, buckshot and splinters flying crazy. Smoke and bits of wadding hung in the air.

He gave it a second, waiting for another blast, then swiveled into the smoke, pointed the Sig through the hole.

The woman was standing in the center of the room, a sawed-off double-barrel broken open on her knee. She was prying a smoking shell from a barrel, fumbling with a fresh one in the same hand. She dropped the new shell, bent to pick it up.

"Don't touch it," he said. "Don't move at all."

She froze, looked up at him, the gun.

"Play this right," he said, "you'll walk out of here."

She straightened, not taking her eyes off him.

"Drop the shotgun," he said.

She let it clatter to the floor. The room was thick with the smell of gunpowder.

"Now stand back."

When she did, he lifted a boot, slammed the sole into the bottom half of the door, below the knob. It flew open, rebounded off the wall, hung from one hinge. He went in.

The room was slightly larger than the other bedroom, with a closet in one wall, the door closed. He saw her glance at it, then back to him.

He came closer, kicked the shotgun away.

"You live here?" he said.

She didn't respond.

"You want to get out of here, answer my questions. You live here when you cook?"

She nodded.

"Where's the rest of them?"

"Gone. We finished cooking yesterday." She had a hard Philadelphia accent, a hollow in her cheek where she'd lost teeth.

"What are you doing here?" he said.

"We're supposed to watch the place tonight. Tomorrow they're going to come with another truck, take it all apart. You going to kill me?"

"Maybe not. Why are they breaking it down?"

"They do it every once in a while. The longer a place is around, the more people know about it."

"Just the three of you here?"

"Yes."

He shot her twice. The first shot jerked her around, the second slammed her into the wall. She slid down to the floor, lay still.

He looked at the closet door, listened, heard a faint scraping inside. He pointed the Sig at the door, moved closer. The sound came again.

He turned the knob, pulled, stepped back. The door swung open slowly. Inside was a stack of cardboard boxes. In the space

143

behind them crouched a boy of about five, eyes closed, hands over his ears.

He lowered the Sig. The boy was trembling, silent streaks of tears running down his dirty face. The closet smelled faintly of urine.

He pulled the ski mask off, pushed it into a pocket.

"It's okay," he said. "Come on out."

The boy opened his eyes, looked up at him. Johnny flicked the safety on the Sig, lowered the hammer. The boy wore pajamas with race cars on them, the front of the pants dark where he had wet himself. His blond hair was long, uncombed. Johnny wondered if the woman had made him practice hiding here, knowing a day like this would come.

"Come out," he said. "Nobody's going to hurt you."

He raised the tail of his jacket, stuck the Sig in his waistband and crouched, held his arms out. The boy backed farther into the closet.

"Come with me," Johnny said. "I'll get you out of here."

He reached, got his hands under the boy's armpits and there was no resistance. He pulled the boy toward him, lifted, got him up against his chest. The boy's arms locked around his neck.

"Close your eyes now. Tight. Until I tell you to open them again."

The boy shut his eyes, put his forehead on Johnny's collarbone. Johnny lifted him out of the closet, shifted the boy's weight so he could carry him with his left arm alone. Then he pulled the Sig back out with his right hand, held it down by his leg.

"Keep them closed," he said. "Just a little bit longer."

He carried him past the woman's body and into the hallway, moving slowly, listening, hearing nothing but the generator. They went through the main room, out the door and into the night.

He carried him past the cooking shack and up a slight hill, the boy beginning to shiver with the cold. Johnny brushed snow off a fallen log with his boot, set the boy down on it.

"Sit right here," he said. "I'm going to get you some shoes."

He put the Sig on the ground, took off his jacket and draped it around the boy's thin shoulders. The boy pulled it tighter around himself, almost disappearing into its folds.

Johnny picked up the Sig, went back to the shack.

There was a cheap dresser in the bigger bedroom, adult and children's clothes mixed together. He got a pair of socks for the boy, found a sneaker under the bed, looked around until he found its mate. The woman lay where she'd fallen, facedown, one leg bent sideways under her.

He thought about what it must have been like for the boy to live out here, what he would have seen. He wondered if either of the dead men was the father. He put two more bullets into the woman's back and moved on.

The boy was trembling, his nose running freely, when Johnny went back out to him. He knelt in the snow, set the Sig down and rolled a sock up each foot, slipped on the sneakers and tied them.

"Where's Mommy?" the boy said when he was finished.

Johnny looked at him, stood up.

"You wait right here," he said. "Don't go back inside. Don't go anywhere until I come back to get you, understand?"

"I'm scared of the woods."

"Then just stay right here and you'll be all right. I'll come back and we'll go to the car, get you warm, okay?"

The boy nodded, looked at the ground.

Johnny left him there, went back down into the clearing. In the moonlight, the blood was black on the outhouse wall.

He went around the shack, back up the way he'd come, stepping quietly in the snow. This time he went deeper into the woods. When he came out of the trees, he was behind Tuco. The Mexican had the Mossberg up, was pointing it down the path toward the shacks.

"Hey," Johnny said.

Tuco spun, saw him. The shotgun stayed up for a moment, then lowered.

"Don't do that shit to me, homes." He exhaled.

"Sorry."

"How'd it go?"

"Okay."

"You get 'em?"

"Yes," Johnny said. "Got you too."

He brought the Sig around and fired twice. When Tuco hit the snow, he put two more into him for insurance, watched the body jump. Then he put the safety back on the Sig, tucked it in his belt.

He found the Explorer keys in a front pocket. Grabbing the parka with both hands, he dragged Tuco face-up down the slope toward the shack. His eyes were open, staring up at the moon.

Johnny was out of breath by the time he got him into the main room. He left him just inside the door, went back out and got the nylon bag and the Mossberg, carried them inside.

He was still breathing heavy when he got back to the trees. The boy was where he'd left him, shivering uncontrollably now.

"Here," Johnny said. He picked him up, held him tight. They went around the shack and up the path, the boy trembling against him. He carried him all the way back to the Explorer, knowing the path now, the moonlight enough. When he saw the shape of the vehicle, he got the keypad out, touched it and heard the doors unlock. He opened the passenger's-side door, set the boy in the seat, reached up and turned on the dome light.

"You wait here, okay?" he said. "Just a few minutes more. Don't get out of the car." He closed the door.

Going back, he didn't use the flashlight, was able to anticipate the reflectors before he saw them. The adrenaline was wearing off now and he was feeling the cold.

On the side of the shack was a five-gallon gasoline can used for feeding the generator. Shaking it, he heard the heavy swish inside. He carried it to the cooking shack, used an elbow to break two of the windows, the acrid chemical smell welling out.

He hefted the can, fed its plastic feeder tube through the broken glass, heard gasoline *glug-glug* out onto the floor. He did the same at the second window, then splashed gas over the two vehicles, the outhouse, the first biker's body. He poured a trail to the open door of the shack, tossed the empty can inside.

One of the fifty-five-gallon drums was only half-full, manageable. He wrestled it around the side of the shack and through the door, pushed and pulled it into the center of the room. He dragged the woman's body from the bedroom, left her next to the barrel, rolled Tuco beside her.

The longest fuses were thirty minutes each. He fit a fuse and blasting cap onto each stick of dynamite, carried them outside. At the cooking shack, he broke two more windows—away from the gasoline spill—lit two of the sticks with his Zippo, dropped them through, heard their fuses hissing. The third stick he set against the full fifty-five-gallon barrel in the yard. The fourth he propped against the drum in the living room.

The moon stayed with him. He found the Explorer again easily, thumbed the keypad to unlock the doors. From the corner of his eye, he saw the empty shell box in the snow. He picked it up, climbed into the Explorer, tossed it in the back.

The boy was still shaking, looking out the window, expressionless. Johnny started the engine, turned the heater vents toward the boy and switched the fan higher. Then he reversed down the road until it was wide enough to turn around in. He turned on the headlights, started back the way they'd come.

He was almost at the Parkway when he felt the low rumble through the tires. In the rearview mirror, he saw a glow in the darkness of the woods, rising into the night sky. A ball of red, then another, and then the flicker of flames high above the tree line.

He stopped at the same rest area near Atlantic City, fed money into the pay phone outside, dialed Lindell's number. The sky to the west was orange and red, a sunset at 3 A.M.

When Lindell answered, Johnny said, "It's done."

"Tuco?"

"No," he said after a moment. "This isn't Tuco."

Silence on the line, then: "What happened?"

"He's gone. There was nothing I could do."

"You okay?"

"Yeah."

"Then get away from there. Go back where you're staying. Keep the rig with you. We'll pick it up."

"Yeah," Johnny said and hung up.

There was a twenty-four-hour Burger King there. Johnny could see someone pushing a mop around inside. He went back to the Explorer, opened the passenger-side door.

"Come on," he said. The boy was half-asleep, dead weight as Johnny lifted him down, set him on his feet. He unzipped the field jacket, got it off him.

"Sorry," he said. "But I need this."

The boy didn't resist. Johnny pointed at the front door of the restaurant.

"Go on in there," he said. "It's warm. They'll take care of you."

The boy didn't move.

"Go on," Johnny said. He put a hand on the boy's back, pushed him gently. "Go."

The boy looked back at him, then began to walk toward the brightly lit restaurant as if in a dream.

Johnny pulled the jacket on, the lining still warm, got back behind the wheel. He looked toward the restaurant, saw the boy reach up, tug the front door open.

He started the engine, pulled out of the lot, got back on the Parkway. The inside of the Explorer smelled like gasoline and gunpowder. He stripped his gloves off, powered down the window, dropped one out, then the second twenty minutes later. Then he settled back for the long drive north.

SEVENTEEN

IT WAS A SMALL PARK—A SWING SET, PLASTIC SLIDES, A TEETER-totter. There were maybe a half dozen kids playing, parents watching them from benches. Alongside was a small lake, year-round geese walking the banks, two children feeding them bits of bread from a plastic bag. The afternoon was cold and clear, a light dusting of snow still on the ground.

Harry pulled to the curb, parked behind an old Honda. As he got out, a woman on a bench turned to look at him. She was in her mid-thirties, long red-brown hair tied back, a waist-length fake fur coat.

He had the card out before he reached her.

"Ms. Wicks?" he said. "Sherry?"

She turned back to the children.

"Janey!" she called. "Be careful on that."

Halfway up the slide ladder, a golden-haired girl turned, looked at them for a moment. Then she scrabbled over the top and down the slide.

"I'm Harry Rane," he said. "We spoke on the phone."

She took the card, looked at it, the handwriting on the back.

"Mind if I sit down?"

He sat beside her, the wood slats cold against his back.

"Sorry to make you come here," she said. "But I promised Janey I'd take her. And I've got work later."

"I understand. I appreciate your giving me the time. How old is she?"

"Four next month."

"Must keep you on your toes."

"I don't mind it. She's the best thing that ever happened to me."

149

He wasn't sure how to respond to that. Didn't.

"It was a shock. Hearing from Nikki like that. Out of the blue."

"I'm sure."

"Two years, not a letter or a phone call. I didn't know if she was dead or alive. Then the phone rings this morning. I never even knew she was back."

"It's only been a couple months."

"Long enough. If she wanted to call me, she could have. But I don't blame her. I'm sure I remind her of things she wants to forget. What I don't understand is why she came back at all."

She slipped the card in her coat pocket, took out a pack of menthol cigarettes, lit one. Behind them, geese squawked.

"She tells me you had some contact with him," he said.

She nodded, not looking at him. Janey was on the swings now, she and two other girls her age taking turns pushing each other.

"He came by the Heartbreak," she said. "Looking for her."

"How did he seem? Was he angry, agitated?"

"Johnny? Johnny's never agitated. Even when he's angry, you can't tell. That's what's scary about him."

"What did he say?"

"He said he was looking for Nikki. Wanted to know if I'd heard from her. I told him I hadn't. And it was true. Then."

"Did he threaten you?"

"You don't know him well, do you?"

"No."

"Johnny doesn't threaten. Like I said, he's always calm. He told me if he found out I knew where she was and hadn't told him—or if I tried to warn her—he'd come back to see me." She blew smoke out.

"That sounds like a threat to me."

"Maybe. But I really didn't have any reason to worry about that, did I?" She looked at him. "Until now."

"There are things that can be done."

"Like what? If Johnny wants to find me, he'll find me. Like I said, you don't know him."

"Maybe there's someplace you can go. Stay with a friend. For a little while at least."

"And what about work? Are you going to pay my bills? Is Nikki?"

"Maybe we can work something out."

She shook her head, dropped the cigarette and put it out with her shoe.

"Janey's father," he said.

"What about him?"

"Is he around?"

"He's dead."

"I'm sorry."

"I'm not. She's better off without him. And so am I. He wanted to be a musician, but all he ever really was, was a junkie. And a liar."

"Is there anybody in your life . . ."

"To look after us? Is that what you mean? No. I do all the looking after. I told Johnny there was, because I didn't want him to think I was alone. But I don't think it made any difference."

"Did he hurt you?"

She looked away, didn't answer.

"If he hurt you," he said, "if he's breaking the law, then that's all we need."

"Is that what I am?" She turned to him. "A means to an end?"

"That's not what I meant."

"If anyone gets Johnny sent back to jail, it'll have to be someone besides me. Johnny doesn't forget anything. Ever. Nikki knows that."

"I'm sorry. I know you feel like you've been caught in the middle."

"Is she paying you for this? To look after her?"

"The agency I work for, yes."

"But there's more to it than that, isn't there?"

"What do you mean?"

"Nikki always knew how to get what she needed, especially out of men. Always. That's what she did with Johnny, Joey, everyone. I used to admire it, her ability. Envy it. She was always thinking ahead. She still is, I guess."

"You sound angry."

"Not at all. I was happy to see her get out of here, try to get her life together. I even went out to visit her in California, right after she got there. Before Janey. She asked me to stay. I thought about it."

"Why didn't you?"

"She wanted me to stay for her, not me. She was homesick, I

guess. But I saw some of the things she was getting into out there, and I didn't want anything to do with them. Dancing was bad enough. I took a bus home."

"What sort of things?"

"You'll have to ask her about that."

He let that go.

"Have you had any contact with Harrow since that night?"

She shook her head.

"But every time I come home, I'm looking in the mirror for headlights. Wondering if it's him."

"He know where you live?"

"I don't know. But if he wants to, I'm sure he could find out."

She reached into a coat pocket, came out with a black matchbook, handed it to him. There was no type on it, just the outline of a green neon heart with a crack through it. He opened it, saw the number written inside.

"That's the number he gave me. To call if I heard from her."

"Is this where he's staying?"

"I don't think so. He told me he wouldn't be there, but if I left a message he would get it."

"You didn't call."

She gave him a sad smile.

"Did you think I would?"

"I guess not. I'm sorry."

"She did the right thing, leaving. I loved her like a sister back then. Still do, I guess. And I still wish her luck. Tell her that."

"I will. Can I keep this?"

"Go ahead. I don't want it around. I don't want anything of his around."

He put it in his jacket.

"And this," she said. She took a folded bill from her pocket, put it on the bench. "Take it. Give it to her. Throw it away. Do whatever you want to do with it. I don't want it."

He picked up the bill, saw it was a hundred.

"He gave this to you?"

"He thought I needed it. I do need it. But not from him. Not for that."

She looked at him. He met her eyes.

"Then I'll give it back to him," he said. "When I see him." He put the bill in his shirt pocket.

One of the other mothers was collecting her children from the swings, getting them ready to go. The sun was low in the west, the sky brushed with scarlet.

"There're two numbers on that card," he said. "The front is the agency number. Ray Washington is the guy that runs it. You can ask for him. On the back is my home phone. One way or another, you'll always be able to reach one of us, day or night. You hear from Harrow, you're worried he's around, you just want to talk, anything, you can reach me at that number."

Her playmates gone, Janey began to run toward the bench. Sherry stood, put out her arms. Janey ran into them, out of breath and red-faced.

Sherry hugged her tight. Janey peered out from around her shoulder, looked at Harry.

"Come on," Sherry said. "Let's get you home and fed. Alex will be there soon."

"Who's Alex?" Harry said.

"Her sitter. She watches her at night. When I work."

He nodded, stood up, feeling out of place now, excluded. The little girl watched him.

"Hold on to that card," he said. "Make sure the sitter has those numbers too. She sees, hears anything . . ."

"Thank you," she said and lifted Janey up. The girl buried her face in her mother's jacket, peeked at Harry, smiling, hid her face again.

"I'm sorry," he said.

Sherry looked at him.

"About what?"

"About all of it."

"Don't be," she said. "We all make our own lives, don't we? With what we have to work with?"

"Yes," he said. "I guess we do."

"And nobody owes us anything. So we do what we have to do. And that's just the way it is."

He waited as they made their way to the Honda. When they got to the car, Janey looked over her mother's shoulder at him, waved good-bye. He waved back.

He was still standing there in the fading light, the empty playground behind him, when they drove away.

EIGHTEEN

"WHAT THE FUCK HAPPENED DOWN THERE?" CONNOR SAID.

Johnny blew smoke out, looked at the ocean. They were on the Asbury boardwalk, the day bright and cold, the sun flashing hard off the water. Gulls argued above.

Connor's topcoat was buttoned to his neck, hands deep in the pockets. The wind was whining through the holes in the Casino roof.

"I don't know," Johnny said. He propped one boot on the pipe railing overlooking the beach. "What did you hear?"

"Don't give me that bullshit. I didn't drive all the way down here for that."

Johnny finished his cigarette, flipped it onto the sand.

"Whatever," he said. "I guess you'll believe what you want."

"What I believe is when a meth lab—owned and operated by rivals of Joey Alea—gets torched and all the hired help gets whacked, that Joey Alea's involved in it. And if Joey Alea's involved in it, then you should know about it."

Johnny said nothing.

"But there's one thing I do need to remind you, John, though I hoped that I wouldn't. You better not have been personally involved in what went on down there. You start doing wetwork for this guy again and there's no way I can protect you. We went over that down in Glades. You know the deal as well as I do. You get back into the heavy stuff and we'll need to terminate this relationship."

Johnny looked at him, met his eyes. Connor stuck it out a few seconds and then turned away, looked out at the barren beach, the waves beyond.

"As long as we understand each other," he said.

Johnny didn't answer.

"Fucking freezing out here," Connor said.

"You said you had something for me."

"I do. Let's walk."

They started down the empty boardwalk, the wood warped and uneven beneath their feet. There was little chance of anyone seeing them here. The wind and cold were keeping even the homeless away, and the boards were too treacherous for joggers.

When they reached the boarded-up entranceway to the Casino, Connor stepped into a pigeon-stained alcove to get out of the wind. He unbuttoned his topcoat halfway, took out a manila envelope, handed it over.

Johnny undid the clasp. Inside were two thin, banded packages of money and a Xeroxed sheet of paper. He left the money, pulled out the sheet.

"That's a copy of the original paperwork," Connor said, buttoning his coat back up. "It doesn't give the specific town or the family. Just the regional office it was handled out of. That's the way it went into the computer. I'm working on getting the whole case file."

Johnny read the sheet.

"Chicago," he said.

"That's where they lived at the time they signed the papers. Doesn't mean they haven't moved somewhere else since. But whoever they are, they were in or near Chicago at that time."

"It's a big city."

"Like I said, I'm working on it. But that's what I've got so far. Thought you'd want me to share it with you."

Johnny slid the paper back into the envelope, shook out the money, saw new hundreds.

"Five grand," Connor said. "It'll have to do for now. We make some progress, I'll see what else I can shake loose."

"Thanks." He put the money back in the envelope.

"It isn't Christmas yet, you know. That's not a gift."

"I didn't think it was."

"We need to get down to it. I want you to wear a wire at your next meeting. Try to get him to talk about the meth lab. That mess could be the leverage we're looking for. But we need him on tape."

"I'll see what I can do."

"When you have a meeting set up, you call me. There's a Bureau tech owes me a favor. He's put together a simple rig, smaller than a pack of cigarettes. I can wire you up myself."

Johnny nodded, looking off at the beach. Thinking about Chicago.

"But don't lose sight of one thing, John. We did—and still do—have a deal. But if you stop holding up your end, then we don't have anything. You go back to Glades and neither of us gets what he wants."

"I heard you."

"So you need to start producing. You're on the books as a TE now. You know what that means?"

"No."

"A Top-Echelon source. That means you and I cut our own deals, do what we want, nobody knows about it, it's all confidential. You don't testify, you don't show up in reports, you don't have any exposure at all. But you need to earn your keep. You're on the payroll now. You need to justify that."

"I understand."

"Good. But maybe what you don't understand is that the only reason this has been such a sweet deal for you so far is that I'm your handler. Me. No one else. I go to my SAC, tell him I'm having trouble with a CI, he takes me off it, reassigns you or closes your folder. Then you're on your own."

"I'm not going to deal with anybody else. Not now."

"You might not have a choice."

"There's always a choice."

"We need results, John. Results I can use. Not talk, not guessing. And we need them soon."

"And you'll get them," Johnny said. "Soon."

"I DON'T know," Mitch was saying. "Just pick up and leave like that."

They were sitting in a booth at Pratt's, a half-full pitcher of beer on the table between them. They'd left the Firebird at the Sea Vista, walked the two blocks to the bar in the wind and cold.

"Up to you, Mitch," Johnny said. "But you should think about it. Things are coming together now. I had an idea the other night, set something in motion. I'm going to be making some moves soon."

In the back of the room, two pimps were playing pool, a pair of bored-looking women watching them, one milk white and bleached blonde, the other light-skinned black. On the jukebox, Prince was singing about going crazy.

Mitch drank beer, lit another cigarette.

"It's a good thing you have here," Johnny said. "I understand. The woman. The girl. Place to come home to. People there waiting."

"You could have that too, Johnny, you wanted it."

Johnny shook his head.

"Maybe once," he said. "Not now."

"Why not?"

Pool balls cracked loudly. Wind rattled the big front windows.

"Too much has happened," Johnny said. "I used to think it was easy. You see what you want, you move toward it, you take it. But you've got to keep it too, keep it together. And that's not always so easy to do."

"But you're out now, man. You can do whatever the fuck you want. Anything."

"Not that simple. Since I've been away, I've done shit that . . ." He trailed off. Mitch was watching him.

Johnny drank from his mug, feeling the beer now on his empty stomach. He watched one of the pimps circle the pool table, heard balls thump into pockets.

"I've been thinking a lot," Johnny said. "About what happened. In Florida."

Mitch watched him, waited.

"I had a lot of time," Johnny said. "To think. And you know what I kept coming back to?"

"What?"

"After my trial, after the sentencing, Joey sent Tuco down there to take out Cardosa."

"Yeah?"

"Why'd he wait?"

Mitch didn't answer. Johnny got a cigarette going, drank beer.

"I should have seen it," he said. "It was a setup, all of it. He wanted to get rid of me, but he didn't have the balls to do it himself."

"Johnny, I had no idea . . ."

"Doesn't matter now. It'll all be settled before this is through. Everything. That's why I came back."

"Are you sure about Joey? I mean, I never liked the guy, but—"

"I'm sure. And I'll deal with it. But we need to think about what comes after."

"You say 'we.'"

"Get me straight, Mitch. I didn't come back here to fuck up your thing. I'm happy for you."

"I'm glad to hear you say that."

"But I'm blowing out of here soon. For good. I have to settle some business, make a side trip and then I'm gone. You come with me. After things get settled, you can send for Sharonda and the girl."

"Where you gonna go?"

"North. Someplace clean. Far away from here. I have a place in mind, I've been looking into it. I'm putting together the cash. That thing I told you about. Enough to last us a long time there."

"I don't know, John. I think I'd just be in your way, you know? I mean, I was never in your league. Even back in the day. I'd just slow you down."

"I'm done with ripping and running. This isn't about that. This is about family. This is about what happens now."

Mitch looked at him, couldn't hold his eyes, looked away.

"I don't know, man."

"Think about it. When the time is right, we'll have to jump fast. I'll try to give you as much warning as I can, but there might not be much."

He took out some of the money Connor had given him, counted out ten hundreds. He folded them, tucked them under the ashtray.

"What's that?" Mitch said.

"That's for you."

"Why?"

"Because I feel like it."

Mitch looked at the bills.

"Go ahead. Take 'em."

Mitch slid the money out.

"It's only a grand," Johnny said. "But there's more when you need it. Buy some things. Whatever you need."

"Pay some bills."

"Whatever. When you need more, let me know."

Mitch put the money in his shirt pocket.

"Thanks."

Johnny poured beer into their mugs.

"You seen Frazer around?"

Mitch shook his head.

"Not since that day."

"Good."

"Johnny, I know the way you feel about him and all, but . . ."

"But what?"

"He's an old man. Maybe you shouldn't treat him like that."

"Your memory must be fucked up."

"What's past is past, John. I mean, what happened then . . . He's still the guy that raised us."

"And a good job of it he did too, didn't he?"

"I'm just saying—"

"When Belinda was fourteen, he put his dick in her. You forget that?"

"You don't know that, John."

"No. I do. And it happened more than once. Why do you think she got out of the house as soon as she could? Got fucked up all the time like she did? When her car went off the road, hit that abutment, he was as much to blame as she was."

"John, you weren't even around when that happened."

"If I had been, I would have put that old bastard down then and there. It was good for him I was gone."

"That was cold. Their not letting you go to the funeral."

"Like you said, it's ancient history."

They grew silent. The pitcher was almost empty.

"There's some shit you can't control," Johnny said. "That's always the way it is. You live in pain and you die in fear and there's nothing anybody can do about it. But some things you can control. You can get a handle on them, make them go your way. You just need the balls to do it."

"You always had it wired, Johnny."

"You think so? That what you call sitting on my ass for seven years? Having it wired? Let me tell something, no matter how tough you think you are, how much you eye-fuck the world, there's one thing gets stolen from you every day. And there's no way to steal it back, no matter how hard you try. No fucking way at all."

"What's that?"

"Time," Johnny said.

NINETEEN

Harry had poured himself a glass of wine, was sitting on the back steps looking up at the stars, when the phone rang.

"Hey," Nikki said when he answered. Noise in the background, people talking, laughing.

"I tried to call you all day," he said. "I left three messages on the machine at the house."

"I've been out, I'm sorry."

"Where are you?"

"Like I said, out. Listen, I have to be quick. I'm on a pay phone. I need to ask you a favor."

"What kind of favor?"

"I need a ride."

Automatic Slim's was a small, low-ceilinged club set on the block of businesses that South Belmar called downtown. He walked into clouds of noise and smoke, saw her at the bar.

It was a mixed crowd here, middle-aged black couples dressed to go out, gray-haired bikers in denim vests over T-shirts. Instruments sat unattended onstage, but a handwritten sign tacked to the wall behind advertised Billy and the Bluesbreakers.

She was at the bar, her back to him, wearing jeans and a man's white shirt, her hair moussed and ragged. She was ordering a drink from the elderly black bartender, counting out bills. Men in the crowd were watching her.

He came up on her right.

"You really think this is a good idea?" he said. "With all that's going on?"

She turned to him. The top two buttons of her shirt were undone. She wore a small gold crucifix on a chain.

"I was wondering if you'd come," she said. "Let me buy you a drink."

"No, thanks. What's going on?"

She lifted her drink, nodded toward the back of the room. There was a raised section with tables there. At a table by the wall were Jack and a man at least ten years his junior, with curly black hair and delicate features. He seemed to find everything Jack said amusing. A bottle of champagne stood in a pewter bucket beside the table.

"He did manage to break away for a couple minutes on his way to the men's room," she said. "Asked me if I could find another way home. I didn't know who else to call." He could smell the liquor on her breath.

"Where's Reggie?" he said.

"Please. As Jack gets older, his interests get younger. He'll be an old queen before long and he knows it, so he thinks if he screws men half his age it'll keep him young."

"Does it work?"

"Who knows? Occasionally, someone will recognize him, though, from the movies. And then he can't keep them off him."

He looked at her face.

"That ever happen to you?" he said.

She met his eyes.

"So you are a detective, after all. But I guess the answer would be not lately. At least not out here."

"I'm sorry. That was wrong."

"Never mind. I've had worse said to me by better."

She sipped her drink.

"You look awful funny standing there with your coat on, not drinking," she said. "Let me get you something. A beer. Soda."

He shook his head.

"I'm fine. And I wasn't planning on staying long."

"Let me finish this at least," she said. She raised her glass. "I've given up just about everything else in my life. I felt I had to hold on to at least one vice. So I told him easy on the vodka, and don't spare the cranberry juice. This is only my third."

"My concern would be this," he said, turning his head to indicate the club. "Being out. If I were worried about someone looking for me, I might try to keep a lower profile."

"Every once in a while I'm reminded I had a life once, you know? Before Johnny, before the Heartbreak, before California. I had friends of my own, places I went. I used to come here all the time. I felt comfortable here. If I give all that up because of what happened, what does that leave me?"

"I was just asking."

"I've been a prisoner since I've gotten back. At least that's the way it feels. This is the first time I've been out in months. Jack asked me if I wanted to come along—protective coloration, I guess. Make Reggie less suspicious. I couldn't come up with a good reason to say no."

"It's none of my business what you do."

"You're right. It isn't."

She sipped her drink, put it down. The band members were starting to make their way back onstage, drums, bass, guitar and keyboards. The guitarist and keyboard player were white, the others black.

"I'm sorry," she said. "But I was having a good time tonight, not thinking about any of this. Until now."

"Forget it, I'm sorry I brought it up."

She touched his jacket, drew her hand away self-consciously, let it drop.

"No, it's me that should apologize," she said. "Getting all wound up without a reason. Things haven't been easy for me lately."

"You're not armed right now, are you?" Only half kidding.

She smiled.

"Not tonight. You're safe."

"Good. If it's all the same to you, I think I'd like to get out of here."

"Let me get my jacket."

She sipped her drink, put it down on the bar, made her way

through the crowd to the tables. She leaned over, spoke to Jack and took her leather car coat off the back of the chair next to him. He looked up, saw Harry, then leaned close to the dark-haired man, spoke in his ear.

Harry met her halfway to the door.

"I hate it when he puts me in these situations," she said. "I feel like I'm stuck in the middle."

"Ask him not to."

Behind them, the band kicked into "Crosscut Saw." He pushed the door open, held it for her. She zipped up as they went out into the cold.

"Sometimes I think Reggie knows what's going on," she said. "And maybe he tolerates it. I just wish Jack were a little more discreet."

Out here, the music was just muffled bass. He pointed up the street to where the Mustang was parked. She puffed, watched her breath mist, a girlish gesture, bumped shoulders with him as they walked.

"You could have called a cab," he said.

"And gone home without him? Two hours early? How would I explain that?"

At the Mustang, he unlocked the passenger-side door. As he made his way around the car, he saw her lean over, pop the lock on his side.

He got behind the wheel, switched the ignition on, racing the engine slightly to warm it up. She smelled of cigarette smoke and vanilla musk.

"Are you hungry?" she said. "There must be a diner open someplace where we can eat. Kill some time."

"I guess."

"Or you can just take me home. I'll tell Reggie I didn't feel good, that I called you. Jack can fend for himself when he gets in."

"Whatever," Harry said. There was warm air coming from the vents now. He pulled away from the curb.

"You said you called me, left messages," she said.

"I did. You weren't in."

"Are you going to tell me now?"

They stopped at a light. He gave the engine gas to keep it from stalling.

"I talked to Sherry," he said.

"She hates me now, doesn't she?"

"No, I don't think so. She said she wished you luck."

"I lost touch with her. I shouldn't have. She was a good friend. It's just that once I got back—"

"She understands."

"—I didn't feel like the same person anymore."

The light changed.

"When Harrow came by the Heartbreak," he said, "he gave her a phone number, told her to call if she heard from you."

She looked at him.

"She didn't, of course," he said.

"Did you get the number from her?"

He nodded.

"It's in western Monmouth. Englishtown area. I called, a woman answered. I hung up. The number's new, though, we couldn't match it up with the reverse directory. Might be the brother's. Ray's chasing it down. Might take a day or two."

"So Johnny's there?"

"I don't think so. I think he's just using it as a place to get messages."

"He grew up in Englishtown, you know that, right?"

"Yeah."

"He might be staying out there."

"Maybe. Ray should be able to get an address on that number from the phone company Monday. We'll take it from there."

They drove through Belmar, past darkened storefronts, bars with beer signs glowing in their windows. The Christmas decorations that hung from the lightpoles were dark.

She looked around the car.

"This is nice," she said. "How old is it?"

"Sixty-seven."

"It's cute. I meant to mention that the last time, but the mood didn't seem right, if you know what I mean."

He didn't respond.

"You angry?" she said. "That I called you?"

166

"Not yet."

"I bet you're wondering how you ever got involved with me."

"Not really."

"And I bet you're full of questions about me, even though I haven't given you the chance to ask many of them."

"You've told me a lot. More, probably, than I had a right to know."

"More than you wanted to know?"

"I didn't say that."

"I know I'm paying you, but it still feels wrong. As if I'm pulling you into something I have no business involving you in."

"Like you said, you're paying."

"It's not enough, I'm sure."

"Where are we going?"

"I'm not so hungry after all. Can we just take a ride, drive around a little? I don't want to get back too early."

He looked at her, feeling her nearness. She was looking out her window, her face giving nothing away.

"Sure," he said. He turned right, drove down toward the beach, then north on Ocean Avenue. To their left were dark arcades and restaurants, shuttered for the winter. To their right, the empty boardwalk.

"That's what I missed about being out here," she said. "The ocean."

"They have one in California too, last I heard."

"It's not the same. The water's colder there, even though the air's warmer. I don't know why. And the beaches are so crowded. It's not like here."

"You haven't been around in the summer lately then. More people come down here every year. You can't move on the beach sometimes. It's not the way it used to be."

"I missed it, though. You always miss the place you grew up in. Even if it was full of bad memories."

"And was California any better?"

"It was at first."

"And then?"

"It's like every other place. It's who you are. Not where. Turn left here."

He looked at her.

"Here. This street coming up."

They were in Bradley Beach now; dark, empty summer rentals, windblown sand on the road. He turned.

"Up here," she said. "On the right. Over there."

She pointed at an empty oversize lot, a dark bingo hall on one side, a church on the other.

"Can you pull in?" she said.

The Mustang's headlights flashed across the lot, the wooden fence at the back of the property. They were on the potholed remains of a driveway, the blacktop around them cracked and split. Near the fence was what looked like a pile of twisted scrap metal, half-buried in windblown trash. He put the car in neutral, tugged the emergency brake on.

She swiveled in her seat, looked around the lot.

"They used to have a carnival here," she said. "Every weekend during the summer. The church sponsored it. My mother used to take me on Friday nights sometimes, when she got off work. It's been years since I've been back here."

He looked at the pile of metal, switched on his high beams. He saw rusted metal arms a foot thick sprouting from a central mass of once-black steel. In that instant he knew what it was. The Octopus, a ride from his childhood. Eight cars spinning fast at the end of long metal arms. But the cars had been removed, the main mechanism and supports left to rust.

"When I was in California, I used to go out to the pier in Santa Monica all the time," she said. "They had rides, games, Skee-ball. It reminded me of home. Bright lights, noise and then the ocean just going on forever. Have you ever been to California?"

"No."

"You need to get around more."

"Maybe."

"It's the same feeling you get here. Of being on the edge of something. Something that doesn't end."

"It does," he said. "Eventually."

"You know what I mean. When you were a kid, did you come here, to Bradley?"

"Not here. But other places like it. Long Branch mostly, where I grew up. Asbury."

"It was so long ago. Those nights seem like a dream now."

She was looking out the window again.

"Funny," she said, "how a memory like that, something that small, can bring so much back."

"It's selective. We remember the good things, block out the bad."

"No," she said without turning. "I remember the bad too. You have to concentrate to bring back the good things, or something has to set it off. Like this place. But the bad, it's always with you."

A gust of wind blew from the ocean, shook the car almost imperceptibly.

"I'm sorry," she said. "I'm babbling. But I'm not drunk. Really."

"I didn't think you were."

"Whenever we came to the beach, we came to Bradley. We had season badges. I'd stay in the water for hours. My mother would have to drag me out."

"Are your parents still around?"

She shook her head.

"My mother died when I was fourteen. I never knew my father. He left after I was born."

"You grew up on your own?"

"A foster home first. Then some relatives, my mother's cousin. I stayed with them for a while. It wasn't good. Then I ran away."

"Why?"

"I had my reasons. Do you mind if we stay here a little while? I just want to sit."

He shut the headlights off.

After a moment, she said, "It's not fair, is it?"

"What?"

"How all those things that happen to you as a kid, things you had no control over, how you never get out from under them, no matter what happens afterward."

"I guess it's what you do with it that counts."

"That's one of the things you learn in therapy. Sometimes, when you're finally able to talk about something, say its name, it loses its power over you. I learned a lot about myself, my patterns of behavior. Other people's too."

"Good."

"It was, for a while. The therapy, I mean."

"What happened?"

"At the end of one of our sessions, she tried to kiss me. I let her."

"Your therapist?"

"Yes." She turned to him. "Are you shocked?"

"That doesn't sound very professional."

"It wasn't. But I brought it on myself too. I guess I was giving off a certain vibe, flirting with her. I could see the effect it was having. And she knew the business I was in, so I'm sure she figured it would be a safe bet. But I think the only reason I let it happen was because the therapy had started to get a little too on-target, uncomfortable. I needed to take control of the situation again, protect myself. So that's what I did. That's what I've always done, my whole life."

"You go back to her after that?"

"Once or twice, but it wasn't the same. So I stopped going. I'd gotten what I wanted, and after that kiss, she was no good to me anymore. I didn't respect her. Plus, three hundred dollars a week was starting to become a problem."

"So you came back here."

"Eventually. It was Jack that suggested it. He was done with things out there. He and Reggie wanted a quieter life, I think. So I came along. Jack was like the brother I never had. And the only man I'd ever met, since I was fourteen, that didn't want to fuck me."

He looked out the windshield.

"Cute," she said. "To see you can still blush."

"I'm glad you're amused."

"Cut a little too close to home?"

"You don't quit, do you?"

"Sorry." She looked back out the window. He could see she was smiling.

"Your friend Jack. How much does he know about Harrow?"

"I told him most of it. It wouldn't be fair otherwise."

"Nice of them to want to help."

"I know why they're helping me. Jack loves me and Reggie loves Jack. But why are you? Have you thought about that?"

"Like you said, you're paying me. It's a job."

"I don't believe that for a minute. Not totally, anyway."

"Believe what you like."

"Did I offend you? I'm sorry."

"Forget about it."

"I know why you're helping me, though."

"Why's that?"

"You're not that different from other men I've known. You find somebody—especially a woman—that seems to be down on their luck and you want to help them, solve their problems, save them from themselves. But it doesn't work that way. Nobody saves anybody."

"Thank you, Doctor. Can we go now?"

"In a minute," she said, and leaned toward him.

He turned and she cupped the back of his neck with her hand, pulled him close. He tried to get his hands up between them but then her lips were on his, her eyes closed. Her mouth opened and he could taste the sweetness of alcohol. He met her tongue with his own. His hands came up, cupped her face, and she held his wrists as they kissed, then pulled away, smiling. He was breathing shallowly, his heart racing.

"Sorry," she said. She let go of his wrists. "I probably shouldn't have done that, should I?" She leaned back against the door, watched him. "It's just like what I was telling you. The way I deal with things."

He watched her, saw her amusement, felt the first flush of anger.

"Are you mad at me?" she said.

He let his breath out, put the headlights on, let the brake go, shifted into reverse.

"You are, aren't you? I can tell," she said.

"You can? Good for you. You'll be ready to open your own practice soon."

He backed out into the street, turned toward the beach again. She put her left hand lightly on his thigh.

"I'm sorry," she said.

He took one hand off the wheel, used it to gently ease her hand from his leg.

"Now comes the silence, right?" she said after a moment. "You don't say another word the whole way home?"

"Give me a break."

"Take me to your house, I'll give you more than that."

He looked at her. She looked back, not smiling.

He turned left onto Ocean Avenue, shook his head slowly.

"You sure you want to pass up this opportunity?" she said.

They swung around the long turn on Fletcher Lake, the inlet that separated Bradley and Ocean Grove. He didn't answer.

"But you will, won't you?" she said. "Because you want me to know you're different."

He didn't answer, made the right over the bridge into Ocean Grove. After a few blocks, she said, "I ruined your night."

"Just drop it."

He drove by darkened houses, read street signs.

"Make a left on Beach," she said.

He went up two blocks, turned right onto Bath, saw the house ahead. There was no Blazer outside.

"Poor Reggie," she said. "I don't know what I'm going to tell him."

He parked at the curb.

"I guess I should thank you," she said. "For—"

He pulled her to him, cupped her face, kissed her, felt her sudden intake of breath. Her mouth opened and he tasted her again, his fingers in her hair. Her left hand slipped into his jacket, touched his chest. Her right slid quickly up his thigh, stroked his hardness through his jeans.

He began to undo the buttons of her car coat. His hand slid inside and she caught it, lifted it to her left breast. He cupped its warm softness, felt the nipple harden through the cloth.

She broke off the kiss, pulled away, looked at him. He felt dizzy, out of breath. She leaned back against the door.

"Well," she said. "I wasn't expecting that."

He looked straight ahead, tried to slow his breathing. Neither of them spoke.

"I guess," she said after a moment, "I better go."

He turned to her and she leaned toward him, slower this time. She kissed him lightly, then touched the line of his jaw, kissed him quickly again.

She got out of the car without a word, the cold air rushing in. She shut the door and he watched her go up the walk to the porch.

Keys in hand, she looked back at him a final time, then let herself in, closed the door behind her.

He wasn't sure how long he sat there, engine running, waiting for his breathing to return to normal, his heart to slow down.

TWENTY

JOHNNY WATCHED THE HONDA PARK BENEATH THE STREETLIGHT, snow flurries swirling down around it. Sherry got out, shouldered her bag, started up the slate walk to a three-story house with two front doors, mailboxes on the wall between them. Apartments.

He was behind the wheel of a Nissan he'd stolen an hour earlier. The plastic steering column was cracked, colored wires sticking out from where he'd pulled them loose and hot-wired them. The engine was running, the heat on low. He'd followed her from the Heartbreak to Avon, keeping as far back as he could without losing her.

He watched her go in, shut the door behind her. He smoked, waited. Snow was starting to dust the Nissan's hood. He pulled the wires apart and the engine coughed and died.

After a few minutes, the front door opened again. A skinny, long-haired girl in her early twenties came out, stood on the porch talking to Sherry, who was just inside the door. Then, while Sherry watched, she got into an old Plymouth Horizon parked across the street.

Johnny slid lower in the seat. The Plymouth pulled away from the curb, headlights sweeping across the Nissan. But she drove past him without slowing. The front door closed and the porch light went out.

He got the Buck knife from his pocket, opened the long blade and used it to pop the lens off the Nissan's dome light, then unscrewed the bulb. He folded the knife, put it back in his jacket pocket and got out of the car.

There was a driveway on the side of the house, a car parked against a closed garage door. In the back, a wooden stairway doubled as a fire escape. He stood in the backyard, snow blowing around him, saw third-floor lights go on.

The stairs were already slippery with snow, so he went up carefully. All the windows he passed were dark until he got to the top. He stood on the landing, looked through a lighted window into an empty kitchen.

He heard footsteps inside, sat down on the landing. Snow drifted around him. A shadow fell on the landing as someone moved around the kitchen. Then the light went out.

He waited, looking at his watch occasionally, his hair wet with snow. After a few minutes, he heard the low thrumming noise of a shower somewhere inside the apartment.

He got up, brushed snow from his jeans. He'd bought another pair of cotton work gloves, and he pressed his palms flat against the outside storm window, pushed up. It wasn't locked. He slid it up gradually, carefully, so as not to knock it out of its frame. It slipped into its notches, stayed there.

He looked in, the kitchen still dark. Through the door he could see a dim hallway light.

He pushed against the inside window. It was old, set loosely into the frame, hinged horizontally so it opened into the room. It swung in a quarter inch, stopped, and he could see the hook and eye that held it shut on the right side. He got the Buck out again, held the window open with one hand, used the straight side of the blade to pop the hook out of the eye.

He put the knife away, climbed into the kitchen, tracking snow on the linoleum. In the darkness a clock ticked, an old-style radiator clanked.

He could still hear the shower. He went into the corridor. To the left, at the end of the hall, was a closed door, light beneath it, the sound of the water coming from within. There were two other doors, both partially open, lights out. To his right, the corridor opened onto a small living room, lit by a single lamp.

He got the Mag-Lite out, went left down the hall. He shone the thin beam into the first room he came to. Inside was a child's bed, a

175

dollhouse, toys on the floor. A Mickey Mouse night-light glowed in an outlet on the wall. A girl of about four was sleeping in the bed, her breathing regular and undisturbed.

He backed out, flashed the light into the second room, saw a neatly made bed, a dresser, a full-length mirror against one wall. On the nightstand was an ashtray, a tiny ceramic carousel horse figurine and a rosary. No sign of a man's presence anywhere.

He switched the Mag off, walked quietly down the hall to the small living room. There were paper cutouts of Santa Claus and reindeer taped to the walls, smiling snowmen. Lights blinked on a miniature artificial Christmas tree, maybe two feet tall, on a table. There was a low shelf filled with children's books, videos, a VCR atop the TV.

He sat on the couch, unzipped his jacket, left his gloves on. On the coffee table in front of him was a phone, a glass ashtray, a pack of menthol cigarettes and a cheap lighter. He pulled out drawers, looked through them. Bills, children's drawings. No address books. Then he moved the phone, saw the card that had been hidden beneath it.

He picked it up. RW SECURITY embossed on the front. On the back a handwritten name—Harry Rane—and a phone number.

He heard the shower shut off. He closed the drawers, put the card in the pocket with the Buck. He could hear her humming softly to herself down the hall. Then the sound of the door opening, the smell of steam.

He waited, one arm thrown over the back of the couch. She came into the room without seeing him at first, wearing a terry-cloth bathrobe, toweling her hair.

"Hey, Sherry," he said.

She jumped, choked the scream off. He lifted an index finger to his lips.

She backed into the doorway and froze, as if deciding whether to turn and run.

"Johnny," she said. "What are you . . ."

"Take it easy," he said. He pointed at an ancient recliner to the left of the couch. "Come sit down."

"Janey's here. She's right down the hall."

"I know. I saw her. Have a seat."

"Let me get dressed first, it's cold in—"

He shook his head. He could see the fear in her, knew she would do whatever he said. He picked up the pack of menthols.

"Go on," he said. "Sit down."

He took a cigarette, slid the pack across the table. She looked at it, settled slowly into the recliner, her arms wrapped tightly around herself.

He broke the filter off his cigarette, used the lighter. He blew smoke out, put the lighter atop the pack. She leaned forward, the robe opening slightly, got a cigarette out. He could see her hands shaking as she lit it.

"How'd you get in?" she said.

He didn't answer, leaned forward again, tapped ash in the ashtray.

"What do you want?" she said.

He sat back, looked at her.

"Heard from her?" he said.

"From who?"

He smiled, turned his head to the side, blew smoke out softly.

She had the towel in her lap, her long red hair dark and straight and wet. Ash fell from her cigarette to the floor unnoticed.

"Come on, Sher. I only want to talk to her. Just once. Is that too much to ask?"

"Johnny, I told you everything I know."

"Did you? I've been thinking about it and I wonder if you did. Tell me everything, that is. You're a good friend to her. Always were. You'd protect her if you thought she needed it, right? Even lie to me. But there's no reason to. No one's going to hurt her. And lying to me . . . well, it just makes things worse."

She looked away.

"Why are you doing this, Johnny?"

"Doing what?"

"Why can't you just leave things alone?"

"I've come a long way, Sherry. A lot of miles and a lot of time. Look at me."

She did.

"I'm owed," he said.

She blinked and he saw wetness in her eyes.

"She may be around here," he said, "or she may be somewhere

else. Another state. Country, even. But I have the feeling that wherever she is, you know."

She shook her head quickly, noticed the growing ash on her cigarette. She leaned forward to tap it off, missed the ashtray.

"Janey's very pretty," he said. "Like her mother."

She looked at him then.

"Nikki can take care of herself," he said. "We both know that.
You should be worrying about yourself—and Janey."

"Don't say that, Johnny. You would never—"

"Seven years, Sherry. People change."

"I told you all I know."

He took the card out, flipped it on the table in front of her.

"Who's that?" he said.

She dropped the cigarette, picked it quickly off the carpet.

"Just some guy," she said. "That I met."

"At the Heartbreak?"

She nodded.

"You're a bad liar, Sherry. You always were."

"I'm not lying."

"Just some guy. And what's this security business? He do burglar
alarms, locks, that kind of thing?"

"I don't know."

"You should ask. Maybe he can put some in here. You should
have them, living alone like this. You know what I used to get in?
Just this."

He took the folded knife out of his pocket, put it atop the card.
She looked at it.

He stubbed the cigarette out in the ashtray.

"That number I gave you," he said. "You didn't lose it, did you?"

"No."

"But you didn't call. I was disappointed."

She dropped the cigarette again, picked it up and put it out in the
ashtray.

"Don't make this tougher than it should be," he said. "We've got
all night. I can leave here in five minutes—or five hours. It's your
choice. So maybe you want to get your priorities straight. About
who's worth protecting and who's not."

She couldn't look at him now, and he knew it had settled in.

"Two ways to go, Sherry," he said. "You give me what you *do* have—an address, a phone number, whatever. Or you convince me you're telling the truth. But I'm not leaving until you've done one or the other."

"Johnny . . ."

"Come here."

She looked at him, slowly got up from the chair.

"Closer."

He took the towel from her hands, dropped it on the floor, slipped one gloved finger into the knot of her belt.

"Please, Johnny, no. Not here."

He tugged and the knot came loose, the robe falling open.

"Please," she said. "Janey . . ."

He looked at the empty doorway, the hall beyond. Then he dragged her down to him.

HE LEFT the Nissan in Asbury, on a side street near the projects, engine running. He walked the six blocks to the Sea Vista, snow still falling lightly. Up in his room, he took out the phone number Sherry had written down for him. It was a local exchange. He'd known she was near, had never doubted it.

He dropped the paper on the bureau top, then took out the card. He wasn't sure why he'd brought it with him. But he felt it again, the momentum, the energy. The world arranging itself around him, things falling into place. Fate now, or something like it.

TWENTY-ONE

THEY WERE IN ONE OF RAY'S COMPANY CARS, AN OLD FORD STATION wagon Harry had used before. It was innocuous enough for surveillance work, but had a big 400 four-barrel engine that ate up the road.

They were parked behind an abandoned gas station, with a clear view of the trailer park. Separating the properties was a trash-strewn slope, a frozen-over creek and a stand of bare trees. Every once in a while, Errol turned the engine on, let the wagon warm up.

Harry took his field glasses from the dashboard, had another look down at the trailer. Unlike most of the others, it had no Christmas decorations, and its trim was eaten with rust. A broken Big Wheel lay in the small side yard.

"How's the chest?" Harry said.

"Hurt for a while. Then it itched more than anything. Bruise is gone, though."

"Good."

"First time I've ever been shot."

"Hopefully the last."

"Makes you look at things a little differently, though."

"What do you mean?"

"How easy it can happen. I guess that's what I've been trying to get my mind around ever since."

"Don't bother. It won't get you anywhere."

"You think about it much anymore? What happened to you?"

He put the glasses back on the dashboard.

"Only every night."

He brought up the thermos of coffee from the floorboard, unscrewed the cap.

"How sure are we that's the right place?" Errol asked.

"That's the address the phone company gave Ray. Bill's in the name of a Mitchell Sweeton."

"Different last name."

"Yeah, but the first name's the same as the brother's. Too much of a coincidence."

"Heads up," Errol said.

Harry looked down, saw a young black woman leave the trailer, walk the twenty feet to a bank of mailboxes along the road. He put the thermos back down, raised the glasses again.

"You think it's possible this brother's a brother?" Errol said.

Harry watched the woman take a small stack of letters and circulars from the mailbox.

"Or we've got the wrong trailer," he said.

"One way to find out."

Errol opened his cell phone.

"What's that number again?"

Harry gave it to him.

He punched in the numbers, waited. Harry saw the woman lift her head, look toward the trailer, then close the mailbox. She went back up the trailer stairs.

After a moment, Errol said into the phone, "Sorry, I misdialed," and closed it.

"Bingo," he said.

The woman pulled the door shut from within.

"I'd like to have a look at that mail," Harry said.

"Think you missed your chance. And above and beyond the fact it's a federal crime, from the looks of that place I think all you'd find are some bills and maybe a couple termination-of-service notices."

Harry put the field glasses down.

"What now?" Errol said.

Harry shrugged. Errol's phone rang. He answered it.

"Yeah?"

He listened for a moment, nodded.

"It's for you."

He handed it over.

"It's me," Nikki said.

"How did you get this number?"

"Ray gave it to me. I tried your house but there was no answer."

"What's up?"

"Sherry called me."

"What did she say?"

"Not much. She said she was sorry and that was it. Then she hung up."

"She was sorry? That's all she said?"

"When I called her back, she didn't answer."

Errol was watching him now.

"What do you think it means?" she said.

"I don't know. But I guess I should get over there, try to find out. Do you know where she lives?"

"No. All I have is her phone number."

"Give it to me again. I don't have it with me."

She read it off to him.

"Okay," he said. "I'll call you back, let you know what I find out."

He closed the line, dialed the number she'd given him. It rang ten times, no answer. He let it go six more, ended the call.

"Shit," he said.

"What's up?"

"I don't know." He closed the phone, handed it back. "But I don't like the way it sounds."

"The way what sounds?"

"Everything."

ERROL DROPPED him off at Ray's office, headed back to the trailer park. Ray had designated a small room off the main office for their use, and Harry sat at a desk there, pulled a Monmouth County phone book into his lap, looking for an address that matched Sherry's number and name. She wasn't listed. He called Nikki back.

"No luck," he said. "Ray can get the address, but it'll take a while. I'll try her back later, then swing by the Heartbreak tonight, see if she's there."

"I don't like this."

"Neither do I."

182

"What happens if you can't find her?"

"I'll find her."

"Do you want me to go with you, to the Heartbreak?"

"Do you want to?"

A pause, then: "No. I don't think I ever want to go there again."

"Then I'll take care of it."

"Be careful, Harry," she said.

He gave that a moment.

"I will," he said.

WHEN HE got there, the bar was less than half full, a single dancer on the stage. She was barely out of her teens, short blonde hair and a cut-off T-shirt that read I TALK TO STRANGERS.

He took a stool, nodded at the hard-eyed barmaid, asked if Sherry was in.

"No. Later maybe. What are you drinking?"

He ordered a Corona, looked around the bar while he waited. Wondered if he would know Harrow on sight, if he'd changed much since that last photograph had been taken at Glades.

When he was done nursing the beer, he ordered a Coke, looked at his watch. Ten after ten. Two more dancers had shown up, one tall and black, the other a skinny Russian blonde. They worked the bar, smiled at him, but after their third time around, when he hadn't offered any bills, they ignored him.

He was coming out of the men's room when he saw her walk in the front door, dressed in street clothes. She greeted the barmaid quickly, headed for a door in the back. He followed her.

She left the door ajar behind her. It was a small dressing room, a mirror on one wall, lockers on the others. She was working the combination padlock on a locker. When she got it open, he watched her take out a gym bag, fill it with clothes and items from the locker, tampons, two packs of cigarettes.

"Sherry," he said from the doorway.

She turned, saw him, went back to what she was doing.

"What are you doing here?" she said.

She closed the locker, zipped the bag up.

"Where are you going?" he said.

"Away."

"Did Harrow come back?"

She hefted the bag.

"Listen," she said, "I don't have time for his bullshit. I have a life. I have a child."

"We can help you."

"You can?" She looked at him. "And where have you been so far? Forgive me if I don't believe you. But I don't think anyone around here gives a shit about me anymore, except myself."

The short-haired blonde ducked by him into the room, went to her locker.

"Think about this," he said. "We can protect you. And you can help us find him."

"Find him? You're having trouble finding him? Every time I look over my goddamn shoulder, he's standing there. And you can't find him?"

"We will. We—"

"Off-limits, partner. I have to ask you to leave."

Harry turned, saw a broad-shouldered bouncer in a yellow STAFF T-shirt behind him.

"We're talking," Harry said.

"Leave or I'll carry you out."

"Just go," Sherry said. "Just fuck off, please. All of you. And leave me alone."

"I'm telling you, we can help."

"Okay, let's go, pal." The bouncer reached for his arm and Harry shrugged it off, turned to look at him. The bouncer saw something in his eyes, stopped.

"You have to go," he said, not touching him now.

The blonde was getting dressed, as if oblivious to their presence. She pulled her T-shirt off, tossed it into the locker, stood there topless as she got out her street clothes.

He turned and went back into the bar. The barmaid was watching him. His seat was taken, and the singles he'd left on the bar were gone.

He went out the door into the parking lot, sat on the hood of the Mustang and waited. She came out a few minutes later, saw him, walked to an old Honda parked on the edge of the lot. He started toward her.

"Sherry," he said. "I'm sorry for all this."

She put her bag in the backseat of the car, looked at him.

"Are you really? You expect me to believe that? Do any of you—Nikki, Johnny, you, anyone—care about what happens to me, really?"

"Yes. I do."

She looked at him, shook her head slowly, then opened the car door, got behind the wheel.

"Keep that card," he said and she looked at him for a moment, then shut the car door.

He walked back to the Mustang, watched her drive away. As he got his keys out, he saw the bouncer was standing outside the front door, arms folded, watching him.

Harry cupped his crotch, said, "Right here, pal," and got in the car. The bouncer was still watching him when he pulled out of the lot.

JACK ANSWERED the door.

"What do you want?" he said.

"Spare me the attitude," Harry said. "Is she home?"

He turned away from the door.

"Nikki," he called out. "That man's here."

He opened the door wider and Harry came in. Reggie was doing shirtless bench presses in a small area off the living room. He looked at Harry, sat up, rubbed a towel over his chest.

She came down the stairs.

"What happened?" she said.

He looked at the kitchen.

"Let's go in there," he said. "Where we can talk."

Jack watched them, hands on his hips. In the kitchen, Harry told her about his visit to the Heartbreak.

"Where is she going?"

"I don't know," he said. "But maybe it's not such a bad thing after all. Might be safer for them."

"This is exactly what I didn't want to do. Turn everyone's life upside down with my problems. She's got a four-year-old daughter. Where are they going to go?"

"Whatever. It's done. We know more than we did, though, about Harrow. We found where the brother lives. I was out there today."

"Did you see him?"

"Harrow? No. We're watching the place, though. I have the feeling he'll show up sooner or later. We'll follow him back to wherever he's staying, sit on him. He won't be able to do anything, go anywhere without us knowing about it."

"You hope."

"It's more than that."

She looked off into the living room.

"Thank you," she said finally.

"I'm sorry it worked out this way."

"You did your best."

"I should get going," he said. "It's late. But I wanted you to know."

"Hang on," she said. "I'll walk you out."

Jack and Reggie watched them as they went out onto the porch. Nikki closed the door behind them.

"You should go back inside," he said. "It's cold."

"I will. Thank you for coming by."

He shrugged.

"Poor Sherry," she said. "She was a good friend to me, but she never got anything out of it but trouble."

"I'll call her again tomorrow, try to talk to her."

She looked at him.

"What?" he said.

"Nothing." And she raised up and kissed him lightly on the lips.

He felt himself flush.

"You're a good man, Harry Rane," she said. "Don't let anybody tell you different."

AT THE wheel of the Firebird, parked a half block down, Johnny watched her go back inside. At first, he hadn't recognized her. Her hair was shorter, her movements more confident. But it was her.

He watched the man in the leather jacket kiss her, get into the old Mustang. He'd followed Sherry to the Heartbreak, waited there, seen the man come out. He'd trailed the Mustang then, not sure why. And this was where it had led.

He let his breath out slowly, looked at the house, saw figures moving behind the windows. She wasn't alone. But he knew where she lived now; she would keep. As he watched, a second-floor light went on. He looked up at it, saw a shadow behind the shade, knew it was her.

TWENTY-TWO

WHEN HE PULLED THE FIREBIRD UP NEXT TO THE TRAILER, MITCH WAS standing outside in the cold, waiting for him. He rolled to a stop and Mitch pulled open the passenger-side door, got in.

"Keep going," he said. "Don't stop."

Johnny pulled away again, looked in the rearview.

"What's wrong?"

Mitch turned, craned his neck.

"Keep driving. Swing around toward the exit."

Johnny made a circuit of the trailer park, headed back out onto Route 9.

"Go up here and turn around," Mitch said.

"Tell me."

"There was someone watching the trailer."

"Who?"

"I don't know. They were parked up by that old Sunoco station. All day. Old man who lives one trailer over called the cops. Sharonda saw them up there, talking to some black guy in a station wagon."

"What Sunoco station?"

"Behind the park. It's out of business. I'll show you."

They turned around and headed back in the other direction on 9. Mitch pointed out the turnoff to him. He slowed at the boarded-up station. All that was left of the pumps were bolts sticking out of the concrete.

"They're gone now," Mitch said. "Drove off with the cops."

Johnny pulled into the station lot, parked on the gravel.

"What are you doing?" Mitch said.

188

He got out of the Firebird, walked around to the rear of the station. Graffiti covered the back wall. He saw the tire tracks in the snow, where they ended. He stood at the top of the slope, looked across the creek. He had a clear view of the front of Mitch's trailer.

He heard Mitch come up behind him.

"What do you think?" Mitch said.

"Someone was here. Looking for me, I expect."

"Who knows you've been here? Who could have told them?"

Johnny got his cigarettes out, lit one.

"Only one person I can think of," he said.

THE SKY was clear, the moon out, when he eased the Firebird up the dirt driveway. He killed the lights, wondered if the old man had heard the muffler. He shut the engine off, sat there in the darkness. The moon cast the snow-covered ground in a bone gray light.

The Sig was on the seat beside him. He took it as he got out of the car, shut the door quietly behind him. The gun went into his belt in the small of his back, cold against the skin.

There was a single light on in the house, throwing a square of yellow into the side yard. The living room. Johnny couldn't remember the last time he'd been here. This was the house he'd grown up in, had slept in every night until his first time in Jamesburg.

There was a car up on blocks in the backyard, its doors gone, the interior white with snow. Frazer's pickup was parked at an angle near the back door, one tire in a stone-circled area of bare ground that had once been a flower garden.

He waited, listening, heard the low drone of a TV inside. There were trees on three sides of the house, but he could hear the traffic on Route 18 in the distance. Somewhere, a dog began to bark.

He stubbed his boot on a discarded wheel rim, half-frozen in the dirt. He tugged it free with one gloved hand, dragged it over to a window and stood on it. He looked into the mudroom, the kitchen beyond. There were wet footprints on the floor of the mudroom, two white recycling buckets full of Budweiser cans, more cans on the floor. Frazer's heavy red hunting jacket hung on the wall.

He went to the mudroom door, tried the knob. The door was loose in its frame, but held when he pulled. He took the Buck out, sliced an inch-thick sliver of rotted wood from the frame. It opened easily then, creaking on its hinges.

He put the knife away, stepped through. He could still hear the TV inside. He pulled the door closed behind him.

The kitchen smelled of grease and staleness, with the faint undercurrent of rotting food. The lidless trash can was overflowing, the sink full of dishes, faucet dripping.

He didn't need a light in here, knew every step by heart. He crossed peeling linoleum, floorboards creaking beneath, and stood in the doorway to the living room.

The old man was asleep in front of the TV. He wore the same clothes Johnny had seen him in last time and his breathing was labored, a wheezing, tubercular snore. There were two empty beer cans on the coffee table, one on the floor. On the television, a black-and-white documentary, bombs falling, the camera pointing straight down out of the bay, following their flight.

The room was warm, close, and smelled of the old man. He coughed, stirred, then slipped back into sleep. Johnny watched him. The only father he'd ever known.

He settled into an overstuffed chair across from the couch, got his cigarettes out. Only one left. He lit up, blew smoke toward the old man. It drifted around his face. Frazer sneezed, coughed, opened his eyes, saw him there.

Johnny waited. The old man rubbed at his gummy eyes, coughed again, deep and wet.

"John?"

Johnny didn't answer, finished his cigarette.

"What are you doing here?"

Johnny got up, went into the kitchen. He dropped the butt into the sink, ran water on it, then pulled open the latch on the old-style refrigerator. It was empty except for beer, some cold pizza on a plate.

He took out two cans of Bud, kneed the door shut. Back in the living room he handed one to the old man, sat back down across from him.

"You awake now?" he said.

Frazer looked at the beer, pushed moisture away from the pull top with his thumb.

Johnny popped his can open, sipped. It was watery, flat.

"You should have let me know, John. That you were coming."

His words were slurred. Johnny saw the bridge resting on a paper towel on the end table.

"Go ahead," he said, pointing at it. "Put that in."

Frazer looked at him, then reached for the bridge. He turned his head slightly to hide the process, made wet noises as he slid it home, adjusted it. Johnny took another sip of beer.

"What time is it?" Frazer said, his words clearer.

Johnny looked at his watch.

"Midnight," he said.

"Awful late, John."

"Drink your beer. Then we're going for a walk."

"A walk? Where?"

Johnny drank beer, watched him. The old man fumbled with the can, got it open. Foam spilled onto his pants.

Johnny looked at the television screen, a map of Europe with animated arrows spreading across it. He heard the old man slurp beer, felt his eyes on him. Johnny ignored him, drank from his can. When it was almost empty, he shook the contents, set the can down on the coffee table with the others.

"There," he said. "Now we've had our drink together. Get your coat."

"John."

"Come on. Get up."

He stood in the doorway to the kitchen, waited for him. Frazer got up slowly, one hand on the couch arm to steady himself. He broke wind loudly, then stood up, shoulders stooped.

"Where we going?"

"Just out back. I want you to show me a couple things. It's been a long time since I've been here, remember?"

"I don't have my shoes."

"Those slippers are fine. We'll only be a couple minutes."

Frazer looked at him, then twisted his feet into a pair of brown corduroy slippers on the floor. Johnny went into the mudroom, got the hunting jacket off the peg, stood there with it.

The old man shuffled into the kitchen, coughed deeply.

"Wait a minute," Johnny said.

Frazer looked at him.

"The money I gave you. What did you do with it?"

"What?"

"The five hundred. You couldn't have spent it all by now. Where's the rest?"

"I'm saving it, Johnny. For groceries."

"Get it."

"You taking it back?"

"I'm not here to steal your money, old man. I just want to make sure you haven't spent it all yet. Get it."

Frazer went to the sink, leaned down and opened the cabinet beneath it, broke wind again. He reached under the pipes, came out with a Maxwell House coffee can.

"That your bank?" Johnny said.

Frazer put the can on the counter.

"Take it out," Johnny said.

He rooted through it, brought out matchbooks, nuts and bolts, then a roll of cash, wrapped tightly with a rubber band.

"There it is," he said. He put it on the counter. "There's four hundred there. Just like I said. I've still got most of it."

"Good," Johnny said and opened the mudroom door, nodded outside.

Frazer took the coat, pulled it on. Johnny went out first.

"It's colder than a witch's tit," Frazer said. "That's what your mother used to always say. Remember that?"

Johnny didn't answer.

Frazer shut the door behind them, buttoned the jacket up.

"Let's walk," Johnny said.

"Where?"

"Over here a little."

The backyard sloped down through trees to a fallow field, a collapsing barn on one side. With the moon, it was almost as bright as day.

"Used to play out here," Johnny said. "As kids."

He walked down to the field, watching his footing. He looked up at Frazer, who had stopped halfway down the slope.

"Come on," Johnny said. "Just a little ways."

"I need my boots, John."

"No, you don't. It's fine here." He stamped the frozen ground. "You won't fall."

They walked out into the field, the ground furrowed and hard. Frazer had wrapped the coat tighter around himself. He coughed once, spit. Johnny turned his back on him, walked out farther into the field. Through the trees on the far side he could see houses, Christmas lights.

"Who did you tell?" he said.

"What?"

Johnny turned to him. He reached under his jacket, got the Sig out.

"Who did you tell that I was back here?"

Frazer saw the gun then.

"No one, Johnny, I swear."

Johnny worked the slide, locked the hammer back, let the gun hang at his side.

"I don't believe you."

"Put that thing away, John."

"I just want to know who you told. Then we can go back inside."

"Why would I tell anyone about you?"

"Because you couldn't resist. Because you can't shut your mouth for five goddamn minutes. Who did you tell?"

Frazer looked back at the house, then at the trees on the other side of the field, as if comparing distances.

"Nobody special," he said finally. "Just people that know you, that would be happy to see you again."

"What people?"

"Down at the Jumping Brook. At the bar. People you know. That's all, John. Everyone always asks about you, about my sons."

"Who else?"

"That's it, Johnny, that's it, I swear to the Lord Jesus . . ." His voice trailed off into a deep cough.

"I think you're lying. I think you called the police, told them I was back, that I had money. Got them interested in me again."

"No, Johnny, I didn't. Why would I?"

"Because you were scared. Angry."

"I didn't, Johnny. I swear on your mother's grave I didn't."

Johnny looked across the field again.

"Kneel," he said.

"What?"

"You heard me. Face the barn. Do it."

"Johnny, I—"

"Don't make me ask you twice."

The old man turned slowly, coughed, the single one growing into a chain that wracked his body. Then he lowered himself to one knee, a hand on the ground to steady himself. He set the other knee down heavily, nearly lost his balance.

"Shape you're in," Johnny said, "I'd be doing you a favor if I put you in the ground."

"John, I'm your father. I love you. I always loved you, all you kids. I always did my best for you. Raised you like my own."

"Beating the shit out of us, terrorizing us? That how you did it?"

"Times were hard back then, John. Sometimes I drank too much. I know that, but—"

"Did you fuck Belinda?"

"No!" Another cough. "And whoever told you I did is a goddamn liar."

"When we were kids, we were terrified of you. Mitch used to mess his pants when you came home drunk those nights and started going at him."

"John, don't do this, please."

"Three little kids. Fucked for life because of you, because they ended up in your house. We would have been better off on the street."

Frazer closed his eyes tightly, and Johnny saw the dark stain spread down his right pants leg.

"I did my best for you, Johnny. I did." Tears in his voice now.

"It wasn't good enough."

"John, your mother's looking down on us right now . . ."

"No, I don't think she is," Johnny said, raised the gun.

"You'll burn in hell for this, boy."

"Then I'll see you there," Johnny said and fired twice.

The brass was easy to find in the moonlight. He went back to the house, got the money, put it in the pocket with the shell casings. He let himself out the front door, the TV still on.

Fifteen minutes later, he was stopped at a light. The moon was a blue and silver globe in the east, its mountains and shadows visible to the naked eye. He blinked wetness away, breathed in deeply, looked up at the moon. Wished he had a cigarette.

TWENTY-THREE

"IS SHE GONE?" NIKKI SAID.

Harry shrugged.

"I don't think so. Not yet, at least. When I called again, she answered, then hung up. I tried back, but she wouldn't pick up."

They had the house to themselves, Jack and Reggie at a bed-and-breakfast in Cape May, "making up," as Nikki had put it. They had Chinese take-out food in front of them, glasses of white wine. She wore jeans and a red cardigan sweater, no makeup. Behind him, the refrigerator hummed.

"We can help her," he said. "But I don't have the feeling she wants it."

She pushed her plate away, drank wine.

"What happened at Mitch's trailer?"

"A neighbor called the locals. Errol was there alone. He talked his way through it, but we're blown there. If we're going to keep an eye on the trailer, we'll have to find another way to do it."

She refilled their glasses from the bottle.

"You trying to get me drunk?" he said.

"I have the feeling nobody gets you anything you don't want to be."

"Not sure of your grammar there, but you're probably right."

She got up, scraped their plates into the trash, rinsed them in the sink. As she moved, the cardigan rode up slightly on one side, showing an inch of skin. He got up, resealed the leftover food containers, found room for them in the refrigerator.

"Isn't this a cozy domestic scene," she said.

"Make you uncomfortable?"

"I'm not sure. I guess it's just been such a long time since I've led anything even close to a normal life."

"We don't always get to pick and choose how we're going to live our lives," he said. "Things happen." He sat back down.

She leaned against the counter, sipped wine.

"Amen to that. You're an interesting man, you know that? Not at all the way I envisioned someone in your business being."

"I could say the same for you."

"Touché."

"I'm sorry. That was wrong."

"Don't apologize. I know what I've done. I made choices. If I had to make them again, I'd do it differently. But you don't get to do that."

"No."

"I could tell you about things that happened to me, in my childhood. And you'd say, 'Oh yeah, that explains it.' But it wouldn't be totally true, would it?"

"It never is."

"Tell me about this woman. The one in Seattle."

He reached for the wine bottle, turned it to look at the label.

"I'm not sure what to say."

"Is she coming back?"

"I don't know. She said she would. I hope she does."

"You look so sad when you say that."

He didn't answer.

"And will you get married again? Someday?"

"I don't know."

"You're a Man of Mystery, you know that? I'm supposed to be the one with the past. Tell me something about yourself."

"Like what?"

"A secret. Something you're ashamed of. Something that happened in your life. Something you did, something you felt."

"Why?"

"I don't know. Maybe I just want to level the playing field a little."

"I told you a lot."

"Not really. Me, on the other hand, my life's an open book now, isn't it? You know everything I've done, every low I hit."

"I don't judge. It's none of my business."

"You're right, you don't judge. And you don't ask too many questions either. Even when I've volunteered to answer them, whatever they are. Not many men would pass up that opportunity."

"Like I said, none of my business."

"Knowing what I did out there, how I made a living. It doesn't make you curious?"

"You'll tell me what you want to tell me, and when."

"You think I'm embarrassed by it? I'm not. I did what I had to do. I made my choices. It's easy to get hooked up with the wrong people, sure. And that business eats you up. But there's always another factor, a decision you make somewhere along the line. Some women I've known—here and out there—look at themselves as victims. I never have."

"I know that. I admire it."

"I don't hate Johnny. I never did. I hated myself for what I let myself become, how I let things get away from me. But I never blamed Johnny."

"Maybe you should."

She shook her head.

"On one level, it's got nothing to do with him, does it? I've made mistakes. I have to pay for them, find a way through, control the damage. I don't want to see Johnny dead or back in jail. I just want him out of the way so that I can start making things right again. I can't have him here, now, at this point in my life. He'll destroy everything I've built, everything I'm building. He'd ruin everything just to prove he can. For the boy too, if he finds him."

"Then that doesn't leave a lot of choices, does it?"

"I don't know. I've been thinking. Maybe I should just call him, talk to him. You've got that phone number."

"I don't think that's a good idea."

"I've always been able to deal with him in the past. Even the way he was, I could always talk to him."

"He's been in prison for seven years. You think that improved his personality? No, I don't think you should call."

"I feel like I'm running away again. Putting other people at risk, making them deal with my problems. It's an issue I've always had, relying too much on other people. It got me into a lot of trouble. I thought I was through with it, knew better. But now I'm slipping into it again."

"You can't do everything yourself. And there's other issues at stake here. The boy."

"Yes."

"You made the right decision. Don't second-guess it now. Everything's going to be okay."

"I have the feeling that's a phrase you're pretty free and easy with. Meant to reassure. But not always true."

He didn't know what to say to that.

"Excuse me," she said and set her glass on the counter, left the kitchen. He heard her feet on the stairs.

He got up, recorked the wine, took his glass out into the living room. Somewhere a church bell was tolling the time.

He sat on the leather couch, waited. After ten minutes, she still hadn't come down. He went to the foot of the stairs, called up.

"Nikki?"

No answer.

"Nikki?"

He listened, then went quietly up the carpeted stairs. Three doors opened off the hall, one of them slightly ajar, light inside.

"Nikki?"

"In here," she said.

He put his fingers on the door, pushed it wider. It was a small bedroom, a dresser against one wall, a closet. There was a single lamp atop a nightstand, a nylon scarf thrown over the shade, bathing the room in a bluish light.

She had her back to him, was going through the nightstand drawer. She came out with a blue candle in a glass, a pack of matches. She lit it, set it on the nightstand. The flame flickered, and after a moment, the smell of jasmine drifted over to him.

"There we go," she said, switching the lamp off and turning to face him. Shadows fell against the wall, danced.

"You don't have to stay," she said. "I'll understand."

He was frozen.

"You could leave right now," she said. "I wouldn't blame you."

He shook his head. She came closer and he smelled fresh perfume, vanilla musk.

He touched the side of her face lightly, felt her tremble as he trailed his hand down her throat, her collarbone. He could feel the pulse of her, the thump of her heart.

He leaned close and their lips met, hers opening under his. He tasted the sweetness of the wine, broke off the kiss to look at her. She met his eyes as he undid one button on her sweater, then another, exposing the sheer black bra beneath. He reached inside, cupped her warmth, felt her nipple harden. She closed her eyes.

He held the edges of the sweater, tugged gently, and the rest of the buttons undid themselves. One popped off, landed on the bed. He kissed her again, both hands on her now, and slipped the sweater off her shoulders, let it fall silently to the floor. She leaned into him, eyes still closed, mouth open. He tasted her tongue, cupped her buttocks through the jeans. She began to pull at his belt, unsnapping, unzipping, kissing him harder, hungry. He reached back with one hand and gently pushed the door shut.

IT HAD started to snow lightly, flakes blowing up against the window. She had found three more candles in Jack and Reggie's room, along with a package of condoms. The room was filled with a yellow glow, flickering shadows.

He got up, walked naked to the window, the floor cold under his feet. He held the curtain aside and looked down at the quiet street, the Mustang already covered with a dusting of snow.

When he looked back at her she was lying on her side in the tangled sheets, her bare back to him. He could see the yellow and red butterfly just above the cleft of her buttocks.

"Is it snowing?" she said.

"Yes."

"Almost Christmas. The year's gone by so fast."

He went back to bed and she slid over to give him room. He lay on his left side, propped on an elbow, looking at her, put a hand on her hip. He thought of Cristina, imagined for a moment it was her beside him.

She rolled to face him. Candlelight glinted off the small gold ring in her navel.

"How long has it been since you've been with someone?" she said.

"A long time."

"I could tell. For me too, hard as that is to imagine. You're the first man I've slept with since I've been back here. That's the truth."

"I'm flattered."

"Not that much, I hope. It's not like you're part of an exclusive club, you know."

"You don't need to talk about that. About then."

"Sorry. It just feels strange. I used to do it for a living once. And then I stopped doing it altogether."

"So what's strange?"

"This was different. I wanted to be with you because I liked you, was attracted to you."

He reached beneath the sheet, ran his palm along the smoothness of her thigh.

"Nothing else?" he said.

"And I guess, to a certain extent, because I wanted to thank you. For caring. Does that bother you?"

"No, not at all."

"I hope you weren't disappointed."

"What do you mean?"

"Men I met—in California—when they knew I was in the business, they expected some sort of three-ring circus in bed. Especially if they saw some of the movies I was in. They never seemed to understand I was acting."

"Like I said, you don't have to tell me about that. Any of it. It doesn't matter to me."

"You say that, but I'd bet you on some level it does. And I'm sure you were happy when you saw those." She nodded at the open condom packets on the nightstand. "You can't tell me you weren't thinking about that. What I might have."

He didn't answer. She folded a pillow behind her, sat back against the headboard.

"How do you feel?" she said.

"What do you mean?"

"Guilty?"

"I don't know."

"Don't let yourself get deluded," she said. "About this. Don't let it screw anything else up."

He tugged the sheet gently down to expose her right breast, kissed it, ran his tongue around the nipple, felt her respond. There was a thin pale scar about three inches long that curled up from under her breast, visible only from the side. He kissed the skin there, traced the outline of the scar with his tongue.

"Do you know what that's from?" she said.

"I think so."

"When I got out there, everybody told me I should have it done. It took me two months to raise the money. Then, just before I came back here, I went to the same doctor, had him take them out."

"Why?"

"Because I didn't want them anymore, didn't need them. And I'd forgotten what I looked like without them."

He cupped her breast.

"I like them just the way they are," he said.

He kissed her upper arm, her shoulder, felt goose bumps rise beneath his lips.

She touched his stomach, his scar.

"This is where you were shot."

"Yes."

"Did you almost die?"

"Yes. Almost."

She rolled toward him, onto her stomach, traced her fingers down his chest and then splayed her hand over the scar as if to heal it.

"What happened to him? The man who did it."

"It was a woman."

"Did they catch her?"

"I shot her. She died."

She took her hand away.

"I'm sorry."

He shook his head slowly, took her hand, kissed it. She looked at him and then leaned forward, kissed his chest, his stomach, his scar, her tongue lingering there, warm and wet. He felt himself thicken. He reached beneath the sheet, touched her where she was damp. She closed her eyes and he dragged the sheet slowly off her, her skin a pale yellow in the candlelight.

He kissed the nape of her neck, felt her tremble, traced his lips down the bumps of her spine. He kissed the butterfly, flicking his tongue against the ink, tasting the salt sweat of her skin.

Outside the window, snowflakes spiraled up, lifted by the wind. They touched gently against the glass without leaving a mark, and were blown back out into the night.

TWENTY-FOUR

JOHNNY PULLED UP TO THE WAREHOUSE DOOR, WAITED, THE FIREBIRD idling. He flashed his brights and the door began to roll up. There were lights inside, forms silhouetted in them. He opened the glove box, the Sig there in easy reach.

He drove into the warehouse slowly. Ahead, parked on the concrete floor, was the black Explorer and Lindell's Lexus jeep. Viktor the Russian stood between them.

Johnny pulled up in front of the Explorer, shut the engine off, watched the garage door slide closed in the rearview.

Beyond the vehicles was a waist-high guardrail protecting a spiral metal staircase that ran up to a glass-walled office. There were lights inside and the door was open. He saw Lindell come to the glass, look down at him.

To the right was a break room with wide windows, fluorescent lights, vending machines against the wall. There was no one inside that he could see.

The Russian turned away as if uninterested, sat on the guardrail and lit a cigarette.

Johnny got out of the car, left the door slightly open. Lindell and Joey Alea came out of the office, down the stairs. It was the first he'd seen Joey since the meeting in the Escalade.

Joey came toward him, his arms wide. Johnny stepped in, took the embrace.

"Lindell told me what happened," Joey said. "But you're okay, that's the important part. That's all that matters."

Joey nodded at the break room.

"Come on," he said. "Let's go in there. More room."

204

Lindell went in without waiting for them. There were three long tables inside, plastic chairs. Lindell dug in his pocket for change, fed it into one of the machines. There was the whir of a motor then a pop and hiss. He slid a plastic door open, took out a paper cup of coffee.

"There've been some developments," Joey said. "Some ramifications you need to know about. Have a seat."

Johnny pulled a chair away from the table, sat down.

"This is something I didn't anticipate," Joey said. He pulled a chair out, sat down, put his elbows on his knees and began to rub his forehead, looking at the floor. For the first time Johnny noticed the strands of gray in his hair.

Lindell leaned against the machine, sipped his coffee, waited. His face gave nothing away.

"It's the old man," Joey said.

"What about him?"

"He's not happy. It has to do with that thing in South Jersey."

"I thought he was leaving you alone."

"I don't know what the fuck's gotten into him. He had that Frankie Santelli come by the mortgage office yesterday. I mean, the place where I fucking do *business*. Like he didn't care."

"What did he want?"

"Frankie said all of the sudden there's a lot of heat. Some Feds came to talk to Tony at his house, including a DEA guy. Says it's the first time the G has bothered Tony at his house in years."

"Why would they do that?"

"I don't know. Frankie asked me the same thing. I said, 'How the fuck should I know?' But this fuckin' guy . . . he's like a walking *malocchio*. He just looks at me like I know more than I'm telling and he knows it."

Johnny shrugged, got his cigarettes out, lit one. Outside, the Russian was sitting in the front seat of the Explorer, door open, playing the radio.

"So you're scared," Johnny said.

"Scared? *Fuck* him."

Johnny blew smoke out, waited.

"Frankie passed on a message," Joey said. "The old man wants to talk with me, face-to-face."

"And?"

Joey looked at Lindell.

"You believe this guy," he said. "Nothing fazes him, huh? I tell him Tony Acuna wants to talk with me and all he says is 'And?'"

"He's your uncle," Johnny said. "Whatever goes on between the two of you is just that. It's got nothing to do with me."

"You think it's that easy?" Joey said. "You're with me. You think my uncle doesn't know that? He knows you're out, you're back here. He might get the wrong idea."

"Which is?"

"That I brought you up here so I could make some kind of move against him. If he thinks that, he might try to move first."

Johnny shook his head.

"What?" Joey said.

"This whole thing. All this 'friend of ours, friend of mine' bull-shit. I thought you were done with it, anyway."

"It isn't that easy."

Johnny looked at Lindell. A single drop of sweat had crept out of his pomaded hair, was crawling down his left cheek.

"So you're thinking," Johnny said, "maybe you go to this meeting and you don't come back?"

Joey said nothing.

"When is it?"

"Monday night."

"Where?"

"Down the Shore. Long Branch. Some locksmith shop. Friend of my uncle owns it."

"You know the place?"

"Yeah."

"So we get there early, take a look around."

Joey looked at Lindell, smiled.

"See, already he's thinking," he said. Lindell didn't respond.

"You think I'd let you go alone? Leave you out in the wind?" Johnny said.

"No. I didn't. But it feels good to hear you say it."

"Who's going to be there?"

"My uncle. Some of my uncle's people, probably. Santelli, I'm sure."

"And he said just you?"

"Just me. I can bring a driver but he can't come in."

"Now that shit right there worries me already," Lindell said.

"Things go bad while you're inside, there's not much we can do about it," Johnny said.

"You can make sure that, if I don't come out of there alive, no one else does either."

"Why would I want to do that?"

"Because if I get clipped, you and Lindell are next. My uncle wouldn't want you around, not know what you were planning, whether you were going to come back at him in some way—"

"Now, wait a minute . . ." Lindell said.

Joey looked at him.

"What? You think it'll be some other way? You want to go to my uncle, throw yourself on his mercy, go ahead. I'm just telling you the way it is. I go, we all go. And I'm sure I don't have to remind you, both of you"—he looked at Johnny—"the only juice either of you have is with me. My uncle could put paper out on your heads tomorrow and no one would care, no one would speak for you. Hell, I'm blood, his sister's son, and for all I know, right now he's got someone digging a grave for me down in Ocean County."

He got up from the chair, went over to the window, looked out onto the warehouse floor. Johnny pinched out his cigarette, put it back in his pocket.

"Thought you were all done with this, didn't you?" he said to Joey's back. "You thought it was all just going to be real-estate deals and counting money from here on."

Joey didn't answer.

Johnny stood up.

"Have Lindell call me tomorrow, at the motel. We'll work out the specifics. I'll need some things."

Joey turned to him.

"I knew you wouldn't let me down, John."

Johnny shrugged.

"You keep forgetting," he said. "I owe you."

AT A rest stop on the Turnpike, he pulled up to a bank of outdoor phones, rolled down the window. Tractor trailers idled in the lot beyond. He dialed Connor's beeper, then punched in the number of the phone, hung up and waited. It rang almost immediately.

"Yeah?" Connor said.

"I've got something for you, straight up. But you better have something for me too."

"I do."

Johnny breathed out.

"What's going on?" Connor said.

"I just met with him, up in Newark, some warehouse near the port."

"You should have called me beforehand. We could have gotten you set up."

"No time."

"So what happened?"

"Some beef with his uncle. Over the Pine Barrens thing. He's worried."

"He should be."

"He says his uncle got visited by some federal men."

"I know."

"How's that?"

"I sent them."

Johnny watched a truck roll out of the lot, back onto the Turnpike.

"Why would you do that?" he said finally.

"I can't just wait around, sitting on my hands, for you to come up with something. I wanted to rattle Joey's cage a little bit. So I put together a bogus CI report that said Tony Acuna knew something about that meth lab going up in flames. I made sure it got copied to the right people. Then I just sat back and waited."

"You should have told me."

"Why? If I'd been getting useful reports from you, I wouldn't have had to make one up."

"I might have been in danger."

"Hey, you told me you had nothing to do with it, remember?"

"You played me."

"And you haven't been playing me?"

He didn't answer.

"So, what's the deal?" Connor said. "His uncle want to meet?"

"Yeah."

"When?"

"This week. Somewhere down the Shore. I don't know where."

"Yes, you do. Or if you don't now, you will. No way Joey Alea's walking into a meeting with his uncle and you're not around somewhere. He'd be too worried about coming out of there with half a dick."

"He didn't give me the specifics. He's calling me tomorrow."

"And you're going?"

"He wants me to."

"Who else?"

"Lindell. Maybe this Russian Joey has working for him."

"Viktor Ismayla."

"I didn't get his name."

"We know who he is. Out of Brighton Beach. He's a nobody."

"You know all this, why you need me?"

"I've asked myself the same thing."

He lit a cigarette.

"What have you got for me?"

"An address. You got something to write with?"

"Hold on."

He opened the glove box, pushed the Sig aside, found a cracked ballpoint pen, an envelope. He scribbled on the paper until the ink started to come.

"Okay," he said.

"Before I give you this, let me emphasize something, John. I don't know what you're planning on doing—"

"I just want to see him. Once. That's all."

"Let me finish. I had to call in a lot of favors to get this, bend some rules. My ass is on the line here. Now, you want to make contact with that boy, see him, that's one thing. You try to take him, harm or threaten the parents at all, that's something else. If that happens, I will turn the full resources of the Bureau over to finding you and making sure you go back to prison for a long time. We understood on that?"

He blew smoke out.

"Yeah."

"Good. I'm taking a big chance here. And I'm trusting you."

"Let's have it."

"George and Lynda Haynes," Connor read off. "Twenty-two Eleven Green Bay Road, Lake Bluff, Illinois."

Johnny wrote it down.

"What's his name?" he said.

"What?"

"You saw the file, right? The whole thing?"

"Yes."

"What's his name? What do they call him?"

Connor sighed.

"Matthew," he said finally.

Matthew, Johnny thought. *A good name. Matt.*

"Let me tell you how this is going to work," Connor said. "Are you listening?"

Matt Harrow.

"Yeah."

"You're going to call me when that meet's set up. And then we're going to get you wired. This is nonnegotiable."

"I understand."

"You ready to do what needs to be done?"

"Yes. I am."

"Good. The sooner the better."

"I'll call you."

"Oh, yeah, and one other thing. I almost forgot."

"What?"

"The mother."

"What about her?"

"You know she was with Joey for a while, right?"

He watched the trucks in the distance, didn't answer.

"At this point, you probably don't care anyway, though, right?"

"Tell me."

"Maybe some other time."

"Tell me now."

"After you went away, things got tough for her, with the baby coming and all. Hard to make ends meet, you know? Doctor bills, hospital, rent. So she went to Joey."

"That's what I told her to do."

"I guessed. So yeah, he helped her out. Put her up in an apartment. He used to visit her, if you know what I mean. We were watching him all the time then, but he didn't know it. Pretty ballsy of that guy, huh, mess with the woman of someone who'd just gone to prison for him? The guy's ego is huge."

"Why are you telling me this?"

"Come on, John. You can't tell me you didn't suspect it. You know the kind of guy Alea is. Nothing's free with him. Everything comes with a price."

"What happened?"

"What do you think? He got bored with her, started nailing some nineteen-year-old who was dancing at one of his other clubs. He and Nikki got into some pretty good fights over the phone about it. We've got a bunch of them on tape if you want to hear them someday."

"Go on."

"Finally he shipped her off to California, get her out of his hair, I guess. He paid her way, got her started. He knew some people out there in the fuck-film business. It was a natural fit. She leaves it all behind, goes out to the coast, makes some movies. Everybody's happy."

Johnny said nothing.

"You mean you didn't know all this already? Sorry to break it to you, John. I thought you did."

"What else?"

"Not much. I did have a look at those field office files, though, from Florida, after you got taken down. Odd, isn't it? That sting operation down there, nothing to do with you, and you walk right into it, bam?"

"What are you saying?"

"Doesn't take a genius to figure it out. They knew you were coming. It was in the files. They got an anonymous tip—phone call—that someone was coming down from Jersey to take Cardosa out. Now who could have made that call?"

Johnny didn't answer.

"He punked you. Face it, John. I'm the only one who's ever given a shit what happened to you over the last eight years. Just me, no one else. When you realize that, all of this will go easier."

"I'll call you tomorrow."

"You may think I'm winding you up, but I'm not. I'm just letting

211

you know what the situation was. In case you have any doubts that you're doing the right thing. Because you are. You know that, don't you?"

"Yeah," Johnny said. "I do."

BACK AT the motel, he smoked another cigarette out on the balcony, watched the ocean. He thought of Nikki and Joey Alea, Joey struggling to remember her name at that first meeting above the porn shop.

He scaled the cigarette away, went back inside. He sat on the bed, pulled the phone into his lap and punched nine for an outside line. He got the envelope out, dialed Information and got the Chicago area code. When he reached the Chicago operator, he gave her the name and address, had her read the number back to him twice while he wrote it down. Then he hung up, called, got an answering machine. A man's voice read the number back, said no one was home. Before the beep, the phone was picked up.

"Yes?" The same voice. Dead air, then a woman in the background, asking who was on the phone.

"Hello?" the man said.

Johnny set the receiver back down.

TWENTY-FIVE

Errol leaned back in his chair until it creaked, feet up on the desk. He lobbed the football easily and Harry caught it without getting up. They were in Ray's side office, where they each had a metal desk and phone, shared a single computer terminal against the wall when they needed it. The rest of the office was lunchtime quiet.

"You're in a pretty good mood this morning," Errol said. "If I didn't know you better, I'd say you were smiling."

Harry hefted the football, tossed it back.

"That mean you had a good night?" Errol said.

Harry's desk phone rang, saved him from having to respond. He picked it up.

"Hi," she said.

He felt the smile come to his face. Errol was flipping the football into the air, catching it, watching him.

"I tried your home phone," she said, "but there was no answer. So I called here and they switched me to this extension. I hope it's okay."

"Sure," he said. "It's fine."

He held Errol's gaze. Errol took his feet from the desk, tossed the football in the air a final time, caught it. He got up, humming something to himself, went out into the corridor that led to the reception area.

Harry shifted so he wasn't facing the door.

"I'm glad you called," he said.

"I feel a little funny."

"Why?"

213

"That maybe I put you in an awkward position."

"Don't worry about it. We're adults. These things happen."

"I guess they do." A pause. "Do you regret it?"

He looked to the corridor, saw Errol walk by, still humming, carrying a paper cup of water from the cooler. He was smiling but went by without looking in.

"No," Harry said. "I don't regret anything."

"We didn't violate some sort of professional ethics code? Like one of those doctor-patient relationships?"

"Not as far as I know. I'll check on it. Get back to you."

She laughed.

"Well, I was wondering if you could stand to see me again," she said. "Maybe get some dinner."

Errol went by again, in the other direction.

"I think I could manage that," Harry said.

"Good. So when do you think we could make that happen?"

"I don't know," he said. "How about tonight?"

THE RESTAURANT was in Ocean Township, almost hidden in a strip mall. They had Italian food, glasses of wine on the table. Christmas lights blinked in the windows.

"This almost feels like a date," she said when they were finished eating. "I can't remember the last real one I had."

The waiter brought them coffee, left the check in a leather booklet. Harry slipped his credit card inside it.

"You feel bad, don't you?" she said. "About last night."

He sipped coffee.

"I don't know," he said.

"You shouldn't. It's like you said, we're adults. And anyway, I'm more to blame than you. I meant it when I said don't let this screw up anything else for you. That would be wrong."

"I know."

"And there's one thing I should make clear. About something I said last night."

"What?"

"About wanting to thank you. I'm afraid that part of it came out wrong. That it sounded like I was somehow paying you off. That's not what I meant."

"Don't worry about it."

"No, I want to get this right. It's important to me."

"Okay."

"When I said I wanted to thank you, I didn't mean for what you've done for me. I meant for the way you've treated me, the way you act toward me. You make me feel like, what I was before, the things I'd done—that they don't matter to you."

"Should they?"

"They would to most men."

"We've all done things we're not proud of, when we had to."

"You sure it's that simple?"

"To tell the truth," he said, "these days, I'm not sure of much at all."

When they left, she linked her arm through his. The night was frigid and clear, the moon bright.

"Let's walk down this way," she said. "I want to show you something. Or try to, at least."

"What?"

She didn't answer.

There was a video shop four doors down, between a Radio Shack and a vitamin store. She reached for the door.

"What are you doing?" he said.

She ignored him, pulled the door open, an electric chime sounding within. A teenaged girl with short spiked hair and a pierced lip looked down at them from behind a high counter.

The store was almost empty. She led him between long racks of videos and DVDs until they came to the curtained-off doorway at the back, a small neon ADULT sign above it.

"No," he said.

She tugged on his arm.

"You should know," she said.

She pushed the curtain aside, looked in. There was no one inside.

"Is this really necessary?" he said.

"Come on."

They stepped through into a smaller room, about ten by twenty feet. Wall racks were lined with adult videos and DVDs, naked women and men gazing out from glossy box covers.

"Don't tell me you've never been in one of these places," she said. "I wouldn't believe it."

She let go of his elbow, started browsing the racks. He stayed where he was, near the curtain. She picked up video boxes, looked at the backs, replaced them. She carried one back to him.

"Here," she said.

He took the box. On its front was a full-color picture of a brunette in black lingerie and pearls, leaning back against the brass headboard of an old bed. The title was *Eager to Please*.

"It's pretty restrained," she said. "Compared to some of the other covers."

"I noticed."

"Higher production values too, not like most of the direct-to-video junk they shoot nowadays."

"Why are you showing this to me?"

"Turn it over."

On the back was a paragraph-long synopsis of the plot, six inset photos of different couples, most naked or close to it, making love in various positions.

"Second one from the bottom," she said.

He looked. In the picture, a naked woman with long blonde hair was kneeling on a bed, leaning back against a muscular man with her eyes closed. He was kissing her neck, one hand cupping her right breast, the other covering her pubic area. It took him a moment to recognize her. He felt his face grow warm.

"I'm surprised they still have that," she said. "It's about five years old. Usually the turnaround is much quicker. They sell the used tapes off to make room for newer titles, rougher stuff. I guess I should be grateful for that. Every year there are fewer copies out there."

There was a cast list in small type on the bottom of the back cover. "Nikki Lynn" was next to last.

"That's me," she said. "Original, huh? That was my third film. I got a thousand dollars for it. I did fourteen in all. But they get so chopped up, re-edited into compilations and best-of tapes, you never know how many are floating around out there. But I never got above fourth or fifth billing anyway. It didn't take long to play itself out."

He handed the tape back to her.

"I wanted you to know who I am," she said.

"I already did."

"Different, though, isn't it? Seeing it in color like that?"

"I guess. But I didn't need to."

"Stoic, as always. It's attractive in a strange way."

"Can we leave now?"

She ignored him, turned the box around, looking at it. She held it up again so he could see the brunette on the cover.

"You think she's attractive?" she said. "Sexy?"

"Sure."

"I did a three-way with her once. In a movie. Another one."

"You feel obligated to tell me that? I know what you did."

"You know some of it."

She replaced the video, came back and took his arm again, led him through the curtain.

"You're bright red," she said. "I'm sorry if I made you uncomfortable."

"That wasn't your intention?"

"Not entirely."

The kid at the counter ignored them as they went past and out the door.

"Sorry if I embarrassed you," she said as they walked to the Mustang. "But like I said, I wanted you to know who you were getting involved with."

"I heard you."

"I didn't want you to have any false ideas about me. Because I don't have any about myself. I could never have been a good mother, or a good wife. I know that. I'm not pretending otherwise."

"I would have taken you at your word."

"You know what they say—'Ten steps to heaven, five steps to hell.' It's always easier to do the wrong thing."

When they got to the Mustang, he unlocked the passenger-side door, held it for her, shut it. She leaned over, unlocked his side and he got in, started the engine.

"You shouldn't look so shocked, though," she said. "Porn keeps mom-and-pop stores like that in business. There will always be a market for it. It's a fantasy. A world where every woman loves sex and there's no consequences or messy emotional issues. Everyone just wants to fuck and suck their lives away. The act without the complications. That world doesn't exist. But the fantasy sells."

He pulled out of the lot and onto Route 35, heading south.

"You didn't feel exploited?" he said.

"I don't know. Maybe on some level. But I was a participant in it, not a victim. It was almost more honest than dancing, you know? And hard to believe as it might be, most of the people in the business are pretty nice. Sweet. At least at the production level. The money men, that's another situation."

"Then why'd you leave it?"

"A lot of reasons. One of them was marketability. That business ages you quickly. By the time you hit thirty, you're washed up. At least if you're a woman. And there's always another wide-eyed eighteen-year-old getting off the plane, happy to take your place."

"I can imagine."

"But you know something about those tapes? It's almost nice to have a record of yourself when you were young and attractive, before things started falling apart. When you could still compete."

"I think you made your point."

"I'm sorry. I'll shut up. Did I offend your sensibilities?"

"Don't worry about it."

"Are you religious?"

"Not very. Not these days."

"Why not?"

"I had my share of it, I guess. Twelve years of Catholic school. That's enough for anyone."

"You wear a uniform and everything?"

"Most of the time, yes."

"You must have looked cute. So what did you get out of it?"

"Out of what?"

"Twelve years of Catholic school."

He thought about that for a moment.

"I'm not sure. But I guess it cured me of Catholicism."

"No, it didn't," she said.

THEY LAY side by side, sweat cooling, her head on his chest. Candlelight flickered.

"Jack and Reggie will be back in the morning," she said. "I don't think it's a good idea if you stay tonight."

"Then I won't," he said. He stroked her hair, kissed it. He bent his left wrist so he could see his watch. Eleven o'clock.

"I should go now," he said. "Let us both get some sleep."

She turned, kissed him. He ran his hand down the smoothness of her back. She traced her lips down his jaw, the side of his neck, the hollow of his throat.

"This isn't exactly pushing me out the door," he said.

She laughed, kissed his chest, moved lower. Then, when he was ready, she swung atop him, took him deep. He arched up into her and she moaned, their shadows rising and falling against the bedroom wall.

HE LOCKED the front door behind him, zipped his leather jacket up. The frozen porch boards creaked under his feet.

He pulled his gloves on as he walked to the Mustang. He still had the smell of her on him, her taste on his tongue.

At the Mustang, he stopped and looked back at the house. He could see the warm glow of the candles in the bedroom window. Wished he were still up there.

JOHNNY LOOKED up at the lighted window, then down at the Mustang. He heard the engine start, saw the lights go on.

He was in a stolen Mazda, parked halfway down the street. He'd been out here for three hours now, in the cold, watching.

He twisted the ignition wires together and they sparked, the engine catching immediately. He watched the Mustang pull away, then looked up at the house again, saw a shape moving behind the window.

The Mustang was at the end of the street now, signaling to turn. He took a last look up at the window, then pulled away from the curb, his lights off.

TWENTY-SIX

RIVING BACK TO COLTS NECK, COLD AIR STREAMING THROUGH THE wing window, he found himself thinking of Cristina again, of their days together. Back when his life still made some kind of ragged sense.

Halfway home, he knew he'd need a drink if he wanted to sleep. He pulled into the lot of a storefront bar and liquor store on Route 33. All the diagonal spots in front were taken, so he steered into the alleyway, parked beside a Dumpster.

The bar was crowded, a sea of cigarette smoke, noise and laughter, a Christmas party in full swing. The bartender wore a Santa hat. The Ronettes' version of "Sleigh Ride" was playing on the jukebox.

Harry chose a bottle of red wine from the wall rack. A TV high on the wall was showing *It's a Wonderful Life* with the sound off. Jimmy Stewart running down a snow-covered street past bars and dance halls, flashing neon signs.

He paid for the wine at the bar, pocketed his change and went back out into the cold, the bottle in a paper sack in the crook of his left elbow.

At the Mustang, he got his keys out, sniffed the air. Cigarette smoke. Close.

He turned just as the figure stepped out from behind the Dumpster, still in shadow. On the wall above, a security light flickered.

"Hey," the figure said. "Got a light?"

He let the wine bottle slide easily down into his hand, grasped its neck through the paper. The man's face was still hidden, but Harry could see jeans, heavy work boots, a dark army jacket. A hand came up into the light, holding an unlit cigarette.

"Sorry," Harry said. "I don't smoke." He unlocked the driver's-side door.

"Too bad," the man said. He took a lighter out, flicked it open. It flared, the flame illuminating his face for an instant.

Harrow.

The lighter clicked shut, went away. The tip of the cigarette glowed. Harry stepped slightly away from the Mustang to give himself room, let the bottle hang at his side, half hidden by his leg.

"Nice car," Harrow said. He stepped out of the shadows, hands empty, looking at the Mustang, the cigarette hanging from his lips.

Harry watched him, waited.

"So tell me something," Harrow said.

"What?"

"Are you fucking her?"

Silence between them. Harrow grinned, no humor in it. He nodded at the bottle in the bag.

"You going to hit me with that?"

Harry didn't answer.

"Shame to waste it, whatever it is."

The alley light buzzed, flickered.

"Why don't you just step back from the car?" Harry said.

Harrow raised his hands, backed away.

"Sorry," he said.

"I know who you are. So cut the bullshit. Just walk away."

Harrow nodded, took another half step back, looked at the ground, pushed at gravel with the toe of his boot. Harry hefted his keys in his right hand, ready to throw them.

Harrow took the cigarette out of his mouth, blew on the tip until it flared. Then he flicked it casually onto the back window of the Mustang. It burst into sparks on the glass, rolled onto the trunk and lay there glowing.

Harry looked at it. He'd have to cross in front of Harrow to knock it off. A school yard game, a line in the sand.

Harry let his breath out slowly, centering himself. He set the bottle upright on the roof, shifted the keys to his left hand. With his right, he reached out, plucked the butt off the trunk lid, saw the penny-size burn it left on the paint.

Harry looked at the cigarette, turned back to Harrow.

"Talk about a waste," he said. "There's plenty of tobacco left here." And he flicked the cigarette at those blue eyes.

Harrow jerked his head back, but not in time. The cigarette hit his left cheekbone, ashes flying. Harry grabbed the bottle, swung it backhanded as Harrow came forward. The bottle thudded into an upraised arm and Harry punched with his left, keys angled out from between his fingers. He felt them scrape flesh and then pressure exploded in his left knee, bent it inward. He went down, dropped the bottle, heard it shatter, took a knee to the chest that flung him back up against the car.

He tried to roll away, caught a kick in the low ribs that stole his breath. Harrow loomed over him and Harry saw him pull something from beneath his coat. He heard the snick of metal, a slide being racked back.

"Cock *sucker*," Harrow said and pointed the gun at his head. Harry looked into the muzzle of a suppressor, smelled gun oil.

Harrow touched the cut on his cheek just below his left eye. His fingertips came away bloody. His gloved finger tightened on the trigger.

Harry turned his face away, the suppressor inches from his right temple.

"I should," Harrow said. "I fucking should."

When the shot didn't come, Harry turned, looked up at him again.

Harrow snapped his wrist and the steel suppressor cracked against the bridge of Harry's nose. Water filled his eyes, pain shooting back through his sinuses. He put his hand to his face and blood came from his nostrils.

The alley light flickered. Harrow's face fell into shadow, lit up again.

The suppressor touched Harry's forehead, pushed his head back against the car. He could taste blood in his mouth. Harrow crouched, reached around and pulled Harry's wallet from his jeans. He took the gun away, sat back on his haunches, looked through the wallet. He came out with Harry's driver's license, read it, looked back at him.

"I should have known," he said. "That lying bitch."

He dropped the license on the blacktop, the smell of wine rising around them.

"Now I know who *you* are," Harrow said. "I know where you live. I know the car you drive. I know every fucking thing I need to know if I want to find you."

Harry coughed, spit blood onto the blacktop.

"So I'll ask again. Are. You. Fucking. Her?"

Harry looked at him, didn't respond.

"A gentleman," Harrow said. He let the hammer down on the gun, slid it into a jacket pocket. From the other he took a folded Buck knife.

"But you know what they say." He opened the knife. The alley light glinted on the blade. "About virtue untested."

Harry watched the knife.

"Open your legs," Harrow said.

"Fuck you."

Harrow's left hand closed around his throat, pushed his head back. He jabbed him on the inside of his right thigh with the point of the knife. It punched through the material of his jeans, broke the surface of his skin. Harry's leg jerked away involuntarily and he felt the warmth of blood on his skin.

"That's better," Harrow said and pushed the tip of the blade into Harry's jeans just below his scrotum, the blade angled up. The point broke through the material.

"I wouldn't move if I were you," Harrow said. "I wouldn't even twitch."

Harry could feel the knifepoint against his skin.

"I'll ask a third and final time. Are you fucking her?"

Harry looked into his eyes.

"No," he said.

The knife jerked up, slicing easily through the material of the jeans, from seat to zipper. Coldness flooded in.

Harrow took the knife away, closed it.

"I'm not sure if I believe you," he said. "But you should know this. She's taken, partner. Trust me. I don't know what she told you, what she wants from you, but you have to ask yourself if it's worth getting your balls sliced off. Is it?"

He put the knife away.

"Because I promise you that is what will happen if I catch you around her again."

Harrow rose, took the gun back out. Harry could hear his knees creak.

"Or maybe I'm making a mistake, letting you go," he said. "Maybe I should tie this up right now."

He flicked Harry's nose with the suppressor, then touched it to his upper lip, pressed until his head touched the car again, lip mashed back against his teeth. Harry could taste oil and gunpowder. The suppressor moved down, scraped against his teeth, pushed into them. He kept his jaws clamped.

"Don't want to give it up, huh?" Harrow said. "Good for you."

He took the gun away. Harry tasted fresh blood.

"Next time," Harrow said, "we won't dance. We'll just get to it."

The gun disappeared under his jacket again.

"You may think you know me," he said. "But believe me, you don't."

Harry felt blood in his throat, gagged. He leaned to the side and vomited, a thin fluid of blood and bile and stomach enzymes. He coughed, spit. When he looked back, the alley was empty.

HE PULLED into an Exxon station on Route 33, left the engine running while he got out, fed change into a pay phone next to the air machine. He dialed the number Sherry had given him, waited. The air hose hissed behind him.

She answered on the third ring.

"Hey, baby," he said.

Silence.

He watched cars go by, heard her breathing.

"Long time," he said. "Nothing to say to me?"

"Johnny."

"You knew I'd find you, right? That it was only a matter of time?"

"How did you get this number?"

"Does it matter? One way or another I would have found it, found you."

"Where are you?"

"Close. We need to talk, babe."

"I don't think that's a good idea."

"You scared of me? You shouldn't be. Everything that happened back then . . . it's forgotten. You want to get on with your life, I understand. That's fine. But you owe it to me, to meet me face-to-face. One time. That's all I'm asking."

"Johnny, I don't have anything to tell you. Nothing I can say is going to change—"

"Face-to-face, Nicole. You can't deny me that. Seven years is a long time. How do you think it feels, after all that, coming back, finding the mother of my child with another man?"

"Another man? What are you talking about?"

"Don't fucking lie to me, Nicole. After all this time, please don't fucking lie to me."

"Johnny, what did you do?"

"Not much. He didn't put up much of a fight. But I don't think he's going to be coming around anymore. Look at it this way: I did you a favor. You can do better than him."

"Why, Johnny? Jesus Christ, why?"

"Because you and I need to have a serious conversation. And the last thing I need is some boyfriend of the moment running around with a hard-on, thinks he's protecting you. I don't have time for that bullshit, Nicole. This is between you and me."

She didn't answer.

"Come on, babe," he said. "You knew this day would come. Don't pretend otherwise."

"What do you want?"

"To talk, like I said. Get some things straight. Give me that. Then you can do whatever you want, with whoever. I'll leave you alone, you'll never see me again."

"Why did you come back?"

"Things to do. But once they're done, I'm gone. I'll call you tomorrow night at nine at this number. You make sure you answer.

226

We'll work it out, arrange a place to meet. If not, then I have to come find you, and neither of us wants that."

"Don't stay, Johnny. Leave. Tonight. For your own sake. There's nothing for you here anymore."

"Maybe," he said. "Maybe not."

"Nothing at all."

"Tomorrow," he said and hung up.

He got back into the Mazda, pulled out onto the highway. He was breathing normally again, his hands steady.

One more stop to make.

TWENTY-SEVEN

YOU NEED TO GO TO THE HOSPITAL," RAY SAID. "X-RAYS."

Harry shook his head, limped into the kitchen and got the ice trays out of the freezer. He spread a dish towel on the counter, emptied the trays onto it.

"There's nothing broken," he said. "I can tell. Are you sure she's safe?"

"I sent Errol and another man over as soon as you called me from the bar. "They'll spend the night parked outside. No sign of Harrow so far. Tomorrow we'll take her to a hotel, check her in."

He twisted the towel around the ice, pulled up a kitchen chair, rolled up the leg of the sweatpants. The ruined jeans were in the trash.

"Sorry to wake you up," he said. "But I didn't want to wait."

"I understand. This changes everything, though. You know that, right?"

Harry settled the ice pack on his swollen knee, held it there.

"This looks worse than it is," he said.

"Well, it looks pretty bad. And you ain't kissing anybody with that lip anytime soon either."

"He was just trying to scare me off."

"And did he?"

"What do you think?"

Ray pulled up a chair, sat down.

"We should talk strategy here. She told Errol that Harrow said he was going to call her tomorrow. That he wanted to meet."

"Not much chance of that."

"Maybe we should let her take that call. Set something up."

228

"Why?"

"So we can get the locals involved. Arrest him for assault, battery. Gun charge. Enough to send him back."

Harry shook his head.

"What?" Ray said. "You want to take this further? Keep fucking around with him, see what he does next? Enough."

"I'm not going to the locals. Not for some bullshit assault charge he'll walk on overnight."

"And then when he parks a bullet in your brain, you'll leave it up to me to deal with, right?"

"Like I said. He was just trying to scare me."

"You've got fingermarks on your throat. You know that?"

Harry touched the tender spot under his jaw.

"They'll go away."

"How did he find you?"

"He followed me from her house, that's all I can figure."

"And how did he know where she lived?"

"I don't know."

"And I'm not supposed to ask what you were doing there, ten-thirty at night?"

"You can ask." He put the ice pack on the table, got up and limped to the refrigerator, took a Corona out. He waved the bottle at Ray, who shook his head. He twisted the top off, sipped, sat back down.

"I don't know if I want to ask," Ray said. "Because I'm worried what the answer is going to be. Are you nailing her?"

Harry looked at him.

"What?" Ray said. "That's a simple question."

"He asked me the same thing."

"And we both hope the answer is no, I'm sure. What did you tell him?"

Harry put the beer on the table, the ice pack back on his knee, didn't answer.

"Okay," Ray said. "But you know I've got to take you off this now, right?"

"Why?"

"If you can't figure that out, then I think he scrambled your brains as well. There's Errol, and others. We'll look after her."

"You're missing the point. This makes things easier."

"How's that?"

"Now we've got bait. For him."

"Bait? What bait?"

"Me."

"That is total bullshit," Ray said. He stood up. "And you don't get to call the shots on this anyway. I do."

"This guy isn't going to wait around, bide his time, Ray. He's got an agenda and he's on the move. This was just the beginning."

"More reason to keep you out of the picture."

"He's got to be stopped. One way or another."

"He will be."

"I'm the best chance we've got of finding him again."

"And that's something you're anxious to do? It doesn't look like that first meeting went too well."

Harry touched the bridge of his nose, tested the soreness there. He hadn't told Ray about the knife, or the wallet.

"He had an advantage. Surprise. Next time he won't."

"You hope."

"Well," Harry said. "We'll just see what happens, won't we?"

AFTER RAY left, he checked the front and back door locks, then limped upstairs to the bedroom. In the closet, he pushed clothes aside until he found the leather gun case against the wall. He pulled it out, set it on the bed, unzipped it. Inside was the Model 1300 Winchester twelve-gauge pump he'd bought the year before.

He got the box of shells from the top shelf of the closet, spilled them out on the bed. He took the sportsman's plug from the magazine, fed five thick red shells into the receiver. Bracing the butt on his right thigh, he worked the pump to chamber a shell, slid another into the receiver to replace it.

With the safety on, he carried the gun downstairs. There was a closet in the short hallway between kitchen and living room. He cleared the top shelf, set the shotgun there within easy reach, covered it with a folded blanket. He wasn't sure if it made him feel better or not.

Later, he lay in bed with the lights out, the whole thing playing through his mind again. There was a dull ache across the bridge of his nose, and when he touched it his eyes stung and filled with water.

When he couldn't take it any longer, he got out of bed, walked down the dark hall to the bathroom. He pulled the light cord, looked at himself in the mirror. There was a patch of purple bruise between his eyes, the skin around it still slightly swollen. His upper lip was puffy, scabbed with dried blood where it had split. He traced fingertips along the marks on his throat, remembered how Harrow's hand had felt there, his grip like stone.

He got the Percocet bottle from the cabinet, shook one out. He started to break it in half, then stopped. He swallowed it whole instead, washed it down with water from the sink. Then he switched the light off, walked back to his bed in the darkness.

TWENTY-EIGHT

COPE," JOHNNY SAID.

The Russian unwrapped it from the chamois, handed it over, watching. Johnny fit it into the runner atop the AR-15, slid and locked it into place. He wore rubber surgical gloves, could feel the coolness of the metal through them.

"Is good, no?" the Russian said. "Like M-16?"

He didn't answer. They were sitting on the floor of a storage room on the third level of an old house that had been converted into offices. The only illumination came from the parking lot lights.

He pulled the black gym bag toward him, took out one of the loaded clips. With the rifle in his lap, he thumbed the shells out one by one, rubbed his thumb along the polished tips. They were 7.62s with full metal jackets, one-shot stops anywhere in the body. He tested the springs in the clip, then began to fit the shells back in. He'd never used the rifle before, but he knew what it could do. He slid the clip home again.

"Have a look out the window," he said. "See if they're there yet. Be careful."

Viktor stood, went to the window that looked out on the parking lot, parted the blinds with a finger.

"Not yet," he said.

Johnny stood up, his knees aching, leaned the rifle against the wall.

"Help me with the desk," he said.

They hauled it from the center of the room, pushed it toward the window, raising dust. He felt the Russian's eyes on him. When he looked down, he saw the patch of dried day-old blood on his jeans leg, the size of a half dollar. He hadn't noticed it before. Had worn the jeans all day without knowing it was there.

He pushed the blinds aside, looked out. Across the parking lot was the back door of the locksmith shop, one window lit. Snow flurries flew in the parking lot lights.

There were metal folding chairs along the wall. He opened one, dragged it to the desk, sat down. Viktor took another, straddled it.

"They come soon, I think," he said. He tapped his watch. "Is time."

Johnny looked over the gun, engaged the safety, then set it on the desk, lit a cigarette.

"One for me," Viktor said. Johnny ignored him.

Fifteen minutes later, they saw headlights in the parking lot. Johnny went to the window, parted the blinds again. A dull black Cadillac and a gray Lincoln Town Car cruised slowly through the lot, parked behind the locksmith shop, facing it. Their headlights went off.

"Stay down," Johnny said. He pulled the cord, raised the blinds halfway, then tugged the window up. There was no screen. Cold air swirled into the room.

There were heavy plat books atop a filing cabinet and he carried two of them to the desk, stacked them, sat back down. As he watched, another light went on in the back of the shop.

He rested the front stock of the AR-15 on the books, shifted his chair until he got the angle right. He fit the butt against his shoulder, looked through the scope. He twisted the focus dial until the scene below leaped into clarity. He tracked the crosshairs across the back door of the shop, lingered over the lighted windows.

Car doors opened. He watched men get out, two from the Town Car, three from the Cadillac. One of the three was Tony Acuna.

As he watched through the scope, the back door of the shop opened and someone greeted them from inside. The two from the Town Car went in while Acuna waited outside with the others. He spoke to a man with silver-gray hair combed straight back, a top-coat and scarf. Frankie Santelli.

Johnny let the crosshairs drift over them. Acuna wore a heavy coat, thick glasses, a hat with a feather in it, leaned on a cane. If Johnny were to fire, he knew he would have to compensate for the angle, aim high, take into account the bullet's drop. He had a sudden image of the heavy shell striking home, vaporizing skull and skin, Acuna's body catapulting forward, nearly headless when he hit the ground.

The two Town Car men came back out. There was a brief discussion and all five went into the shop, closed the door behind them.

He set the gun on its side, sat back.

"Is him?" the Russian said. The room was cold enough now that his words misted in the air.

Johnny didn't answer, zipped his field jacket up, buttoned the collar.

Five minutes later, he saw Joey's Escalade pull into the lot. It parked sideways, using two spots. The headlights went off.

The cell phone in Johnny's pocket trilled. He opened it.

"Yeah?"

"We're here," Lindell said.

"I can see that. Acuna's in there. Four others too."

He heard Joey take the phone.

"You have a clear shot?" he said. Johnny could hear the tension in his voice.

"Yes."

"If this goes bad, I want you to open up on those motherfuckers as soon as they come out the door. All of them. You understand?"

"Easy shots," he said.

"Good. 'Cause remember what I said. My uncle won't take any chances. If I go, we all go." The call ended.

He put the phone on the desktop, set his cigarette on the edge, lifted the gun again, put his eye to the scope.

For a few moments, there was no movement from the Escalade. Then both front doors opened, Lindell getting out from the driver's side, Joey from the other. Johnny squinted into the scope, could see their breath. The back door of the shop opened, threw warm light onto the blacktop. They went to the door, spoke with someone there. Johnny could see a hand come out, touch Lindell's chest. More talking and then Lindell turned around, went back to the Escalade. Joey went inside the shop and the door closed behind him.

Lindell got back behind the wheel, and Johnny saw the plume of exhaust as he started the engine. Lindell would be running the heater, waiting, nervous. He let the gun rest again, took his cigarette from the edge of the desk. The cell phone rang. He picked it up.

"Yeah?"

"He's in," Lindell said.

"I saw. You should stay off the phone. Someone'll look out a window, see you, wonder who you're talking to."

"I don't like this, man. This waiting."

"No way around it. Sit tight. If they were going to take Joey out, they wouldn't have left you outside. They would have let you go in with him, done you both."

"I still don't like it."

"Follow the plan."

He ended the call, put the phone back on the desk.

"What's wrong?" the Russian said.

Johnny shook his head, picked up the rifle, leaned into it, feeling the coldness of the stock against his cheek. Through the scope he could see figures moving behind the lighted shop windows.

After twenty minutes, the back door opened again. Joey came out alone. He went to the Escalade, pulled open the passenger door and climbed up. The headlights came on as it pulled away.

The phone trilled again. Johnny set the rifle down, answered it.

"Get out of there," Joey said, anger in his voice. "Clean the place up after yourself. Meet me at the warehouse."

"What happened?"

"I'll tell you there." He ended the call.

Johnny looked at the phone, closed it. The Russian was on his feet, watching him.

Johnny picked up the rifle, ejected the clip, worked the bolt to clear the breech. A shell clattered out onto the table. He fit it back into the clip.

"We go?" the Russian said.

"We go."

JOEY WAS pacing the break room. Johnny was in the same chair he'd had last time. Lindell sat across the table, watching Joey.

"That son of a bitch," Joey said. "That cocksucking old *bastard.*"

He picked up a metal napkin dispenser, hurled it across the

room. It hit a soda machine with a loud clang, bounced off and fell to the floor.

"What's the deal?" Johnny said. "How much?"

Joey wheeled on him.

"How much? Two hundred and fifty fucking K, that's how much. Can you believe that?"

"Could be worse." He took his cigarettes out. "A couple days ago you were worried about even coming out of there alive."

"That's beside the point. That old bastard wants two hundred five from me—*my* money, that *I've* earned—to keep the peace."

"It's the nature of the business," Johnny said. "You kick up."

"'Kick up'? *Fuck* him. What did he ever do for me?"

"I don't see you having a lot of options."

"Options? How about I option to take out that old man and his whole fucking crew?"

Lindell looked up. Johnny turned away, looked out the window into the bay.

"And I could do it too," Joey said, quieter now. "I've got the muscle, the people. I could do it."

Johnny lit his cigarette.

"Don't talk nonsense," he said.

"What did you say?"

Johnny let smoke out, looked up at him.

"Two hundred and fifty grand," he said. "It's not worth it. Pay him. Get it over with."

"Pay him? *You* fucking pay him."

"It's a one-shot deal. Get the money together, give it to him. It keeps the peace, lets him know you're a serious player, lets you stay in business with his blessing. He's not going to be around forever."

"Not if I have anything to do with it."

"You talk like that and people hear you, you might not be around very long yourself. Give him the money, consider it an insurance payment, an expense. You'll earn it back triple within a couple years."

"It's not your money."

"You're right," Johnny said. "It's not. You want to go after him, start taking out his guys? Just say the word. I'll do it. But I'm telling you I don't think it's a good idea. You think about it awhile, you'll realize I'm right."

Joey turned away, looked out through the glass.

"When does he want it?" Lindell said.

"Four days from now," Joey said. "Can you believe that? Four days to get that kind of money together and give it to him. Who the fuck does he think I am?"

"He thinks you're somebody that can raise that kind of money in four days," Johnny said. "Which means he knows you're serious, that you're for real. Play it right, Joey, you'll come out of this way ahead."

"And what's to keep him from whacking me as soon as I hand it over? I get the money up, give it to him, one of his fucking guys pops me, I end up buried at a chicken farm. What's to keep that from happening?"

"Me," Johnny said. "I watch your back. I take the money to him myself if need be. Keep you safe. If he knows you can get the money, are capable of coming up with it, he won't fuck with you in the interim, endanger that."

"You sound like you're sure about that."

"I am," he said.

TWENTY-NINE

YOU REALLY THINK THIS IS NECESSARY?" SHE SAID.

She set her suitcase down on the floor. Harry got up from the Italian couch. Errol was on the other side of the room, looking at the titles of books on the shelf.

"He followed me," Harry said. "He knows where you live."

He picked up the suitcase, felt a jolt of pain in his knee.

"Are you going to tell me what happened?" she said.

"Later. Let's get moving."

"Where are you taking her?" Reggie said from the kitchen doorway. Behind him, Harry could see Jack at the kitchen table. He'd been fighting tears since they'd arrived. "We have a right to know."

"No, you don't," Harry said. "And it's better for you if you don't. Might be a good idea if the two of you thought about going somewhere yourself for a couple weeks."

"And why's that?"

"He knows about this place. He'll come back, looking for her."

"I wish he would. Then I'd settle this whole thing."

"Maybe," Harry said. "Maybe not."

"She's safer here."

"Please, Reggie," Nikki said.

He looked at Harry, his anger unconcealed, went back into the kitchen.

Errol had taken a book off the shelf, was paging through it. Harry could see the title: *Sodomy and the Pirate Tradition.*

"Who's paying for the hotel?" she said.

238

"Ray, at the moment. It's a place he uses, puts people up. Can you get the door for me?"

He carried the suitcase out to the station wagon, stowed it in the back. She followed him out.

"Jack hates to see people leaving," she said. "It upsets him."

"I understand."

He shut the tailgate, nodded at the house.

"I wasn't joking," he said. "They should go somewhere. It would be better. You should talk to them."

"I will . . . but Reggie—the both of them—can be pretty stubborn sometimes."

"Not a good quality in this situation."

She reached up, touched his cheek gingerly.

"Did he do that?" she said.

He moved her wrist away gently.

"Come on," he said. "Let's get the rest of your stuff."

They went back inside. Errol shook his head, closed the book, replaced it on the shelf.

"I need to get a couple more things upstairs," she said, "then say good-bye to Jack and Reggie."

"We'll wait outside," Harry said. "Warm the car up."

Out in the station wagon, Harry at the wheel, Errol said, "That true, what you said? About that blond guy being an actor? Making those movies?"

"That's what I heard. Why, you find him attractive?"

"I'll forget you said that."

Harry turned the heater up, raced the engine.

"He don't look like much," Errol said. "Built like a mop handle and you couldn't call him pretty. Must have a big one."

"Ask Reggie."

"Thanks, but that definitely falls into the too-much-information category. That's an image I can do without."

"You asked."

They watched her come out of the house, carrying a shoulder purse.

"That is a fine-looking woman, though," Errol said.

She pulled open the back door, got in.

"Ready to go?" Harry said. "Get everything you needed?"

"Yes," she said. "It just feels strange, leaving like this. This is the first real home I've had in a long while."

"You'll be back," he said.

THE HOTEL was off Route 35 in Old Bridge. She used the key card to open the door, held it for him. He set the suitcase on the bed.

"You can call out," he said, "but don't give anyone this number or tell them where you're staying. That includes Jack and Reggie."

"They'll be worried."

"Give them my number. They can call me, I'll tell them what they need to know, get a message back to you if that's the issue."

"That sounds like a roundabout way of doing things."

"It's the safest."

He went over to the window, looked down onto the parking lot.

"How am I supposed to get around?" she said. "I'm sure that T.G.I. Friday's downstairs is a delight, but I'll get a little tired of it after a while, don't you think?"

"I'll be around. Take you where you need to go. That includes meals too."

"So you're going to stop by, take care of all my needs?"

He saw her half smile, felt himself blush.

"Errol's waiting," he said. "There's some things we need to do. I'll call you later tonight, see how you're doing."

"That's something to look forward to, I guess."

"In the meantime, any questions, problems, just call."

"I only have one question so far," she said.

"What's that?"

"How long do I have to stay here?"

"I don't know. Until this is over."

"Over? Will it ever be?"

"Yes," he said. "It will."

THEY WAITED in semidarkness, only one light on in the living room. Harry sat in shadow, Errol in the light, half-asleep, feet propped up on an ottoman. Reggie and Jack were in the kitchen, cleaning up from the late dinner they'd made.

The phone on the coffee table rang. Errol looked up.

It rang again. Harry leaned forward. He was aware of Reggie and Jack in the kitchen doorway.

He picked it up on the third ring, said, "Right on time."

Silence on the line.

"What's wrong, sport?" Harry said. "Forget what you were going to say?"

Errol was watching him, frowning.

"Is she there?" Harrow said.

"No. She's gone. Just you and me now."

"Is that right?"

"Yeah." He touched his split lip.

"Then that's bad news for you, *sport*. Like I said, the next time you won't even see me coming. Just *pop, pop* and that's it."

"Any time," Harry said. "Any place."

"It'll happen," Harrow said. "Sooner than you think." He hung up.

THIRTY

THEY WERE HEADED SOUTH ON ROUTE 34, CONNOR DRIVING HIS unmarked Crown Victoria. He'd picked Johnny up at the motel, stopped for coffee at a Dunkin' Donuts along the way. Their cups rested in plastic holders on the console. Connor had turned the police radio off when Johnny got in, and they'd driven the last few miles in silence.

"Under the seat," Connor said.

Johnny looked at him, then reached under, felt the cardboard box there.

"Go ahead," Connor said. "Have a look."

He pulled the box out, opened it on his lap. Inside, nestled in bubble wrap, was a microcassette recorder. Beside it, coiled and bound with a black twist tie, was a thin cord and a tiny microphone.

"Voice-activated," Connor said. "Microphone can go in your jacket, collar, anywhere. I can show you how to rig it up. Take five minutes. They have newer models now, wireless, but this one was sort of borrowed off the books, if you know what I mean."

"I'm supposed to wear this?"

"Like I said, it takes five minutes to put on. After you get comfortable with it, you'll forget it's there. You have to tape it on, though. I'll show you how to do that as well. You'll need to shave in a couple places, make it easier to get the tape on and off."

"So you're solo on this, huh?"

"Far as it goes. When things develop, I'll bring my SAC in. Not until I have some of those tapes in hand, though. Last thing I need is a clusterfuck, other people trying to horn in."

242

Johnny closed the box, slid it back under the seat, took his coffee from the console.

"There's extra tapes in there too. I'll show you how to load it."

Johnny peeled the plastic lid back, steam rising out, sipped.

"You do anything with that address I gave you?" Connor said.

Johnny shook his head.

"Maybe it's better if you don't. Ever think about that?"

Connor pulled into a strip mall, parked, took the lid off his coffee. The nut smell of it filled the car.

"The people you work for," Johnny said, "how much they know about me?"

"Like I said, they know I'm working a CI. But your name's not in the files. Nobody knows who you are."

"That the way things are normally done? Or am I special?"

"I did what I thought was best."

"And when Joey goes down, you get the credit. No one else."

"I don't deserve it? All I did? I recruited you, got you out of Belle Glades, cut the deal. I gave you two years of life you would have pissed away down there otherwise. I did that. No one else."

"Seems odd, that's all. You doing this on your own."

"Let me worry about that. I have my reasons."

"Yeah, I'm sure you do. Don't get me wrong. I respect a man that looks out for himself."

"There's a flip side to that too."

"What's that?"

"By Department of Justice guidelines, if an informant is involved in a 'serious act of violence,' as they put it, the agent in charge is required to consider closing his file and targeting him for arrest."

"Consider? That's all?"

"That's the way it's written. Now, I don't know exactly what you're doing for Alea on a day-to-day basis, but I imagine you're not selling real estate, you know? Any other agent, you would have been closed down, probably be back in Glades already."

"I'm never going back to Glades."

"You sound pretty certain of that."

"I am."

"I'm just trying to give you the whole picture. There's more to it than you think."

Connor looked out the window. Johnny sipped coffee.

"I'll take you back," Connor said. "Show you how to set that rig up so you can do it yourself. When is he going to meet with Acuna?"

"Day after tomorrow. We'll know the place soon."

"Close as you can get, John. And as much as you can get."

"I understand."

Connor put his coffee back in the holder, put the car in gear.

"Do this my way, John, and we'll both come out of it with what we want."

"I believe you," Johnny said.

THE TRAVEL agency was in Freehold and catered to Central American immigrants and illegal workers. There were signs in the window offering phone cards, check cashing, money transfers. He chose it because he knew they would take cash, ask no questions. The heavy Latin man at the counter watched as Johnny counted the bills out, took them without a word.

When he left the office ten minutes later, he had a round-trip ticket to O'Hare on United leaving the next day, three one-way Amtrak tickets from Newark to Vancouver with open dates. The total came to $750 and he gave the man $800, didn't ask for change.

Mitch was waiting in the Firebird, the engine running. Johnny got in, put the ticket envelopes in the glove box.

"You all set?" Mitch said. He pulled away from the curb.

"Yeah. But I need a ride tomorrow."

"No problem. Where to?"

"The airport."

Mitch looked at him.

"You going away?"

"Just for a day or two. And when I get back you should think about what we talked about. Because it's going to happen. Soon."

BACK AT the motel, he called Joey.

"How are you doing on that thing?" he said.

"Getting it together," Joey said. "Another day or two, maybe. I'll get there."

"Good." He looked at the recorder and the mike laid out on the bed. "I have to go away for a couple days. I'll be back."

"Go away? Where? I need you here."

"Relax. It'll only be for a day or so. There's something I need to take care of. Then I'll come back and we can settle this business with your uncle."

"I talked to Santelli, about you being the go-between. He agreed."

"Good."

"You sure you want to do this?"

"I told you I would."

"You might be taking a chance. Maybe a big one."

"We'll see," Johnny said.

THIRTY-ONE

HE HURT YOU, DIDN'T HE?" SHE SAID.

Harry looked across the table at her. They were in the hotel restaurant, Christmas music playing faintly over the PA. It was late for dinner, nearly nine, and only about a half dozen tables were occupied. They'd finished eating, Nikki barely touching her food, and Harry was on his third Corona, Nikki her second vodka and cranberry juice. She'd worn the sleeveless black sweater, jeans. She looked tired, the lines around her eyes deeper.

"I'm fine," he said. "Don't worry about me."

"You say that, but have you looked in a mirror lately? And you don't think I've noticed the way you've been walking?"

"Like I said, I'm fine."

"Have you heard from Sherry?"

He shook his head.

"Errol went by yesterday. Her car was there but no one answered the door. I'll go by tomorrow, talk to the neighbors."

"You went back to the house last night, didn't you?"

He looked at her, didn't answer.

"Because I told you he was going to call."

He shrugged.

"And did you talk to him?" she said.

"Just for a minute."

"What did he say?"

"Not much. I think he was surprised. He knows you're not there now, though, so hopefully that will keep him from going by again. Though Reggie seemed pretty anxious to have that happen."

"Reggie hasn't got a clue."

"Have you given any thought to going somewhere for a while yourself?"

She looked at him.

"Is that what you'd like? Are things getting too complicated for you?"

"No. I was thinking about you."

"This is my home. I've finally come back. And I'm not leaving now. Not because of him. And if I left, I'd have no idea how . . . close he was getting."

The waitress brought the check. Harry signed it, charged it to the room.

"What about the agency?" she said.

"You were right. It's part of a larger, national one, based in D.C. I've already got a phone number, names. I'll make some calls, see what we can find out, who we can talk to."

"You work fast."

"So does Harrow. We need to keep that in mind."

"When I asked you last night," she said. "About when this would be over."

"Yes."

"You said soon. What did that mean?"

"Just a feeling."

"Because John works fast."

"Maybe."

"So if he keeps looking for me, if he doesn't give up, it'll be resolved soon, right? One way or the other? Is that what you mean?"

"I don't know. But one thing at a time. The object right now is to keep you safe."

She looked off across the restaurant, then back at him.

"Getting involved with me," she said. "It's cost you a lot, hasn't it?"

"Come on. I'll take you up to your room. I need to get going."

In the elevator, he pushed the button for 9 and when he turned to her, she kissed him. Her tongue darted out, bumped against his teeth. He opened his mouth, his upper lip a dull pain, tasted the sweet tang of the vodka, felt the softness of her breasts against his chest.

The elevator bonged and the door opened onto the corridor. She smiled and pulled away from him.

He followed her to her door. Down the hall, an ice machine hummed and clattered.

"Come on in," she said, opening the door. "If you want, we can still call room service, get a drink."

"No, I'm good," he said. He looked around the room, went to the window, looked out.

"See anybody?" she said.

He shook his head.

"Then why don't you close the curtain?"

She went into the bathroom and he heard water running. He pulled the curtain shut along its track.

There was a closet with a mirrored sliding glass door in the room. He turned a nightstand lamp on, stood in front of the mirror. The marks on his neck were fading, his lip still slightly swollen.

He heard the water shut off.

"Admiring yourself?" she said when she came out.

"Just taking your advice."

She came up beside him.

"You're still handsome," she said. "Don't worry about it."

He turned to her. She touched his chest, then kissed his upper lip, his neck where the bruises were.

"You're shaking a little," she said.

"You should feel my heart."

She slid a hand under his sweater, touched his bare chest.

"I can feel it." Her fingers drifted over his nipple, then down his chest. She rubbed him softly through his jeans, then her hands went to his belt.

"Wait a minute . . ." he breathed.

"Shhh." She put a fingertip to his lips.

She reached down, caught the edge of her sweater, drew it up over her head, shook her hair free of it. The bra was sheer white lace, her nipples hard beneath it. She tossed the sweater on the bed behind them, reached for his belt again, unsnapped his jeans. He watched in the mirror and she tugged slightly, freed him.

She looked into his eyes, started to kneel.

"You don't have to do this," he said and then he was in her mouth and he felt himself cry out softly, almost involuntarily. He looked at her in the mirror as she worked him with her hand and mouth, felt the heat rising inside.

"Here," he said. He reached down, started to pull her up. She resisted at first, her hand and mouth moving faster, but he drew her up and off him. She looked at him, puzzled at first, and he kissed her hard, feeling the pain in his lip. His tongue slid into her mouth and she sucked on it, closed her eyes, her right hand still on him, stroking. He bent, tucked his right arm beneath her knees, lifted her up.

She looked up at him as he carried her to the bed, set her on the sheets.

"You're beautiful," he said and she touched his swollen lip again, shutting him up.

"Don't talk," she said.

THEY LAY there in bed, her head on his chest. He couldn't tell if she was awake or not.

Tired as he was, he couldn't sleep. Whenever he closed his eyes, Harrow was there. He could feel the coldness of the knife blade, the oil taste of the suppressor as it pushed into his teeth. He could see Harrow taking the license out, reading it.

Lying bitch.

But what had she lied about?

He looked down at her, breathing softly, eyes closed. He touched her hair and she curled tighter against him.

When Harrow had called her two nights ago, it was the first time they'd spoken in years. But that was after the alley.

And then he knew.

He jostled her awake as he reached for the phone. He looked at his watch. Eleven-thirty.

"What's wrong?" she said sleepily.

He didn't answer. He was too busy dialing. And hoping it wasn't too late.

THIRTY-TWO

WHILE ERROL DROVE, HARRY USED HIS CELL PHONE TO TRY THE NUM-ber again. After the tenth ring, he ended the call.

"Nothing?" Errol said.

Harry shook his head, closed the phone.

"Well, we're almost there," Errol said. "Here's the street."

"That's her car, the Honda."

Errol parked behind it.

"Same place it was last time," he said.

Harry took the heavy aluminum flashlight from the floorboard, got out. Errol took a smaller one from the glove box.

He shone the light in the back of the Honda, heard Errol's car door shut. A suitcase in the back, the car seat, toys on the floor. The car was locked.

He started up the walk, Errol behind him. There were two rolled-up newspapers on the porch in front of the door, wrapped in plastic.

He pushed the bell with a gloved thumb, held it down. Did it again.

"I'll look around back," Errol said.

Harry tried the door, locked. He looked at his watch. A little after midnight.

"Harry," Errol called.

He went around the house. Errol stood by the wooden fire escape, shining his flashlight beam on the first steps. There were footprints there in the frozen snow.

"Boots," Harry said.

"Maybe we should call the locals."

Harry looked up to the third-floor window.

"I'm going up," he said.

He stepped carefully, avoiding the footprints already there. He heard Errol coming up behind him, doing the same. When he reached the landing, he turned, saw Errol had the .380 out. They could hear a TV on somewhere inside.

"If she's in there," Errol whispered, "we're going to scare the hell out of her."

Harry looked through a window into a dim kitchen, saw the outside storm window had been pushed up in its frame. He put gloved fingertips against the inside window. It swung in easily. He could see puddles of melted snow on the linoleum, footprints.

"Careful," Errol said.

Harry pushed open the window, swung his legs in. When he got both feet on the floor he waited, listening. The TV still, nothing else.

He held the window open. Errol came in behind him.

"Sherry," Harry called out. No answer.

He started for the hallway and Errol touched him on the shoulder, pointed at the refrigerator. He turned the flashlight on, saw the bloody handprints on the refrigerator door, a juice carton on the counter, marked with small red fingerprints.

He felt his stomach tighten. Errol had put his flashlight away, had the .380 in a two-handed grip, muzzle pointed at the ground. He looked at Harry, raised an eyebrow.

They went into the hall together. The TV noise was coming from the living room to their right. More bloody handprints here on the wall, knee-high, dark against the pale blue paint.

"Janey?" Harry said.

No answer. He felt the cold now, the draft sweeping through the open kitchen window. There was a thermostat on the wall. Sixty-four degrees. He felt the pull of the draft around his ankles. There had to be another window open. He looked to his left, saw a closed door at the end of the corridor.

Errol cocked his head at the living room and they went down the hall slowly. He put the .380 in first, swiveled to cover the room, his back to the wall.

Harry went in beside him. The room was empty, an infomercial on the television. There was a Disney video half wedged into a dark VCR, bloody fingerprints on the label. Half a dozen children's videos lay scattered around, out of their cases, daubed with blood.

The phone lay on the coffee table, off its base, fingerprints there too. His eyes followed the cord across the floor. It ended abruptly, sliced through, the last part of it missing. Something caught his eye beneath the couch. He knelt, reached with his left hand, picked up a cigarette filter that had been broken off, tossed away. He set it on the table.

"Time to get on the phone," Errol said.

Harry went back into the hallway, down to the closed door. There was another door across the hall, slightly open. A third door opened onto a dark bathroom.

He tried the first door, turned the knob, pushed it open. Knowing what he was going to find.

Sherry lay on her side on the floor, in between the bed and the wall. There were sheets tangled around her legs. A child's blanket had been pulled over her, up to her neck, red fingerprints on it.

"Oh, Jesus," Errol said behind him.

There was blood on the carpet, blood on the wall, blood in the bed. All dried. Cold air whistled through an open window above the headboard.

Harry knelt. Sherry's eyes were half-open, staring at the wall. Near her head was a plastic sippy cup, marked with tiny red finger-prints. He touched the bare flesh of an ankle, felt the coldness.

Slowly, he pulled the blanket away from her. She wore a long night-shirt, once white, now dark red and stiff with blood. He could see the stab wounds to her chest and stomach, the material of the nightshirt torn where the knife had gone in. He laid the blanket back over her.

They waited outside the second door, listening, not wanting to go in. Then Harry put his fingers against the door, pushed it open.

Muppet posters on the walls, a toy box in one corner, a dollhouse beside it. A Mickey Mouse night-light. In the bed, the golden-haired girl from the playground was wrapped in covers, clutching a stuffed rabbit, breathing softly.

Harry exhaled. Errol came in behind him, holstered the .380. He took the cell phone from his jacket pocket, stepped back into the hall.

Harry reached for the light switch, saw the bloody fingerprints there too. He flicked it up and an overhead light fluttered, went on.

Janey stirred, gripped the rabbit tighter. There was blood on the rabbit, blood on the sheets, blood on everything she had touched.

He crouched down.

"Janey?"

She rolled tighter into the covers.

"Janey, honey, are you all right?"

She sat up then, blinking in the light, looked at him, not letting the rabbit go. She wore pale blue pajamas with feet, a cartoon lion on the front.

"Are you hurt, sweetheart?" he said.

She knuckled sleep from an eye. Her face was smeared with dried blood where she had rubbed it. He could hear Errol talking on the cell in the hallway.

"Who are you?" she said.

"I'm a friend of your mother's," he said. "Remember? From the park?"

"Mommy's sick," she said. "I tried to help her, but she won't wake up."

He rose slowly to his feet, looked down at her.

"Will you take care of my mommy?" she said.

Harry leaned in the doorway, felt a bone-deep tiredness. She looked at him, impassive. But he couldn't meet her eyes.

THEY WERE sitting in Ray's Camry, engine running, watching uniformed people move in and out of the house like ants, red and blue lights bathing the front of the building. Neighbors stood bundled on porches, watching. He could see Errol on the front walk, talking to an Avon cop.

"She was going to leave town," Harry said. "Get away from here. Her and the girl."

"Not soon enough, I guess," Ray said. "She shouldn't have waited."

When Harry didn't respond, Ray looked at him.

"This wasn't your fault," Ray said.

Harry watched two EMTs carry the covered stretcher out the front door, balance it gingerly as they came down the porch steps.

"You're wrong," he said. "It was."

They slid her into the back of the EMT van, one tech climbing up inside. The other shut the door, went around and got in the passenger side. The van pulled away from the curb, no flashing lights, no siren.

They'd told their story twice already. Errol knew one of the first Avon cops to arrive and that had helped them, smoothed the way for when the county people had shown up. Harry watched the lights and the movement around him, felt an echoing emptiness inside, a leaden weight in his limbs.

"Did you call her?" he said.

"Not yet," Ray said. "I will."

"I'll do it."

"Better if you let me. You're not in too good shape yourself right now."

Harry reached into his jeans pocket, pulled out the hundred-dollar bill Sherry had given him. He looked at it, turned it over in his hands, put it back in his pocket.

Branson, the county man, came out the front door, looked around. A uniformed Avon cop came up to him, spoke, pointed at the Camry. He started toward them.

"Here we go again," Ray said and shut off the engine.

Harry opened the door, got out. Ray did the same. It was colder than before, the wind stronger now. Harry pushed gloved hands deeper into his pockets.

Branson had a shaved head, dark goatee. He wore a black overcoat over a suit. Harry felt Ray come up, stand at his shoulder.

"We hit the trailer," Branson said. "Picked up the brother. There was a woman and a little girl there too. No sign of Harrow. The brother says he doesn't know where he is, the woman too. We're holding on to him in the meantime, though, and we've put out a BOLO with Harrow's description. No word yet."

Harry nodded, saw flashes in the third-floor windows, then a constant bright light. Photographers from the mobile crime scene van, stills and video.

"From what you've told me, it sounds like Harrow won't go down easy," Branson said. "So when we get a location on him, we'll go in with a tactical team. Sooner or later he'll show up."

"The little girl," Harry said. "Janey. Who's got her?"

"DYFS for the moment. We're trying to track down some relatives. She'll be safe."

"That's good," Harry said, hearing the flatness in his own voice.

"I'm sorry," Branson said to him, "that you had to be the one to find her. I know what it's like. Looks like the mother was dead a day at least, maybe longer. So the kid was trapped in there the whole time with her. I guess the only thing to be grateful for is he didn't hurt the little girl."

"He did," Harry said.

Branson looked at him, then understood. He looked away.

"Yeah," he said. "I guess you're right. She won't be much of a witness, though, when it comes down to it. It's like having no witness at all. The only thing we can hope is she's young enough, she might forget most of this, you know? Move on."

Harry shook his head slowly.

"She'll never forget."

Errol came down the walk toward them.

"We'll need all three of you tomorrow," Branson said. "Down in Freehold. Make an official statement. Get it recorded."

"You got it," Ray said. "We'll be there."

"If anything comes up in the meantime, if we get a hit on Harrow or the brother, I'll let you know."

"Thanks," Ray said. They shook hands.

Branson looked at Harry.

"Then that's it, I guess. See you gentlemen tomorrow."

He turned and headed back to the crime scene van.

Ray looked from Harry to Errol and back.

"Come back to the office," he said. "We can talk this thing through, try and figure out what happens now. And both of you look like you could use a drink."

"You're right on that," Errol said.

"You go back with Ray," Harry said. "I'll follow."

They both looked at him.

"Go on," he said. "I have a phone call to make."

RAY HAD taken a bottle of Chivas from the credenza behind his desk, splashed some into three glasses. He pulled his chair out from behind the desk and the three of them sat in a triangle, Harry look-ing at the floor, Errol with his elbows on his knees, turning the glass around in his hands.

Ray sipped scotch, set the glass on the edge of the desk.

"There's a couple things we should go over," he said.

"It was my fault," Harry said. "I thought he'd come after me."

"There's no way you could have known what would happen," Ray said.

"If I hadn't gone to see that woman, talk to her—pressure her—she'd still be alive today."

"You don't know that," Ray said.

Harry set his untouched glass on the carpet.

"I thought I was being smart," he said. "Heading him off. And instead I got her killed."

Errol drained half his scotch, went back to turning the glass around.

"They'll get him," Ray said. "And when he goes away this time, he won't ever be coming back."

"She didn't have much in life, you know?" Harry said. "But she wanted more for her daughter. Better. She didn't deserve what happened."

Ray didn't answer.

"But you know something?" Harry said.

"What?"

"*He* will."

HE KNOCKED, waited. When she opened the door, he stepped in and she came into his arms. He pulled her close, buried his face in her hair.

He held her like that, in the open doorway, felt her tremble against him, her sobs as soft as a child's.

THEY LAY atop the bed, fully clothed, her head on his chest. She'd cried herself to sleep.

Outside, sleet rattled the hotel room window. He felt her stir, looked down and saw her eyes open. He kissed the top of her head and she put a hand on his chest, feeling his heart, looked off at nothing.

"We need to call the agency," she said. "Tell them what happened. They should know."

"Ray's on it. He's going to make the calls first thing in the morning. Simmons first, then the D.C. people. He'll take care of it."

"I called Jack," she said.

"And?"

"Reggie's finally agreed. They're going to go out to the Hamptons the day after tomorrow. Jack has a friend with a house there."

"Good. The sooner the better."

"Will they catch him? Because of this."

"Yes. There are other people involved now, other agencies. It's not just about you anymore. They'll catch him."

She rested her head back on his chest.

"I wish I could believe you," she said. "I wish I could listen to that and know it was true."

He pulled her tighter, felt her breathing, the beat of her heart. But he didn't answer.

THIRTY-THREE

JOHNNY PAID THE CAB DRIVER, GOT OUT. IT HAD BEEN NEARLY AN hour's ride from O'Hare and it was dark now, bitter cold. He saw the street sign that said GREEN BAY ROAD, waited on the corner until the driver pulled away, disappeared in traffic.

He was in a neighborhood of big hedge-enclosed yards, wide tree-lined streets. Outside the airport there had been snow everywhere, but here the streets were plowed clean, salted, the sidewalks cleared.

He pulled the collar of his field jacket higher, started down the street, keeping close to the hedges. It would also be a neighborhood with regular police patrols, he knew, where just the sight of a pedestrian was reason enough to stop and question him.

The wind whipped around him. He'd had the driver stop at a hardware store outside the airport, and he'd bought another folding Buck knife. If he saw a cop now he would just toss the knife away, lose it in the snow.

He passed a suburban train station, the lot carefully cleared, a pair of cabs waiting with engines running. He kept walking, watched mailbox numbers, the houses set too far back from the street to identify. When he reached 2204 he crossed the street.

Twenty-two eleven was smaller than some of the other houses on the block, two stories with a big backyard, separate garage. The front porch was strung with Christmas lights.

He walked by it, went to the next house. It was a two-level stone structure, driveway still covered with snow, no footprints or tire marks. No one home.

He pushed through bare bushes into the yard, boots crunching in the snow. There was a shoulder-high skeleton hedge separating the two properties. He followed the line of it, out of sight from the street, until he reached the stone house. He looked in a dark living room window, searched for light or movement. None.

With his back to the stone house, he looked through the gaps in the hedges at 2211.

There was a bay window in front, and through parted curtains he could see a living room, bookshelves, pictures on the walls, a Christmas tree in one corner.

A woman came into the room and he backed up a step, into the shadows of the stone house. She was in her thirties, blonde, a baby balanced on one shoulder. She looked around the room, turned to speak with someone out of view, left the room again.

He moved down the hedge to the next lighted window. He could see the short hallway that led from the living room, a brightly lit kitchen beyond, smell food cooking. There was a man at the head of the table, his back to the window. To his right sat a small boy, dark hair and glasses. Maybe seven, eight.

Matthew.

The woman set the baby down in a high chair, kissed the top of its head, began to put platters of food on the table.

He watched them, not feeling the cold anymore. The boy went for a basket of bread on the table, couldn't reach it. He laughed, strained as if hyperextending his arm, and the woman laughed too now as she ate, the father moving the basket closer so the boy could reach it.

Johnny looked beyond them for signs of movement, someone else in the house. Nothing. Just the four of them.

He backed up a step, decided to risk a cigarette, got one lit. He stood there smoking, watching them. The boy wore a green sweater with reindeer on the front. He talked as he ate, the story occasionally causing him to put his fork down, wave his hands to make a point. The woman had finished eating, was feeding the baby now from a bowl balanced on the plate of the high chair.

He sucked in the harsh smoke, let it out. He felt the warmth of the room, could almost taste the food.

He couldn't see the father's face. He imagined it was his.

When he was done with the cigarette he pinched it out, put it in his pocket. Then he walked back to the street.

HE GOT a cab at the train station, spent the night at a motel near the airport. When he checked out the next day, he left the knife behind.

After landing at Newark, he waited outside the terminal, watching the long line of cars queuing to pick up passengers. No Firebird.

He looked at his watch, smoked a cigarette, waited. After a half hour, he went back into the terminal, used a pay phone to call the trailer. Ten rings, no answer.

He waited another half hour, then headed for the cab stand.

THEY ROLLED slowly up the main street of the trailer park.

"Which number?" the driver said.

"I'll tell you when to stop," Johnny said.

He saw the trailer, the Firebird outside, no lights on within.

"This it?" the driver said.

"No. Keep going."

A dark Chevy was parked up the street, two men inside drinking coffee. Cops. Johnny looked away as the cab passed them.

"Well?" the driver said.

"My mistake. Wrong place. Take me to Asbury."

"This is going to be extra, you know."

He fished a hundred from his jeans pocket, dropped it over the seat. He looked back at the Chevy, still parked.

"Swing around here," he said. "It'll take you back to the entrance."

"Anything you say, boss."

THE DRIVER let him out two blocks from the Sea Vista. He crossed over to the boardwalk, came out behind a boarded-up taffy store across from the motel. He stood in the shadows, watched. No lights in his room, no cars out front he hadn't seen before.

He should leave now, he knew, not even try to get back in. But the duffel was in the room, the Sig, the money. The tickets.

He waited, the wind off the ocean cutting through his jacket. Then he crossed the street.

HE MOVED quickly, got the duffel from the hidden space in the closet ceiling. The money was all there, the Sig too. He pushed it into his belt, crossed to the sliding glass door and pushed the curtain aside, looked out. Nothing.

He called Connor's beeper, left the motel number. It rang back in two minutes.

"What the fuck is going on?" Connor said.

"What do you mean?"

"What do I mean? There's a murder warrant out for you. Do you know that? Your brother's in custody too."

"That's bullshit. He never did anything to anybody."

"Who killed that woman?"

"What woman?"

"You're a bad liar, you know that, John? Don't fucking give me that. What did we talk about, about shutting your file down? You think I can get you out of this? You're wrong."

"How should I know who killed her? They're trying to pin it on me because I've got a jacket, that's all. Because I did time. It's bullshit."

"It better be."

"It is."

"I don't get you, John. This whole thing's going to hell and you seem awful fucking calm about it."

"What am I supposed to do? Like I said, it's bullshit."

"It changes everything."

"Maybe not. I've got what you want."

Silence on the line for a moment.

"What do you mean?"

"The wire. I wore it to a meeting we had in Newark. I've got Joey A., Lindell, others, all clear as day, talking about the meth lab, the trouble with Tony Acuna. That's what you wanted, isn't it?"

A pause.

"Yeah, that's what I wanted."

"You don't sound too happy."

"You have it with you?"

"Right here. Right now."

"I need to hear it, see what we've got. Then we'll talk about what we're going to do."

"You listen, you tell me."

"When can I get it?"

"I'll be in touch," Johnny said.

THIRTY-FOUR

MY GUESS," HARRY SAID, "IS HE DOESN'T KNOW ANYTHING."
They were standing in front of a two-way mirror at the State
Police barracks in Holmdel, watching Mitchell Sweeton smoke cigarettes, look at the floor and occasionally offer an answer to the two
detective lieutenants sitting across the table from him. His left hand
was cuffed to a D-bar on the table.

"Maybe not," said Vic Salerno. "But he's the only connection
anyone's got to Harrow right now."

At a desk behind them, Branson was on the phone. There had
been others watching at first, but it was Sweeton's second hour in
the box and most of the curious had lost patience and interest.
Salerno had flicked off the external speaker a few minutes previ-
ously, so the scene inside now played out in silence. Sweeton looked
exhausted. Every few minutes he would rest his forehead on the
table, look at the floor.

"Where's the woman?" Harry said.

"In another room, second floor. They've kept them separated the
whole time. DYFS has the kid."

"Anything from her?"

Salerno shook his head.

"She knows who Harrow is. She's seen him around. He's been by
the trailer, that's it. Says she doesn't know where he is now. I'm
inclined to believe her. They're threatening to take the little girl
away, for good. They found some pot, paraphernalia in the trailer,
and some goods that will almost certainly turn out to be stolen. It's
bullshit, not enough to even go to court with. Good enough to use
as a threat, though. We'll see what happens."

Sweeton had his face in his hands now, cigarette burning unattended in the tin ashtray.

"I never got a chance to thank you," Salerno said. "For calling me. This is the kind of break we wait for."

"What about Alea?"

"We sent some people to his house. Nonconfrontational was the brief I gave them. Said he hasn't seen Harrow in years, didn't even know he was out."

"You believe him?"

Salerno shrugged.

"No evidence he's lying, unfortunately. He'll be a stone wall until we get something to use against him. That's what I was hoping Sweeton would give us."

Inside, the two detectives looked at each other. One of them, whom Harry knew by sight but not name, got up from the table. He stepped out into the hall, shut the door behind him.

"Yeah?" Salerno said. "Anything?"

"Maybe," the detective said. "You guys ever hear of a motel called the Sea Vista?"

THE SWAT team rolled into the motel lot in a pair of black vans with tinted windows. Salerno's Ford pulled in behind them, Harry in the passenger seat.

Salerno parked on the edge of the lot. They watched half of the team—wearing black flak jackets, helmets, and carrying stubby H&K machine guns—go in the front door. Others raced around the back of the building to cover the other exits. Three more state police cruisers pulled into the lot, flashers and sirens off. One blocked the entrance.

Salerno looked up at the building. They could see helmeted figures on the roof now.

"What do you think?" he said. "He in there?"

"We'll find out."

From the back of one of the vans, two SWAT members brought out a four-man battering ram. They carried it through the front door.

"Nice place," Salerno said. "Good for the kids. You don't have to

264

worry about cooking dinner. They can just eat the paint chips off the walls."

"I hear it's coming down. This whole block. The Heartbreak, Pratt's. Everything."

"Couldn't be too soon, you ask me. Places like this, what this town's become, sometimes you just have to drop a big bomb, start over."

As they watched, a fifth-floor balcony door opened. A curtain was pushed aside and a team member carrying an H&K came out onto the balcony. He signaled to those on the roof.

"He's gone," Harry said.

"Looks like."

Two SWAT men came out the front door, huddled with a pair of plainclothes detectives. One of them was Branson. Salerno powered down the window as he came over.

"Gone," Branson said. "No luggage, no clothes. But he was there. Room 503. Bed's unmade, cigarette butts everywhere."

"So he's in the wind," Salerno said.

"Manager hasn't seen him since yesterday. He paid in advance for the month. Doesn't look like he's coming back, though."

Salerno looked at Harry.

"Ideas?"

Harry shook his head.

"His brother's in custody, the trailer's being watched. So he's not going back there. He must have another hole somewhere."

"What are you two going to do now?" Branson said.

"Rattle some cages," Salerno said. "And wait."

THIRTY-FIVE

THE MOTEL WAS IN NEPTUNE, FEW CARS OUTSIDE, GRAFFITI ON THE walls. He filled out the registration form with a false name, address. The old black man behind the bulletproof glass took his money, gave him a key on a diamond-shaped plastic tab.

There were no phones in the rooms, so he had to use a pay phone in the parking lot. He made the call, spoke for ten minutes, had to feed in more change halfway. When he was done, he went back to the room, lay on the thin mattress and looked up at the discolored ceiling. Next door, a black couple argued. He closed his eyes, slowed his breathing, found the Valley.

HE WAS standing outside, finishing a cigarette, when Connor's Crown Victoria pulled into the lot. It was a gray day, clouds scudding by overhead. He'd slept a long, dreamless night, felt awake and alive. Focused.

He tossed the butt away, waited for Connor to unlock the passenger-side door, got in. Connor swung the car around.

"Nice place," Connor said. "Only the best, huh?"

"You don't always have a choice."

They pulled out onto Route 33, headed west.

"Well?" Connor said.

Johnny fished the recorder, wires and mike out of his left jacket pocket, put them on the seat between them.

Connor looked at them, then back at the road.

"I have to say, John, I doubted you."

"Why?"

"I didn't know if you could go against your nature like that, keep your end up. Do the right thing."

"Was this the right thing?"

"Yes, it was." He looked at him. "You doubt that?"

"I don't know."

"It's a good thing, John. For both of us. You won't regret it. It's just the beginning, though."

"What do you mean?"

"If what's on that tape is half as good as you say it is, it's a start. But we'll need more. This needs to be rock solid, no questions."

"Or you won't get your promotion?"

Connor smiled.

"This is a marathon, John. Not a sprint. The tape itself isn't admissible. You know that as well as I do. But it's the bedrock we can build a case on. We'll know what to look for, what doors to knock on. It all comes out of this. But there's more work to do, for both of us. This is just the first step."

There was a Dunkin' Donuts up on the right. Connor pulled into the lot.

"Get you something?"

"Regular," Johnny said. "Easy on the sugar."

Connor got out of the car, went inside. Johnny turned the AM-FM on, scanned the dial until he found music, WCBS, an oldies station. The Four Seasons' "Rag Doll" came on.

After a few minutes, Connor came out carrying a small cardboard box with two coffees in it. He got behind the wheel, set the box on the dashboard.

"Yours on the right," he said.

When they pulled out of the lot, Johnny said, "Let's get off this road. Too many cars around. It's not good like this, when it's still light out."

He took his coffee from the box, peeled the plastic lip back.

"You feeling the irony?" Connor said.

"What do you mean?"

"Here you are, murder warrant for your arrest. Cops all over, looking for you. And you're riding around with an FBI agent."

"It occurred to me."

They turned off the highway onto the access road for an industrial park.

"That's the beauty of it," Connor said. "And something you shouldn't forget."

"What's that?"

"When you're with me, nobody can touch you."

They pulled into the empty parking lot of an electronics company, parked around the side, out of sight of the road.

Connor put the car in park, left the engine running. Johnny handed him his coffee. Del Shannon on the radio now. "Runaway."

Connor took the lid off the cup, sipped.

"Like I said, John, you did the right thing. The only thing. You'll see."

"I guess I will." He put his coffee on the dashboard, flexed his fingers inside the gloves. They were still stiff from the cold.

"Big nor'easter coming," Connor said. "They're talking ten, twelve inches of snow. Going to be a fucking mess." He brought the cup to his lips.

Johnny waited until Connor had a mouthful of coffee, then took the Sig out of his right jacket pocket and shot him in the side of the head.

Even with the silencer, the shot was loud in the closed car. Connor's head cracked against the glass. Coffee and blood splashed against the window, dripped down the door.

Johnny watched him slide down in the seat, twitching, his eyes wide. He pushed the silencer into the folds of the overcoat until he felt ribs, then pulled the gun back an inch, fired twice more. Connor jumped, shook, then seemed to relax. His chin settled on his chest, his eyes half-closed. Bits of scalp were stuck to the window with blood.

Johnny put the Sig on the dashboard, finished his coffee. Then he reached over and turned the key, cut the music off.

He got out, opened the trunk. A briefcase inside, a cardboard box with files. The briefcase was unlocked. He went through it—papers and a bound planning calendar. Nothing with his name on it. Nothing in the files either.

He pushed them to the side, opened the driver's-side door,

caught Connor as he slumped out. He got him under the arms, dragged him to the back of the car. He hitched him up and into the trunk, went through his pockets, careful to avoid the blood. He found Connor's Bureau ID in his suit jacket, a wallet with $150 in cash in his pants. He took the money, tossed the ID and wallet in the trunk. There was a Smith & Wesson .38 in a belt holster on his hip, a set of handcuffs in a loop on the back. He took them both, dropped them into his jacket pockets, shut the trunk.

There were some napkins in the box the coffee cups had come in. He used them to wipe the window, the steering wheel. The blood on the glass smeared, but he got most of it off and all of the hair. There was almost no blood on the seat.

He tossed the bloody napkins in the back, got behind the wheel and shut the door. He started the engine, pulled around and back out onto the access road, careful not to rub up against the blood on the door.

He headed back to Route 33, drove for five minutes and turned onto Route 66. The storage facility was right before the Parkway entrance. He pulled up to the electronic gate, used the key card he'd been given when he rented the unit. When the gate slid open, he drove through.

The unit was toward the back, away from the highway. He pulled up to the door, turned the headlights on. The day was almost gone, the sky an unbroken gunmetal gray.

He found the key, got out and bent over the padlock. He opened it, slipped the lock off, rolled the door up on its tracks.

The unit was empty. He'd rented it two weeks ago for just this purpose. Pulling the car in, he parked nose-first against the far wall, killed the engine. He opened the glove box, looked through the papers there. Nothing but the registration, insurance. He shoved the recorder inside, shut the glove box door. If they ever found it, it wouldn't matter. The tape was blank.

He got out, locked the doors. There was a climate control thermostat on the wall. He turned it all the way off. He had paid for the unit in advance for six months, cash. There would be at least two more months of cold weather, maybe more. By then he would be long gone.

He went out, pulled the door back down, reset the padlock. He let himself out a pedestrian gate, crossed Route 66 and walked a half mile to a Home Depot, where he used a pay phone to call a cab.

He smoked a cigarette while he waited, then dropped Connor's keys into a storm drain. The padlock key went into another one. Then he broke the key card into four pieces, put each in a separate trash can outside the store.

He was back at the motel before dark.

THIRTY-SIX

NOTHING YET?" RAY SAID.

Harry shook his head, poured coffee for both of them from the office machine.

"He didn't leave much behind that was useful," he said, putting the cup on Ray's desk. "Except cigarette butts."

"What?"

"Cigarette butts. Unfiltered Camels. That's what he smoked."

"So?"

"I found a cigarette filter in Sherry Wicks's apartment, broken off. He smoked her cigarettes, snapped the filters off first. He was there."

He sat down opposite the desk, sipped coffee.

"And the brother?" Ray said.

"Still in custody, but not for long, I wouldn't think. They don't have much to hold him on."

"How involved do you think he is?"

Harry shook his head.

"He's small-time. His sheet is minor. He and his brother don't play in the same league. And he's got a live-in girlfriend now, a kid."

"What's Salerno say?"

"They'll go back to Alea, keep at him. And someone will stay at the trailer, watch it."

"You think he'll go back there?"

"Not a chance."

"You heading back to the hotel?"

Harry nodded.

"For a while. See how she is."

"Errol will spell you later. I'll give him a call. He can stay outside in the wagon, watch whoever goes in or out. The girl will be safe."

"Good."

"Maybe if we're lucky, Harrow's had enough. He'll figure it's not worth the effort, fuck off back to Florida."

"Not this one," Harry said. "He's not going anywhere."

"THE SEA Vista," she said. "I should have known. If I'd thought about it—"

"What do you mean?"

They were in a dark corner of the hotel restaurant, food untouched in front of them.

"That place . . ." she said. "It's close to the Heartbreak."

"I know."

"It was the first place Johnny and I ever went . . . to be together."

He nodded, pushed back slightly from the table.

"I should have thought about it. I could have told you. Then they could have found him before . . ."

"There was no way you could know," he said. "And you had no reason to think he'd be there, that he'd stay so close."

"When you think about it now, it all makes sense, though, doesn't it?"

"How's that?"

"The places he went back to. Places he knows. From the past. Places that meant something to him."

"I suppose."

"If I'd thought about it that way . . . I could have saved her."

"Maybe not."

"But there would have been a chance."

He let his shoulders rise and fall.

"What have you heard about Janey?" she said.

"There's an aunt coming down from Minnesota. She may already be here. She'll take her back."

She grew quiet, looked away. He leaned forward, touched her hand, didn't speak.

"Are you going to stay tonight?" she said.

"I was thinking about it."

"Don't. They're talking about a snowstorm. You should go home. I'll be okay."

"If I don't stay, someone else will be here, outside."

"I'm never going to be able to pay for all this, you know."

"I don't think Ray's even worrying about that at this point."

"But he's got a business to run, doesn't he? I must be monopolizing a lot of his time, resources. Not to mention yours."

"What else do I have to do with my time?"

"Live your life?"

"What life?" he said. "And speaking of that . . ."

"What?"

"Ray asked me to mention to you, since Christmas is in a couple weeks—"

"I'd lost track."

"—he's having dinner at his house. He wants you to come."

"With you?"

"That's what he implied."

A ghost of a smile played across her face, disappeared.

"In the middle of all this craziness," she said, "it's hard to think about that."

"I know."

"I don't know if I'm up to it."

"Me neither. No pressure, though. It's your choice. And there's plenty of time to decide."

"Is there?" she said.

THIRTY-SEVEN

WHEN JOEY ANSWERED THE PHONE, JOHNNY SAID "IT'S ME."

"What the fuck is going on? Where are you?"

"Back here now."

"There were state cops at my house, asking about you. What the fuck, John?"

"It's nothing. They haven't got shit."

"It didn't sound that way. They said it had to do with a homicide."

"What did you tell them?"

"*Ugatz.* What do you think? But you owe me an explanation, John."

"Just calm the fuck down."

"What did you say?"

"I said calm down. They're grabbing at straws. They're trying to railroad me back inside."

"This is no good, John. We've got business to take care of. I talked to that guy today. The one with my uncle."

"And?"

"They're ready. They want to do it tonight."

"Are you ready?"

"Ready, yeah. Happy about it, no."

"Where?"

"Same place as last time. Midnight. Tell the truth, I don't like it."

"We have much choice?"

"Lindell will drive you, wait outside. You two get there and you don't like the looks of it, feel like you're walking into something, you turn around, come back."

"You think it's a setup?"

274

"I don't know. But if it is, then we move on to the next stage. And then we'll see who comes out on top."

THE LEXUS jeep slowed, steered to the curb. Johnny pulled the passenger door open, got in.

"Yo," Lindell said.

"How's it going?"

They pulled away. The first flakes of snow were starting to fall, glistening on the windshield.

"Man's not too happy," Lindell said. "Cops around. Bad news."

"Life's bad news. That's all it is."

Lindell turned the stereo on. Music seemed to surround them. Marvin Gaye. Johnny could feel the bass through the seat.

"I was talking to Joey," Lindell said. "We were saying, after tonight, you should take some time, man. Hit the road."

"Joey afraid I'm going to fuck up his thing?"

"Ain't that, man. He's thinking about you. Heat's on right now. You need to chill somewhere, let some of this shit blow over."

"Blow over?" He had the sudden image of Connor's head snapping back, blood hitting the window.

"That," he said, "is never going to happen."

THE CASH was banded in stacks of $2,000. Johnny watched as Joey counted it a final time. They were in the office above the store, the money laid out on the desk, a plastic suitcase open on a chair.

"This is a fucking crime," Joey said when he was finished.

Lindell pulled on his goatee, looked at the money. Joey began to stack the bills in the suitcase.

"This is the last fucking money that old man ever sees from me," he said. "Not another fucking dime is he getting. Ever."

The suitcase filled up quickly. They watched without speaking. When Joey was done, he closed the lid, snapped the latches shut. He hoisted the suitcase up.

"Shit's heavier than you'd imagine," he said, set it on the floor.

Johnny got his cigarettes out, lit one.

"Where's Viktor?" he said.

"Storeroom. Doing inventory," Joey said. "I didn't want him in here, see all this, get ideas."

Johnny blew smoke out, looked at the suitcase—black plastic pregnant with green paper. He checked his watch. Almost time.

Joey settled down behind the desk, sighed.

"This is what they don't tell you," he said. "You can get what you want, what you deserve, but you always have to pay a price. You always have to put up with someone else's bullshit along the way."

"That's the nature of it," Johnny said.

"The nature of what?"

"Getting what you want. It's never as simple as it looks."

"That's for goddamn sure."

Lindell pulled a chair away from the wall, sat down.

"And what about you, Johnny Blue Eyes?" Joey said. "You get what you want?"

"Working on it."

"Still? Even with the cops looking for you? You should be in the wind, brother. Back to Florida or somewhere. South America, even better."

"And what would you do without me?"

"After we settle this business with my uncle, maybe we get a little breathing room, coast for a while. You want to take an extended vacation, you let me know."

Johnny walked over to the window, looked out. The parking lot was empty except for Joey's Escalade and Lindell's jeep. It was snowing steadily now, both vehicles covered.

"Let's wrap this up," Joey said. "And let me buy both of you a drink." He opened a drawer, took out a bottle of Johnnie Walker Black, set it beside the phone.

Johnny watched the dark car roll into the parking lot, lights off. It pulled up alongside the Escalade.

Joey had three glasses out, was pouring drinks. Johnny reached under his jacket, took the Sig out, turned away from the window.

"Here's a toast," Joey said. "To greedy old bastards. May we all live long enough to become one."

Johnny raised the Sig and Joey looked up then, saw it. The first bullet shattered the scotch bottle, hit him in the chest. The second punched into his left shoulder, sent him and the chair over backward.

Lindell was getting up quick, reaching beneath his suit coat. Johnny tagged him before the gun came out, high in the right chest, the impact spinning him around and over the chair. When he hit the floor, Johnny fired once into his back. The smell of cordite drifted through the room.

He turned, spit his cigarette out, pointed the Sig at the storeroom door. When Viktor Ismayla came through, he shot him through the forehead, watched him crash back into a pile of cardboard boxes. He hit the floor and lay still.

Johnny turned back, walked around the desk. Joey lay face-up, the back of his head against the wall. He grimaced in pain, his white cotton shirt soaked through with blood. Johnny kicked the chair away. There was blood on the wall too.

Joey coughed, spit blood, looked up at him, raised a hand as if to ward him off.

"You surprised, Joey? You shouldn't be."

Joey closed his eyes, opened them. His face was whitening.

"It's like you said," Johnny said. "There's always a price." He lifted the Sig.

"Stop!" Joey said, blood on his lips. "Just fucking stop!"

Johnny waited.

"Is this about Nikki?" Joey said. "That whore? Is that was this is about?"

"No," Johnny said and fired twice.

He turned away, went to the window, saw the car still waiting outside. He hoisted the suitcase up, surprised at its heaviness, headed for the door.

He heard the noise, the scrape of the chair, and turned to his left, saw Lindell there, on one knee, the silver gun in his right hand. Johnny tried to bring the Sig up but the angle was wrong. His arm hit the door frame. He lifted the suitcase, heard the crack of the gun, felt the hammer blow as the suitcase smashed into him.

His legs tangled and he fell back into the hallway, Lindell still firing, the bullets chipping the doorway, whizzing off into the hall. Johnny snapped a shot, heard it strike a metal cabinet. Lindell aimed, fired and plaster flew from the wall over Johnny's head. Johnny kicked the suitcase away, lifted the Sig. Lindell fired again, the shot high and to the right, and then the slide on the gun locked back empty. Johnny took careful aim and shot him in the face. Lindell toppled backward, didn't move again.

Johnny lay there for a moment, trying to catch his breath, feeling the pain in his side where the suitcase had hit him. He set the Sig down, felt for a broken rib, and his fingers touched wetness, warmth. Lindell's first shot had passed through the suitcase and money, out the other side and into him.

He rolled to his knees and the pain hit him then, taking his breath away. He stayed like that for a moment, then rose slowly, leaning against the wall for support.

He righted the suitcase, saw the matching holes in each side. Then he went to Lindell, rolled him over, found the jeep keys in his jacket pocket. He picked up the Sig, let the hammer down, pushed the gun into his belt.

He dragged the suitcase through the door, saw he'd left bloody handprints on the wall. Halfway down the stairs he let the suitcase go, watched it tumble to the bottom. He followed it down, wiped his palm dry on his jeans, pushed open the fire door.

The Town Car still waited, exhaust billowing behind it. The headlights went on, pinning him there, the snow dancing in their beams. He raised his right hand in front of his face to shield his eyes.

A door opened and he saw a figure in silhouette get out. The lights went off then and he could see the figure wore a black overcoat. He gestured at the open door, the lighted interior. Johnny picked up the suitcase, felt the pain, let the fire door shut behind him. His breath was coming in pants now, frosting in the air. He carried the suitcase to the car, looked in.

Frankie Santelli sat in the far corner of the wide seat, gloved hands in his lap. He looked at Johnny, expressionless. Johnny hefted the suitcase, got it in the car, then slid in behind it, sat down. The suitcase rested against his legs. The man in the overcoat got in, shut the door behind him, killing the interior light, sat in a jump seat facing Johnny. He was in his early forties, slick black hair shot with gray, jaws working as he chewed gum. His right hand stayed in his overcoat pocket.

"Well, here we are," Santelli said.

There was tinted glass separating them from the driver's compartment, and Johnny could see two men up there. Overcoat watched him, chewed gum.

"We should get this over with," Santelli said. "The weather and all. Everybody wants to go home."

Johnny unsnapped the hasps on the suitcase, let it fall open. Some of the bundled bills fell onto the floor.

"You all right, John?" Santelli said. "You look a little pale."

"I'm fine," he said. "Let's do it."

Overcoat took his hand out of his pocket, reached up and turned the interior light on. He opened the case wider, money spilling out.

"You count it?" he said.

"No. But I watched it get counted. It's all there."

"You take your share already?" Santelli said.

Johnny shook his head.

Overcoat picked up one of the banded stacks, looked through it. He set it on the floor, picked up another, looked at it, then held it up. Johnny could see the dime-size hole through the bills where the bullet had gone through.

"Leave that one," Johnny said. "I'll take it."

Overcoat reached under the seat, came out with a black canvas bag. He opened it wide, set it on the floor, began to count money.

Johnny could feel sweat on his forehead, his hands. He wiped his right palm on his jeans, flexed his fingers. Overcoat saw it, looked at him. After a moment he went back to counting.

"Our friend?" Santelli said.

"Gone."

"And the *mulignan*?"

"Both. The Russian too."

Santelli nodded.

"I have to say, John, we're impressed. Anthony and I both. We didn't know if you could pull this off or not. When you reached out to us . . . well, who would have thought?"

"I'll take the bag," Johnny said. "You keep the suitcase."

Overcoat looked at him.

"I'm traveling light," Johnny said. "I need something I can carry easily."

Overcoat looked at Santelli, who nodded. Overcoat began to set bricks of money inside the bag.

"I'll count it when you're finished," Johnny said.

"You've got nothing to worry about, John," Santelli said. "When Anthony makes a deal, it's a deal. When people are straightforward, when they keep their part of the bargain, he'll do whatever it takes to keep his. His word is his bond."

"I know," Johnny said. The pain was back, a low throbbing, and a sharper pain inside, deeper.

The bag was starting to fill with money.

"What happened, with Joey," Santelli said. "It's best for everyone. It allows us all to get back to business. It's a better world without him, safer too. You did the right thing."

The bag was almost full when Overcoat looked up and said, "One twenty-five."

"Not a bad little nest egg," Santelli said. "Good traveling money. You still planning on traveling, right?"

"Yeah."

"Then you'll need these." He reached into a coat pocket, came out with a white envelope. He set it on the seat beside them, patted it.

Johnny took the envelope. Inside was a blue passport. He opened it, saw a picture of himself from years ago, before Glades, and the name Richard Martins. Also in the envelope was a New Jersey driver's license and a Social Security card, both in the same name.

"You could pay an arm and a leg for those things," Santelli said. "Have some scumbag do a crappy job, take your money and then turn you in to the Feds a month later when they start squeezing his balls about some Arabs coming in from Canada. But this . . . flawless work. And the guy who did it has no idea who you are, never saw you, except for that picture we gave him. Its clean, perfect. Like gold. It's a gesture, from Tony."

"It was part of the deal."

"It was. And he's kept it."

Johnny put everything back into the envelope, dropped it in the bag, zipped it up.

"I guess that's it," Santelli said.

"Thanks," Johnny said and reached for the door. Overcoat got it first, pushed it open. Johnny stepped out into the snow, felt a wave of dizziness sweep over him, then settle. He breathed in the cold air, dragged the bag out. There was a quarter-size blood spot on the seat where he'd been. Santelli looked at it, then up at him. Over-coat was watching him too.

"You sure you're all right?" Santelli said. "You need a doctor?"

Johnny shook his head.

"You sure?"

"I'm sure." He took another step back from the car.

Santelli and Overcoat looked at each other. Overcoat shrugged. Santelli turned back to him.

"Look out for yourself then," he said. *"Buona fortuna."*

Overcoat reached over, pulled the door shut. The Lincoln backed away, turned around in the lot. Johnny watched its taillights as it pulled back out onto the highway.

He stood there in the snow for a moment, then got Lindell's keys out. The first button he pushed set the jeep's alarm off, the second silenced it. The third unlocked the driver's-side door with a click.

He climbed in, wincing with pain, set the bag on the passenger seat. He turned the engine on and the stereo started up. Background chatter, voices as if at a party, then Marvin Gaye singing, *"Mother, mother . . ."*

He took his gloves from his jacket, put them on, turned the wipers on, adjusted the rearview. He took a last look up at the lighted office window as he pulled out of the lot and onto the highway.

BACK AT the motel, he upended the bag from the twenty-four-hour drugstore, spilled its contents into the bathroom sink. He shrugged off his jacket, let it fall to the floor.

The left side of his sweatshirt was sodden with blood. He raised his arms, peeled it off, feeling the pain. The wound was a few inches above his hip, the area around it puffed and discolored. The hole was smaller than a dime, edged in black, dried blood crusted around it and down his hip. The left thigh of his jeans was stained and stiff with blood.

He soaked a washrag in warm water, dabbed gently at the wound. As he touched it, blood began to seep out again. He wiped at it, saw the dark blue bulge just under the skin an inch or two away. The slug.

He turned the Mini Mag on, moved closer to the mirror, shone the beam into the wound. There were flecks of green inside, bits of money that had been driven into him by the bullet. Using the tweezers he'd bought, he picked at them, dragged them out piece by piece, sodden with blood. The pain brought nausea, dizziness. When he got all he could see, he dropped the bloody tweezers in the sink, opened the bottle of rubbing alcohol and half filled a plastic glass. Then he got the Buck knife out, opened it, swirled the blade in the alcohol.

After a few moments, he went to work. He pressed the point of the blade against the skin above the slug, sliced carefully. As the skin parted, blood began to ooze out. He put the knife down, squeezed the new wound with both hands until the slug eased through the incision and clattered into the sink. It was small, a .32 at best. Anything larger would have punched through the ribs, taken the lung.

He rinsed the blade again, scraped at the hole where the bullet had gone in, brought fresh bleeding. When he was done, he washed both wounds with alcohol and hot water, dried them with a towel and then slapped gauze pads over them. He got two banded stacks of money from the bag, set them against the gauze pads to hold them there, then wrapped everything with an ace bandage, cinched it tightly around his waist. Every breath hurt, but the dressings stayed in place.

He washed four aspirin down with a palmful of water from the sink, then got a fresh work shirt and jeans from his duffel, pulled them on. He put the canvas bag with the money on the bed, unzipped it. Into it went the rest of the money from the duffle, the tickets, the Sig, the extra clips and Connor's .38. He'd leave the rest of his clothes, his books. They were baggage from another life, another time.

When he was done, he put the bag in the jeep, shoved his bloody clothes into a Dumpster. He climbed into the jeep, turned the wipers on. It was snowing heavier now, the ground covered, the wind picking up.

Lindell's cell phone was plugged into a charger on the console. He picked it up, punched buttons until he got a signal. He dialed Mitch's number, waited. On the tenth ring it was answered.

"Yeah?" Mitch's voice.

"You're home," Johnny said.

"Jo—"

"Don't talk, just listen. Are there people with you now?"

"Just Sharonda and Treya."

"Cops still outside?"

"I don't know. Probably."

"We'll keep this quick. That thing I told you about. That trip. It's happening tomorrow."

"Tomorrow?"

"There's a place for you too, if you want to come. But you have to walk away from there tomorrow, with whatever's on your back. If they follow you, you'll have to lose them."

"What about clothes?"

"We'll buy what we need."

"I don't know. . . . Sharonda might not—"

"Not Sharonda, not Treya. Just you."

Silence on the line.

"We've been apart for a long time, Mitch. When I was in James-burg, then later in Glades. Things got fucked up. We've got another chance now. But I'm not coming back—ever."

"I didn't want to tell them anything. I didn't. But they were going to take Treya away."

"Forget about all that. It doesn't matter anymore."

"But I've been thinking . . ."

"About what?"

Johnny unzipped the canvas bag, took the Amtrak tickets out. A man he'd known in Glades, a French-Canadian Hells Angel named Latourre, had told him Vancouver was one of the most beautiful cities in the world. A place to start over. Wilderness, mountains. Cold. Clean.

"It's just that . . . I've never really had anything before, you know? Nothing worth holding on to, at least. I mean, I'm a fuckup from the word go, right? I've screwed up everything I've ever tried to do."

"You come with me, you start over. You can forget all that bull-shit."

"What I mean is . . . it doesn't feel right, leaving them here. It feels like running away."

Johnny watched the snow, listened to the wind.

"You there?" Mitch said.

"I'm here." He dropped the tickets back in the bag.

"I wish I could, John."

"We all walk our path, Mitchy."

"What?"

"Our path. We all have one. It's laid out in front of us from the day we're born, whether we recognize it or not. And there isn't a goddamn thing we can do about it."

More silence.

"Take care of yourself, Mitch. And take care of that little girl."

"Where are you going? How am I going to reach you?"

"Bye, Mitch," he said and ended the call.

Wind shook the jeep. He started the engine. Snow seemed to blow at the windshield from different angles. He turned the wipers on.

Tomorrow I'll be gone, he thought. Out of here for good, forever. The loose ends tied now, his destiny come round. And only one last stop to make.

THIRTY-EIGHT

AT HIS FIRST KICK, THE BACK DOOR EXPLODED INWARD, SHOWERED glass on the kitchen floor. Johnny went in, tracking snow. He raised the Sig, stepped into a hallway. Suitcases here, ready to go. In the living room, a thin blond man, staring at him, frozen.

"Reggie!" the blond man said.

Johnny looked at him, confused, heard thumping steps on the stairs behind him. He turned, saw a man built like a weight lifter come quickly down the stairs, wearing sweatpants, a T-shirt with the sleeves cut off, arms thick and veined. He came at him without hesitation and Johnny raised the Sig, shot him through the left shoulder.

It spun him to the side, checked his momentum, but he kept coming. Johnny stepped back, lowered the Sig and fired again. Blood burst from the weight lifter's right thigh and he went down onto his knees.

Behind him, he heard the blond man pulling at the front door, working the locks. Johnny moved quickly, caught him by the back of his shirt, spun him around and kicked his legs out from under him. He went down hard and Johnny leaned over him, touched the warm silencer to his forehead. The blond man closed his eyes.

Johnny sucked air, the pain in his side flaring. The weight lifter was moaning on the floor, holding his injured leg. Johnny twisted the silencer into the soft skin between the blond man's eyes.

"Where is she?" he said.

The blond man's eyes opened.

"You're him, aren't you?" he said.

"I'm him."

"She's not here."

285

Johnny looked around the room, caught the collar of the man's shirt, dragged him farther away from the door. He put the silencer behind the man's right ear.

"Where is she?" he said again. "I'm not going to ask much longer."

The blond man had gone rigid, eyes shut, tears leaking. The weight lifter was watching them, hands clasped over his bleeding leg.

Johnny turned to him.

"You know, don't you?" he said.

"Fuck you."

"You do know," Johnny said. He used the Sig to pin the blond man's head to the floor.

"Leave him alone."

"Tell me where she is," he said. "And tell me now. Or I'm going to shoot your friend through the head."

"This is bullshit," the weight lifter said, pain and anger in his voice. "This hasn't got anything to do with us."

"Not the point," Johnny said. "Counting to ten. One, two—"

"Stop it."

"Three—"

"She's at a hotel. They took her there."

"Who?" Johnny said. "Who took her there?"

"Those people. That man."

"What man?"

The blond man was shaking now, as if with a seizure.

"What man?" Johnny said.

"Harry," the weight lifter said. "His name's Harry."

Johnny took the Sig away, straightened. The blond man didn't move or open his eyes.

"What hotel? Where?"

"I don't fucking know, man. They didn't tell us."

"You talk to her since?"

"Jack has."

"Today?"

"She called. She didn't say where she was. I'm telling you the truth. We *don't know*."

Johnny eased the hammer down on the Sig, slipped the safety on. He reversed the gun in his grip, raised it and brought the butt down hard on the blond man's right knee. He cried out, shuddered, but his eyes stayed closed.

"You stay there," Johnny said to him. "Don't move."

He went past them into the kitchen, saw the weight lifter begin to crawl across the floor to the blond man.

There was a cordless phone resting in its base on the counter. Johnny picked it up, hit Star 69, got a local number back. He dialed it and a hotel operator answered.

"I need you to help me," he told her. "Someone called me, left this number but not the room they were in."

"What's the name?"

"Might be registered a couple different ways. Try Ellis first."

Computer keys clacked. He saw a phone book atop the refrigerator. He set the Sig on the counter, pulled the book down, began to flip through the pages.

"No guest by that name," the operator said. "Want to try another?"

"Rane." He spelled it.

More keys clacking. He paged quickly through the book to the INVESTIGATIONS heading, traced his finger down the listings until he got to RW SECURITY. There was a small ad for it in a corner of the page, with a silhouette of the state of New Jersey. At the bottom of the ad, in smaller type, was RAYMOND J. WASHINGTON. NJ STATE LICENSED. BONDED. INSURED.

"No one by that name either, sir."

"Let's try another. Washington."

The sound of keys and then "That would be a Miss Washington?"

"Yes."

"That's Room 916. Should I connect you?"

"No," he said. "That's all right. I'll call back."

He hung up, flipped through pages until he found the listing for the hotel, the address. He ripped the page out, went back and tore out the RW ad as well. If he had the wrong hotel, or if she'd already left, it would be a place to start again. But he knew it was the right hotel, that he'd find her there. Things were falling into place again, the path revealing itself.

He took out the Buck knife, used the blade to slice through the cord that led from the phone base to the wall outlet. Back in the living room, the blond man was sobbing softly, the weight lifter cradling him in his arms.

On an end table by the couch, a cell phone was plugged into a charger. Johnny unplugged it, dropped the phone on the floor and crushed it with a boot, heard it snap and splinter. He kicked the pieces across the floor.

"I should kill you both," he said.

"Just get out of here," the weight lifter said. "Leave us alone. Just go."

He raised the Sig, pointed it at them.

"You try to call her, warn her," he said. "And I'll be back."

"We don't know where she is," the weight lifter said. "I told you that."

"And why should I believe you?" Johnny said. He thumbed back the hammer.

The weight lifter looked straight into the muzzle.

"If you're going to do it, do it," he said. "If not, then just leave us alone."

Johnny looked into his eyes, lowered the gun.

"Brave man," he said.

He eased the hammer down, raised his jacket and slipped the gun into his belt.

"Don't hurt her," the weight lifter said.

Johnny shook his head.

"I'd never do that," he said. "She's my girl."

Then he went back through the kitchen and out the ruined door into the night.

HE CRUISED the hotel parking lot, wipers on, looking at cars. There was a station wagon parked near the front entrance, a black man at the wheel. No Mustang.

He drove around the side of the hotel, parked near the dark restaurant. There was a service entrance back there by the Dumpster, fire doors. He got out of the jeep, walked through the snow and climbed up onto a loading platform. The first door he tried was locked, the second opened when he pushed on it. He stepped through into a dark kitchen area. The wind shut the door behind him.

HE RODE the elevator to the ninth floor, walked down the carpeted hall counting room numbers. When he got to 916, he knocked twice, stood at an angle away from the peephole.

"Who is it?"

He knocked again.

He heard the chain being undone. When the door started to open, he put his hand against it, shoved. She stumbled back and the door thudded into the wall.

He stepped in, shut the door behind him, heard it lock.

"Hey, baby," he said.

THIRTY-NINE

HARRY STOOD ON HIS PORCH, WATCHED THE SNOW. THE WIND WHISTLED through the weeping willows, their bare branches fluttering.

He went back inside, put kindling and logs in the fireplace, poured a glass of wine. He turned on the television, switched to the Weather Channel. The local forecast ran as a crawl across the bottom of the screen. Six to ten inches of snow, winds up to forty miles per hour. A good night to stay in.

He drank wine, watched television, looked at his watch. Ten P.M. Not too late.

In the kitchen, he set his glass on the counter, dialed the hotel, then direct-dialed the room. It rang five times, then switched to voice mail. He hung up, looked out the kitchen window into the backyard. The drifts were already collecting against the house, the wind sweeping the snow across the yard.

He finished the glass, tried the number again. Five rings and voice mail. After a few minutes, he dialed Ray's home number. Edda called him to the phone.

"What's up?" Ray said.

"You sleeping?"

"Watching the news. Feeling grateful I'm not out tonight. What's the problem?"

"It's probably nothing. I called Nikki at the hotel a couple times. There was no answer."

"How long ago?"

"Just now."

"How many times did you let it ring?"

"Enough. Is Errol still out there?"

"He was. But he called me twenty minutes ago to say he was going home. He was worried about getting stuck there with this weather. I told him to go, we'll pick it up again tomorrow. Nobody's moving out there tonight, anyway, with this snow."

"Maybe I should head over there."

"This could be nothing, you know. She could be down in the hotel bar. Night like this, that's where I'd be."

"You're probably right."

"But if it's really bothering you, call the desk. Have them send someone up to check. If she's in the bar, they can page her."

"Maybe I'll do that."

"Listen, if you have a bad feeling about this, I'll call Errol's cell, have him go back. He wouldn't be home yet, anyway."

"No, that's okay."

"I wouldn't go out there if I were you, not in that thing you drive. It'll be all over the road. You'll end up in a ditch until morning."

"I'm not sure what I'm going to do."

"I'm sure there's nothing to worry about. Try her again, see if she answers."

"I will," he said. "I'll call you back later."

He dialed the room again. When the voice mail picked up, he hung up, got his leather jacket from the peg by the door. He found his car keys and headed out into the storm.

"LONG TIME," Johnny said.

She was sitting on the bed, watching him. He'd pulled a chair away from the desk, sat facing her. The phone was behind him and she would have to cross in front of him to reach the door. His side was stiff and ached dully, but the sharpest pain was gone.

He studied her, seeing the changes. The crow's-feet around her eyes. Her long brown hair lighter, chopped short. She wore jeans, boots, a dark sweater.

"You look good," he said.

"Did you do it?" she said.

"Did I do what?" He got his cigarettes out.

"Kill her?"

He looked at her, lit a cigarette, put the lighter away, didn't answer. He saw the fear in her eyes, but something else too.

"You shouldn't have done it, John. There was no reason to."

"Easy to look back, say that," he said. "But in the actual situation? Things don't always go as planned."

"You shouldn't have done it."

"She was warned. Face-to-face. She wanted to send me back inside. I couldn't let that happen."

"She never did anything to you, Johnny."

He blew smoke out.

"Well, it doesn't matter now, does it?" he said.

He looked around the room.

"You're here alone," he said.

"Yes."

"Where's your boyfriend?"

"Why are you doing this, John?"

"A guy back in Glades once told me women are like monkeys. They never let go of one branch until they have a firm grip on another. And you've just gone from branch to branch to branch, haven't you?"

She didn't answer, wrapped her arms around herself.

"And you always land on your feet, don't you? No matter what. Because the world's still full of guys you can fuck to get what you want, isn't it?"

"What do you want, John?"

"I went through a lot to get here right now," he said. "To be with you. I just want to talk."

"I never did anything to hurt you, John. Ever." He could see she was trying to get her edge back, her composure. Trying to turn the situation to her advantage.

"Well, I guess that's all relative, isn't it?" he said.

"How did you find me?"

"Wasn't hard. Did you really think you could hide from me? I mean, Christ, babe, seven years. I'd hope you'd at least want to see me once. For old times' sake."

Snow blew against the window.

"You have any idea what I've gone through since I went away?" he said. "The things I've done? The things I've had done to me?"

"Why, Johnny? Why all this? You were out of there. You could have gone anywhere."

"You think so?"

"Why come back?"

"I don't know. Maybe because I wanted to see you. See my son."

She looked at the floor.

"He's not here," she said. "Not anymore."

"I know. And I didn't have a say in that either, did I?"

"I did what was right."

"Because you didn't want him growing up with a father like me?"

She shook her head, looked away.

"Then what? What were you trying to protect him from?"

"Me," she said.

He looked at her, blew smoke out, said nothing.

"Wherever he is," she said, "he's better off. He has a chance now. We were all out of chances, even back then."

He got up, walked to the window, looked down into the parking lot. The station wagon was gone. Snow swirled in the lights.

"You're right," he said. "He is better off. I've seen him."

He turned to her, met her eyes.

"I found him," he said. "I thought I wanted to take him away, take him with me, do whatever I had to do to make that happen. But I guess I really just wanted to see him. Once. Something you never gave me the chance to do."

"I had no choice, Johnny. It was the right thing. The only thing."

"Maybe," he said. "Maybe it was."

He moved back to the chair, swung it around to straddle it, winced at the pain. She saw it in his face. He sat down, the Sig digging into his back. He pulled it out, set it on the bureau beside him. She looked at it.

The phone began to ring. They turned to it. It rang five times, fell silent.

"How is he?" she said.

He looked back at her, shrugged.

"Good," he said. "As far as I could tell. Big house. Family. A life. A real life."

"It tore me apart to give him away. You think it didn't? He was my baby. I had to lay there, watch them take him out of the room, knowing I'd never see him again. Do you think that was easy? But I did what I had to do."

"And taking up with Joey A. after I was gone? That something you had to do?"

"I needed money. I needed to get by. He offered to help me. I wasn't in a position to turn him down."

"Yeah, I guess. And what's another fuck more or less, right?"

"I loved you, Johnny. But I had to go on. You'd left me with nothing."

He felt the anger then. He dropped the cigarette on the carpet, ground it out with a boot.

"Did your boyfriend tell you what I did to him?" he said. "Did he tell you I had him on his knees? He was practically crying when I let him go. If he'd been in Glades with me, I would have made him my bitch, then passed him around the tier. You couldn't do any better than him?"

"He wanted to help me."

"And look where it got him. I have to hand it to you, Nikki. You were always a piece of ass. Better than most. But to get somebody to risk their life, for you, take a beating for you . . . well, you must be a better fuck now than you ever were then."

"He's got nothing to do with this, with us."

The phone rang again. Five times, stopped.

"You're popular these days," he said. "Ten o'clock at night and people calling you. Think that was him? Maybe next time I'll answer."

"Leave, Johnny. For both our sakes, just go."

"So you can invite him over? Think I can live with that? Knowing that five minutes after I left, some guy's over here fucking you? How do you think that makes me feel?"

She looked at the floor.

"Please, John."

He felt the heat in his face.

"I loved you," he said. "But all you did was use me. Just like everybody else in your life."

"That's not true, Johnny." She looked up, met his eyes. "It's not."

The fear was strong in her now, he could see it. But she didn't look away.

He stood up.

"Take your clothes off," he said.

She watched him.

"You heard me," he said. "Why should everyone else be getting some, and not me? Doesn't make much sense, does it."

"Johnny, please—"

"Take them off."

"Johnny, I—"

He hit her high in the right forehead with his open hand, knocked her onto her side on the bed. She tried to curl up and he caught her throat with his left hand, straightened her out and pinned her there, leaning his weight into her. She slapped at him, kicked, and a knee thudded into his thigh. Pain shot up through his side and he reached into his pocket, got the Buck out. He opened the knife one-handed, snapped his wrist so that it locked into place. She stopped fighting, looked at the blade.

He could feel sweat on his face, wet warmth against his side, fresh bleeding. Pain like a tearing inside him. He touched the point of the knife to her face, just below her left eye.

She looked up at him, met his eyes. He knew then he didn't want her, would never want her again. He took the knife away, held her there with his hand, his weight still pinning her.

"You're beautiful," he said. "You always were."

He felt her relax slightly under him.

"And that was the problem all along, wasn't it?" he said and dragged the edge of the blade from her left cheek to her chin.

She closed her eyes as the blood welled up, didn't scream. He let go of her throat, stood up. The phone rang again. Five times, then silence.

"You had it coming, baby," he said. "You can't say you didn't."

She touched her hand to her face, began to shudder and sob silently. He wiped the blade clean on the pillowcase, folded the knife and put it back in his pocket.

She curled up on the bed, shaking, still making no noise. Blood dripped from her face onto the comforter.

He was breathing heavily, the pain inside deeper now.

"You got off easy," he said. "Look at it that way."

He got the Sig, pushed it back into his belt. He caught a glimpse of himself in the mirror above the bureau. His face was white, dark circles under his eyes.

He turned to her and she wasn't on the bed anymore, was kneeling on the floor, a shoulder purse in her lap, hand inside.

"What are you—" he started to say and then the hand came out and there was a gun in it.

He reached under his jacket for the Sig but she already had the gun up, was aiming. A flat crack and the mirror behind him broke. He raised his left hand and she fired again. Something hard slapped his palm and hot blood spotted his face. He reeled away from her, his legs hitting the chair, and then he was falling. He landed on his side, the pain tearing through him, heard a bullet hit the chair, saw splinters fly from the leg.

She was aiming now, and a bullet whizzed past his ear, punched into the bureau. He kicked the chair at her, rolled onto his knees, felt a flash of fire along his neck, wet heat in the collar of his shirt. She was still aiming, still firing, and he lurched toward the door, heard bullets hit the wall behind him.

The door flew open, a uniformed security guard standing there, and Johnny slammed into him, drove him back into the hallway. They fell together, the pain stealing his breath. Then Johnny was on his feet, moving toward the stairwell, the guard still on the floor.

Johnny hit the fire door, drove it back against the wall, went down the stairs fast, his footsteps echoing. He looked at his left hand, saw the hole where the small bullet had neatly pierced his palm.

He took the steps two at a time, was gasping when he reached the emergency exit, red sign glowing above it. He hit the panic bar with his shoulder, stepped out into blowing snow.

He could hear sirens in the distance. He headed for the jeep, got the door open and pulled himself up into the driver's seat. His left hand was numb, but he could move the fingers, so he knew the tendons were intact. He looked at himself in the rearview, saw the line of red on his neck where her fifth shot had grazed him. There was blood on his face, the taste of it like salt and copper on his lips.

He dragged the Sig out, put it on the passenger seat, got the engine started. He could see flashing lights maybe a half mile back. He slammed the jeep into gear, gave it gas and headed for the exit, steering one handed, the wheels spinning slightly when he hit the highway.

He put the pedal to the floor, felt the big engine respond, turned the wipers on against the snow. Thick flakes flew wild in the headlights. In the rearview, he saw the flashing lights slow, turn into the hotel lot.

His hand was throbbing now. He moved his fingers, saw fresh blood ooze from the wound. He pulled his jacket open. The side of his work shirt was dark where he'd torn open the wound, blood seeping through the dressing.

He smiled then, thinking of her, what she had done to him. The Sig slid off the seat, thumped onto the floor. He left it there.

Bleeding, he drove into the night.

FORTY

HE HAD TO FIGHT TO KEEP THE MUSTANG ON THE ROAD. EVERY TIME
he slowed, braked, he could feel the rear end swinging, the tires
losing traction. No sand trucks yet and every half mile a car was
stranded by the side of the road, hazard lights blinking. The Mustang's wipers thumped back and forth at full strength, but the snow
was coming down thicker, heavier, the road a field of white in front
of him. No telling where the yellow lines were or where the road
ended and the shoulder began.

When he rounded the final curve, he could see the hotel ahead.
There were flashing lights outside the entrance—red, yellow and
blue. Police cars, an ambulance. Dread bloomed inside him.

THEY HAD her in a treatment room by herself, two cops standing
outside the half-open door. He went past them into the dim room.

She was lying on the treatment table, face turned to the wall, a
pillow propped under her. A wide swath of gauze covered her left
cheek.

"Hey," he said.

She turned to face him.

"Harry?"

She sat up and he held her, saw the tears. Her sweater was stiff
with blood.

"Easy," he said. "Easy." She put her right cheek against his chest
and he held her there, felt her tremble against him. He kissed her
hair.

298

He turned, saw the cops watching from the doorway. They looked at him, then turned away.

"They gave me something for the pain," she said. "But I don't feel it yet."

"You will."

"Did they get him?"

"Not yet."

"I shot him."

"I heard. They'll find him soon."

"I hurt him, I know I did."

"Easy. Easy."

"All this time, I thought I was smarter than him. That when it happened I could still handle him. Look him in the eye."

"Shhh."

"Fifteen stitches, Harry. That's how many it took. I'll never be pretty again."

"Don't say that."

"It's true."

He kissed her forehead, squeezed her.

"Lie back."

"He didn't kill me. Why didn't he kill me? Why Sherry and not me?"

"I don't know," he said. "Relax, breathe deep." He eased her back onto the table, felt some of the tension go out of her. She gripped his hand.

There was a shadow in the doorway and he looked up, saw Branson, the county detective, there. Branson bent his head toward the corridor. Harry nodded, watched him go.

Whatever they had given her was kicking in now. She lay back, touched his face.

"You'll always be beautiful," he said. "Nothing can ever change that."

She shook her head slowly and the tears started again. He touched the line of her jaw, kissed the gauze gently, then brushed his lips over hers. She looked at him through half-closed eyes, her grip tighter.

They sat like that for a while, until he felt her breathing steady and deepen as the painkiller took effect, watched her slide gradually into sleep.

Branson was out in the waiting room with Ray and Errol. Through the automatic emergency doors, Harry could see a snowplow with flashing yellow lights clearing the area outside.

They turned to face him as he came out. Branson had a cup of coffee from a vending machine.

"She's sleeping," Harry said.

"She'll stay the night," Branson said. "I've already talked to the nursing supervisor. They'll put her in a room if they can. I'll leave the officers here as well."

Through the doors, Harry watched snow swirl in the parking lot lights.

"Any word?" he said.

"Nothing yet," Branson said. "But in this weather, he's not going to get very far. He might have run off the road somewhere already. We'll find him."

"I called the Neptune cops," Ray said. "Asked them to go by that house in Ocean Grove, in case Harrow had been there. He had. They'd already had a call out."

Harry looked at him. "What happened?"

"One of them—the musclehead—was shot, leg and shoulder, but they think he'll be all right. The other one was roughed up, had a broken knee. The one who was shot managed to make it to a neighbor's house before he passed out. He crawled all the way. The neighbor called the police."

"Harrow's been a busy boy," Branson said. Then to Harry: "I called Vic Salerno, told him what was going on. No way he can make it down here through this, though. You hear about Alea?"

Harry shook his head.

"Springfield police got a call earlier tonight, shots fired at this porn store Alea owns on Twenty-Two."

"Yeah?"

"They found him in there, along with a couple guys work for him. One named Lindell, another named Ismayla, a Russian. You know them?"

"No."

"All three shot to death. Shell casings all over the place."

"Sounds like a labor-management dispute," Ray said.

"There's blood all over the walls," Branson said. "Some of it might be our boy's. This Lindell had a weapon too, looks like he got off a full magazine. Could be Harrow was wounded before he walked out of there. Either way, the woman says she tagged him too, at the hotel, with a little twenty-five she had."

"I've seen it," Harry said.

"Could be he's dead already. Bled out somewhere."

"I don't think so," Harry said.

"When the snow slows down—if it slows down—we'll get a state police helicopter up, start searching the area around the hotel. Until then, though, there's not much we can do except wait for him to show up somewhere."

"Won't be long," Ray said. "Way he's been going, his string must be about run out."

"Don't count on it," Harry said.

HE HAD the heater on full, but it seemed like the jeep would never warm up. He was trembling now and every few minutes his hand would spasm in his lap. There was dried blood on the seat, on the steering wheel. He was headed up Route 34, watching for Parkway signs, the road unbroken white in front of him. Once on the Parkway, he'd go north, find a motel to hole up in for the night, ditch the jeep.

The snow danced in his headlights, made kamikaze runs at the windshield. He felt his eyelids grow heavy, sleep stealing up on him. It was shock, he knew. Loss of blood. He had to fight it. He powered the window down a crack, the cold air whipping in, turned on the stereo. Marvin Gaye singing about mercy.

Headlights came at him, high beams. A horn blew and he realized he'd drifted into the oncoming lane. He steered back, braked, felt the rear wheels lose traction. The car passed him as he fought the skid. He worked the brake and gas and the jeep did a one-eighty on the ice and ended up on the shoulder, facing the opposite direction.

He sat there for a moment, trying to control his breathing. He closed his eyes, waited for the Valley. It wouldn't come.

Wind rocked the jeep. When he opened his eyes, the snow seemed to be blowing almost horizontally. Another car went by him without slowing, disappeared into the storm.

One-handed, he got his cigarettes out, pushed in the dashboard lighter. When it popped out, he lit the cigarette, dragged in smoke. Then he pulled onto the road, gave it gas, headed back the way he'd come.

THEY LEFT the Mustang at the hospital. Errol drove him back to Colts Neck in the station wagon, never getting above twenty-five miles an hour. Errol's fists were tight on the wheel, the wind stronger than before. At times it felt like it was going to push the wagon off the road.

"No way you're going to make it home to Asbury in this," Harry said. "You should stay at the farm tonight."

"We're going to be lucky if we make it there."

"There's a turn-off up ahead. Stay to the right."

After a few minutes, Errol said, "I shouldn't have left."

"No way you could have known. They say he went in through a service entrance anyway. You probably wouldn't even have seen him."

"Maybe I would have."

"And maybe not. Or maybe he would have seen you, popped you before he went up there or after he came out. No sense thinking about it. It'll just make you crazy. The driveway's up here, on the left."

"I see it," Errol said when the lights of the house came into view. "Hope you got something to drink in there, because I need it."

"Find something, I'm sure."

They turned into the driveway, the wagon's back wheels spinning before they caught hold.

"No way that Ford was going to make it up here in this," Errol said.

"You're probably right."

They went up the slope of the drive carefully, pulled into the side yard. Snow swirled wildly in the security light above the barn. Errol shut off the engine and lights, the wind howling around the wagon.

Harry got out of the car, his legs heavy. Anger had given way to exhaustion, left him stranded someplace between them. He felt empty, spent.

They walked in the teeth of the wind to the back door. Harry got his keys out, and Errol caught the storm door to keep the wind from yanking it off its hinges. Harry unlocked the main door and they went into the kitchen. He pulled the storm door closed, latched it, locked the main door behind him.

"Started building a fire earlier," he said. "Never got a chance to light it. I'll do it now."

"Sounds good to me."

Harry stamped his boots to get the snow off, hung his jacket on the peg by the door. Errol did the same.

"Go on in the living room," Harry said. "Beer all right?"

"Cold beer on a cold night. Can't beat it."

"I'll be right in and get that thing lit."

He opened the refrigerator, took out two Coronas.

From the living room, he heard Errol say, "Harry?"

The roar of the gun filled the house. Errol flew back into the kitchen, crashed into the table, took a chair down with him as he hit the floor. Harry dropped the beers, saw Harrow standing in the doorway to the living room, the Winchester pump up at his shoulder. Gunsmoke drifted in the air.

"Two points," he said. "What do I win?"

FORTY-ONE

HARRY LOOKED INTO THE MUZZLE OF THE SHOTGUN. HARROW WORKED the pump and a smoking shell flew from the breach, landed on the floor as another shell chambered. The gun didn't waver.

He wondered what he would see in the final moment. A blur from the barrel, flame and smoke? Or nothing at all. Just the crushing impact as the twelve-gauge pellets hit him. He looked at the gun, the face beyond it, didn't move.

Harrow lowered the shotgun, held it at port arms, the butt against his right hip. His left hand was bandaged, swollen.

"You rush to her rescue?" he said. "She call you?"

Harry didn't answer. Harrow pointed the shotgun at him one-handed, then at the living room.

"Come on in," he said. "It's your house."

Harry went into the dim living room. There were red-stained bandages on the floor, a box of gauze he knew had come from his own medicine cabinet, an empty bottle of hydrogen peroxide. On the coffee table, the Percocet bottle lay open on its side.

"Helped myself," Harrow said. "Hope you don't mind."

He pointed the shotgun at the couch.

"Sit down. Turn that light on."

Harry sat, reached over, switched the lamp on. Harrow blinked. His face was pale, vaguely yellow in the light, and there was a line of dried blood across his neck. His shirt was partially unbuttoned and Harry could see the Sacred Heart tattoo, the edges of a bandage.

Harrow sat down in a club chair, the shotgun across his lap. On the floor beside him was a black canvas bag and the box of shotgun shells.

"Almost didn't make it here," he said. "Jeep too, four-wheel drive. I parked near some woods, walked a fucking quarter mile here through the snow. Didn't think I was going to find it."

He picked up the box of shells, fumbled with it one-handed, got it open. He took a shell out and the box fell from his knee, its contents spilling out on the floor. A shell rolled under the coffee table, came to rest against one of the legs.

"Fuck," Harrow said. He thumbed the shell he held into the receiver.

"You don't look so good," Harry said. "You look like you need a hospital."

"You don't know the half of it."

With the shotgun on his lap, he reached into his jacket pocket, took out a pack of Camels. He shook one out, got it in his mouth, lit it with a silver Zippo from the same pocket.

"Problem is," he said, "I'm getting low on options."

He reached into his other pocket, came out with a pair of hand-cuffs.

"You might as well put these on." He tossed them at Harry. They hit his thigh, clattered to the floor. "We'll be here a little bit."

Harry looked at them. The muzzle of the shotgun shifted, pointed at him.

"Go on," Harrow said.

Harry picked up the cuffs, slipped one over his left wrist, ratcheted it closed.

"All the way," Harrow said. His index finger was on the trigger of the shotgun. Harry slid the teeth home, heard them lock. He closed the second cuff over his right wrist.

"That one too," Harrow said. Harry pushed on the cuff until it locked.

The shotgun muzzle lowered.

"Have to admit," Harrow said, "I did underestimate you once. My mistake. I figured after what happened, you'd take off, not even say good-bye. But you didn't, did you?"

"You're running out of road. Time to give it up."

"Is it?"

Harry nodded.

"You could be right," Harrow said. He lifted the shotgun. "Fucking thing's heavy." He set the butt on the floor, tried to lean the barrel against the chair. It slid off and hit the floor, the muzzle pointing at Harry's feet.

"Oops," Harrow said. "That would have been a fuckup, wouldn't it?"

He'd taken the automatic from his jacket pocket. Harry saw it was a Sig, nine-millimeter, eleven shots at least, suppressor screwed into the barrel.

"I'd planned to dust you as soon as you walked in the door," Harrow said. "Just like the other guy. Not sure why I didn't. Maybe it's because we have something in common. What do you think?"

"There's a hospital not far from here. Even with the snow, I could get you there in a few minutes."

Harrow nodded, blew smoke out.

"And that would be a very Christian thing for you to do. But I think we're just going to wait here, till this weather clears. Then I'll take that wagon you drove up in and be on my way."

The house shook in the wind. From somewhere upstairs, they heard the whistle of a draft.

"Fucking cold in here," Harrow said. He looked at the fireplace. "Why don't you get that thing going?"

Harry looked at him, got up. There was a box of wooden matches on the mantel. He got it open, awkwardly took one out, lit it. He pulled the screen away, leaned down, dropped the match in. The paper there caught, yellow flames rising around the kindling. The fire crackled, grew.

"Now sit back down there," Harrow said.

Harry did as he was told. Yellow light spilled out onto the hearth as the logs caught.

"That's better," Harrow said. He cocked his head, looked out the window onto the porch.

"Still coming down," he said.

Harry slid his right foot out, put it over the shotgun shell that had come to rest under the table. Harrow looked back at him.

"Maybe a foot of snow before it's over," he said. "I have the feeling I'm not going to make that train."

"What train?"

Harrow pulled the canvas bag closer to him, opened it. He took out an envelope with tickets in it, tossed it into Harry's lap.

"The big getaway," he said. "What a fucking joke."

Harry looked at the tickets, saw the final destination.

"Vancouver," he said.

"Yeah, one was for me, one for my brother. One for my son."

Harry looked at him.

"But things don't always work out the way you want them to," Harrow said. "Maybe I was just fooling myself all along."

He dropped the cigarette on the floor, put it out with a boot. A log fell and cracked in the fireplace. Shadows flared.

"Your brother," Harry said.

Harrow nodded.

"Didn't want to go. Can't blame him either, I guess. He's got a woman now, a little girl. I should have let them be. Instead, I fucked everything up for him. I always thought I was protecting him, you know? Our whole lives. But he was better off without me, always was."

"Police will be after him, try to find out where you are."

"And he won't know. It's all bullshit. Mitch had nothing to do with any of this, since I got out of Glades. Somebody should know that. Somebody should tell the cops that. I would, but they wouldn't believe me."

"I'll tell them."

"That's being a little optimistic now, isn't it?"

"Maybe."

He could feel the warmth of the fire now, the heat on his legs. He dragged the shotgun shell closer to the couch.

Harrow looked at him.

"You think after all this shit I'm just going to let you go?" he said. "Walk away, leave you behind?"

"I don't know."

Harrow aimed the Sig at him.

"If I was smart, I'd do you right now. Get it over with. But then I'd be stuck here the rest of the night with the both of you. Don't get the wrong impression, though. Whatever happens, you won't have any fucking say in it. If I'm telling you things, it's because I need to say them. But don't flatter yourself. You were in the wrong place, the wrong time. And that's just fate."

Harry didn't respond.

"I do have one question for you, though," Harrow said.

"What's that?"

"Was she worth it?"

"What do you mean?"

"I know how it is. Man starts thinking with his dick, he doesn't want to hear any opposing viewpoints. But look where it got you."

Another log cracked, fell.

"We've got a lot in common, you know?" Harrow said. "I had this whole thing figured out, every detail. Except for Nikki. I couldn't leave her alone. I let her get to me again. And I fucked everything up."

He reached back into the bag, came out with a banded stack of money, tossed it on the coffee table. It slid to the edge, fell over.

"A hundred and twenty-five grand in this bag, give or take," he said. "And the more I carry it around, the heavier it gets. So what does that mean, huh?"

Harry reached down, picked up the stack. He moved his foot, closed his right hand around the shotgun shell. He dropped the money on the table, brought his hands back into his lap.

Harrow was getting another cigarette out.

"She played us," he said. "All of us. You know that? Me, Joey. You too." He put a cigarette between his lips, flipped the lighter open, got it lit. He coughed as he sucked in the smoke, put the lighter away.

"But you don't even know what the fuck I'm talking about, do you? What any of this is about. I'm rambling, I guess. Must be that shit I found in your medicine chest." He nodded at the Percocet bottle. "They're finally starting to work, though."

"It's not too late. We can end this before anyone else gets hurt."

"You're wrong," Harrow said. "It is too late."

His eyelids dipped for a moment, opened wide. The room was warm now, close. He shook his head as if to clear it.

"Long day," he said. "Almost over, though."

"She loved you," Harry said.

"What?"

"Nikki. She loved you, you know."

"Once maybe."

"She did. She told me."

"She had a strange way of showing it last time we met."

"Doesn't change what was, though, does it?"

"Enough bullshit. Why don't you put another log in that fire, then sit your ass back down? You're making me regret not popping you."

Harry got up, went to the hearth. There was a metal bucket with split logs to the right of the fireplace, next to the rack that held poker and shovel. He pulled the screen away, used both hands to take out a log, could feel Harrow's eyes on his back. He leaned forward, felt the heat on his face, let the shell roll out of his hand into the embers, set the log atop it. He moved the screen back into place.

"Sit down," Harrow said. Harry moved back to the couch. Flames started to creep up around the fresh log. The room got brighter.

Harrow finished the cigarette, put it out with his boot, looked into the fire. Harry saw his eyelids flutter, close, open wide. His grip tightened on the Sig.

"Just can't seem to get warm," Harrow said. "I don't know what it is." He turned to Harry and then the fireplace exploded.

Harry raised his arms to cover his face, turned away as the screen blew out. Steel shot rang off stone, whistled away, ash and smoke filling the air. Harrow twisted, tumbled out of the chair.

Harry pushed himself off the couch, ran into the smoke, got his hands on the poker, dragged it from the rack, spun. He saw Harrow roll and come up fast onto his knees, the Sig extended. There was a blur from the barrel and Harry heard the bullet go past him as he swung. As if in slow motion, he saw the poker connect with Harrow's wrist, saw the Sig fly away, hit the wall, fall behind the couch.

They both looked at the wall for an instant and then Harrow went for the shotgun.

Harry swung the poker again, missed, overbalanced. Harrow rolled onto his back, kicked up with both boots. They took Harry in the stomach, knocked him backward. He came down hard on the coffee table and it broke under his weight. He kicked out, tried to swing the poker again. Harrow avoided the blow, came at him, the shotgun forgotten, and then Harry drove a boot heel up into his side.

It folded him. He gasped, bent, and Harry rolled clear of the broken table, dropped the poker, got his hands on the shotgun. He crab-crawled away, got the gun up in front of him, raised it with his right leg, his finger on the trigger. Harrow reached into the black bag, pulled out a revolver, aimed.

They fired at the same time. The shotgun roared off Harry's leg, leaped from his hand, the muzzle rising toward the ceiling. The recoil wrenched it from his grip and the stock hit him in the face as it flew by. He heard it land behind him, raised his head, tasting the blood in his mouth, his ears ringing. He looked into a dissipating cloud of cordite smoke.

Harrow was sitting on the stone hearth, his back to the fireplace, smoking embers all around him. The right side of his jacket was torn, the shirt beneath it darkening with blood. He held the revolver, a .38, in his lap. He was breathing heavily, looking at Harry, but made no move to raise the gun.

Harry looked at the couch, saw part of the arm had been reduced to torn upholstery and splintered wood. It had caught the brunt of the shotgun blast.

Harrow smiled, turned his head and spit blood on the floor. Smoke rose up around him.

Harry felt something warm and wet on the left side of his neck. He brought his bound hands up, the right one numb, touched the side of his face. His left earlobe was missing, nothing there but a nub of torn flesh. His hand came away red.

Harrow shifted, rolled onto his side, got his knees under him, began to stand. Harry used his boot heels to push himself along the floor, put distance between them. He looked under the couch, tried to see where the Sig had fallen.

Harrow got to his feet, wavered. He spit blood again, then brought up the .38.

Harry looked up. From the angle he was at now, he could see into the kitchen. He saw the overturned chairs, a dark stain on the floor. Errol was gone.

Harrow cocked the gun loudly. A shadow seemed to move behind him. Harrow saw it from the corner of his eye, turned, and there was Errol, the front of his sweater torn, leaning against the doorway for support, the .380 in a two-handed grip.

No one spoke. Harrow looked from Errol to Harry, his finger still tight on the trigger. Errol was breathing heavily, but the .380 was steady, pointed at Harrow's chest, wrists braced against the door frame. Through the torn material of his sweater, Harry could see the blue of the Kevlar vest beneath.

"Enough," Harry said.

Harrow looked at Errol.

"Just put it down, John," Harry said. "You need to get to a hospital."

Harrow shook his head slowly.

"No," he said. "I don't think so," and then he pointed the .38 at Errol and fired.

The roar of the two handguns came as one. Harrow staggered back and Errol spun away from the door frame, took a half step and went down on the kitchen floor. Harrow turned the gun back to Harry, but he was already moving, slamming into the couch, shoving it away from the wall. Harrow fired and the bullet passed through the couch, blew bits of upholstery into the air. Harry's hands closed on the Sig. He raised it up, stood, using the back of the couch for cover, and squeezed the trigger.

The Sig made a dull cough and Harrow spun to his left, turning on his heel. He made a complete circle, came up with the gun again. Harry dropped to the floor as Harrow fired, heard the bullet hit the wall behind him.

Another shot and the couch jumped. Harry kicked it away, started to rise up, the Sig out in front of him, and he heard the loud click of the .38's hammer coming down on an empty chamber.

Harrow aimed, worked the trigger again. Another click. Harry centered the suppressor on his chest, finger tightening on the trigger. The .38 stayed steady, clicked again.

Harrow lowered the gun, looked at it, then back at Harry. He smiled, spit again, then dropped the .38 on the floor and turned away, walked calmly into the kitchen.

Harry aimed at his back, couldn't fire. And then Harrow wasn't there anymore. Harry heard the back door open, felt the cold draft blow through the house.

He came out from around the couch, gun up, went into the kitchen. Wind caught the storm door, blew it back against its hinges. Snow drifted in, settled on the floor.

He went to the door, looked out. Through the wind and snow, Harrow was a dark blur moving toward the woods. Harry aimed at his outline, began to squeeze the trigger, stopped. In another moment the figure was gone, lost in the snow and the howling wind.

He lowered the Sig, stood there for a moment, looking out into the night and the snow. Then he turned away, shouldered the main door closed. The wind whined, stopped. The door thumped and shook in its frame as if something were trying to gain entry.

He put the Sig on the counter, reached with bound hands for the phone.

HE DIDN'T feel the cold.

He was conscious of the wind pulling at him, the wetness blown under his collar. His boots were heavy and each step took him shin-deep into snow. He was deep in the woods now, the house a warm glow in the distance. He tried to remember the way he'd come, where he'd left Lindell's jeep.

He took another step, stumbled, fell to his knees in the snow. His fingers and side were numb, but there was no pain. He pushed himself to his feet, walked on, knowing he was lost now.

He took shelter from the wind behind a thick tree, leaned against it. Blood rose in his throat again. He hacked it up, spit, looked back the way he'd come, at his footprints already disappearing.

He reached inside his jacket, shirt stiff with drying blood, felt the four small holes the shotgun pellets had made on the upper right side of his chest. Below them the larger hole, still bleeding, where the black man had shot him. He moved his hand until he touched another entry wound, through the center of his tattoo, where the last bullet had hit him, one from his own gun. His fingertip explored the hole and he was amazed he felt no pain.

He laughed, reached into his pocket, took out the cigarettes. He shook the pack, his fingers numb, until one came out. He lifted it to his face, got the end of it between his lips, let the pack fall. Then he pushed numb fingers into his pocket, came out with the lighter. He thumbed it open, worked the wheel. The flame caught, blew out, caught again. He got the cigarette lit, pulled the smoke in, closed the lighter, dropped it back in his pocket.

He leaned back against the tree, smoking, looked up at the sky through the bare branches. Thought of the boy. Safe and warm on this wild night.

The cigarette was done sooner than he expected. He dropped the butt in the snow, pushed away from the tree. He started to walk again, but his steps were slower, heavier. He fell, pushed the snow-covered ground away from him, stood up, walked on. It was somewhere right ahead of him, he knew. It was waiting for him.

When he fell the final time, he smiled, because he could see it then, right in front of him, where it had been all along. Always just a few steps away. And now, finally, close enough to touch. The Valley.

FORTY-TWO

"DID I GET HIM?" ERROL SAID.

"You got him."

Errol was flat on his back on the kitchen floor. Harry pulled the torn edges of his sweater apart. The vest had caught most of the shotgun charge, but Harry knew at that range the bones beneath it might be broken. Two of the pellets had hit above the vest on the left side, leaving small holes in the thick muscle connecting neck and shoulder. Blood oozed from them.

"Go find him," Errol said, pain in his voice. "Make sure."

"I will. Just take it easy for now, partner."

The vest still held the imprint of the pellets that had hit it. On the right side was a deeper dent where Harrow's last shot had impacted. Harry undid the Velcro fasteners and Errol gasped. A misshapen slug fell from the vest to the floor.

"Mother*fucker*," Errol said.

Harry peeled the Kevlar back. Errol's chest was purplish, swollen, but there were no other puncture wounds.

He winced, caught Harry's hand.

"I'm okay," he breathed. "Just . . . let me lie here."

Harry went to the couch, pulled a cushion free, carried it back and propped it under his head.

"Help's on its way, partner," he said. "Hang in there."

Errol nodded, shuddered. "Go on," he said.

Harry took the Sig from the counter, ejected the magazine to check the load. There were still a half dozen shells in it. He angled his bound hands so he could slide the magazine home again, then

314

got a red plastic flashlight from under the sink. He went out the back door, the Sig in his right hand, the flashlight in his left.

The snow seemed to be slowing, fewer flakes visible in the beam of the barn light. He turned the flashlight on. Immediately he saw the footprints, the snow in them stained pink.

It was an easy trail to follow. When he got to the willows, he saw where Harrow had jumped the creek and fallen. He pointed the Sig out in front of him, knowing the flashlight made him a good target if Harrow was out there and had another weapon.

He followed the blood and the footprints, saw the places where Harrow had fallen, gotten up again. He went deeper into the woods, the wind whining through the bare trees.

Ahead, a dark bundle at the base of a tree, fresh snow already settling over it. He pointed the Sig at it, then went down on one knee. Harrow's blue eyes were wide, the left side of his face in the snow.

Harry put the Sig down, touched his neck, felt the cooling skin there, the stillness. Then he went through the jacket pockets, found the handcuff key. He worked it in the locks, got the cuffs off, dropped them, rubbed snow onto his welted, red wrists.

After a moment, he reached into his pocket, pulled out the hundred-dollar bill. He leaned down, stuffed it into Harrow's jacket pocket. Then he stood back up, reclaimed the flashlight and the Sig. Snow whirled around him.

He started back to the house. Somewhere in the distance, far away but clear against the silence of the snow, he could hear the first sirens.

WHEN THE ER doctor left, Harry touched the bulky bandage over his left ear, winced.

"Hurts, doesn't it?" Ray said.

Harry nodded. They were in the same treatment room Nikki had been in earlier that night. He sat on the table, Ray in a plastic chair. In the hallway, Harry could see a handful of cops, Branson talking on a cell phone.

"A couple inches to the left," Ray said, "he would have taken your head off."

"I know. How's Errol?"

"Three broken ribs, hairline crack in his sternum, plus a couple of puncture wounds. No internal injuries as far as they can tell."

"Nikki?"

"I looked in on her. She's upstairs. Three-eleven. They gave her something for the pain. She's out."

Branson came into the room, looked at him.

"Busy night," he said. "I should have just gotten a room here. Would have saved me a lot of driving."

"Sorry," Harry said.

"You're a lucky man."

"Doesn't feel that way."

"You're alive. Others aren't."

"That's true, I guess."

"I meant to tell you earlier. We had to cut the brother loose, the woman too. Nothing to hold them on."

Harry shook his head.

"He had nothing to do with anything."

"You could be right."

"I am. And it's over anyway, isn't it?"

"I don't know," Branson said. "Is it?"

HE MADE his way down the dim hall to 311. The door was partially open.

There was a curtain drawn between the beds. Hers was on the far side by the window. It had stopped snowing.

She was breathing softly, steadily. The bandage on her face was smaller now, secured by two Xs of surgical tape. He sat on the edge of the bed, touched her hair, the right side of her face. She slept on.

He kissed the top of her head, smoothed her hair. She stirred, didn't waken.

He sat with her that way for a while, until the gray sky began to lighten. And then he left as quietly as he had come.

FORTY-THREE

T WAS ALMOST NOON WHEN RAY PULLED UP THE DRIVEWAY, PARKED behind the station wagon. The sun was bright off the snow, birds chirping, looking for food and finding none.

He left the Camry's engine running.

"You want me to come in?"

Harry shook his head.

"Not now. I'll be fine."

"Still a mess in there, I'd guess. I think the crime scene van only left a half hour ago, if that."

"I'll be okay."

"Don't worry about the girl. They'll release her later today. We can find her a place to stay if she needs one."

"Thanks. What about Errol?"

"CAT scan, MRI were all negative. He'll be okay. And financially he won't have to worry about anything. Company insurance will pick up his hospital bill. Yours too. It was all work-related."

"Hard to remember that," Harry said. "Hard to remember that had anything to do with anything."

Ray put out his hand. Harry took it.

He got out of the car, shut the door, watched as Ray cut the wheel, tried to K-turn in the side yard, back wheels spinning briefly in the snow. He got the car turned around, raised his hand a final time. Harry waved back, watched him disappear down the slope of the driveway.

The living room still smelled of smoke. The fireplace was cold and black, ashes and carbonized wood littering the floor, the hard-

317

wood scarred with burn marks. Blood too. On the hearth, in the kitchen. He would leave that for later.

He filled a plastic scoop with birdseed, opened the back door. He threw the feed out onto the hard snow, one scoop, then another. Birds descended noisily, a carpet of black against the whiteness, fed and flew away.

When he was done, he went back into the living room. The Percocet bottle lay on the floor near the couch. Half a dozen pills had spilled out. He gathered them up, replaced them in the bottle, capped it. He brought it into the kitchen, dropped it in the trash.

At the closet, he reached up under the blanket, dragged out the canvas bag he'd hidden there. He took it to the couch, unzipped it, looked at the bills within.

Whose money, finally? Joey Alea's? Tony Acuna's? It was Harrow's getaway money, he knew that much. Enough to kick the door open on a new life.

He dumped the money out on the couch, counted it twice. One hundred and twenty-six thousand.

He thought of Luther Wilkins, head shot in a hospital bed, eyes bandaged. He got out the phone book, made some calls, and within fifteen minutes had Wilkins's address and his mother's name. He put $30,000 aside. He'd FedEx it to her tomorrow, with an unsigned note. When the boy got out of the hospital he would need a lawyer as well, other things. It was a start.

He divided the rest of the money in half, put $48,000 back into the bag, the Amtrak tickets on top, zipped it closed. In the closet, he found a cardboard box, duct tape, a pair of scissors. When he was finished, he had a package about the size of a shoe box. He put the other $48,000 inside, found paper and pen and went into the kitchen. He righted a chair, sat down at the table, trying not to look at the dark smears of dried blood on the floor.

Nikki, he wrote. *This belongs to you. Trust me. Don't ask where it came from, because I won't tell you. But believe me when I say it's yours.*

I have to go away for a while. And when I come back, I might not be alone. While I'm gone, Ray will do whatever he can for you. If you have any questions, problems, let him know. He'll take care of it as best he can. But know this—the danger, the things you've worried about all these years, are gone. And they're never coming back.

And you were, are—and forever will be—beautiful. Know that too. Some bad luck—and a handful of stitches—could never change that.

His hand began to cramp. He put the pen down, worked the muscle beneath his thumb, picked up the pen again.

I'm leaving this package with Ray, to give to you when he sees you. You don't need to tell him what's in it. And he won't ask.

Take care of yourself. Whatever happens in your life now—maybe for the first time—is up to you, no one else. The past is dead. Bury it.

He signed the letter quickly, folded it, put it in the box, taped the end shut.

After a while, when it was late enough, he found the number, used the kitchen phone, listened to the forlorn buzz of the ring a continent away.

"Ellen?" he said when she answered. "It's Harry."

"Harry, she's been trying to call you, but nobody answered. Hold on."

She put the phone down. After a moment, Cristina picked up the line.

"It's me," he said.

"Harry? I had a dream last night, a bad one. It was dark out, you were lost. When I woke up I was crying."

"I'm fine," he said. "Everything's okay. I'm coming out there."

"Here?"

"Yes." He waited, listening to the silence on the line, wondering what her next words would be.

"When?" she said finally.

"I'm leaving tomorrow. I have some things I need to settle here first. I'm driving, taking the Mustang. It'll take me a few days. But I should be there by the end of the week."

Silence again. He didn't interrupt it. Waited.

"Good," she said. "That's good."

He felt the warmth in his face, a dampness in his eyes.

"Soon," she said. "Make it as soon as you can."

"I will," he said. And then there was nothing else to say. He replaced the receiver, sat down in the chair, the kitchen bright with the reflected light off the snow outside.

As simple as that, he thought. After all that time.

He sat that way for a long time. And then he started to get ready.

FORTY-FOUR

HE KNOCKED TWICE, STEPPED BACK, WAITED. HE'D PARKED THE MUS-
tang behind the Firebird, left the engine running, exhaust
swirling up. The sun was sinking behind bare trees, dark and cold
settling over everything. He knocked again.

The door cracked open, the black woman looked out at him. She
was dressed in a basketball jersey, jeans. Beside her, a little girl
watched him with unashamed curiosity. He could feel the warmth
of the trailer, smell cooking food inside.

The woman said nothing, looked at the bandage on his ear.

"Is your husband here?" he said.

"Who?"

"Your husband . . ." then catching himself: "Mitchell."

"What you want with him? When you people ever going to
leave him alone? He had nothing to do with those folks got
killed."

"I'm sorry. I'm not here to cause trouble. I just want to talk to
him."

"You're a policeman, aren't you?"

He looked at the ground, shook his head, then back at her.

"No, ma'am," he said. "Not anymore."

Footsteps behind her, then Sweeton was standing there. He wore
jeans and a flannel shirt.

"It's all right, Sharonda," he said. Then to the little girl. "Treya,
go back to your room."

"Why?" she said.

He put his hand gently on her shoulder, still looking at Harry.

"Daddy needs to talk," he said.

"You don't have to talk to him," Sharonda said. "You don't have to talk to nobody."

"It's okay," he said.

Harry stepped back as Sweeton came out, closed the door behind him.

Harry looked to his right, saw the little girl peering out through kitchen curtains before her mother took her away.

"What is it?" Sweeton said, fear and uncertainty in his voice.

"You know who I am?"

Sweeton shook his head.

"Doesn't matter anyway," Harry said. He held the black canvas bag out.

"What's that?" Sweeton said.

"It's yours. It's from your brother."

"My brother?"

"Yeah."

"How did you get it?"

"He gave it to me, for you. And them." He nodded at the door. "Don't worry. No one's going to come looking for it."

"I don't understand."

"You don't have to. Take it." He raised the bag. Sweeton looked at it, took it from him, surprised at its weight.

"No one knows," Harry said. "And at this point no one's left to care. It's all yours."

Sweeton looked at the bag, sensing now what was in it. Harry took another step back.

"You, uh . . . want to come in?" Sweeton said.

Harry shook his head.

"No. No need. Merry Christmas."

He turned and started back to the Mustang. When he got to the car, he opened the door, looked back. Sweeton was still standing there, watching him.

"Merry Christmas," Sweeton said and seemed to mean it.

Harry raised a hand, got into the car. As he pulled away, the suitcases clunked in the trunk. The cardboard box slid off the passenger seat onto the floorboard.

One more stop. And then the road.

He pulled out onto the highway, gave it gas, the heater blowing warm against his legs. He drove west, darkness in his rearview mirror, stars already sparkling coldly in the sky.

The sun was now just a violet glow on the horizon. But still a glow. A beacon, however long it lasted. And if he drove long enough it would return, as bright as ever. All he had to do was believe it. Hard as that was sometimes.

The night at his back, he drove on.